Last Guard

Last Guard

A PSY-CHANGELING TRINITY NOVEL

NALINI SINGH

BERKLEY
New York

BERKLEY
An imprint of Penguin Random House LLC
penguinrandomhouse.com

Copyright © 2021 by Nalini Singh
Penguin Random House supports copyright. Copyright fuels creativity, encourages diverse
voices, promotes free speech, and creates a vibrant culture. Thank you for buying an authorized
edition of this book and for complying with copyright laws by not reproducing, scanning,
or distributing any part of it in any form without permission. You are supporting writers
and allowing Penguin Random House to continue to publish books for every reader.

BERKLEY and the BERKLEY & B colophon are registered trademarks of
Penguin Random House LLC.

Library of Congress Cataloging-in-Publication Data

Names: Singh, Nalini, 1977– author.
Title: Last guard / Nalini Singh.
Description: First edition. | New York: Berkley, 2021. | Series: A psy-changeling trinity novel ; 5
Identifiers: LCCN 2021004457 (print) | LCCN 2021004458 (ebook) |
ISBN 9781984803658 (hardcover) | ISBN 9781984803665 (ebook)
Subjects: GSAFD: Adventure fiction.
Classification: LCC PR9639.4.S566 L37 2021 (print) | LCC PR9639.4.S566 (ebook) |
DDC 823/.92—dc23
LC record available at https://lccn.loc.gov/2021004457
LC ebook record available at https://lccn.loc.gov/2021004458

First Edition: July 2021

Printed in the United States of America
1st Printing

This is a work of fiction. Names, characters, places, and incidents either are the product
of the author's imagination or are used fictitiously, and any resemblance to actual persons,
living or dead, business establishments, events, or locales is entirely coincidental.

Last Guard

Anchor Point

ANCHORS ARE THE foundation of the PsyNet.

They aren't simply integral to the psychic network that the Psy rely on for life.

They *are* the PsyNet.

Without Designation A, there is no PsyNet.

Akin to a band of rubber stretched too tight, the PsyNet will snap into a crushing ball of death should the anchor points fail, the whiplash eradicating an entire race from existence.

Yet . . . the vast majority of Psy never give a thought to anchors.

As humans and changelings give no thought to the foundations of their home.

The foundations just are.

Anchors just are.

Until they vanish, the last gasp of a dying race.

Chapter 1

While I am yet close to my Silence and may remain so for the rest of my life, I do not come close to the robotic coldness of Payal Rao. There is something fundamentally defective about her, something that puts her in the same category as those we term psychopaths, and I have no compunction in saying that openly.

—Excerpt from the April 2083 edition of the
Singapore Business Quarterly: "Interview with Gia Khan"

PAYAL HAD RISEN to her position as CEO of the Rao Conglomerate by being ready for anything. Surprise was an enemy to be conquered—because unlike what seemed to be the majority of her race, she wasn't sanguine about the utopia of a world beyond the emotionless regime of Silence.

A century the Psy had spent shackled to the pitiless ice of the Protocol. Payal didn't have enough data to say whether Silence had been a failure, but she knew that emotion brought with it countless problems, exposed endless vectors of weakness.

She had felt once. It had caused her visceral pain—and nearly led to an order of psychic rehabilitation. Had she not been a cardinal telekinetic, valued and not exactly plentiful on the ground, the medics would've wiped her brain and left her a shuffling creature without a mind.

Far better to be thought a psychopathic robot—as she'd so memorably been described by Gia Khan earlier that year—than drop her Silent shield and give her enemies a soft, quivering target. Payal had no intention of ending up dead and forgotten like her grandfather, uncle, and eldest sibling, Varun.

So it was noteworthy that the missive currently displayed on her private organizer had caught her unprepared. It wasn't only the contents, either. No, what was even more unexpected was the address to which the message had been directed: an e-mail address she'd set up after she watched her father execute his firstborn for the crime of conspiring against him.

Pranath Rao was not a man to forgive disloyalty.

Older than Payal by fifteen years, Varun had been caught because—in an act of arrogant stupidity—he'd used official channels to make his seditious plans. He must've believed their father wouldn't bother to check up on the child being groomed to one day take over the Rao empire.

He'd been wrong.

In punishment, Pranath had held his son down using telekinesis, then ordered a combat telepath to crush Varun's brain, crush it so hard that blood had leaked out of his eyes and brain matter out of his ears. Varun's screams had gone on and on until they were nothing but a whistling gurgle.

Payal knew because both she and her next eldest sibling, Lalit, had been forced to stand witness.

The medic who'd certified Varun's death as natural was in their father's pocket.

Even as nine-year-old Payal watched her brother's casket head to the crematorium after a "respectful" funeral service in accordance with the rules of Silence, she'd been thinking. Strategizing. Learning.

She didn't intend to be fed into the fire. Pranath Rao had still had two living heirs at that time, *and* he was young enough to father and raise more.

Which he'd done twelve years later, adding Karishma to his list of heirs. The long gap had been very much on purpose—Pranath waiting until his living children were adults to show them that their lives were in no way invaluable to him.

He could write them off and start again at any moment.

Payal's secret e-mail account had been just one prong in her plan for survival.

Even now that she held a certain degree of power, she still only accessed it through an encrypted organizer she'd set up with its own IP address—one that bounced off so many servers around the world that there was no straight line to Payal Rao, CEO of the Rao Conglomerate.

So for this individual to have identified her displayed a deadly level of skill and knowledge.

But in the text . . . there lay the real danger.

Payal, we've never met, but we have something critical in common.

Put bluntly, I know that you're a hub-anchor—and the reason Delhi's section of the PsyNet has suffered so few fractures and failures. That it's suffered any at all is because you shouldn't be anchoring the Net on your own with the limited assistance of secondary anchors and fail-safes.

I'm in no way denigrating the role they play, because we both know we'd be dead without them, but the fact is that you should have at least three other hub-anchors around you whose zones of control overlap yours. That was how it was when you first initialized.

I'm a hub-anchor in the same position, strained to the limit, with no room for error. And the situation is deteriorating by the day. I believe it's time we stopped relying on the rulers of the PsyNet to watch over our designation. The Ruling Coalition has barely been born and they might turn out to be better than the Psy Council when it comes to Designation A—but we don't have the luxury of waiting.

Anchors are critical to the PsyNet.

But we're ghosts.

Protected. Shielded. Coddled.

Trapped. Suffocated. Controlled.

We—Designation A as a whole—are as much at fault here as Psy Councils recent and past. You and I both know that most As are barely functional outside of their anchor duties, and prefer to remain insulated from the rest of the world.

You don't fall into that group. You are the CEO of a major and influential family corporation. You're well beyond functional—to the point that no one who doesn't already know would ever guess you to be an anchor.

That makes you the perfect person to speak for Designation A at every meeting of the Ruling Coalition—because the PsyNet is dying and *no one* knows the PsyNet like those of us who are integrated into its fabric.

There will be no Rao family if the PsyNet collapses.

There will be no anchors. No Psy.

This could be the twilight of our race.

Unless we stop it.

Rising from her desk, Payal walked to the large arched doors to the right of her office. They'd been made of warped and weathered wood when she took over this space, but though she'd kept the wooden frame, she'd had the center sections of both doors changed to clear glass, so that she could look down into the apparent chaos of Old Delhi even when the doors were closed.

The Rao family's central home and executive offices were located inside what had once been a mahal—a palace full of ancient art, its floor plan quixotic, and its walls studded with odd-sized windows that glowed with stained glass, such as the mosaic of color behind Payal's desk. It even had a name: *Vara*.

Blessings.

A name given long ago, before Silence, and before the slow creep of darkness into Vara's aged walls.

Beyond its limited but well-maintained grounds, Vara was surrounded by smaller buildings of a similar vintage, and looked out over a mishmash of more ancient structures and rickety new buildings that appeared held together by not much more than hope and the odd nail.

Gleaming Psy skyscrapers rose in the distance in stark contrast.

Yet even that clinical intrusion into the heart of this ancient city hadn't been able to tame the controlled disorder of Delhi. Her city had its own soul and wasn't about to bow to the whims of any civilization.

Every now and then, she still spotted monkeys scrambling up into the fruit trees on the grounds, and the pigeons had no respect for any of the bird deterrents trialed by the maintenance staff.

Through it all, Vara stood, solid and enduring.

Her father had once considered bulldozing it and rebuilding out of steel and glass, then decided the mahal was an important symbol of their long-term power. "The Raos were here long before others who might think to defeat our hold on this city," he'd said as they stood at Vara's highest viewpoint, the rooftop garden hidden from below by decorative crenellations. "And we'll be here long after they're dead and buried."

It was silent and cool in her third-floor office, but she knew that should she step out onto the stone balcony, she'd be hit with a tumult of horns and cries and scorching heat—the monsoon winds hadn't yet arrived, bringing with them a humidity that was a wet pressure on the skin.

Payal would then wait for the rains to come wash away the muggy air.

Her office was situated at the front of Vara, only meters from the street. She could see motorcycles zipping through traffic with apparent insouciance, while multiple auto rickshaws stood lined up in front of Vara, hoping for a passenger.

A Psy in San Francisco or Monaco might turn up their nose at that mode of transport, but Psy in Delhi knew that the small and nimble vehicles were far more adept at navigating the city's heavy traffic than bigger town cars. The more intrepid drivers even dared take on Old Delhi's narrow lanes—but it was far smarter to travel via motorcycle in those mixed pedestrian/vehicle zones.

The traffic chaos was an accident of history. Delhi had grown too fast at a time when it had more pressing issues to address, and now there was simply no room to expand the roading or underground rail. The rickshaws were here to stay.

Even Payal was known to hail one on occasion despite the fact she was a teleport-capable telekinetic. It helped her keep a finger on the pulse of the city. She'd seen too many powerful Psy fall because they had no idea what was happening beyond their insulated bubble.

Nikita Duncan was the perfect example—the ex-Councilor held considerable financial and political sway, but she'd lost her once-tight grip on her home base. The DarkRiver leopard pack had grown exponentially in power right under her nose. San Francisco would never again be Nikita's city.

Payal kept an eye on multiple small groups like DarkRiver that wielded more power than they should—she watched and she learned. Always.

After spending several minutes focused on the patterns of movement out on the street, she glanced down at the signature at the bottom of the unexpected e-mail: Canto Mercant, Mercant Corp.

Mercant.

Talk about a small group that held an excessive amount of power. Though the rumored scion of the family was now one of the most famous faces in the world, the Mercants didn't generally seek fame or overt political power. Rather, they were the primary shadow players in the PsyNet, with a network of spies so skilled they were said to have something on everyone.

Payal knew the latter to be an overstatement for the simple reason that they had nothing on her. The fact she was an anchor wasn't any kind of a smoking gun or threat. No doubt she was on a list of As somewhere in the Ruling Coalition's archives. But she didn't exactly advertise her status. Not when the most well-known telekinetic anchor of recent years had ended up a serial killer.

So how had Canto Mercant worked out her root designation?

Anchor minds weren't visibly different on the PsyNet, couldn't be pinpointed that way. And because A was an "inert" designation during early childhood, when Psy were sorted into various designations for the necessary specialized training, it would've appeared nowhere on her early records.

In point of fact, *all* her public-facing records listed her as a Tk.

Canto Mercant shouldn't have the data on her true status. She certainly hadn't known the Mercants had an anchor in their midst. Not only an anchor but a hub, born to merge into the fabric of the PsyNet. Chances were Canto Mercant was a cardinal.

Non-cardinal hub-anchors were rare inside an already rare designation.

Setting aside her organizer on her desk, she used her intercom to contact her assistant: *Ruhi, bring me our files on the Mercants.*

Before

Severe behavioral and psychic problems that manifest in physical disobedience. No medical issues found to explain sudden bouts of uncoordinated motion, loss of balance, and apparent migraines that lead to blackouts.
Full re-education authorized by legal guardian.

—Intake Report: 7J

THE BOY FOUGHT against the psychic walls that blocked him in, made him helpless. His brain burned, a bruise hot and aching, but he couldn't get through, couldn't shatter the chains that caged his child's mind.

"Stand!" It was a harsh order.

He'd long ago stopped trying to resist the orders—better to save his energy for more useful rebellion—but he couldn't follow this one. No matter how hard he tried, his legs wouldn't move, wouldn't even *twitch* anymore.

He'd been able to drag himself through the corridors earlier that day, even though pain had been a hot poker up his spine, and his legs had felt as numb and as heavy as dead logs. Now he couldn't even feel them. But he kept on trying, his brain struggling to understand the truth.

Nothing. No movement. No sensation.

Each failure brought with it a fresh wave of terror that had nothing to do with his tormentor.

"You think this is a game? You were warned what would happen if you kept up this charade!"

A telekinetic hand around his small neck, lifting him up off the schoolroom floor and slamming him to the wall. The teacher then walked close to him and used an object he couldn't see to physically smash his tibia in two.

He should've felt incredible pain.

He felt nothing.

Terror might've eaten his brain had he not become aware that the man who'd hurt him was stumbling back, clutching at his neck, while children screamed and small feet thundered out the door. Thick dark red fluid gushed between the teacher's fingers, dripped down his uniform.

As the man stumbled away, the child crumpled to the ground, the trainer's telekinesis no longer holding him up.

No pain, even now.

He should've been scared, should've worried. But his entire attention was on the wild-haired little girl who'd jumped up onto a desk to thrust a sharpened toothbrush into the teacher's jugular. *"Run!"* he cried. *"Run!"*

Chapter 2

"The boy has encompassed the newborn in his shields."
"Is the infant under threat?"
"Unknown."

—Ena Mercant to Magdalene Mercant (February 2054)

CANTO HAD NO way to confirm if Payal Rao had read—or even received—his message. He'd embedded a subtle tracker in the e-mail so he'd know when it was opened, but it had been neutralized at some point in the process. It had been a long shot regardless—Payal wasn't the head of the biggest energy conglomerate in Southeast Asia and India because she was anything less than icily intelligent.

Two of the other hub-anchors he'd contacted had already responded to him, wary but interested. But for this to work, they needed Payal. Canto and the other hubs on his list were outliers in their designation because of how functional they were in external spheres. Payal, however, was the one who'd automatically garner immediate respect from the most ruthless players in the Net.

He looked once again at the image of her he had onscreen, though he'd told himself to stop obsessing years back, when he'd first done a run on her. She was of Indian descent. And she was a cardinal. Those were the only two traits she shared with 3K. That small girl had been a storm of emotion and passion, nothing about her contained and sophisticated.

Children changed, grew up. But for 3K to be Payal Rao, she'd have to have had a total personality and temperament transplant. No, she wasn't the one for whom Canto searched—and fuck, yes, he knew 3K had to be dead, but he couldn't stop looking. She'd saved him. How could he just abandon her?

But whoever 3K had been, her family had scrubbed her from the system with such brutality that even the might of the entire Mercant network hadn't been able to locate her. Canto might have begun to doubt his memories and believe her a ghost—but he had a scar over his left tibia that was a physical reminder of the warped "school" that had been his home for five hellish months that had altered the course of his life.

Payal Rao, in contrast, had been educated at a private girls' school in Delhi. Because he *was* obsessive, he'd checked the records, even located the class photographs.

There she was on the attendance rolls and in the images. The photos from her earlier years were blurry and of low-resolution—that had raised his suspicions until he'd looked back and seen that all the school's uploads from that period were of the same low quality. Her name had also shown up on athletic and extracurricular lists.

According to Canto's grandmother, Payal had even been considered for a Council position at one point. "Nothing official," Ena had said. "But Santano Enrique noticed her intelligence and ambition. In the end, the Council decided that Gia Khan and Kaleb made the better candidates. My guess is it's because Payal appears to have a black-and-white view of the world. Gray isn't her strong point."

And politics in the time of the Council had been all about the gray. Canto could do gray—he was a Mercant, after all—but not only did he prefer the shadows, Payal had a presence about her that couldn't be counterfeited. She took over a room, was a cold burn of determination.

Canto wanted that icy flame on their side.

He wasn't planning to give up if she didn't respond. This was too important.

"Mercants never give up," Valentin had rumbled to Canto once. "You just get sneaky." A scowl on the bear alpha's square-jawed face. "Sneaky-cat Mercants." Then he'd smiled with unhidden delight. "Beautiful sneaky-cat Mercants. *My* sneaky-cat Mercant."

Canto hadn't needed to turn to see that Silver was walking toward them. Valentin Nikolaev made no bones about the fact that he was madly in love with his mate. To most people, Silver probably appeared cool and standoffish in return. Most people didn't know Canto's younger cousin.

Silver would cut out the heart of anyone who dared hurt Valentin.

It had been unexpected to see her fall—yet not at the same time. Because Canto knew about Arwen, about the Mercant who'd altered the course of the Mercant family . . . altered the shape of Canto's heart.

Without 3K, he'd be dead.

Without Arwen, he'd be a bitter, twisted monster.

He'd protected Arwen in turn, paid back that gift. He'd never been able to do anything for 3K, and it would haunt him till the day he died.

"Fruitless obsession will lead you to your grave, Canto," he muttered, repeating words his grandmother had said to him.

Ena had also added: "Mercants have a gift for obsession. It's led to prison sentences, epic heroism, great works of art, and madhouses. Choose your path."

Turning to the screen to the left of his workstation with a scowl, he brought up the Trinity Accord Convention newsfeed. As he watched, Silver delivered her speech with poise and confidence. She gave no indication that she was in any way intimidated by being in a physical forum filled with the intelligentsia of all three of the world's races.

Psy. Changeling. Human.

Neither did she appear the least ruffled by the knowledge that her speech was being broadcast to every corner of the globe. As director of EmNet, the worldwide Emergency Response Network, she'd learned to live in the spotlight and use it to advance the aims of EmNet.

"We will fail if we permit petty squabbles and power plays to divide us. There are those who are counting on your minds and hearts being small and mean and without generosity. They intend to break the world by putting pressure on those fracture points. Do not allow it."

She walked off the stage on that crisp order.

Pushing away from the main workstation, Canto rolled back the wheels of the chair designed for his long and solid frame. It had a hover function for those times when access was otherwise impossible—but as he'd wanted a streamlined chair devoid of armrests, those controls, as well as his backup computronic brake controls, were on a small side panel on the right-hand side of his seat.

Black on black, the panel mimicked the curve of his wheel and looked at first glance to be nothing more than a design feature. As it was, Canto rarely used the hover mode, far preferring to manually operate the chair.

The constant physical motion helped keep his upper body strong. Not that he relied only on that. He'd set up a full gym in another section of his home, complete with a robotic physiotherapy device that helped him exercise the legs that were a part of his body, but that he couldn't feel.

He had, however, long ago rejected the full-body robotic brace designed for bipedal motion. Of a far more streamlined design than in its original iterations, the brace worked well for many. Canto wasn't one of those people. The few times he'd tried it, he'd felt as if he had insects dancing on his spine and buzzing in his brain.

"Electro-biogen-feedback loop," the robotics expert had muttered. "Might be caused by the innovative wiring in your spine."

Whatever the cause, Canto far preferred his sleek black chair with its highly maneuverable wheels. Heading to another area of his large, windowless, and temperature-controlled office area—a place Arwen had termed his "computronic dungeon"—he picked up his phone and sent a message to Silver: *You were brilliant.*

Pride was a conflagration inside him.

Canto had said "fuck it" to Silence long before its official fall. That was what happened when a child empath lived inside your airtight anchor shields, and the PsyNet flowed through your mind in an endless river, bringing with it the flotsam and jetsam of the lives of millions of people, powerful and weak, brave and cowardly, good and bad.

Then there'd been his childhood—the school had been the final part of a play that had run since his birth, and it had nearly broken him. Without 3K, without the example of her stubborn fury and refusal to surrender, he might have given up. But if she, so small and physically far weaker, could fight on, he had no excuse. But the fight had burned any hope of Silence right out of him—he'd run on pure rage.

Sometimes, in his dreams, he still heard 3K laugh, though he'd only ever heard it once in real life. In a moment when their teacher had turned his back and Canto had made a face mimicking the man's bulging eyes and puffed-out cheeks when he laid down the rules.

Bright, brilliant laughter, unafraid and wild.

She'd been the strongest of them all. And the people in charge had *hurt* her for it.

Not expecting a quick response from Silver, he was turning his attention to one of his multiple screens when his phone chimed. He glanced at it to see: Zdravstvuyte, *Canto. Silver's talking to the brains. She was dazzling, wasn't she? My magnificent Starlight who takes no prisoners.*

Temperamentally, Valentin was at the opposite end of the spectrum from Canto. "You now hold permanent grump status," Arwen had declared of Canto a month ago. "Silence falls, no more threat of psychic rehabilitation hanging over us for daring to feel, and instead of choosing sunshine, you decide to ramp up the surly. Repent now or I'll never visit again."

Canto had scowled. Arwen had groaned. And continued to drop by with ferocious regularity. *Empaths.* Once they decided you were one of their people, it was like trying to shake off a tick.

Arwen had grinned when Canto muttered that, then returned to opening up the box of new shirts he'd bought as a gift: "Because your definition of acceptable clothing offends my eyes, Canto. That shirt isn't frayed—it's a sorry bunch of threads held together by nothing but fear of your bad mood."

Yet Canto and Valentin got along fine. More than fine. Strange as it was, they were becoming friends. *Yes*, he replied to the bear. *It's good you're with her. There are problematic ripples in the PsyNet. Eyes looking her way.*

Silver wasn't the only target of those eyes, either, and he'd received the vague impression that she and the others being watched were in the way of some larger goal. But it was all foggy and without edges, much like the fortunes peddled by weak F-Psy who set themselves up as high-Gradients in order to scam the gullible.

That was the trouble with having so much of the PsyNet running through his mind; he didn't always catch anything but the merest wisp of information. Even then, he had to fight hard to hold on to it, the rush of the Net a massive waterfall that pounded at the back of his brain every instant of every day.

He dreamed of thunder in his sleep and woke to an avalanche.

We have her protected on all sides, Valentin reassured him. *Physical and psychic. Now I have to go and remind two idiots that she is mated and they should stop making cow eyes at her. We will talk again soon.*

Had Valentin not known Canto so well, that last line might as well have been a threat—the bear version of "talk again soon" was "we're throwing a party and you're invited!" Canto had survived one bear party so far—the one the StoneWater clan had thrown to celebrate their alpha's mating to Silver. It had been . . . an experience.

At one point, he'd ended up with a drunk bear changeling in human form on his lap. Dressed in sequined shorts and an equally dazzling top, she'd regaled him with stories of how she'd "slapped the smug" out of two bear males who'd thought they could beat her in a fight. She'd then fallen asleep with her head against his shoulder.

Canto had taken her to one of Valentin's sisters.

Stasya had laughed and thrown her snoring packmate over her shoulder. "Sorry, Canto. You're cute, no? Many of my packmates want to take you to bed, and they think they're being subtle and flirtatious."

A subtle bear?

Canto snorted.

Not that he minded the bear tendency toward openness. For a man whose work was to trawl the darkest shadows, it was refreshing to interact with people who wore their hearts on their sleeves and made no bones about showing anger or fury, either.

As for the rest—well, his hair was currently in a brutally neat cut, but given that he only shaved when his scruff got itchy, and his face was all hard angles, he'd never before been described as "cute." But he accepted that there was a lot he'd never understand about bears and left it at that.

When it came to the bed part of Stasya's comment, Canto already had the PsyNet rushing through his mind each and every second of the day. He barely tolerated even the people he liked. He didn't have the desire or the capacity to have anyone else that close to him for any appreciable length of time.

Anchors were loners for a reason.

Now he had to make them into a working unit. Or they would die. All of them.

DRAFT FRAMEWORK OF FERNANDEZ–MERCANT FERTILIZATION AND CONCEPTION AGREEMENT: 7 MARCH 2044

Preamble: The aim of this advice letter is to set out the main points of the proposed contract between Binh Fernandez and Magdalene Mercant for the procreation of a child for each party from their shared genetic material.

Our firm has also been asked to do further research and provide a concluding opinion, which is appended to the end of this draft framework.

Fertilization: Sperm will be provided by Binh Fernandez within three months of the final agreement, at a mutually agreed-upon medical facility, under the supervision of Fernandez-and-Mercant-approved medics.

Eggs will be extracted from Magdalene Mercant one week prior to the date above.

Once both parties have provided their genetic material, one viable embryo will be created and implanted in Magdalene Mercant's womb within a medically suitable time period. Given the current success rates of implantation, failure is unlikely, but should that occur, two more attempts will be made.

Should all three fail, this genetic match will be deemed unsuitable, and all remaining genetic material destroyed. The fertilization and conception contract will then be voided on a no-fault basis except for Binh Fernandez's financial obligations as follows.

Financial Agreement: As this is a dual fertilization/conception agreement, neither party will pay the other a fee. Magdalene Mercant will carry each child to term. In recompense for that physical risk and task, Binh Fernandez will pay any and all associated medical expenses. This includes pre- and post-natal care, as well as the costs involved in egg extraction and implantation attempts. Failure of implantation will not discharge Binh Fernandez from such financial obligations.

Issue: Binh Fernandez will have full custodial and parental rights to the first child carried successfully to term. Magdalene Mercant will have full custodial and parental rights to the second child carried successfully to term.

Dissolution: The proposed contract will end:

after the birth of the second child, at which point, Binh Fernandez will no longer have any financial obligations to Magdalene Mercant excepting any post-natal care prescribed by her physician up to six months post-birth; or

after the failure to achieve a second pregnancy after three attempts*; or

after the birth of the first child, if that first child displays physical or mental abnormalities—or if the child is stillborn. At that point, the genetic match will be deemed deficient, and both parties will be absolved of any further obligation under the contract excepting any post-natal care prescribed by Magdalene Mercant's physician up to six months post-birth. Should the child be born alive, it will become part of Binh Fernandez's family.

In case of significant injury or death to Magdalene Mercant as a result of any part of the pregnancy or pregnancies, the compensation terms of Addendum 1 will come into effect.

*Should this match only produce a single viable child, a "familial disadvantage" fee will be negotiated per the rates in Addendum 2.

Coda: Per the Mercant Family Group's practice, a coda will be added to the contract stating that while the first child will be part of the Fernandez Family Group, Magdalene Mercant will be consulted should there come a time when a terminal—or apt to be terminal—decision has to be made in relation to the child.

Violation of this coda will result in the rejection by the Mercants of *all* future contract proposals by the Fernandez family, including in business, for intelligence information, for contract work, and such other matters as may arise.

This coda would survive the dissolution of the contract.

Standard terms for fertilization and conception agreements (attached) apply where not contradicted by this personalized framework.

Opinion: As legal counsel for the Fernandez Family Group, we note that the coda is the only unusual point in this draft framework. Research tells us that the last time a family group breached this coda was in 2001. The Mercants have never again interacted with them—and neither have their allies. As a result, that family group has gone from a power to being all but unknown. There is no room for give on this point.

However, if the other party follows all contractual terms, the Mercants have a track record of maintaining ties with any child who is genetically linked to them—and of assisting those children in various ventures. While this has the effect of growing the Mercant network, it also benefits the other party, as the Mercants prioritize such contacts when it comes to information requests.

Furthermore, Magdalene Mercant is from the central branch of the Mercant family, a branch that has consistently produced high-Gradient Psy. There is no one lower than a 6.5 in her direct line. Given that Binh Fernandez comes from a similar line, the chances of producing high-Gradient offspring is significant.

Therefore, it is our considered opinion that the proposed contract is fair, and of significant future value to the Fernandez Family Group. We advise commencement of negotiations to finalize this contract and set up a timeline for the necessary medical procedures.

Before

Subject exhibits significant psychological and mental deficiencies.
Likelihood of recovery and/or return to the family unit is nil.
All necessary measures authorized by legal guardian, but they are to be
consulted prior to a decision to permanently discontinue treatment.

—File Update: 3K

SHE DIDN'T RUN to the door. She ran to him, to the boy who'd made her laugh and slipped her extra food when the teachers weren't looking. "Come on," she said, tugging at his hand.

The teacher was choking on his own blood and making gurgling sounds, but she didn't look, tried not to hear. She'd done a bad thing, a very bad thing, but he'd been hurting the boy. He'd *broken* a bone!

"Come on!" She tugged again. "We can go before they come looking!"

But the boy shook his head. "My legs don't work anymore." A rasp. "Not just heavy and half-numb. Nothing." Breaking their handclasp, he pushed at her leg. "Run! Go! Get away before they find you!"

She couldn't go and just leave him here. They'd hurt him again.

Running to the door, she began to shove a desk against it. It was heavy. But she got it done. The teacher had stopped making noises by the time she got the door blocked. Coming back to the boy, she sat down next to him and took his hand again, held on tight.

"No," she said when he told her to run again. "I'm no one. I don't have anywhere to go."

Chapter 3

Please advise status of Canto Fernandez, minor, age 8, with a genetic link to my family group. It has been brought to my attention that he is no longer an active member of your family unit.

—Ena Mercant (CEO, Mercant Corp.) to
Danilo Fernandez (CEO, Fernandez Inc.) (29 July 2053)

AFTER ABSORBING ALL the data her family had on the Mercants, Payal had gone hunting on her own. She was highly skilled at unearthing information. But locating anything on Canto Mercant after he hit eight years of age had proved impossible.

Even before that, she'd almost not found him. It had been a small notice in the *PsyNet Beacon*'s Births and Deaths column that had alerted her to the fact he'd begun life with a different name.

Binh Fernandez is pleased to announce the result of his F&C Agreement with Magdalene Mercant. The resulting male child is to be named Canto Fernandez.

That had to be him. The first name was unusual and there was the Mercant connection.

The now-deceased Binh Fernandez had been the eldest son of the

Fernandez Family Group out of Manila, and Canto had been listed as his first child on a family tree she was able to dig up. Mercants, Payal had discovered during her research, didn't enter into many conception or fertilization contracts, preferring to keep their family unit relatively compact.

Most of them had muted public profiles at best. Canto's might as well not exist.

Even before the transfer of guardianship from Fernandez to Mercant, information on him was sketchy at best. As indicated by the birth notice, the Fernandez family had been eager to announce their link with the Mercants. Two months later, Binh Fernandez had repeatedly mentioned his "son and heir" in an interview.

Then dead silence.

No images of the child Canto anywhere.

No school records.

No mentions by Binh in future interviews.

Which told Payal that Canto Mercant had a flaw that had become apparent in the months after his birth. Given what she'd seen in her own family, she was skeptical of any such judgment. Her psychopathic brother had long been considered perfect, while she'd fallen into the "problem" category, and fourteen-year-old Karishma would be termed a liability should the information about her rare genetic disorder make its way to their father.

The only reason Payal's younger sister was even alive was because testing for that disorder wasn't part of the standard battery run on all newborns. Yet "flawed" Kari was in every way more of an asset than outwardly perfect Lalit.

You simply had to have a brain that could see beyond the most obvious gains.

Which the Mercants had if they'd ended up with a hub-anchor in their midst without any apparent protest from the Fernandez family.

Binh had died at the same time Canto disappeared off the Fernandez family tree, so the transfer could've been related to that, but Payal didn't think so.

Psy didn't let go of genetic capital.

That was the sum total of all she knew about Canto Mercant. She hadn't been able to locate a single image of him. That spoke less to a low profile and more to a conscious effort to remain unseen.

Even Ena Mercant, head of the Mercant family, wasn't that difficult to pinpoint.

Was it possible the Mercants hadn't truly accepted Canto, that they forced him to stay out of sight? *No.* The Mercants were known to prize family loyalty; they would not have rejected a child they'd claimed. Which left one other possibility—that Canto Mercant was so invisible because he *ran* the Mercant information network.

That was how he'd found her.

Still thinking, she walked out onto her balcony. The air was hot but clean thanks to a smog-dissolution device invented by the local tiger pack. Payal had recently negotiated a deal to license a related device designed to eliminate the limited pollution currently created by certain Rao industrial interests.

Despite the clear financial returns forecast as a result, her father had stated she was an idiot for "dealing with the animals," but her father was no longer CEO. Pranath Rao might have an ace in the hole that meant he could pull her strings, control her on a personal level, but he knew she'd choose the nuclear option if he tried to hobble her business decisions.

This was a new world, and Payal intended to take the Rao empire into it, not be left behind. Which is why she lifted her phone with its encrypted line to her ear after inputting the call code Canto Mercant had included with his letter. She had no idea of his physical location, so she didn't know if it was night or day there, but when he answered after four rings, his tone, though gravelly and deep, was alert.

"Canto." A single hard word.

"You sent me a letter," she said without identifying herself, even though he had to have sent letters to more than one A.

"Payal Rao." No hesitation. "You sound exactly as you do in the interviews I've watched."

She wondered if he was referring to the "robot" description that had stuck to her like glue. True enough if he was; she took care to never allow her shields to drop, never allow the world to see through to the screams hidden in the deepest corner of her psyche. To do that would be to sentence herself to death.

The Rao family had made an art form of the term "survival of the fittest."

"You're attempting to set up an anchor union," she said, wanting him to lay out his cards, this invisible man who knew too much. "To what purpose?"

"The Ruling Coalition has—from all evidence so far—good intentions, but they're making decisions without knowledge of a critical factor. You're a hub. You know full well what I'm talking about."

Payal's hand tightened on the phone at the brusque challenge in his tone. "We need to talk face-to-face." Negotiating with a faceless voice was not how she did business; she liked to see her allies—and her enemies. "For all I know, you're a clever twelve-year-old hacker from Bangalore."

Payal hadn't meant it as a joke. She didn't do jokes. But she had enough life experience to know that a human or changeling would've laughed at the comment. Perhaps an empath, too. The rest of her race was yet coming to terms with being permitted to feel emotion.

She hadn't worked out where Canto Mercant fell on that spectrum, and his response to her comment didn't offer any additional insight. "I'll message you an image for a teleport lock. Can you meet in fifteen minutes?"

"Agreed."

Hanging up, she stared at her vibrant city. The slow feline stride of a woman below caught her eye, and she knew even from a distance that one of the GoldenNight tigers had ventured into the city streets.

Unlike many feline changeling groups, the tigers and leopards of India didn't mind interacting with city populations, but they didn't live in the urban centers. The spaces were too constrained, the pathways too cramped.

As the changeling prowled out of sight, a scooter swerved around a town car, while three pedestrians with shopping bags decided to stop traffic by simply stepping out onto the road to cross.

She'd once hosted a meeting with a Psy business associate normally based out of Geneva. The man had recoiled at the energetic beat of her city. "How can you live here?" he'd asked. "So many people, so much noise, everything . . . unorganized."

He was wrong.

Delhi was highly organized. You just had to be a local to see it. But before being a denizen of this old city, before being the Rao CEO, Payal was an anchor.

That thought in mind, she picked up her encrypted organizer once more. Canto Mercant had sent the image as promised: of an oasis in a desert, one made unique not only by the placement of certain palms, but by the etchings on the flat gray stones that had been placed on the sand in a wide pathway that led gently down to cerulean blue water.

The sands were a fine gold that made her wonder if she was teleporting to the Gobi desert, that place where the dunes sang and sunset turned cliffs to fire.

Focusing on the image, she felt her mind begin a trace and lock. One second. Two. She had it, the knowledge a hum in her blood. Had the image been imprecise or generic, she'd have gotten a feeling of sliding or bouncing off things, her brain unable to settle.

She'd always wondered if other teleport-capable Tks felt the same sensations but had never trusted one well enough to ask. Even the most minor mental deviations could be cause for concern when it came to one of Designation A. Because anchors as a whole weren't stable.

Councilor Santano Enrique's psychopathic murder spree had just cemented that belief in the minds of those who knew what he'd done. The vast majority of the population *didn't* know, but Payal wasn't the vast majority of the population.

She was a cardinal telekinetic.

She was an anchor.

She was exactly like Santano Enrique.

Before

Find Magdalene's son. Find Canto Fernandez.

—Priority 1 mission alert from Ena Mercant to entire
Mercant network (1 August 2053)

THE BOY KNEW his small rescuer's makeshift barrier would fall at
the first strong push, but he didn't say anything. The truth was, even
if she ran, there was nowhere for her to go. This re-education facility
was in the middle of snowy wilderness—and they both had cages
around their minds, imprisoning their psychic abilities.

"I'm sorry," he said to her, as molten arcs of pain shot up his spine
in painful contrast to the lack of sensation in his legs. "That you had
to do that."

She used her free hand to pat the hand she held. "You didn't make
me." It was a firm statement. "He hurt me, too."

But he knew she'd killed in that moment because of him, because
of the threat to his life. The teacher wouldn't have stopped, not today.
The adult male had known that no one would care if Canto died. The
children in this school were all flawed, all unwanted. He and the girl
were the only cardinals, but even their great psychic abilities hadn't
been enough to make up for their imperfections.

If he hadn't been a cardinal, he'd have wondered why his father hadn't simply strangled him when it became obvious he wasn't a "normal" baby. Even at just over eight years of age, he knew his father's family wielded a lot of power. Enforcement wouldn't have looked too deeply into the "accidental" death of a baby.

But a cardinal, even a broken one, could be useful. So he'd been allowed to live. Until his brain began to act too strangely to accept. His father had told him that this school was his "last chance to step up and be a Fernandez." As if Canto could just *fix* the misfires in his brain that meant he heard voices—as if he could will his body to work as it should.

Looking up into his small friend's cardinal eyes, he wondered at her power, but didn't ask. As his power meant nothing here, so did hers. Not with their minds trapped in psychic barbed wire. So he said, "What will you do when you get out, are free?" He wanted freedom for her more than he did for himself—she'd been here longer, suffered longer.

She was younger, her starlit eyes stark with reality, but she got all bright and happy at his question. "I watched a recording of pink blossom trees once, all in a row. The blossoms were falling and I wanted to walk under them. I'll do that." She squeezed his hand. "What about you?"

He told her, asked her more questions. She was so smart, so vivid. He liked being around her, liked listening to her dreams. She was telling him about her favorite animal when the door smashed open. Then the girl who'd saved him was being wrenched away from him, and he realized he'd never asked her name. No one used their names in this place. They were just numbers and letters.

Neither one of them screamed.

They knew these people had no mercy.

Rather, they stared at one another in a silent rebellion that only ended when she was literally carried out of the room. One of the teachers kicked him in the gut. When he choked out a cough but didn't move, the numbness now halfway up his chest and his breathing a stuttering beat, the man looked at the woman who was checking on the dead teacher.

"Looks like a real medical issue. We'd better get instructions from the family."

"Sure. It's part of the protocol. But you know what they'll say—he's here because he's problematic. No one will authorize lifesaving measures." Cold green eyes on his face. "Guardians will tell us to dump him on his bed and let him die a 'natural' death. He'd be better off if I slit his throat."

Chapter 4

Current percentage of anchors diagnosed as psychopathic: 14%
Current percentage of anchors diagnosed as borderline: 27%
Current percentage of anchors with significant mental health risk factors: 43%

—PsyMed Census Bureau: 2067

CANTO ARRIVED AT the oasis five minutes prior to his meeting with Payal Rao. "Thanks for the teleport," he said to Genara.

Lifting two fingers to her temple, her ebony skin gleaming under the desert sunlight, Genara shot him a salute that was just a little too crisp to come off as anything but martial. Her hair, the tight curls buzzed close to her skull with military precision, echoed that impression, as did the way she stood lightly on her feet.

Always ready to snap into motion.

"Nice shirt," she said.

He scowled. "Arwen calls the color distressed steel. It's fucking gray."

Genara's flat expression didn't alter. "Heard he stole your other shirts and burned them."

"Go away," Canto growled, because while Genara appeared as

Silent as they came, she was tight with Arwen. Which told Canto all he needed to know about this new member of the Mercant clan.

Ena rarely adopted in family members, but when she did, it was law. Trust was given at once. Because Ena Mercant was the toughest of them all—if she said Genara was to be trusted, was to be treated as family, that was how it would be.

Canto had said "Yes, ma'am" and gotten on with creating an unbreakable new identity for Genara. The only thing he'd asked his grandmother was where in hell she'd managed to unearth an unknown teleport-capable Tk. Canto ran their intelligence operations, yet Genara was a mystery who'd appeared out of thin air.

Ena had taken a sip of her herbal tea and said, "You know I want you to act as Silver's right hand when she takes the reins of the family." Her eyes—unreadable silver at times, fog gray with a hint of blue at others—had been serene, her silky white hair in a pristine knot, and the pale bronze silk of her tunic without a wrinkle. "I had no such right hand until Silver came of age, and life is far easier with one."

"As long as that right hand lives in the shadows, I have no problem with it." Canto had about as much desire to live in the public eye as he had to wear the chartreuse horror of a shirt Arwen kept threatening to gift him. "What does that have to do with Genara?"

"A little mystery to keep you sharp."

"I should quit," he'd muttered, making a face at the tea she'd insisted on pouring him. "See who you can find to put up with this disrespect."

Ena's gaze had altered, holding a warmth he'd first seen when he was eight and motionless in a hospital bed, scared and lost in a way that had come out as childish rage. She'd been so cold then, a woman aflame with ice—except for when she'd looked at him. "You're home now, Canto," she'd said in that calm voice that hit down to the bone. "You're safe. No one will *ever* again hurt you."

Canto hadn't believed the stranger she'd been, but she was all he had. *What about her?* he'd demanded telepathically, while the machine pumped air into his paralyzed lungs. *The girl who helped me. 3K?*

"There's no record of her in the school's system, and all those staff who had contact with the students are dead, so we can't scan their minds." Not even a single flicker in her at the idea of smashing open people's minds to reveal their innermost thoughts.

Canto had held the implacable steel of her eyes. *Did you kill them?*

"I would have but only after getting all necessary information. Never act without thought, Canto. That is how your enemies win." Her cool and smooth hand on his brow, brushing back his hair. "However, they were already dead when we came to bring you home. It appears one of the other students broke their mental bonds and struck out."

The other kids? Canto had asked.

"We've found safe homes for them and will monitor their lives to ensure they have the help they need. Mercants do not abandon children. Remember that. Never will we abandon a child in need. But we found no other cardinal. We'll do everything in our power to track down your 3K—your mother has already begun the search."

It was the only promise to Canto that Ena hadn't been able to keep, 3K being so far under the radar that she'd been a ghost. All these years and Canto hadn't accepted that the ghost imagery might be harsh reality, that 3K was long dead. Magdalene, he knew, continued to run the search in the background of her other tasks.

Canto and his mother shared the same obsessive streak when it came to things that mattered.

On the subject of Genara, his grandmother had taken another sip of tea before saying, "No one else would put up with my games, dear Canto. Which is why I play with you." And because she was Ena Mercant, the woman who'd taught a broken, angry boy the meaning of family, the meaning of loyalty, he was now hitting his head against the brick wall that was tracking down the true identity of his new cousin.

Never would he admit to Ena that he relished the challenge.

Today, Genara said, "Next time Arwen should steal your jeans, too," before she teleported out.

Canto's jeans were well-washed and shaped to his body. Arwen knew full well that Canto would hunt him down without mercy should he lay his stylish fingers on them. Shirts were shirts. Jeans? A whole different story.

Rather than staying inside the three-walled shelter at this end of the pathway, he made his way to the edge of the water that reminded him of the haunting azure glow of the Substrate. The late-afternoon sun was warm on his face and the skin of his exposed forearms, the dark brown leather-synth of his half gloves soft and supple from use.

He'd switched chairs for this, the wheels on this one wider and more rugged, better able to handle the desert environment. The chair's computronic components were also designed to survive the fine particles of sand. It had taken him only a single teenage mistake to realize that this particular sand got everywhere and could freeze complex computronics.

The chair did still, however, have hover capacity—along with a hidden compartment that held a sleek and deadly weapon. As a cardinal telepath, he could blow out Payal's brains even as she picked him up and smashed him against the nearest hard surface. In other words, they were both as dangerous as the other.

The weapon wasn't redundant. It was practical.

A flicker in the telepathic scan he'd run continuously since his arrival. He couldn't enter the mind that had appeared in his vicinity, but he knew it was there. Angling his chair to the left, he sucked in a breath as he watched Payal Rao walk along the paved path toward him. She was smaller than his mental image of her—though that made little sense, since he'd looked up her height.

But Payal had a presence that demanded attention, took over a space.

In raw physical terms, she was a bare five feet two inches tall. Her body curved sharply inward at the waist and flared at the hips. She had curves on her upper body, too, her shape not one that was favored among the majority of Psy. He knew damn well why—because it was considered inherently sensual.

That prejudice held even now, but according to his research, Payal had never capitulated to the societal pressure to get cosmetic surgery. Neither did she make any effort to downplay her body. She dressed with perfect businesslike sharpness, without ever blunting her edge; he wondered if she was conscious of the fact that her refusal to back down just added to her reputation as a woman of steel.

Payal Rao, a recent *PsyNet Beacon* article had stated, *is a predator as deadly as any changeling panther. The last rival who forgot that is currently picking up the pieces of his life after a coldly calculating play by Rao saw his company's valuation dive by seventy-five percent. When asked for comment, Rao said, "He began the skirmish. I ended it."*

Today, the predator wore a top of a lightweight material, the sleeves long and cuffed at the wrists and the neck featuring two long ties that she'd knotted loosely above the generous curves of her breasts.

It was smoky blue, a hue that complemented the honeyed brown of her skin.

According to his research, her father was a Gradient 7.9 Tk of Czech-Indian descent, while the maternal half of her genes came from a Gradient 8.8 F-Psy with a mix of Spanish and Indian ancestry.

The genetic mix had given her a softly rounded face with lush lips and long lashes that belied her reputation. Out of context—and if you ignored the night sky of her eyes—she'd appear a pretty and sensual woman, no threat at all.

As for the rest of her clothing, she'd tucked the blue top into wide-legged pants in a dark gray that flowed over her hips all the way down to just above the ground. Canto caught flashes of spiked black heels as she walked. He knew about those torture devices because Silver in-sisted on wearing them, too.

"They're a weapon, Canto," she'd said once when he'd asked. "Each element of how we dress is a weapon and a warning to the world. Even yours."

Canto had briefly considered putting on businesslike clothing today, but as Payal was who she was, so was Canto. There was no point pretending to be otherwise if they were going to be working together for any length of time. The new short-sleeved shirt with its aged steel buttons was about as dressed up as he got.

She didn't stare at his chair when she reached him; no doubt she'd seen and processed the sight when she first teleported in. But she would comment. Most Psy did. It was rare for them to see one of their kind using a device that assisted with motion. The Psy as a race had some very ugly decisions in their past; those decisions included a goal of perfection that had been a de facto program of eugenics.

Now they were all paying the price for those choices.

Right then, Payal *did* begin to stare. Hard.

Eyes narrowing, he went to snarl at her to take a photo if she was that interested.

Then she said, "7J."

And his entire world imploded.

Chapter 5

Tests confirm that the child's unusual ocular structure has no effect on his vision.

—Medical report on Canto Fernandez, age 12 months (17 June 2046)

"YOUR EYES ARE like galaxies," Payal said. "The white spots aren't scattered across the black, but grouped in a highly specific and memorable pattern. You're the only cardinal I've ever met with such eyes."

Canto couldn't speak, his throat drying up. He'd tried so hard to remember the pattern of 3K's eyes, but he'd been a traumatized child, his memories too broken up to be of any use. "How can you be sure?" It came out harsh, a challenge.

"Telekinetic memory."

Telekinetic.

It crystalized then, the unimaginable torture of what had been done to her. The most free of Psy hobbled by chains. He knew this wasn't a lie or a con—only a strictly limited number of people knew about that school, and about what had taken place there. Yet he had to be certain. "Have you done what you wanted to do when you got free?"

A frozen moment before she said, "There are no blossom trees where I live."

A tremor shook his psyche, and it was his turn to stare—this time, with the eyes of a man who'd been searching for her for three decades without success.

The knotted and overgrown bangs were gone; Payal's wavy hair was pulled into a ponytail that gave the impression of being carefree while keeping every single stray strand of hair off her face. Undone, he estimated it would reach just past her shoulder blades. Her face was no longer thin and bony, her features filled out, and just as he wasn't that scared and angry boy, she wasn't the waif who'd killed to help him.

A pinch in the region of his heart, a startling sense of loss.

She glanced down at his chair at last. "So, you had successful treatment."

No Psy outside the family who'd ever commented on his physical state had deemed it a success. But Payal hadn't minced words as a child and didn't do so as an adult. She meant what she said. "Yes."

He angled his chair back around to face the water as she moved to stand at the edge, the two of them side by side. The blue was shocking to his vision now, the entire world in high contrast.

"I can feel everything except for my legs. Medics said if they hadn't removed the spinal and other tumors when they did, it'd have been too late. I'd have died." The tumors had been tiny spots of virulence, obscured by the normal machinery of the body until his grandmother ordered a massive battery of tests.

"How long were you in the infirmary?"

"Years, in and out." He glanced at the line of her profile. "What happened to you?" The question came out raw, unadorned. "I've looked for you every day since."

PAYAL'S gut churned.

7J. 7J.

Half of her had begun to believe that the boy whose hand she'd held had been a figment of her manic and disturbed mind, a fantasy she'd created out of a need for care of any kind.

It was clear Canto hadn't known her identity as 3K until she'd blurted out his ID in a moment of shock that had devastated her control. Now this man knew more about her than anyone else in the universe. Even her father wasn't fully aware of all that had happened— all she'd *been*—in that hellhole where he'd abandoned her.

She could still remember every question 7J had asked her as they sat there, waiting for the inevitable. Not test questions. Not questions to dig up information he could use to his advantage. Just questions about her dreams, about food she liked, about what made her happy.

It had been the first time in her life anyone had wanted to hear her speak.

Inside her crazed, lost mind, she'd secretly called him a friend. Had the adult Payal permitted her Silence to fall when emotion became legal, she might've felt pity for that small, lost part of herself. So deprived of kindness and care that she'd turned fleeting interactions into a friendship. The boy on whose shoulders she'd laid her foolish childhood dreams had been so thin, his body no longer responding to his commands.

Only his eyes had never changed: fierce and fascinating and . . . protective. She'd probably misread them. She'd been an insane child after all. But . . . he'd given her food, saving things from his own meager meals to tuck into her hand when no one was looking.

That thin boy with fierce eyes had grown into a man with long legs and strong, wide shoulders, his arms ropy with muscle. Veins stood out along the olive skin of his forearms, and his thighs pushed up against the faded denim of his jeans. The latter meant he either had a level of lower limb mobility or used machines to exercise those muscles.

Regardless, that kind of strength couldn't be achieved overnight. He had to have maintained a punishing regime over many years. She'd do well to remember that—it was an indication of relentless determination and stubbornness.

People that driven didn't give up on a goal.

Right now, his goal was to rope her into a position that would take her time and attention away from the Rao empire. There was still so much she needed to do there, so many changes she had to make to ensure that Karishma could come home—and that no more innocents would die or suffer.

As for Canto's question, she decided on an honest answer after calculating whether it could be used against her in any way and deciding it couldn't; the paper trail had been wiped clean. "My family almost lost an heir to an accident, decided they might be able to bring the flawed one up to scratch after all."

Varun's car accident had saved her—but it had signaled the beginning of the end for her brother. It was during his recovery that he'd had the time to start fomenting traitorous thoughts. All that downtime to see how tightly their father held the reins, and to chafe against Pranath's control.

"Your shell profile is brilliant." Canto sounded like he was gritting out the words, his tone crushed gravel. "You're in childhood school photos at a time when I know you were with me. The images aren't the sharpest, but add in all the other details and the shell holds."

"My deceased brother Varun," she said. "He was gifted at such photographic and computronic manipulation. My father also had the money to grease plenty of palms. The teachers were bribed to 'remember' me after the fact—and it didn't matter if the children didn't. After all, I was only six when I was pulled out of that prison masquerading as a school."

Payal had a reputation for bluntness, but this was the one topic on which she didn't speak. To anyone. To be so open . . . it made her chest expand, her breath suddenly huge. "What happened to you?" She'd been too young to search for him, but she'd never forgotten the boy who'd held her hand and asked her about her dreams as if she had a right to those dreams.

She'd also done a number of clandestine searches on cardinals with unusual eyes, but of course, he'd never come up.

"My grandmother came looking for a grandchild who'd vanished without a trace." Canto shoved a hand through the short strands of his silky black hair.

"You weren't hers, though. All your documents state you belonged to the Fernandez family."

"Ena Mercant never forgets her children or grandchildren—and *no one* is permitted to sentence us to death." He shrugged, the motion fluid with muscle. "My father tried to lie his way out of it, because in his arrogance, he'd broken their contract. He didn't survive that lie."

"A formidable woman." Too bad no one like Ena had existed for Payal; she'd had only Pranath Rao, who'd considered her an "unfortunate" mistake.

The Rao line's tendency to birth strong Tks—and hold on to them against the might of the Council—was a powerful element of their identity. But they'd birthed no cardinals in the line until Payal. And she'd turned out to be mentally defective. "Was it the physical deterioration that made Fernandez hide you, then sentence you to that place?" A private question, but it looked like 3K and 7J were answering such questions.

"It had a strong role to play," he said. "I had seizures as an infant, couldn't walk until age three, and even then my coordination was problematic. But the final straw was my mental state—I began to hear voices."

Payal's breath caught, a hard lump in her throat. "Delusions?"

"No. It turns out I was hearing the NetMind before my initialization as an anchor." He leaned forward, forearms braced on his thighs and the steel color of his shirt stretched across the breadth of his shoulders. "I've done some research, and it's a rare but not unknown phenomenon with child As."

The NetMind was a neosentience and the guardian and librarian of the PsyNet . . . or had been, until it began to disintegrate into chaos. Payal hadn't sensed its presence for a long time.

Canto turned those galaxy eyes on her. "And you? Why were you abandoned?"

Payal never spoke about this. She couldn't do so, even to 7J. There was too much risk that he could use it against her—because unlike with Canto, her sanity or lack of it had nothing to do with the NetMind.

So she gave him a different truth. "I didn't fit my father's idea of perfection. I'm neurodivergent in ways he couldn't accept. My emotional range has been stunted since childhood." That no anchor was truly Silent was an accepted fact between them that didn't need to be articulated.

"B.S.," he muttered, his features dark. "Even if that were true, why would Pranath care? It'd just make you better at Silence."

"I was also prone to flying into uncontrollable rages."

Canto's words were hard when he spoke. "You were never violent at the school unless they pushed you to it. Was your brother Lalit doing something to set you off?"

Payal blinked slowly, her hands fisting inside her pants pockets. "What do you know about Lalit?"

"Rumors of psychopathic behavior."

Deciding that was too much trust even between 3K and 7J, she said, "Cardinal what?"

"Telepath." A scowl. "Imagine the fucking chaos we could've caused if we'd been free."

"Could've-beens are a waste of energy." She'd learned that lesson young; once in that place, half-crazed by all the small tortures her brother had inflicted on her, she hadn't been able to think with any kind of clarity for a long time.

When she had finally found a path to sanity, she'd castigated herself for allowing Lalit to get what he wanted. He'd been too young to influence or attack Varun, but Payal had been easy prey. Soon, however, she'd seen that such thoughts couldn't help her; she'd been stuck in that prison, alone and without help.

Her eyes went to Canto again.

Did he remember giving her food? The teachers had put them on strict diets meant to keep them weak. She'd been hungry all the time. But every time they passed in the corridor, Canto's—then—halting walk familiar to her, he'd slipped her food he'd saved from his meal.

A nutrient biscuit.

A slice of dried fruit.

A nut bar that was the biggest-energy item on that day's menu.

Payal remembered every single gift.

Her chest began to tighten up, her skin to heat. She felt as she hadn't since she'd been that small, helpless child. She couldn't go back there. Not now. Not when she'd made it out. Taking a deep breath, she stared out straight in front, the world a blur.

Her next comment was rote, words to buy her time. "An interesting location. How did you discover it?"

"I'm a Mercant." It seemed an answer as flat as her question had been. Then his shoulders locked and he shifted his chair to face her. "Payal, we are not doing this."

"You asked me to come here."

"No, we're not going to pretend to be two strangers having a conversation about the fucking desert or the weather."

Chapter 6

"Our histories tell us that anger can be either a weapon or a weakness, Canto. Decide what it will be for you."

"No, Grandmother. Sometimes, I just want to be *angry*. I don't want to pretend to be civilized—because I'm not, and never will be. And I'll never wear masks."

—Conversation between Canto Mercant and Ena Mercant (2063)

PAYAL COULD FEEL the heat blazing off Canto—but that had to be her imagination, for they stood in a sunlit desert. Yet the urge to go closer to his flame was a tug. It had always been there, since she was that feral little girl. The boy who'd given her food and who'd stealthily passed over a folded-up piece of paper bearing answers to a test she was meant to fail, he'd meant something to her.

Some part of her insisted on seeing that same boy in this man. But he wasn't. He was a Mercant. A man whose job it was to gather information—so it could be used against his targets. "We're strangers now," she said as coldly as she could, and took a step to the left, putting more distance between them. "The girl I was, she's dead. She had to die so I could survive." A simple, inexorable fact.

Canto's eyes shifted to pure black, the galaxies eclipsed by emotion. "What did they do to you?" Rage thrummed in every syllable.

"It's all in the past." She glanced at her timepiece, steeling herself so her arm didn't tremble. "Why don't we talk about why we're here today? I don't have endless time."

"You mean the extinction of Designation A?" It was a near-growl. "Yeah, why don't we?"

"Using the word 'extinction' is a touch hyperbolic." She had to keep this rigidly practical. "The PsyNet has its issues, but much of it has to do with the damage done by Silence, and by the rise of the Scarabs." Deadly, unstable Psy who were unleashing their abilities on the Net in a fury of violence.

When he didn't respond, she couldn't help herself from glancing at him.

It was as big a shock as the first time she'd laid eyes on him, her stomach muscles clenching reflexively. She couldn't understand it, why he had this impact on her when they'd both grown and changed so much in the years between what had been and what was now. His cheekbones were striking, his cardinal eyes extraordinary—it was as if he held the universe in his eyes.

Even had she forgotten everything else about him, never would she mistake those eyes for those of any other cardinal. The eyes and the cheekbones weren't the whole of it, however. His skin held a glow that said he often spent time out under the sun, and his eyes were subtly tilted, his jaw square. His short hair was silky black, but the unshaven bristles on his face held a dusting of gray.

Binh Fernandez had been of mainly Filipino and Turkish descent, with a smattering of other genetic factors. The Mercants, meanwhile, had multiple lines of descent through their family tree, but the primary one through Ena was Caucasian—however, that split again in the Mercant matriarch's offspring.

It was the rare Psy who was full-blooded in any genetic sense. Not when their race was about psychic power above all else. Matches were on the basis of increasing the chances of powerful offspring.

Payal didn't know much about the Mercant—Magdalene—who'd carried Canto in her womb. She needed more data on Magdalene. More data on him. Data made sense of the world. Data would help her understand why she felt the impact of him like a kick to the stomach.

Data would stop the feral girl inside her from screaming for freedom.

It had to be a remnant of their childhood interaction, especially those final minutes when she'd locked her hand around his and held on, just held on. She'd known that pain lay on the horizon for both of them, but for those murderously stolen minutes, they'd been free of punishment, free of being watched.

Just free.

But that had been in a different lifetime. Canto's impact on her would fade as soon as she learned more about him and his motives. People were never what they appeared on the surface; while Canto Mercant was beautiful in the structure of his features and in his musculature, physical beauty had nothing to do with personality and ethics.

Payal's brother was considered handsome and sophisticated, one of Delhi's most eligible bachelors. Yet Lalit's version of recreation was to cut bloody lines into the skin of crying men and women who couldn't fight his telekinetic strength.

What she needed to know was the core of Canto Mercant.

Monster or manipulator? Messiah or deluded?

Ally or threat to be eliminated?

Her power crawled under her skin, ready to strike out at the first sign of aggression.

.   .   .

CANTO couldn't read her, this enigma of a woman who'd once killed to protect him. She gave every appearance of being distant and cold, yet there were moments when he could swear emotion licked the air, a wild dark wave viciously constrained.

His muscles knotted with a sense of wrongness.

He'd been older, he reminded himself, more likely to hold on to his sense of self. But the girl he'd known . . . even so young, her will had been titanium. He wouldn't have thought anything could force her into a shape she didn't choose.

He hated the idea of her being coerced and smothered into a form acceptable to her father. "Thank you," he said, his voice rough.

"For what?" She didn't look at him as she asked the question, her eyes on the palm fronds that waved in the slight breeze.

"For stopping that teacher from murdering me."

Payal's dark eyes—no stars now, nothing but endless black—landed on him. "Would he have gone that far, do you think? We were, after all, the children of important people. Certainly they must've needed to get authorization before terminal action."

"They had so much power—were bloated with it." A deep psychic corruption. "My father also hadn't come to see me since abandoning me in that place. To him, I was a genetic mistake he wished would vanish without a trace."

"My father had me tested for psychotic and psychopathic tendencies after the school reported what I'd done." Payal's tone was dangerously even. "He'd already decided to take me back, see if I could be brought up to an acceptable standard."

"Wrong fucking child to test." It came out harsh as crushed stone. "Is he truly so blind that he doesn't see which one of his children is the problem?"

"The fact that I'm CEO and Lalit isn't is the answer to your question" was the cool response, before she shifted the direction of the conversation. "The PsyNet has begun to heal since the re-emergence of the empaths."

Canto forced himself away from their private history, away from the compulsion of Payal Rao, and toward the heartbreaking clarity of the water that fed the oasis. "I thought I was imagining that."

"You're not." Payal's voice, so flat, so without tone, so *wrong*. "The problem is that as soon as it heals, it fractures again. The fractures have now begun to cascade one after the other, which gives the impression that the empaths aren't helping at all."

A rustle of fabric. A soft waft of air that brought with it a subtle scent. It was . . . nice, he supposed with an inward grimace. But it held none of the passion and intensity of the girl who'd sharpened a toothbrush into a knife because she intended to escape, or the wonder of the girl who'd told him about walking under blossom trees with a dreamy light in her eyes.

"The truth," Payal continued in that toneless voice, "is that half the Net would already be dead and desiccated without the empathic network—their Honeycomb, as I believe they prefer for it to be called."

Her mind, the acute sharpness of her intelligence, hadn't changed. "You've studied it."

"I'm an anchor." A faint rebuke.

He'd take it. He'd take any emotion he could get from her. Because he had the sickening feeling that while she'd saved him . . . no one had saved her. Payal had had to fight for survival every day of her existence, and she'd done so by withdrawing so deep within her core of steel that the girl she'd once been had no voice.

She turned to face him. "Haven't you kept an eye on the grid that underlies the Substrate?"

"I can't," he admitted with a grimace. "Turns out not all anchor minds work the same. When I look into the Substrate, I see the wider picture, and what I see reveals extreme stress, buckled sections, others that are stretched thin."

Payal paused, seeming to chew that over. But her question had nothing to do with the foundation of the PsyNet. "How did you know I was an A?"

Most of the other As had assumed he had the knowledge because he was a Mercant. But that wasn't Payal Rao: cool, contained, and ruthlessly intelligent. "I can link A minds in the Substrate back to their PsyNet presence." This wasn't about lies. Especially between them. "After that, I used my usual skills to put a name to the target mind."

The stars had returned to her eyes and those stars bored into him. "No one has ever claimed to be able to identify anchor minds on the PsyNet."

"I'm not delusional," he grumbled with a scowl. "And I didn't say I could ID anchor minds on the PsyNet—I said I can ID them in the *Substrate*." A place accessible only to Designation A. "Think about it—when was the last time anyone asked anchors anything about how our minds work?"

She continued to regard him with a vague air of suspicion. He wanted to growl at her—his grandmother was right; he'd been hanging around the bears too much. But he felt more at home with the rowdy changelings than he did with all Psy outside of his family.

Payal was the sole exception.

What they had here, now, it was awkward and it made his guts twist with a sense of frustrated fury, but he still didn't want to pull away. He wanted to get closer, see inside her. Figure out if that wild girl was just buried . . . or had been erased out of existence.

"Let's head to the shelter," he muttered when she didn't respond. "I want to show you a set of specs."

PAYAL turned to walk up with Canto. "Were you ever Silent?" This level of emotional depth hadn't grown in the time since the fall of Silence. It appeared too ingrained an aspect of his personality.

"No." A grim smile, his eyes glittering. "That was one of the many issues that got me thrown into that place—my Silence was erratic as hell."

As Payal considered that, she couldn't help noticing that he wasn't using either the hover capacity or the drive built into his chair to ease his way up the incline. His muscles were defined against the olive brown of his skin as he maneuvered the chair along the path, and a tracery of strong veins ran under that skin, his jaw set in concentration.

Another data point: this was a man unused to taking no for an answer from himself or from others.

He might prefer jeans to suits and speak with a confronting frankness that eschewed any attempt at sophistication or manipulation, but that was because Canto Mercant fed his determination and energy into other areas.

He was dangerous.

Her fingers curled into her palm, holding on to the sensory memory of a piece of dried apple being pressed into her hand behind the backs of the teachers. A part of her—a quite insane part she'd kept caged for decades—wondered if any element of that protective, kind boy existed in the no-doubt sophisticated surveillance operative he'd become.

Not that it mattered.

Childhood's end had come for both of them long ago.

Upon reaching the shelter—the roof of which held multiple solar power panels—he went to the refrigerated cooler in the corner and removed two bottles of water. A fine layer of ice had formed on the outside of each.

She accepted one, the cold welcome against her palms. Had she been alone, she'd have put the bottle against her neck or cheek, but a robot didn't do that. A robot displayed no weakness. A robot was never vulnerable.

Payal had spent too long building her public persona to allow it to fracture now.

He already knows.

It was a whisper from the maddened heart of her.

He's seen you at your absolute worst, with the blood of another living being on your face and hands.

Chapter 7

A: The designation from which it all begins. I, fortunate to be privy to the writings of a seer of legend, do find it my sad duty to share that this is the designation with which it will all end one day.

—Iram's *Almanac of Designations, Annotated with Thoughts of the Author* (1787)

PAYAL HAD PRETENDED to be sorry for her actions during the psychiatric evals ordered by her father. Only six years old and she'd already learned that her natural tendency to tell the truth was a handicap. But she'd never actually been sorry. The man she'd killed had been a torturer who'd been brutally hurting a boy worth a thousand of his cruel mind.

Payal had never permitted her mask to drop during childhood. Had she done so, however, she'd have spit at the name of that so-called teacher. As a child, she'd have danced on his dead body and not cared.

Yes, that caged part of her was quite, quite mad.

Taking a seat in a chair across from Canto, she checked the seal of the water bottle, then unscrewed the lid and drank straight from the

bottle. He put away the glass he'd been about to offer her, before un-
screwing his own bottle and drinking down half of it in gulps that
made his throat muscles move in a way that caught her attention,
held it.

His neck was strong, his skin touched with a hint of perspiration,
the color appearing darker where—

Going motionless as she realized her small obsession, Payal shored
up her shields.

She couldn't give way to such primal impulses. They came from the
murderous girl who crooned in her head in the quietest hour of night,
wanting freedom. Wanting to *live*.

Capping the water with hands that wanted to tremble, she put it
on a small table to the side. Canto had already placed his own bottle
on the same table. Uncapped.

Payal resisted the temptation to use her telekinesis to lift the cap
from where he'd forgotten it on top of the cooler and screw it on. It'd
be a good use of the micro-Tk skills she'd had to learn to pass her
training modules, but it would also be giving in to her compulsion for
order. Order was how she stayed sane, but she refused to permit it to
become another kind of madness.

Having reached into a side panel of his chair to pull out a paper-
thin large-format organizer, Canto brought up a file on the screen.
"Look."

She took the organizer. On the screen was an image of the PsyNet
as it had been pre-Honeycomb. "Where are the empaths?"

"Several levels up." He moved his chair so he was right next to her,
the warmth of him a quiet assault against her senses. "This is the basic
structure of the Net—the bones, so to speak."

Payal tried not to breathe in his scent. It made her skin prickle, her
pulse want to kick. "I see." She used every trick in her arsenal to narrow her focus to the organizer. What he'd sketched out was the Net

without all the surface chatter—a sea of black with only the finest faded pinpricks to show the minds that existed on the layer above . . . except . . . "Why are there fluctuations in the fabric?"

Reaching out with a hand partially covered by a glove, Canto tapped one of the fluctuations, a point where it appeared that the fabric of the Net was being sucked inward. Like a whirlpool frozen midmovement. "This is you."

Payal went motionless.

"I always thought we could all see each other," he said in that deep voice that held a gravelly edge. "I only recently realized I'm not normal there. But that's not the point. Do you see the pattern?"

Payal's mind saw patterns as others saw the sky or grass. "Your modeling is incorrect," she said with the same bluntness that had led to the robot moniker. Such honesty had been part of the insane girl, too, and it frustrated her that to interact with the world, she had to so often stifle her natural tendency.

"Why?"

"There are no overlaps between anchor zones. There should be overlaps."

"Yes, there should."

She was so involved in examining the model that it took a moment for his quiet agreement to penetrate. Looking up, she met those extraordinary eyes that held the universe, and once again she was nearly lost, falling into them as she had when they were children.

"We'll go walking under the blossoms." A rasp of air through his abused throat. "Or maybe I won't be able to walk. But I'll be there."

"Can we eat cakes as well? The small pretty ones they have in the windows of the bake shops?"

"Payal?" A rough softness to Canto's question.

Hauling herself back from the brink, she broke the searing intimacy of the eye contact while fighting off the keening need from the part of her forever impacted by those fleeting minutes so long ago. "I know there's no overlap in my region due to a recent death." An older anchor had passed away three weeks earlier. "Are you telling me there are zero overlaps across the Net?"

"Seventy-five percent lack of overlaps between anchor zones."

"Impossible." Payal snapped her head to face him. "That would mean a single anchor death could plummet the Net into a fatal spiral."

The Architect

The occurrence of Scarab Syndrome in the general population continues to climb.

Patient Zero is maintaining coherence, and Memory Aven-Rose, now permanent primary empath on this team, has significantly increased her success rate in stabilizing new cases, but she can only attempt to stabilize those we find.

I have grave concerns that the graph charting patients, though upward-trending, isn't as steep as it should be—despite our efforts, a number of those with Scarab Syndrome are falling through the cracks.

While my job is medicine, not politics, I do believe that a large percentage of those lost patients are being scooped up by the bad actor known as the Architect, their aim being to use the patients' growing psychic powers with no thought to the mental decline and death that is the inevitable result of untreated Scarab Syndrome.

—Report to the Psy Ruling Coalition from Dr. Maia Ndiaye,
PsyMed SF Echo

THE ARCHITECT HAD plenty of contacts inside the PsyNet, including many who agreed with the old way of things. After all, what had happened since the fall of Silence but the disintegration of their race?

The Ruling Coalition might be trying to sell the idea that the problems had begun in Silence and that what they were now experiencing was the destructive aftermath, but the intelligent saw through that smokescreen. It was in the Coalition's interest to say such things, part of their grand plan to keep the populace weak and cowed.

The Architect didn't much care for the masses, not when the Psy were so much lesser than she and those of her kind.

Scarabs.

The new power.

The new people.

The Psy would be nothing but slaves for her to rule once she achieved her benevolent dictatorship. She'd inducted so many more soldiers into her network over the past weeks, had spread infinite tendrils through the PsyNet. She was also getting better at persuading her newborn children as they came to their true consciousness.

No longer would her kind be imprisoned and poisoned by so-called medics. No longer would her kind be made lesser so that the Psy could feel strong. No longer would she and her children be anything but world-annihilating powers.

Now the weak ones in power were saying that the PsyNet needed to be broken into pieces in order to be saved. She could not permit that. How could she rule over the entire race if the PsyNet was no longer whole?

No, that course of action had to be stopped.

At the same time, she could see why the Ruling Coalition had come to their foolish decision. Perhaps she'd been hasty in ordering attacks that so significantly weakened critical PsyNet structures. But to fragment the PsyNet? No. Never.

She sat, thought. She wasn't like her children, many of whom were so out of control that she was the only leash on their violence. Not only was she rational, she had telepathic backups of her personality in place should the awesome Scarab power within overwhelm her at any point. A small price to pay for untrammeled power tempered by reason.

Today, she used that sense of reason to make the decision to ask her children to stand down. The Silence of the Scarabs would lull the Psy into a sense of complacency and security, leaving them all the more vulnerable for the strike to come.

The Architect began to make detailed plans, giving no consideration to the fact that the PsyNet was now so damaged that it was beyond being able to heal itself.

In her mind, the Net sprawled endlessly, a black sky unalterable and unbreakable.

Chapter 8

As we walk into a world with emotion, we must accept that for some of our people, it is too late. They were born in Silence, raised in Silence, scarred by Silence. To expect them to forget or "get over" a lifetime of conditioning and interact at the emotional level that may become the norm is cruel—and the Psy have too much cruelty in our past already.

—*PsyNet Beacon* editorial by Jaya Laila Storm (Medical Empath and Social Interaction Columnist)

CANTO COULDN'T STOP himself from watching Payal. It was no longer about the shock of coming face-to-face with the phantom he'd been hunting for so many years; it was *her*. The line of her profile, the way she'd allowed her spine to soften in her concentration—but most of all, the intensity with which she looked at the data.

As if absorbing it into her brain for later recall.

Telekinetic memory.

This wasn't only that. This was Payal Rao, the woman who'd become the CEO of a family where loyalty meant nothing and betrayal was to be expected. She'd had to be smarter, tougher, more ruthless.

And alone. Always.

His hand fisted—at the same instant that she said, "How accurate is this model?"

"Margin of error of a percent at most," he replied, the numbers burned into his brain after all the times he'd checked and rechecked his data. "I did the survey twice to confirm."

Payal didn't respond, her attention on the model.

It gave him time to study her.

She appeared as absorbed as she'd been as a child when she'd drawn precise grids on the screen of her bulky old organizer, the act appearing almost meditative. And once, when they'd been permitted outside for exercise, he'd watched her pick up leaves that had fallen to the ground, begin ordering them by size and color.

"Everything fits together, like a puzzle," she'd said when he joined her. "But the pieces have to be in the right places." Deep frown lines between her eyebrows, the tangle of her hair half falling over one eye. "I like to put the pieces in order."

He'd have thought it a desperate attempt to find control in a situation where they had no control, but she'd always looked so content when she worked with her grids and organized those leaves.

She'd clearly noted a pattern about adult Canto—because, his anger about it aside, she treated him with suspicion due to a dangerous and skilled cardinal who was a stranger. As a threat. Full stop.

His mobility level didn't factor into her equations as a negative when it came to her assessment of his strength. It wasn't that she didn't see the chair. Her comment about his successful surgeries had made that clear. But Payal hadn't fixated on it like so many Psy. To her, it was just one element of the whole pattern that was Canto.

His chest expanded on a rush of air.

He hadn't realized until that moment that he'd been holding his breath on a psychological level, waiting for her to hurt him. Because she could.

Fuck.

Canto had stopped being concerned about the opinions of others long ago. The PsyMed psychology specialist his grandmother had made him see had told him that his "distancing behavior" was a coping mechanism for the "unusual circumstances of his life to date."

In other words, Canto didn't give a fuck because his father had slated him for death when he proved imperfect. The Mercants had brought him back from that enraged and broken edge, but he still cared for the opinions of very few.

Payal Rao would always be one of those people.

Foolish and illogical and goddamn stupid when he hadn't seen her for decades, but it was what it was; he'd been forever altered by her courage and refusal to surrender. The only way his emotions toward her would change for the worse was if she proved to have become a monster.

Head of the Rao empire, Canto. That doesn't happen by being kind and generous.

His grandmother's voice, what he imagined Ena might say were she able to hear the direction of his thoughts. But the thing was, Canto knew Payal could be dangerous. He was alive *because* she was dangerous.

When she raised her head at last, her eyes were obsidian. Heavy processing power, psychic and/or mental. "That's why I'm tiring quicker," she said, as if they were midconversation, her voice clipped. "Because there's almost no overlap in my entire country. The secondary anchors can't take the weight a hub-anchor is built to handle, so the hubs are under unrelenting pressure."

The same pressure was a heavy weight on Canto's mind—and his region wasn't as bad as Payal's. Anchor zones were meant to overlap by at least a quarter, so that when one A tired, the As around them took the load. It was done so instinctively that neither party was ever aware of it—or that was how it was meant to work.

"There's no longer any downtime built into the system," Payal continued. "If anchors were machines, we'd be overheating." She leaned back in her seat, her obsidian gaze unblinking.

It should've been eerie, but Canto had often seen the same inky black in the mirror. Usually when he'd pushed his telepathy too far, or if his emotions were running high.

"Is this a recent problem?" Payal asked, her gaze still distant as that beautiful mind worked at a speed far faster than the vast majority of the population.

"No." Careful not to accidentally brush against her even though he wanted to steal that contact, he touched the screen of the organizer to bring up a chart. "Occurrence of As in the population."

Payal went silent as she examined the bleak downward curve.

He could almost hear her thinking. And there he went, being a quasi bear again by feeling smug that she was already comfortable enough with him to retreat that way—on the other hand, she was a cardinal Tk who could snap his bones in half with a thought. He *had* to stop thinking of her as 3K, stop searching for hints of that wild girl.

Her next question was abrupt. "When did you become aware of the problem?"

"I initialized late," he said to her. "Not until age nine. Probably why I began hearing the NetMind—things were leaking through because of the delayed initialization."

Obsidian eyes on him, her attention a laser. "As far as I know, anchor initialization starts at age five, with the top edge being age seven."

"Yeah, I was an outlier." Unaware of the A ability slumbering inside him, waiting to wake. No one had ever worked out a way to test children at birth to see if they were or weren't anchors. Initialization just happened at a certain age, the Substrate opening up to them as their minds became the weights that kept the fabric of the Net in place.

"Might be because I came into it so late, but I was curious." It had also given him a focus that took him away from the hospital rooms that had so often been his home. "The more I researched anchors—and there wasn't much, even with the weight of my family's resources behind me—the more it didn't make sense."

Magdalene had sat quietly with him, teaching him how to run the searches—because Ena had decreed that he was to do the legwork himself. She hadn't been born yesterday, his grandmother. She'd known he needed a mental distraction—and time to come to terms with the mother who'd contracted him away.

Payal leaned toward him. "How so?"

His skin grew tight, his muscles tense in readiness, not for an attack but for contact. A small part of him still couldn't believe she was real. He wanted to break every rule in the book and touch her, make certain she was here.

Shoving aside the irrational need, he said, "I've never accepted the known wisdom that anchors are rare and always have been. That doesn't make sense in any self-supporting system."

He continued when she didn't interrupt. "But I had nowhere to go from there—until two years ago, when the weeds in the Substrate began to multiply at a suffocating pace." The layer of the Net in which anchors did their work was meant to be a pristine blue ocean aglow with an inner light. It shouldn't be dull and infested with fibrous brown material dotted with hooks that constantly caught onto anchor minds. The things were a bitch to shake loose.

"I assumed the fibers were an extension of the rot in the Net."

"Yeah, probably." Canto scowled. "Doesn't change that it's a screwed-up situation."

Payal stared at him. "Afterward—did you ever try to return to Silence?"

"Nope. Was too pissed off." A broken boy rejected by the only family he'd ever known, his body betraying him more and more with each day that passed.

Then had come Arwen, and it was all over. No one in the family had ever figured out the mechanics of it, but Canto had enclosed Arwen in his shields seconds after Arwen's birth. His shields were anchor tough—perfect to protect a baby empath. But having an un-trained E inside his shields had nixed any attempt at Silence. Those same shields, however, had protected him from exposure.

He waited to see if Payal would take the opening, venture deeper into the past, but she shifted her attention to the organizer once more. "If your figures are correct, the shortage of As didn't begin with the implementation of the Protocol—but it did speed it up. Was it because of our unstable Silence, our mental instability?"

"No." It was accepted fact in the corridors of power that anchors were more susceptible to murderous insanity than the rest of the pop-ulation, but when he'd crunched the numbers in detail, they hadn't borne that out.

"Anchors do have higher levels of mental instability," he told her, "but in the vast majority of cases the only negative impact is on the A in question. Designation A produces murderers at the same rate as most designations." He showed her that data file.

"The Net needs anchors," he said as she examined the information, "and will always need us regardless of emotion." Canto leaned back in his chair. "Silent anchors are just as good as non-Silent anchors—the Council never cared to discipline us, especially since anchor shields mean that nothing leaks out, even if we do feel emotion." Had Canto initialized prior to banishment to the death chamber disguised as a school, no one could've stifled his telepathy, no one could've chained his mind.

He could've helped Payal, helped the other children.

PAYAL glanced up from the organizer . . . and her control broke. He was so close, close enough that she could touch him, this man who was the last person she'd ever *truly* touched. "What happened to your jaw?" His skin was dark with bristles there, and she had the irrelevant thought that it would feel rough against her fingertips.

"The scar?" He rubbed his fingers over the lower right side of his jaw. "Accident when I was trying out a robotic suit." A heavy scowl. "Why?"

"You didn't have it when we last met."

"You didn't have that dot on your left cheekbone."

"Lalit stabbed me with a pencil," she said without any change in her tone, the incident one she'd long put behind herself. "I broke his fingers in self-defense—he wasn't expecting such a fast response."

Canto's muscles went rigid, the line of his jaw brutal. "No one ever teach him that the strong are meant to protect the younger or weaker?" A sudden glitter in his eyes that made her breath catch and spawned an odd sensation in her abdomen. "Or the ferocious are meant to protect whoever the hell they damn well want."

Her, he was calling her ferocious. Perhaps she had been. Once. "I'm a cardinal Tk. My father expected me to take care of myself. The weak don't thrive."

"You're also five years younger than your asshole brother," Canto said in a voice so deep and rough it was a growl that brushed over her like fur. "How in the fuck was that a fair fight? It's not like he's psychically weak. A better-trained Gradient 9.1 Tk against a much younger cardinal? Your father should've kicked his ass for laying a finger on you."

A rising scream in the back of her mind, a vicious torrent of forbidden emotion.

Chapter 9

It is our duty to further the aims of our fathers and mothers. Some of them have faltered in their path, but that is to be expected. They are not Silent natives. We understand this world as they will never have the capacity to do; this is their twilight, and our dawn.

—Council Member Neiza Adelaja Defoe (2016)

SHUTTING DOWN THE incipient emotional storm with harsh abruptness because to listen to that broken part of herself was to lose everything, Payal tapped at the screen. Graphs and numbers and data, she could process those. What she couldn't process was a man who seemed to see her as a person worth protecting.

"What happened seventy years ago?" That was when the decimation of Designation A gained steam.

"The first generation born in Silence began to take control of the power structures of the PsyNet. Before that, the majority were holdovers from the time before Silence—an old guard, so to speak."

Payal looked out at the desert so she wouldn't stare at him, at those eyes full of galaxies, at that jawline bristled with stubble. "People whose decisions would've been informed by the emotions—and the ethics—of the time before Silence."

"Look here." Tapping the screen, he brought up images of the people who he told her had sat on the Psy Council just before the beginning of the end for Designation A. "Three of them had science backgrounds, three business, and the last came from a family previously known for great works of art—but he was a curator and seller of that art, not a creator."

"Effectively another business brain." Cut away the fat, get down to the core, and this man had been about numbers and money. "Business and science can work well in concert, but they can also form a dangerous confluence when devoid of the balance provided by empathy." Even Payal understood that art came from emotion—good and bad. That was why Psy had stopped being poets and painters, sculptors and composers post-Silence.

"Exactly." His attention was aggressive, threatening to see too much—right down into the heart of her stifled screams.

She fought by going on the offensive. "I may be a robot in my social interactions, but I factor all elements into my decision-making matrix." It was a testament to her years of self-training that her tone didn't alter, her breath didn't hasten.

"Recent events have made it clear that empaths exist for the same reason as anchors: they are crucial to the effective and safe functioning of our society. A Council devoid of their input would have been perilously unbalanced."

The way he looked at her . . . "Your brain is a thing of beauty, Payal Rao."

Her stomach grew tight, hot. "What did this unbalanced Council decree?"

He shifted in his chair to lean toward her, the action drawing her gaze to the muscles of his shoulders as the scent of him—warm, oddly rough—wafted over her. "It was less a decree than a subtle change in culture born at the top. The aim of Silence altered from mental survival to perfection."

"I see." Returning the organizer to him, she said, "You exhibited physical defects as a young child—as judged by the PsyNet. I had mental defects on that same judgment. I know that at least one A in my region suffers from a degenerative condition."

Canto nodded, his scent wrapping around her until she inhaled it with every breath. She should've pulled back, but she didn't. A test, she told herself, to see if she could maintain control even when pushed to the extreme.

Nothing to do with the need to be closer to the only person in this world who had ever *seen* her.

"My census is nine-tenths complete," he said in that voice deep and gritty, "and it looks like roughly sixty percent of current anchors have some level of what Silent Psy would consider a defect."

Sixty percent?

The number smashed through her compulsion with Canto, snapping her to icy attention. "Have As always displayed a high incidence of physical and/or psychic defects?"

A hard shake of his head. "The statistics I've unearthed say we were at about the same rate as the general population. It was only after Silence that anchor young began to be born either sick or with hidden genetic defects. Not all, but a slowly growing majority."

The grim darkness of his expression echoed the violent rage in her mad heart.

Anchors were considered so critical that their initialization signs were part of the mandatory post-birth briefing . . . but such signs didn't show until approximately one month prior to initialization. Up to that point, a nascent A appeared no different than any other young child.

"A lot of children have accidents by age five," Payal mused with a determined clinical coldness; anything else would lead to the escape of the manic thing that lived in the back of her head.

The medications the M-Psy had put her on after her father removed her from the school had helped, but she'd been too feral by then to make it out had she not initialized soon afterward. Gritting her teeth and digging in her feet, she'd grabbed hold of the lifeline that was the strong, stable permanence of the Substrate.

Seeing you fight gives me the courage to fight. Quiet, solemn words. *Don't give the monsters the satisfaction of seeing you give up. You're better than all of them, 3K.*

Did Canto remember saying that to her one rainy day when he found her huddled sobbing in a corner, her spirit whimpering in pain? No one else had ever seen her as anything good, anything worthy.

His words had forever changed her.

His faith in her was why she'd survived—and why she'd fought to pretend to be sane—but she'd been a small child with only so much willpower. Without the Substrate, she'd have flown apart into a million tiny pieces.

"Had." The hardness of Canto's voice as he spoke that single word was a hammer. "A lot of children *had* a way of having accidents by age five. The fall of Silence broke the chain of death."

"You're being perplexingly optimistic for a man who is part of a family rumored to know all of the Net's most terrible secrets." Payal couldn't understand him. "Perhaps you have a surfeit of empaths in your zone. They tend to shoot out rainbows and flowers even to those of us who prefer cold reason. I suppose they can't help it."

CANTO almost choked on the water he'd just drunk. Coughing, he wondered what Arwen would make of being described as shooting out rainbows and flowers. A second later he scowled at the realization—not for the first time—of how much his cousin had shaped him. *Softened* him.

Because Payal was right; his statement had been one colored by hope.

Anger was a metallic taste on his tongue as he thought of all the children who'd been eliminated from the population for so-called imperfections. All the children who hadn't had Ena Mercant in their corner. "Did anyone fight for you?" he found himself asking, needing her not to have been so painfully alone.

"In my family, only the strong survive."

Canto's hand spasmed on his water bottle.

Needing to do something—anything—for her, he went to the temperature-controlled storage cabinet and, putting aside the water, pulled out a couple of nutrient bars. He handed one to Payal after returning to his spot by her side. "The teleport would've burned a chunk of your energy. You should refuel. Especially since your anchor zone is also sucking you dry."

She stared at the bar in her hand as if it were a strange, unknown object.

"It's sealed," he said without scowling—he understood that her issues with trust went to the core. They weren't children anymore, and she'd been relying only on herself for a very long time.

He had to get it through his thick skull that she might never fucking trust him.

A hard swallow before she curled her fingers around the bar. "Why do sick As keep being born?" she asked, her voice tight. "Pre-agreement genetic testing of procreation partners should make such matches impossible."

Canto had seen the testing record for his mother and Binh Fernandez. It had been a thing of art in its detail. Yet it had forecast none of Canto's future physical issues. "I have a theory that we only start to sicken after birth—when the first trickle of the PsyNet begins to run through our minds." A slow, relentless drip into pathways built to one day mainline the Net. "It's filthy with rot and we're caught in the stream. No other Psy engage with the Net to the same depth as As."

"I had a tumor, too," Payal told him without warning, almost as if the words had shoved themselves past her rigid control. "In my brain. Medics discovered it a month after my removal from the school."

That was powerful information to have about the Rao CEO. Canto grabbed hold of the small indication of trust—and secreted away the data in a private file about 3K that he would never ever share with anyone else. This? Him and Payal? Theirs was a private bond.

Years of lost time between them, a heavy weight of the unknown, he took the organizer and brought up a profile labeled *Hub-3*. "This anchor suffers from recurring skin cancers, while this one"—a profile labeled *Hub-4*—"has a disorder that causes severe breathing issues that can't be linked to any particular diagnosis."

"You think the PsyNet is doing this to us. That as it sickens and dies, so do we—and because of that, past anchors were murdered as infants and toddlers."

Such a short, concise summation of horrific ugliness. "Prior to initialization," Canto said, "anchors are just ordinary children with medical issues."

"Your theory also explains the high incidence of mental instability in our designation. As the NetMind began to lose coherence, so did we."

"Yeah, that's what I think."

PAYAL knew she had to keep her distance from the relentless force that was Canto Mercant for her own safety. But she opened her mouth and said, "I will assist you." The anchor problem was too critical to the future of their race for her to allow personal concerns to hold her back.

But Canto wasn't done. "Will you be the face of our organization, the one who speaks to the Ruling Coalition?" Galaxies that threatened to suck her under. "Majority of As are ready to join the organization—I don't foresee problems with the more hesitant, either. They just need a little hand-holding."

"I'm considered robotic," she pointed out. "I have no charisma."

"You're wrong." Implacable. Absolute. "When you talk, people listen. You also have a spine of steel—and Designation A needs that steel, because what we're going to say and demand is going to come as a shock."

"Why not do it yourself? Your own will isn't in question." For one, he'd tracked down the loner members of a secretive designation and talked them into becoming part of a group.

"I have zero patience for politicking of any kind." Thunder on his face. "I'd yell. A lot."

Payal blinked. No, Canto Mercant was not predictable. "Why do you believe I can be a politician?"

"You can't. But according to all my sneaky spying—"

Fascination had her interrupting. "Sneaky spying?"

He grimaced. "Damn bears." Not explaining that response, he returned to his previous subject. "You're no politico, but I have plenty of evidence that you never lose your temper. You just keep going until people listen. There's a silent, inexorable grit to you."

"The last time I was in negotiations with Gia Khan, she said I might as well be made out of cold iron, I was so inhuman."

"Gia Khan is full of shit—and a sore loser." Canto shrugged away the insult, as if it was so ridiculous it didn't bear scrutiny. "You're exactly who we need as our general, Payal—generals don't care about hurting feelings or about charisma; they're there for the battle—you didn't break as a child and you won't break as an adult."

No one had ever framed her bullish and often ice-hearted tendencies in such a positive light. It . . . meant something to be valued. Especially by him, by the boy who'd seen her at the very worst, before the medications, before the therapies, before she'd thrown herself into mental and psychic training.

"Fine. I can be the face of Designation A." The screams rising at the back of her mind, she rose to her feet. "I have a business meeting

I can't miss. Are we to have an A advisory board? We can't speak for all As without their mandate."

"I have a list of candidates—most of the other As just want us to deal with the situation and don't care how we do it."

Payal gave a curt nod, then teleported out.

Running from Canto. Running from the past. Running from the keening madness of who she'd once been . . . and could one day again become.

Chapter 10

Honor born
Knight to a king
My blood my coin

—"Loyal" by Adina Mercant, poet (b. 1832, d. 1901)

PAYAL STARED AT the nutrient bar in her hand as she stood in her private apartment in Vara. Her throat was dry and her heart, it beat too fast.

7J had given her food again.

"Not 7J," she rasped. "Canto."

But this bar she held, warm from her body heat, it told her that 7J remained alive inside the stranger who was Canto Mercant. The boy who'd cared to hear her opinions had grown into a man who thought who she was—rigid, robotic, uncharismatic—had value.

He'd compared her to a general.

He'd be disappointed when he discovered 3K was dead, buried so effectively that she'd never again be the girl he'd known. 3K *couldn't* exist if Payal was to live a life of sanity. But he hadn't yet learned the bitter truth, so perhaps she could continue to interact with him in this strange way. With a kind of raw honesty that stripped away the barriers people put between themselves and the world. In Payal's case, those walls were so high that no one else had ever been invited in.

Her sister, Kari, was too young for them to have that kind of a relationship. And though Payal knew there were people in the Rao empire who were loyal to her, those people were all also beholden to that empire for jobs and security. The power imbalance was an ever-present part of their interactions.

Canto, however, needed her for nothing on a personal level.

Even the anchor work—had she said no, he would've been able to find another suitable individual, she was sure. She'd been his first choice, but not his only one. Still, to be anyone's first choice . . .

All her life she'd had to fight and fight. Every role, every position, she'd won it through white-knuckled combat of a kind that left no physical bruises. Canto had just *offered* her the position of head of the anchor union. He'd also done so before he knew she was 3K, so it had nothing to do with the bonds of the past.

Payal allowed herself a quiet exhale, then unwrapped the bar with extreme care before taking a bite. Only after she'd finished the whole thing did she get a sealed bottle of water from her tamperproof cooler and drink. Then she did a foolish thing. She smoothed out the wrapper and placed it within the pages of one of the hard-copy books she had on the shelves in her bedroom.

The book held artwork created by Karishma. Payal only dared display one piece—a large painting of Vara on canvas that her sister had done for her final grade the previous year. Unsigned and with an aged look to it, it could pass as décor that had been in the mansion prior to Payal's usage. Everyone in Vara was used to the amount of art—hidden and out in the open—that lay in its history.

So Karishma's painting could hang openly in Payal's office without anyone noticing it as anything but an appropriate type of decoration for the office of a CEO. Psy might have given up creating art under Silence, but her race had always understood that even the Silent reacted subconsciously to certain elements of their environment.

The book, on the other hand, held pen-and-ink sketches that were nothing if not modern. Payal'd had them bound in a decoy cover that made it appear to be a dusty tome on tax law. Should Lalit ever manage to invade her inner sanctum, he wouldn't bother to look inside those books, would simply dismiss them as another sign that his sister had no life beyond the Rao business.

Good.

Payal didn't want him to look deeper. Didn't want him to remember Karishma, or the others Payal had secreted away to safety. And she never wanted him to find a way to taint the haunting and honest relationship she had with a man who held galaxies in his eyes.

CANTO couldn't settle after returning home, so he went out onto his deck and brooded while staring out at a landscape of lush, thriving green. Though it might seem like he was in the middle of nowhere, he was actually on the public edge of StoneWater land, near the road that led into their wild territory.

His move to Moscow had been unexpected. He'd been based in a small town in Germany for the past decade. But then, while doing his unofficial census, he'd seen that the aging anchor in the Moscow region had started to show signs of a troubling kind of exhaustion. Worried, Canto had reached out to see if he could assist.

Balance of it was that Canto's anchor region had proved "smaller" in terms of energy output. He'd offered to swap regions and the other anchor had gratefully accepted. All of this had happened soon after Silver ended up mated to an alpha bear.

Which explained why Canto had been permitted to set up his base in StoneWater territory. He hadn't asked for it—that would've been an asshole move with Silver so newly mated. Instead, he'd moved into a place on the outskirts of Moscow, taking it over from one of his other cousins—Ivan. A security operative who worked under Canto, Ivan had shifted his home base to San Francisco just prior to Canto's arrival.

Officially, he was there to get up to date on his computronic security certifications by undertaking a highly specialized course. Unofficially, he was there to gather intelligence on the various power players in the area. A lot happened in that comparatively small region, and Ena wanted the family to have a larger presence there.

So it wasn't as if Canto hadn't had a perfectly adequate residence.

Then had come that infamous party to celebrate the mating, when Valentin and his bears decided they *liked* Canto. The bears had liked Ivan, too, but—according to a gossipy older member of the pack—had considered Canto's suave cousin a bit too "slinky" for total comfort. But since the bears adored Arwen, Canto had a feeling the disconnect had less to do with Ivan's sharp dressing, and more with the core of distance Ivan carried within.

The bears could sense it but didn't realize it wasn't personal: of all the Mercant cousins, Ivan was the most remote. Canto knew the reason Ivan was how he was, but no one unaware of Ivan's history could be expected to divine it. The only one who could get him to open up was Arwen—and that was enough. Their empathic cousin would never allow Ivan to lose himself to his demons.

Arwen had even convinced Ivan to attend the celebration of Silver and Valentin's mating.

A month after the event, and Valentin had come to Canto with a proposal. "I think my Starlight should have some more of her family close to Denhome," the bear alpha had said. "My clan is madly in love with her, but if she needs to yell about us to someone not entangled with a bear, who better than a cousin as loyal as a brother?"

"Valya," Canto had muttered, "Silver adores your pack. I went to see her in her office yesterday and found a naked cub in human form trying to hang upside down from a curtain rod." Silver had worked on unperturbed, simply saying "No" when the cub tried to do a dangerous maneuver.

The cub had stopped at once.

And Canto had seen once again why Ena had chosen Silver as her future successor.

"Emergency babysitting when a packmate went into early labor while shopping with her boy," Valentin had explained, eyes of dark brown aglow with a power usually hidden beneath the force of his warm presence.

"Canto, I know from Silver that the Mercants are as much a pack as StoneWater. I never want to cut my Starlight off from her pack—and I want our two packs to become family." A smug bearish smile as he sat back, arms folded. "I'm charming your grandmother, you know."

Canto had snorted. "You wish." But he'd accepted the offer because he understood that it had been made out of love for Silver.

It had taken the bear clan and Canto's family a short two weeks to put up the house according to his specifications. He'd managed the project and done all the computronic hookups, while the bears had provided manual labor, transport of materials, and engineering. Arwen had done the architectural drawings, with Magdalene sourcing the furniture, rugs, and other items to outfit the place.

As it was, he had as many bearish visitors as Mercants.

Such as the dark-skinned man who hauled himself up over the balcony railing just now, a small boy clinging to his back like a barnacle. Bears seemed to find using Canto's front door optional.

"Chaos," Canto said. "Did you know you picked up a butt-naked hitchhiker?" His Russian was passable despite his relatively short period of study—he had a theory it had to do with being an A. The Net was a constant river in his head, and parts of that psychic river spoke Russian.

Reaching back, Chaos pulled off his son with the casual strength bear parents used with their cubs, and threw the giggling boy up into the air. "Dima and I needed fresh air," he said after catching his son in his arms. "He had on clothes until he decided to shift without taking them off."

Dima shrugged, his face mischievous. "I'm a bear. *Grr.*" Then he jumped toward Canto, having learned that Canto was strong enough to take his rambunctious ways. The first time they'd met, the cub had come up to him and very seriously examined his chair, then asked if they could go "zoom."

Canto was pretty sure Dima was his favorite bear.

Today, he hugged the boy and said, "Hungry?" because bear cubs were always hungry. Possibly because they never stayed still.

"Yeah!"

Canto put him on the wooden floor of the balcony. "You know where the snacks are." He kept a stash suitable for small bears in a lower cupboard—the assortment courtesy of Arwen. "Chaos, how many things can he choose?" He'd learned that lesson when he hadn't set any restrictions the first time—Chaos had had to deal with one moaning and stuffed-full cub.

"Two." Chaos's voice was the one Canto had labeled the "bear parent" tone. No argument. No playing. Do as you're told.

Dima ran inside with a big whoop.

Grinning, Chaos hauled over a chair to sit next to Canto and held out a fist for him to bump. The bears, notwithstanding their reputation as rough and tough troublemakers, were highly intelligent and conscious of the Psy aversion to touch. They took "skin privileges" dead seriously.

Even the drunk bear who'd ended up in his lap had asked permission. He'd said yes because he'd been worried she'd otherwise faceplant right onto the asphalt.

Canto liked the changeling idea of skin privileges, of physical contact being considered a gift.

Payal's face flashed in his mind, her skin so smooth and soft looking, her lips lush.

His abdomen tightened, his nerve endings afire. Not ready for the raw physical surge, he almost missed Chaos's question.

Having leaned back in his chair and put his feet up on the deck railing, Chaos said, "You sure you don't get lonely out here?"

It was a quintessentially bear question. They lived in a sprawling den that Canto had been sure would drive Silver insane—yet his cousin was thriving in the midst of a nosy, loving, and occasionally insane pack that loved to throw parties.

"Arwen and Pavel dropped by yesterday for lunch, day before that it was my grandmother, and now you two," he growled as he stripped off the gloves he wore to increase his grip during manual use of his chair; they also protected his palms from constant friction. Now he flexed his fingers and said, "How the hell is a man supposed to get peace and quiet?"

Chaos laughed, big and booming. "You do a good grumble. Almost like a bear."

Small feet running back.

When Dima came around to Canto's side, he saw that the boy held four snacks, not his permitted two. Surprised the small bear had disobeyed his father, he waited for Chaos to discipline him. But then Dima took a pack of dried apple slices from his stash and held it out to Canto. "You like apple."

"Yeah." Heart stretching inside his chest, Canto took the pack, then rubbed his hand over the boy's tight curls.

Smiling, Dima ran over to give his father a pack of something called licorice allsorts that—to Canto—looked like tiny multihued bricks. "Look, Papa, your favorite."

Chaos hugged his boy to his side. "You sure you don't want it?"

"No, I got cookies and this." He looked a bit dubious at his choice of dried mango strips, but determined. "I go play with Canto's blocks now?"

"Sure."

After the boy was happily involved in the play area Arwen had set up on the deck for Canto's small visitors, Canto said, "You must be proud of him."

"Every day," Chaos said quietly, so much love in his voice that it made Canto ache deep within.

With no one in the Mercant clan currently parenting a small child—the youngest Mercant at present was sixteen—Canto had rarely even thought about children before coming to StoneWater territory. Now he knew he'd gut anyone who laid a finger on Dima or any of the other small souls in StoneWater.

Apparently, he had more Ena Mercant in him than he'd realized.

Beside him, Chaos tore open his child-sized bag of sweets. Canto did the same with his apple slices, and in the time that followed, the two of them just sat there, talking now and then, but mostly listening to the trees while Dima talked to himself as he played. It was a good feeling, sitting with a friend . . . but Canto's mind kept being torn away to Delhi, and to a woman who appeared to have no safe haven.

His entire body threatened to knot with rage. He'd find a way to protect her—even if he had to do it in stealth. In saving his life, she'd gained herself a Mercant knight who would always, always be in her corner.

Before

I dream of him every night. And yet he isn't in my arms. I should've never even looked at the proposal Fernandez sent through. I should've listened when Mother advised me to talk to multiple others who had been in my position.

I thought I knew better, thought I understood who I was and how carrying a child in my womb would affect me. I was wrong and I must live with that.

—From the private journal of Magdalene Mercant

"I'M SORRY."

"Why?" He made his voice hard, as hard as he was trying to make his heart. "You did everything legal. You had no responsibility to me."

The small woman with eyes of hazel brown and hair of moonlight gold didn't look away, didn't get up and leave. "It was my responsibility to ensure that no harm ever came to you. In that, I failed." Cool, clear words, with no edge of excuse. "I am a Mercant—and *no one* gets to hurt our children."

He refused to believe her, refused to be vulnerable ever again even though he was scared and lonely and nothing in his body was working right. "Okay, fine. Can I be alone now?"

"I deserve your rejection, but that won't stop me from being your mother. Whatever you need, I will provide—including protection."

He stared out the window of the hospital suite rather than answering, his heart beating too fast and his skin all hot. "I hate you," he bit out. *"I hate you."*

"I know."

Chapter 11

Naysayers shout that Silence will favor the psychopaths among us, but they do not understand the intricacies of the safeguards built into the protocol. They stand in the path of progress out of ignorance and fear.

—Catherine and Arif Adelaja, Architects of Silence (1951)

PAYAL WALKED OUT of the conference room after her meeting and almost ran into Lalit. Her brother—taller than her by a foot, wide of shoulder and hard of jaw, his hair stylishly cut and his cologne crisp—stopped and did up the button on his navy suit jacket. "Agreement reached?"

"Yes."

"Of course. You were in charge." He produced a smile so false she wondered how and why others fell for it.

Payal, however, had no issue with the way Lalit chose to present himself to the world. Her issue had to do with the fact that he was a psychopath. "You're in my way," she said when he didn't step aside. She made sure her voice was lacking in tone, and she didn't break eye contact.

Their father often denigrated changelings as "animals," but her brother was as territorial as any animal, and he had far less reason for the violence in which he indulged whenever he thought he could get away with it. "I have a meeting with Father."

One side of his mouth pulled up. "Off you go, golden child."

She moved on without responding. Both of them knew the truth—after Varun's execution, it was Lalit who'd become the favored child, the one Pranath Rao had intended to succeed him to the throne of the Rao empire.

Payal had initially been a distant third in line, behind Varun and Lalit. Their father had only retrieved her from the school because he was a man who preferred more than one insurance policy. After they buried Varun, her job was to be a silent threat to Lalit. Because by then, their father had caught Lalit torturing a stray cat—and even Pranath Rao knew that to be a bad sign.

The threat had appeared to work, with Lalit toeing the line.

Then three senior members of the staff had caught eighteen-year-old Lalit cutting up the yet-warm corpse of a homeless human man he'd abducted off the street. To Pranath, the problem hadn't been the act itself—but that Lalit had been distracted enough to get caught. The head of the Rao family was fine with psychopathic behavior so long as it didn't draw negative attention to the family.

Payal, still half-mad and with a scream at the back of her head, had nonetheless known that was wrong. She might be a murderer, but she'd acted to protect, and while the kill haunted her, she'd never go back and undo it—because that teacher had been wrong in brutalizing his students.

As Lalit was wrong in harming his victims.

He was the reason why there were no small domestic creatures in Vara, even though a medic had once suggested Payal would socialize better if she had a pet. Therapeutic animals were permitted under Silence in rare cases. Payal now had the power to make such decisions on her own, but she'd never bring an animal into this house.

Lalit would use it as a weapon—and the poor creature would end up abused and dead.

"The beggar is dead," Lalit had said that day, his voice calm. "No one will talk. There is no problem."

Their father had steepled his fingers on his desk, his eyes a pale amber-brown that burned against the darker brown of his skin. Lalit had inherited those eyes, inherited most of Pranath's features. "My investigators tell me that you've been less than discreet on multiple occasions. There is no way to stop the information from spreading, though I'll do my best to ameliorate matters by buying people off."

Their father's face had been a chill blank as he looked at Lalit. "Thankfully, your targets have all been human. They're too afraid of our power to make trouble—and the others who know will keep their mouths shut if paid."

"We can afford it."

"The settlement money is just the start, Lalit." A tone in Pranath's voice that had Payal going motionless—the last time she'd heard it, she'd then had to witness a brother dying in agony. "If it gets out that my heir and successor is unstable, the family will lose millions upon millions. Our race does *not* tolerate mental instability."

"I'm not mentally unstable." No change to Lalit's tone, no hint of fear or of any other emotion. "I know exactly what I'm doing."

"I'd have let it go if you'd been discreet, but I can't trust you now." Pranath had shifted his attention to Payal with the speed of a cobra. "You'll never have Lalit's way with clients and collaborators, but at least you've proven capable of controlling your aberrant mind." A glance at Lalit. "I don't have to be concerned that she'll surrender to the urge to torture someone midnegotiation."

"She's an anchor. They're murderers barely leashed and she's already been blooded."

Pranath's eyes boring into Payal's. "Do you feel any urge to kill again, Payal?"

"No, sir." A lie. The madness inside her had constantly wanted to slam a blade into Lalit's jugular, end his evil. But she'd been too young and untrained, and he had a predator's instincts.

"Payal will be my putative successor for the time being." Pranath's statement had rung around the room. "We can reconvene on the topic in another decade. Keep your nose clean in the interim, Lalit, and anyone who's aware of your indiscretions to date may decide to forget them."

Payal had never been meant to actually take up the mantle. But then two things had happened in quick succession.

Pranath Rao had suffered his accident.

And Lalit had been caught by their paternal aunt doing something for which there could be no rational explanation when he was meant to be in full control of his urges: using a knife to carve shapes into the body of a teenaged maid employed at Vara for domestic duties. He'd been in an unlocked room with an old lattice window that allowed passersby a view inside should they glance that way.

Payal had been lucky that day—she'd happened to walk by as their aunt confronted Lalit. Using Lalit's distraction as cover, she'd teleported to the girl, then out with her to an undisclosed location. She'd made a point of building a mental database of locations Lalit couldn't access, including an old farmhouse that she'd bought with money from a small business venture.

That far in the countryside, it had cost less than nothing—and the caretaker wasn't aware it was in his name. He just knew that the owner paid him handsomely to look after the place and take care of any guests. Because while Payal hadn't been able to save the homeless man, the maid was far from the first person she'd taken to the sanctuary of the farmhouse.

Leaving the wounded maid to be tended to by a rural human doctor who never saw Payal, only the caretaker, she'd then made her way to her father's secure recovery suite—a month after his accident and he was back at work, though under medical watch. He'd also already ordered renovations to the basement area he intended to turn into his long-term base of operations. She'd made her report about Lalit's relapse while her brother was still in the midst of telling their aunt she needed to forget this for her own good.

"I'll be in charge soon enough," he'd been saying when Payal last heard. "You'll be under my control—and I don't like people who get above their station."

After making her report, Payal had delivered her coup de grâce. "Lalit has so little foresight that he was recording the encounter. When I teleported the girl out, I also took the recording—I'll forward you a copy."

"What do you intend to do with this information, Payal?" Pranath's eyes were as motionless as a snake's slitted pupils.

"Hold it over Lalit's head. You can make him your heir, but I'll destroy him and the family in retaliation." The threat had been a carefully calculated gamble, Payal all too aware of the thousands of blameless people who relied on the Rao family for their livelihoods. "He's irrational, Father. He'll take our family name to the gutter. Lalit is driven by his urges, not by reason."

Pranath Rao had smiled the same cold smile Lalit so often mimicked. "Well done, daughter. I didn't think you had it in you." A cool murmur. "You do realize I know every location you could've possibly utilized."

Payal had held his eyes without fear, her ability to wall off the rage of her emotions the best trick she'd ever taught herself. "I've run my own small business since I was fifteen. Did you actually believe I showed you all my profits?" Payal had learned by watching her family, and what she'd learned was *never trust anyone*. "Try to find the girl or the recording. You'll fail."

After a long, tense minute, while Payal stood unflinching, Pranath Rao had brought his hands together in a slow clap. "Brilliant. You are my true heir after all—Lalit never saw you waiting to strike at his back."

Now Payal took the elevator to the basement level of Vara, a windowless and highly secure area that could be accessed only by a limited number of people. All were Psy, and all but Payal and Lalit were fanatically loyal to Pranath Rao.

Which was why their father had other ways of controlling his children.

After exiting the elevator, she keyed in her private entry code on the doors to the main suite, then stood still for the retinal scan. She should've been able to teleport in, but her father had a group of staff on duty whose sole task was to alter elements of his work space in ways that stopped a teleport lock.

The team did this *every single time* after a visit from Lalit or Payal.

What some might call paranoia, their father called good security, and Payal couldn't fault him for it. Lalit, at least, was fully capable of teleporting in while Pranath was at work and slitting his throat.

The doors slid open in front of her. Beyond them moved an M-Psy in blue scrubs, her brown skin dull as a result of all the time she spent underground. The other woman gave her a nod.

"Is my father awake?"

"Yes. He'll see you."

Of course he knew of her arrival. The entire area was monitored. "Thank you."

Turning right, she walked down a wide hallway decorated with artefacts of gold against a black background. Historical treasures captured by their ancestors that should've been verboten under Silence— but the Rao family was never going to give up their history. They'd simply moved the prized possessions to places where no outsider would ever see them.

Her father had added to the artefacts: the two golden swords at the end of the hallway were his. Mounted beside them was a small knife

Lalit had sourced earlier that year. Her brother had never given up on his ambitions; he'd also managed to keep his hands outwardly clean for years.

Payal was well aware she was on borrowed time.

"Payal, come in." Her father sat propped up in the computronic bed he used when working, papers and datapads spread out on the specially built desk that arched over the bed.

The overhead lights were on against the windowless enclosure that was the public part of his suite. Not that the room was clinical—a thick Persian carpet covered the floor, and delicate historical paintings of long-dead royal courts decorated two of the walls.

At the center of it all was Pranath Rao.

Chapter 12

"7J?"

"Yes?"

"Will you remember me? After I'm not here anymore?"

—3K to 7J (August 2053)

PAYAL KEPT HER face expressionless as she stood in what was her father's version of an office. Pranath Rao had lost all feeling below the waist after a riding accident. Horses were one of the few recreational animals that had survived Silence when it came to the Psy. It was considered good exercise to ride.

Pranath had also suffered other injuries, because he'd fallen onto rocks. His facial scarring was significant enough that multiple cosmetic surgeries hadn't been able to soften the pink and patchy places or erase the thick ridges. It turned out his body didn't like healing from surgery and tended to form keloid scars that resisted treatment.

Payal was certain it was the facial scarring rather than the paralysis that had led to his retreat from public life. He hadn't retreated from anything else. She'd had to fight over every major move she wanted to make when she first took on the role of CEO. He'd only begun to release the business leash when it became obvious that she thought five steps ahead and could make them more powerful as a family group.

Despite his partial capitulation, she never forgot that the majority of the people around her belonged to Pranath Rao. Some because that was part of their identity, others out of fear. Payal had turned a number of the latter, but she knew she couldn't fully trust them as long as he lived—fear was a hard taskmaster.

Payal had been afraid once, as a child at the mercy of a monstrous sibling.

"Father." After closing the door behind herself, she locked it.

"Excellent work on the Tiang-Jiao negotiation," he said, his eyes on his organizer. "I had my doubts you'd pull it off with how stubborn they were being, but I shouldn't have doubted you."

Payal said nothing in response, because no response was required. She was always careful to follow the accepted format for Psy interactions when it came to her father. He might consider her more stable than Lalit, but he also never lost sight of the fact that she was an anchor and thus inherently unhinged in a different way.

He made her wait two more minutes before looking up. She knew it for a power play, but such things had no impact on her. She saw them as petty wastes of time. Even more so now because if Canto was right, none of these games would have any relevance soon unless they found a way to fix the dearth of anchors in the Net.

She used the free two minutes to go over data he'd sent her telepathically after their meeting.

Yet even as she did so, she found herself thinking of the wrapper she'd hidden in the book, the *food* he'd given her. Her fingers wanted to curl into her palm, her pulse suddenly an echoing drum.

Her father finally deigned to look at her, his eyes that pale amber-brown. "Are you here for your medication?"

Years of training meant her tone was even when she said, "Yes,

Father." He made her go through this routine every single time—every seven days since he'd made her CEO, when, prior to that, the dosage had been calibrated to last three months. A constant reminder that she could never act against him without putting her life at critical risk.

"It's over there."

She moved to the small table set up against the dark red-brown of the far wall; the color made the room even more claustrophobic for Payal. The familiar injector lay on a sterile tray along with an alcohol swab and the vial of vivid green medication.

Slotting the vial into the injector, she then swabbed the side of her neck, though that step wasn't strictly necessary. It took but a second to punch the medication into her system. The pain was minor at most; she didn't even notice it after so many years.

As a teleporter, she could switch out vials with ease and had done so more than once. But the scientists she'd hired had never been able to reverse engineer the drug her father had sourced from a now-dead chemist. She was ninety-nine percent certain he'd killed the chemist to ensure that Payal could never break free.

Lalit came by his psychopathy honestly; Pranath was just better at playing the role demanded by society.

"Better?" he said as she placed the injector back on the table.

"Yes." The headache that had been building behind her eyes would soon calm, the medicine's effects rapid; and for seven more days, the tumors in her brain would grow no bigger. "Did you want to discuss any other matters?"

He'd returned his attention to his organizer, but he said, "You were away from your office for a long period today."

A sinuous reminder of just how many loyal spies he had in the Rao organization.

"Meeting with one of the Mercants." Payal had always been a bad liar, but at times, the truth was a better mask than anyone expected—especially when used with surgical precision.

Pranath was suddenly not in the least interested in whatever was on his organizer. "The Mercants haven't worked with our family for five generations."

Payal knew that. After being knocked back on a proposed venture that would've brought profit to both parties, she'd made it a point to find out why. It was because a Rao ancestor had betrayed the Mercants after they'd come to an agreement. Canto's family did not forgive.

Yet he expected her to trust him.

Because it was anchor business.

Because it was between 3K and 7J, not Rao and Mercant.

Her stomach squeezed into a tight ball.

"I don't know if they will now, either." Slipping her hands into her pockets, she kept her body relaxed even as her pulse drummed. "It was a preliminary meeting with nothing of relevance on the agenda." All true as far as it came to Pranath's interests.

But her father was no longer looking at her, his attention caught by the idea of an alliance with the Mercant clan. On the face of it, Rao was bigger and held more power, but everyone knew the Mercants preferred to stay out of the limelight—and had more tentacles than any of the mythical beasts created by various cultures.

"All we need is an entry point," Pranath mused. "Word is what one Mercant knows, they all do. So we just need one person and we can crack their hermetic seal of useless loyalty."

So quickly, his thoughts went to betrayal.

"I've kept the door open." Payal always had difficulty breathing in this room, but she'd long ago learned to hide what she knew was a psychosomatic reaction. "I'd suggest you not attempt to track me while I'm with my contact. Mercants are . . . touchy." Her father couldn't actually follow her the vast majority of the time, since she could 'port wherever she wished, but that didn't mean he wouldn't attempt other methods of surveillance.

"Understood." It sounded sincere. "Keep me informed. I want to know the instant this looks like it might go somewhere."

"I will." She began to head to the door.

"Payal."

"Sir?" She made sure to meet his gaze.

"Your brother has brokered several major deals of late, and he's increasingly building connections that will assist the family in the future. A Mercant link would be advantageous for you."

After inclining her head in a silent response, Payal exited. She didn't permit herself to think about what he'd said until she was behind the locked doors to her apartment, a place she swept every morning and night for spyware and that had a number of electronic tripwires designed to alert her to unauthorized access.

Her father wasn't a stupid man. She couldn't risk him figuring out that his final arrow had hit home. She had even less time than she'd thought if he was beginning to threaten her with Lalit.

"You might have killed once, but you don't have your brother's ruthless instincts," he'd said to her the year before. "You expect people to act with logic, to be rational in their behavior."

He was wrong. She used to expect that, but her childhood had shown it to be a false data point—so she'd adapted. In time, she'd gathered enough information to realize that Psy under Silence made decisions for all kinds of reasons, many of them incomprehensible if you took only the rules of the Protocol into account.

Payal, too, didn't always act in a way that fulfilled the tenets of pure rationality. Such as right then, when she reached out to Canto with her mind. He'd given her his telepathic "imprint," for lack of a better word, when he'd sent her the expanded data. She couldn't find that imprint in the telepathic space, which meant he was farther away than her Gradient 4.3 telepathy could reach.

It should've stopped her impulsive act, but she picked up her encrypted organizer and sent him a message: *Initiate telepathic contact.*

The connection snapped into place within seconds: *Payal? Is there a problem?* His voice was crystalline, so pure a sound that it was almost—but not quite—painful to her psychic ear.

Payal didn't understand music, but at that moment, she came as close to that understanding as she ever had. *No problem, just information. To cover our meetings, I've told my father we're considering a business collaboration. I need you and your family to back me up should mine send out feelers.*

It'll be done. A minor pause. *You're the financial head of the Rao family.*

This was why she didn't act on impulse. Impulse led to mistakes. In the end, all she said was *There are other factors in play.*

It's your brother, isn't it? Watch your back, Payal. Lalit is a predator. Another small pause before he added, *If you want him gone, just give the word.*

Payal sat down on the closest surface. It happened to be a seat built into a large curved window that overlooked the city. She could've had an apartment lower down, where the property's opaque fences blocked out the view of Delhi, but she'd never considered that an option. *Are you making an offer?*

Why don't you come over and we'll talk.

She stared at the falling darkness of Delhi, lit up by the yellow lights that lined its streets in tandem with the tiny fairy lights so many of the small businesses still preferred to hang over their awnings or on their rooftops. Now was the time to meet Canto if she wished to do so in absolute privacy. Not even her father could see through walls and into her rooms.

And . . . she wanted to talk to Canto.

Such a foolish, dangerous need, but she couldn't fight it. *Same location?*

It'll be cold now. Come prepared.

First, she took a couple of minutes to touch base with Karishma using an encrypted messaging app, to ensure that Pranath hadn't made any moves that put her sister in jeopardy.

I'm safe, Karishma replied. *Father and Lalit haven't tried to contact me. I think they've forgotten I exist. Visha is fine, too.*

You both remember the exit plan?

Karishma repeated it back to her. *I won't let them kill us*, she promised. *That would leave you all alone.*

Payal never knew what to say to her gentle, artistic sister when she made such statements. *Just worry about yourself and let Visha protect you.* The teenager turned young woman whom Payal had rescued from Lalit's torture was ten years Kari's senior and fiercely loyal to her younger charge. *I'm the elder. I'll take care of myself.*

Yes, Didi. An honorific for "older sister," but not one used among Psy. It held too much emotion, too much affection. Payal didn't chastise her—Kari was growing up in the post-Silent world, and Payal intended for her to grow up in a kinder one, too.

Payal's one experience of kindness as a child had been a boy who'd asked her for her thoughts and slipped food into her small palm. The profound impact of Canto's actions rippled through time in how Payal interacted with Karishma. *Are you still happy with the school?*

Yes. Miss Almeida is my favorite.

Payal responded with interest, and the two of them messaged for several more minutes before she said, *Good night. Keep up your guard.* Though showing emotion was difficult in the extreme for her, she made the effort for Kari—she didn't want her sister to end up like her, damaged in a way nothing could ever fix. *You are very important to me. I won't allow anyone to hurt you.*

I know, Didi. I love you.

Kari's statement clawed into Payal's psyche, the rising emotion a threat that could overwhelm. When she went to reinitiate her shields, the manic, half-mad girl she'd once been fought her with savage fury. Her jaw ached, her neck tight by the time she got things under control.

That was why she didn't crack open the door. It inevitably led to a deluge.

Despite her conversation with Kari and though she took the time to change into fitted black jeans, a sweater in dark green, and work boots she used on site visits, she still beat Canto to the desert.

Lights came on the instant she moved. Small twinkling sparkles wove their way through the trees of the oasis, while the walls of the shelter began to warm with a soft glow that made it welcoming rather than harsh.

Having walked down to the water, she felt Canto arrive, her telepathy strong enough to run patrol scans in this limited area. The mind that appeared with his soon disappeared, the teleporter fast enough that Payal didn't bother to try to catch a glimpse of them. It was hardly a surprise that the Mercant family had access to such services.

As she walked back up to join Canto, she saw that he'd brought nutrient drinks, fruit, and simple food packs in a small box and was setting them out on the table. "Figured you'd need fuel after another distance teleport at the end of a full day," he said gruffly.

Her chest hurt, that ache in her throat threatening to take over her whole body. "Why do you keep feeding me?" she blurted out, angered by him for some incomprehensible reason. "That's not your job."

Chapter 13

I am concerned about the levels of certain hormones in her system.

—Medical report on Payal Rao (age 6)

A CHALLENGING LOOK out of those eyes so hauntingly beautiful—and implacable in their stubbornness. "Yes," he said, no give in him, "it is."

"Why? Because I'm to be your anchor representative?"

His jaw worked. "Don't give me that bullshit, Payal. You and I, we bonded in blood as children. You saved my life. Yours is now mine to protect."

"That's not how it works."

"Take it up with my ancestors." Grabbing a sealed pack of sliced fruit off the table, he lobbed it to her with a scowl. "I can see your cheekbones."

Payal caught the bag; she was a Tk—it was instinct. Since her stomach was gnawing at her in a reminder that she'd missed two meals, she opened up the bag and began to eat. Too late did she remember that she hadn't checked the tamper seal. She should've halted, abandoned the offering.

But she ate on.

Bonded in blood.

"We were children," she muttered, not ready to let this go. It was too important, too seductive. Were it a mirage, it would hurt her. Not too much—not when she hadn't permitted her innermost shields to drop—but enough to scar and damage the strongest and most important memory of her childhood.

"We survived a thing that would break most adults," Canto all but growled, and unscrewed the lid of a nutrient drink, then held it out to her.

"I'm already holding this bag," she argued.

"Fine, I'll hold it for you. But take a drink."

She wanted to rebuke him for giving her orders, but the lines of his face, the tension by his eyes . . . She had the oddest thought that he might actually be worried about her energy state. It was . . . Payal had no word to describe this situation and what it did to her, how it threatened the entire foundation of her existence.

Grabbing the bottle, she slugged down a drink, then handed it to him to hold as they moved down to the water together. "Why aren't you eating?"

"Already ate," he said. "Had friends drop by. One of them is a chef—figured I'd give him a night off and did the cooking."

Payal chewed on a piece of pear. Crunchy, it contained a shock of tart sweetness that was an assault on her senses. The closest she'd come to fruit in her adult life were dried slices infused with extra vitamins and purposefully drained of all taste, but she didn't balk—to reject Canto's gift was an impossibility. "You have friends."

She didn't know why that disconcerted her. Perhaps because she'd begun to think of them as the same in a small way. But of course they weren't. He'd been rescued by the Mercants, whose loyalty to one another was a thing of legend. She'd been sucked back into the bosom of a pit of vipers.

Canto's world was far bigger than hers had ever been.

"You have a sister who adores you," Canto said, as if he'd reached into her mind and read her thoughts.

She froze on the path, ice crackling through her veins. "Is that a threat?" A pulse began to beat in her mouth, and all at once she was viscerally aware of the stupidity of her desire to be with this man.

"What the fuck!" He threw up his hands, his half gloves already familiar to her. "Are you kidding me? Do I look like the kind of man who goes about threatening little girls?" His voice was loud and rough, patches of heat along his cheekbones. "Apologize for that."

Ice melted, her own cheeks hot as her hand clenched around the bag of fruit. "Why?"

"Because you know me!" He pointed a finger. "Pretend all you like that you don't, but you do. You know me to the fucking core in a way no one else has ever done." With that, he moved off down the path at rapid speed.

Pulse pounding in skin that felt too small for her body, Payal saw him turn right onto a path that she assumed went around the water. He soon disappeared into the foliage. She went the other way, to the bottom of the path, then took a seat on a large stone by the water. Where she ate her way methodically through the bag of fruit.

She'd never had an interaction like this with anyone. Ever.

There were no parameters.

So when Canto returned—from her left—she waited for cues on how to react. Social interaction had been difficult for her as long as she could remember, and right now she was lost in a way she hadn't been since she'd realized that to survive, she'd have to suffocate an integral aspect of her nature.

He thrust the nutrient drink at her.

Even furious, he was feeding her.

She didn't *understand* him.

Taking the drink because that she understood, she unscrewed the cap and drank, as Canto moved his chair closer to her. Then, biceps bulging and flexing in a way that drew her gaze and made her mouth go dry, he lifted himself to a position on a slightly higher rock than her own. From the even nature of his breathing, none of his actions had caused him any physical stress.

Her gaze went to his arms again, a crawling kind of heat under her skin. Confused, she looked away. "How long have you known about my sister?"

"Two years," Canto growled, his simmering anger a hot desert wind. "My grandmother likes you better for being protective of a sibling—it's how Silver's father is with my mother. Mercants don't hurt children. It's not who we are."

Run!

A boyish voice that echoed through time, telling her to save herself. "Fine," she muttered. "I'm sorry for believing you'd use my sister as a threat. In my defense, while you can search for information about me, you're a phantom."

CANTO was well aware he'd been an ass. Payal was right—she didn't know him. But he had a bone-deep loathing of her being scared of him or considering him yet another man against whom she had to protect her sister.

"I'm sorry, too," he grumbled, picking up a small white stone from a crevice in the rocks and throwing it from hand to hand. "Shouldn't have jumped down your throat." Seeing she'd finished the fruit, he dropped the stone to pull a protein bar from his pocket.

She looked at him like he was an alien when he held it out, but accepted the offering and began to peel open the wrapper.

"My mother's name is Magdalene," he told her. "You probably haven't heard of her—she's not one of the more visible Mercants. She's quiet, a researcher and a gentle woman who, without warning, had to deal with a boy whose blood was rage."

Payal's gaze searched his face. "You were never meant to be her child."

"The thing is, Mercants never quite let go." Not even the gentlest of them all. "My grandmother was the storm force against my anger, the one who—through sheer grim determination—taught me that I had value, that I wasn't a broken object for Binh Fernandez to throw away."

He took a deep breath of the cool night air. "But my mother, she'd come into my hospital room and read me children's books written by one of my ancestors two hundred years ago. Stories of knights and queens and adventures. I ignored her for months—but she still came."

Magdalene Mercant had her own kind of steel.

He saw Payal swallow before she looked away and to the water. "Did your father really die in an accident on a building site?"

"Says so in the Enforcement report." Canto shrugged. "We live in a dangerous world." He'd never asked his grandmother whether she'd had anything to do with Binh's untimely death—but he knew not a single Fernandez had dared argue or ask for compensation when Ena claimed Canto for her own.

Payal bit off a chunk of the protein bar, chewed almost ferociously. "Mercants aren't known to be assassins."

"Could be because we're very, very good at it." It was also rare for them to take deadly action—but when forced into a situation where protecting the family meant erasing a threat from the board, it would be done.

"We don't start fights, Canto," his grandmother had once said as they sat, faces awash in the spray thrown by the crashing water below her clifftop home, "but we *do* end them."

Payal finished the protein bar in silence and accepted a second one he'd brought down with him. He took the opportunity to look at her, the line of her profile not a thing of hard edges like his own, but of soft curves.

He ached to touch her.

Though he'd hung around the affectionate, touchy bears for months, this was the first time in his life he'd wanted a woman to give him the gift of skin privileges. Was it just an echo of the past? No. The boy he'd been had been too young to have such thoughts.

This was about Payal Rao, the woman.

While the bond they'd forged in blood would never break, he would've never been attracted to her had he discovered that she'd sacrificed her sister to the wolves. He'd have fought to haul her into the light, but his heart would've broken at the realization of who that wild and heroic girl had become.

What he'd instead discovered was a fucking miracle of a woman.

Despite all that had been done to her, Payal could be fiercely loyal, did not harm the weak, and had a mind like a razor. It had begun in blood for them, but there was no road map for where they were now going.

She spoke without warning. "I believe that the wiring for trust—for all positive emotion—was damaged early on in my development. I don't seem to have the capacity."

Canto wanted to kill everyone who'd abused her heart, just crush them out of existence. "You held my hand so I wouldn't be alone." It came out a harsh rasp. "You protected me when I was alone and broken even though you'd been equally brutalized. You have more courage and hope and generosity inside you than most people on this planet."

PAYAL screwed on the cap of the empty drink bottle with infinite care, Canto's words hitting her as hard as a thousand bricks. She didn't know what to do with them, how to make her mind understand them.

Wedging the empty bottle carefully into a space between two rocks and leaving the half-eaten protein bar in the same safe spot, she moved to a succulent garden a bare foot away. "Can I change this?"

"What? Yeah, go for it."

Payal uprooted no plants. This wasn't about harming living things. She just began to rearrange the stones in a pattern that calmed her mind. The manic little girl inside her was as stunned as the woman she'd become, breathing too fast as she tried to see the trap in his words, the betrayal . . . and not finding any.

Her mouth opened. "I'm on medication."

Every part of her believed him, their bond a thing beyond politics and family loyalties. In this quiet desert night lit by the stars strung into the trees, they were just Payal and Canto, 3K and 7J, two people who'd been bathed in blood as children and changed profoundly as a result.

"To help with migraines?" Canto leaned forward with his forearms on his thighs. "I never managed to dig up your medical records, but did hear rumors that you used to suffer from migraines."

"This particular medication is for my brain chemistry," she told him, because this was far more critical to her than the tumors. The tumors could kill her, but her confused brain chemistry could destroy every piece of Payal Rao while leaving her alive. "Do you remember how I was when we were children? Out of control and manic at times, really flat at others?"

She was watching him out of the corner of her eye, saw him frown. "You were being a child. Some of our race just don't accept that."

"No, Canto, it was beyond that—you're being loyal, but you know I wasn't right, Psy or not." When his expression grew dark, this man whose first instinct was to defend her—*her breath short, jagged, her pulse rapid*—she said, "Once, I took a knife from the kitchen and stabbed holes one inch apart in the wall of my bedroom." It hadn't been about anger, but about compulsion. "I felt so peaceful doing it—yet at the same time, I was screaming inside because I couldn't stop."

His expression shifted into an intensity that burned. "These meds. Do they help?"

"Nothing will make me neurotypical, but the medications smooth out the spikes and crashes, so I have brain chemistry more similar to most other people."

"It's not something forced on you?"

"No. My father finally had me assessed after he took me from the school, and the medics recommended the regimen. I didn't want to be on it then, but that was because I was in a manic state after attacking the teacher. After the meds took effect, I began to realize I could actually *think* properly for the first time that I could remember.

"No constant murmur of noise at the back of my head, no sudden periods of darkness, no urges to do compulsive acts over which I had no control." She put a single white stone next to three black ones. "I felt . . . like myself." She glanced up at the starlit sky. "As if the broken pieces of me had been stitched together into a coherent whole."

Coherence.

That was the word that she always associated with her brain-chemistry medication. "I have control over the regimen these days." Her father didn't care about these meds—had probably forgotten about them since she'd been stable for so long. And the one good thing he'd ever done for her was to not tell Lalit about her brain. Else her brother would've found some way to sabotage her. "It's been tweaked and adjusted over the years, but there's no doubt I'll be on this regimen or something similar the rest of my life."

"Okay." Canto picked up her protein bar. "As long as it's your choice, I don't see the problem. Here, you should finish this—you still look drained."

She sat back on the path, her arms hooked around her knees, and stared at him. "I'm telling you the extent of my damage, Canto." She teleported the bar back to the shelter, earning herself a scowl. "The Payal you see, she's the Payal I've constructed out of the ruins of who I once was; my personality is held together by precarious glue that could one day fail."

Canto shifted on the stone to fully face her, the intimacy of the eye contact stealing her breath. "Come here."

Chapter 14

We choose but once. To some we are obsessed madmen. To others, devoted chevaliers.

—Lord Deryn Mercant (circa 1506)

BECAUSE CANTO HAD asked and not tried to command, she rose and walked over to stand next to his empty chair. "What is it?"

"Will you sit in my chair?"

Payal didn't understand the point of his request, but she was feeling exposed enough not to be battle ready. She sat—the chair was too big for her, of course, made as it was to accommodate a much larger frame . . . and it held the scent of Canto. She took a surreptitious inhale, then another.

"That chair," Canto said in his gritty voice, which was like a touch over her skin, "it helps me function in the world. It's a tool."

Payal nodded. "Of course."

"But when they did the operations on my spine, the surgeons never promised me the repairs would hold for a lifetime. There could come a day when they fail and I end up losing function over most of my body."

She saw it now, what he was doing, the pattern he was laying over her own. Her eyes wanted to burn hot, her chest to tighten. "Tools," she whispered.

"Yes, baby, just tools." He reached out a hand.

Her body locked. To touch a male voluntarily? It was an action she hadn't taken in a long time. But when Canto began to drop his hand, she jerked up her own and wove her fingers through his. The skin of his fingers was rough, the fabric of his glove on the top inner part not leather-synth but a softer, more breathable material with light padding behind it.

She tried to think, to absorb all the textures of him, but the shock of the contact was an explosion through her system, overwhelming her capacity to process it in a rational way.

"We're in charge of our tools," Canto gritted out in that way he had—with a confident determination that brooked no argument. "If the fucking things fail one day, or our bodies stop cooperating, we'll find new tools—because you and I, 3K, we're survivors."

Her fingers clenched on his, hard, so hard. "If the meds fail, I won't be rational, not as I am now." She needed him to understand that the screaming little girl would always be a part of her.

"I met you before the meds, remember?" Canto lifted their clasped hands to brush his lips over her skin, the touch slight—and the eye contact constant, so she could deny him at any instant. "Our bond will hold in all our guises. Would you break it if I end up bedbound, only my eyes capable of movement?"

Payal saw then his private nightmare. As losing herself to the compulsions and aberrant impulses was hers. "No," she whispered, her hand spasming tight around his. "Our bond is unbreakable." In speaking those words, she knew them for the truth.

Canto Mercant and Payal Rao were tied by an invisible thread not even the worst horror could break.

She could trust him.

The realization was a cataclysmic shock that sent a tremor through her.

CANTO didn't want to let Payal go. He wanted to wrap her up in his arms and hold on until she could breathe again without grasping herself so tight. But she was like a wary wild bird, one that had barely taken a step toward him.

He had to be careful, not startle her.

So when she flexed her hand open, he released her. And when she rubbed her fingers at her temples and said she had a migraine, needed to return to Vara to rest, he said, "Can you make a meeting early tomorrow afternoon? I want to introduce you to the anchor advisory board."

Payal gave a crisp nod. "I'll make the time." Already, he could see her pulling her walls around herself, the same walls that had led Gia Khan to label her robotic.

Gia Khan was full of shit—and full of envy. The politically active M-Psy who'd been a friend of the old Council knew that Payal was a far better woman and a far better Psy than she'd ever be.

This was no longer her world. This was Payal's world.

"Hey," he said when Payal smoothed her hands over her jeans in readiness for a teleport.

When she glanced at him, he said, "This? Best night of my life."

She went motionless, then was gone. But the imprint of her lingered on his palm, the ferocious strength of her grip a silent testament to trust. Canto curled his fingers inward, trying to hold on to the fragile promise in that grip.

PAYAL slept deep and well that night, though she'd expected to toss and turn. When she woke, it was to a stabbing moment of shock at all she'd shared with Canto, but that passed in a cascade of memory. Of galaxies and tools and the freedom to just *be*. Whatever was happening between the two of them, it had nothing to do with the outside world—and that included anchor business.

Those night hours had been theirs, private and alone.

She almost contacted him and made a request to repeat the experience, but hesitated at the last second. The previous night had been an interaction out of time, lit by starlight and apart from reality; she had no idea what Canto might think of it now. What he might think of her and her chemically imbalanced brain.

Yes, baby, just tools.

Her hand tightened into a fist, holding on to the rough tenderness of his words as she got up to ready herself for the day. Part of that preparation included finishing the protein bar he'd given her—she'd retrieved it before she left.

Foolish, it was foolish to be so affected by his way of giving her food.

She still ate it down to the last bite.

Then it was time to walk out into the battlefield of Vara. She managed to make it through to early afternoon without running into Lalit or being summoned by her father. Surprised by the latter, she glanced at her message stream and saw that Ruhi had responded to a call request from Pranath.

Sir, before I disturb Ms. Rao, I thought you'd like to know that she is deep into planning the upcoming Jervois bid.

Her father had replied that he'd speak to Payal tomorrow.

That had been clever of Ruhi, to gain Payal time without offending Pranath. Payal sent a note to her assistant praising her for the act. Ruhi seemed to be in Payal's corner—if only because she knew Lalit never would have promoted her to her current high-level position. Payal's brother preferred male assistants.

Whether Ruhi was actually "hers" remained an open question. The assistant could have been told to take actions for her boss's benefit exactly so Payal would begin to trust her. Just as well Payal trusted no one.

Except Canto.

A buzz in her blood, she took a moment to compose herself before going to speak to Ruhi. "I'm heading to a meeting. If Father asks, mention it's the Mercant matter. Tell Lalit to speak to my father if he pushes for information." She glanced at her watch. "Actually, have an early day. I'll let my father know."

Ruhi didn't argue—she didn't like dealing with Lalit when Payal was away. "I have some work to finish, but I can log in from home."

Leaving the other woman to gather her things, Payal made her way to her apartment. She didn't intend to change—her wide-legged black pants and simple sleeveless red top with a vee-neck would be fine for the meeting. She'd come down for only one reason—to open up the book of tax law and touch her fingers to the wrapper she'd pressed within.

It wasn't about the wrapper. It was about the care it indicated.

Obsession, whispered the part of her on which hung her sanity, *this is the start of an unhealthy obsession.*

Her hand clenched on the book. Closing it and returning it to the shelf before her mind could spiral, she checked her makeup and hair in the mirror—checked her armor—then teleported to the meeting spot.

Canto was already there, waiting for her in the shelter. He'd parked his chair within a circular arrangement of five other seats. So she'd be meeting with four others today.

"There you are," he said, the galaxies in his eyes warming as if there were a candle within. "Look, I got you this." He held up a small brown box.

Though she had choices, and even though the scent of him disturbed her on a primal level, even though he could look at her and know too much, she took the chair right next to him. Because it was Canto. "What is it? Something for the meeting?"

"No." A faint tug of his lips that tore open places inside her that had long scarred over. "A gift."

She should've treated it as a possible threat, but it took all her control not to grab the box with feral glee. After accepting it with conscious care, she lifted the lid. Inside sat a small artwork of a cake, such as she'd seen in the windows of human and changeling bakeries. It was coated in pink with sparkles of silver, and cascading over one side were tiny flowers made of edible material.

She couldn't breathe.

"You want to try a piece now?" Canto was turning to look over his shoulder. "I have a plate and a knife back there."

"No." It came out a rasp. Coughing, she managed to find her voice again. "No. I'll take it with me." Where she could be alone with the chaos he'd incited inside her, the raw wave of emotion that threatened to swamp all that she was, all that she'd built herself to be.

Getting to her feet in a jerky movement, she closed the box and put it in one of the small cubby-style shelves built into the side wall of the shelter. Every movement felt jagged and hard, her body an automaton pulled by strings out of her grasp.

Unable to inhale past the shards in her lungs, she strode out of the shelter.

Before

THE SMALL GIRL sat in the room where they'd locked her up and stared at her hands. They bore no scabs or cuts, the scars from her previous marks having faded away. She was too young to think in terms of metaphors, but she felt as if the scabs and cuts on her mind were fading, too.

The fuzzy edges had become sharp, the broken thoughts whole.

Putting her hands on the soft stretchy cotton of her black tights, she looked at the wall in front of her, and she made herself *think*. The doctor had said she could soon have her own proper room, where no one would lock her inside.

She wanted that—but she'd seen Lalit spying on her from around the corner. He was waiting for the doctors to stop watching her; he'd hurt her again if she let him. So she had to make sure he never caught her alone—and she had to make her mind stronger and stronger, so he couldn't make her lose her thoughts again.

Don't give the monsters the satisfaction of seeing you give up.

"I won't," she whispered to the memory of the boy who'd said such nice things to her, and who'd looked at her like she was strong and brave and not wrong in the head. "I won't, 7J. I promise."

Chapter 15

CANTO WAS USED to waiting. A man couldn't work in surveillance and not build a tolerance for patience. He was also good at absorbing a lot of information and processing it down to the most critical factor.

But Payal screwed with his calm, turned his patience to dust.

His eyes went to the box that held the cake.

He'd done something wrong, but he couldn't figure out what and it was messing him up. He'd held on to her dreams for an eternity, waiting for the day when he would see her again; to be able to give her this small piece of what she'd wanted, it had made his fucking heart jump like an excited cub's.

"Shit." He shoved a hand through his hair. "Get it together, Canto."

Checking on the time, he saw that several minutes remained until the others would begin to arrive. He moved out of the shelter and down to where Payal crouched by a bed of succulents, quietly re-arranging the stones. Last night, after she'd left, he'd looked at what she'd done and hadn't been able to see anything of substance.

Yet he'd known she hadn't simply been moving stones around without reason, so he'd taken an image and had his computer analyze it. It had linked her design back to a precise mathematical model.

Patterns and grids were the baseline of Payal's mind.

"I screwed up, didn't I?" he asked roughly, because this mattered. *She* mattered.

Payal moved three stones before responding. "I can't—" She broke off, started again. "I function in this world because I work inside a defined set of parameters, within a framework of rules that keep me from becoming erratic and without reason."

Canto waited, unable to see where she was going.

"You . . ." A quick obsidian glance, the stars erased. "When we're together, it speaks too much to the child I once was." Another stone placed before she rose to her feet. "She wants to break out, wants to take control."

Canto bit back his knee-jerk reaction and stared out at the water. He wanted to tell her that was bullshit, that she didn't need all those rules and fences around her mind. She was dazzling in her brilliance, a bright star that had been constrained into an unnatural shape.

But Canto wasn't only the boy who'd almost died because his father considered him a mistake. Canto was also the man who'd spent years harboring a child empath inside his shields. Arwen had altered the core of his nature, taught him things without ever once giving instruction. One thing Canto knew was how to *listen*.

Yesterday and today, what had Payal told him?

That she had a chemical imbalance in her brain that made her feel out of control, obsessive, and without reason. The medications she took helped equalize her brain chemistry to standard levels—and her focus and concentration, the rules she'd made for herself, took her the rest of the way to being the kind of person she wanted to be.

"I'm a risk to your stability," he ground out, the words grating against his insides like sandpaper.

Payal released a shaky breath. "I thought I could handle it, that I could separate our time together from the rest of me . . . but I can't. Being with you, it weakens the walls I keep between myself and the unstable part of my psyche. I need distance."

Canto felt as if she'd stabbed him in the heart, the hilt thudding home against his skin to leave a bruise black and blue. Sucking in the pain, he said, "The anchor work?"

"I won't back away from that." A solemn promise. "But us . . ." A long breath, an exhale. "Whatever this is, it threatens to fracture my foundations. Please help me maintain those foundations."

The last sentence broke him.

He'd promised to stand by her side no matter what, but this was the hardest possible thing she could've asked of him—to help her maintain shields that would keep her distant and separate from him. No more would she reach out a hand and hold on tight to his. Instead, she'd pull back behind the shield of robotic coldness with which she faced the rest of the world.

"Canto?" It was the softest he'd ever heard her voice, and when he looked up, her face was stark in a way he'd never seen.

He jerked his head in a yes. What the fuck else could he do? She needed this. He would not let her down. Not even if watching her reinitiate her shields felt like losing her all over again.

PAYAL wanted to reach out and grab onto the thread she'd just cut, stop it from falling away into the darkness. It took everything she had to remain still and allow the thread to become lost in nothingness.

Loss clawed at her. Inside her screamed the manic, broken girl.

She forced out words of logic, focusing on the one tie to Canto she hadn't brutally destroyed. "In our last meeting, you were adamant that we need to connect with the Ruling Coalition. Why?"

His shoulders were still rigid, white lines around his mouth, but he didn't punish her by withholding himself. His response was immediate. "Because they're talking about breaking the Net into pieces."

The words slammed a fist through the echoes of emotion, snapping her fully into anchor mode. "With all the collapses of late," she said after absorbing the data, "all the fractures, the PsyNet is going to tear apart regardless." She saw it now, why the Ruling Coalition had made a choice of such violence. "Better to do it in a controlled fashion."

"I don't disagree with the idea of breaking the Net into smaller pieces—the problem is that it can't work as posited."

"Show me." Payal heard how she sounded, added, "I'm sorry. That sounded like an order."

Canto was already turning to head back up. "No, it was just you being blunt and honest." He glanced at her, the galaxies missing from his gaze. "Don't change that part of how we interact, Payal. Don't add niceties and politeness to make yourself palatable to me. Speak without filters."

That, she could do. That was her natural state. It was the politeness and the not accidentally offending people that took work. "All right," she said, and shoved her hand into her pocket to stop from reaching out to him.

Never had she reached out to anyone as an adult. That was why Canto was so dangerous to her, why she'd decided to push him away. A choice between a precious and rare connection, and her sanity and reason.

Not fair. But the world had never been fair to them.

CANTO had managed to get his raw emotions under unyielding control by the time he reached the shelter. He'd rage when he was alone. Right now, Payal had asked him to help her maintain her foundations—

to help her live as Payal Rao and not a wild and out-of-control falling star—and he would not let her down.

"Here." Sliding out the large-format organizer he'd put in the case built into the side of his chair, he brought up the plan his grandmother had received from Kaleb. Canto had read the signs in the slipstreams of the PsyNet, knew the Ruling Coalition had to be considering this dangerous solution, and asked his grandmother to feel things out.

She'd just gone ahead and asked the most powerful man in the Net.

It was a measure of Kaleb's respect for Ena that he'd passed on the classified plan titled "Sentinel"—though he had asked why she wanted to know. When informed that the request had come from a Mercant hub-anchor, Kaleb had apparently become very interested in return.

"He doesn't know the whole family yet," Ena had told Canto when she sent him the Sentinel papers. "Had no idea we had a hub in the mix—he wants to meet with you."

Canto wasn't ready to talk to the cardinal Tk. Not yet. He had to figure this out with Payal and the other anchors first. This was an A problem, the subject so specific and esoteric that it had been forgotten by the rest of the world. "I think all of us should talk about Sentinel," he said. "You, me, and the four As who've agreed to be part of the advisory panel."

Payal—who'd once more taken the seat next to him—didn't look up from her intense focus on the severance plan, her skin no longer pale as it had been when she'd looked at him with such open vulnerability. She was once more Payal Rao, CEO, and her skin held a honey-eyed glow under the filtered sunlight. Canto had set the walls of the shelter to medium clarity—a setting that allowed in light but muted it to a more comfortable softness.

"The members of the advisory board," she murmured. "They agree with the decision to face off against the Ruling Coalition?"

"More or less."

She raised her head.

He rubbed his face rather than give in to the compulsion to touch the curve of her chin. "None of us are used to working as a team—or being so visible—but they're all intelligent people. I don't think we'll have too much trouble." He'd made sure not to choose anyone so insular and isolated that they'd panic at the idea of being exposed to the world.

"We'll allay their concerns by making it clear I'll be the face." Payal zoomed in on part of the plan. "You're willing to be my lieutenant? To step in if I can't?"

"According to my grandmother, Mercants were knights to a king at the beginning of our history and rode into battle at his side," Canto said. "Only one of us was left standing by the end." He looked into a face he'd never be permitted to touch. "We're good at standing by our generals."

"Such language makes us sound like an army going into war."

"That's exactly what we are." There was no getting around that. "We're battling for the survival of the entire PsyNet. We are the last guard against a total system failure." And Payal—strong, determined, unbending against pressure—would go into battle at the forefront, the anchor flag held high.

He'd fight to the death to protect her as she fought for Designation A.

A flicker at the corner of his eye, the first of the advisory board members being teleported in. It was the only non-cardinal in the group: Bjorn Thorsen.

Almost eighty-seven years old with gray hair and gray eyes, his skin white with a tinge of pink, the senior anchor took a look around the oasis, then glanced inside the shelter and did a double take. "*You're* an A?"

Payal crossed one leg over the other, while holding the organizer on her thighs. "Yes."

"Payal Rao, meet Bjorn Thorsen," Canto said, "professor of mathematics and hub in California."

Next to come in was Suriana Wirra, a twenty-seven-year-old woman of medium height with skin of darkest brown, softly rounded cheeks, and thick hair she'd pulled back into a single braid. Her teleport was thanks to the second Mercant teleporter, since Genara would've flamed out if asked to make all the 'ports.

Shy and quiet, Suriana just nodded as she settled in.

The next person to arrive did so under his own steam: Arran Gabriel, with his black hair and brown skin, his body tightly coiled under his torn jeans and faded black T-shirt, was another telekinetic with teleport-capable abilities. As a result of the latter—and because his family hadn't held the power of Payal's—he'd been taken from his family unit at age four and thrown into a strict martial training program.

He'd initialized at age seven, but somehow, no one had realized what was happening, what he was. Arran was the only hub of whom Canto was aware who hadn't immediately been tagged as an A upon initialization. His experiences had left him angry in a way Canto knew was dangerous. But at twenty-four years of age Arran had that violent anger under vicious control.

The man was now a mercenary with zero acknowledged alliances or connections.

Canto had fully expected Arran to tell him to fuck off. But while emotionally damaged on a deep level, Arran wasn't a psychopath. His A core wouldn't allow him to ignore the oncoming annihilation of their race.

Now he grunted in greeting, his gaze flat and starless.

Genara brought in the last of their number right then: Ager Lii. Bent slightly at the back, with one hand leaning heavily on a cane, they were androgynous in appearance and claimed no gender. Their eyes were unusually elongated and their hair a soft and snowy white that hit shoulders covered by the linen fabric of the cream-colored tunic they wore with slim brown pants, their skin papery white and spotted with age.

Most Psy got those spots removed, but Ager had moved beyond that.

They were all here. The general and her lieutenants.

Chapter 16

Silence is a gift we need to cherish.

—Unknown A (1981)

CANTO SAW THE others take in Ager as Genara teleported out. Payal, who was closest to the frail A, got to her feet and offered her seat in a silent show of respect; Suriana murmured a quiet greeting, while Bjorn raised a hand in hello.

Arran, who'd blinked when Ager appeared, now moved subtly closer.

To catch the elder should they fall.

Yes, Arran might be angry and dangerous, but he wasn't evil. That had been Canto's only qualification for the anchors he wanted on this advisory board. That they not be so damaged by life and by what was being fed into them through their bond with the Net that they'd become as twisted as the dark twin of the NetMind.

The twins were gone now, merged into one chaotic and mindless creature that made Canto want to break the world. To him, the Dark-Mind and NetMind had been the soul of the Net. Split in two, but still extant, a source of hope that life could come from the worst mistakes. But all that remained of the burgeoning twin neosentiences were faraway echoes of who they'd once been.

"Ager," he said, "welcome."

Five of them arranged themselves around a low table Canto had positioned prior to their arrival. On it he placed nutrient drinks and bars. Having surrendered her chair to Ager, Payal took the one next to the older A. Bjorn sat down on Canto's other side, Suriana between Bjorn and Payal.

Arran didn't sit, a barely leashed creature who prowled the open end of the shelter.

Canto made no comment on the younger male's restlessness as he did a round of introductions. Afterward, Ager was the first to speak. "They're all wondering what I'm doing here, young Mercant." They coughed on the heels of their words. "That wolf child in Psy skin is expecting me to keel over at any moment."

Arran—who did remind Canto of one of the changeling wolves— paused midstep but didn't argue with the statement. And the question hung in the air. They all wanted to know why Canto had brought in an anchor so very old.

"Ager should have retired by now," he began, because accepted common knowledge was that anchors began to decrease their zone of influence at around Bjorn's age and had only a highly limited area of control by age ninety to ninety-five.

That meant three to four decades of life where an A could sleep without the constant huge pressure of a massive piece of the PsyNet at the back of their brain. Yet total retirement was an impossibility. They'd break at the absolute loss of that inexorable pressure, for they'd been born as anchors and would die as anchors.

"But," he continued, "we don't have enough As in the Net." A manifest fact. "As a result, Ager continues to maintain a full zone of influence." The other A had to constantly be on the verge of exhaustion.

Bjorn sucked in a breath. "If I may ask your age . . ."

"A hundred and ten" was the quick reply—because there was nothing wrong with Ager's mind.

Bjorn leaned forward, his hands tight on the arms of his chair. "I want to disbelieve you. I'm already starting to feel the need to reduce the size of my zone, and I'm decades your junior."

"You sure about your age?" Arran muttered, his eyes narrowed.

Ager took no offense. "Heh! Look older, don't I?" Their words were clipped, their accent soft. "I'll save the waste of a question. It's because it turns out the reason we're meant to retire around the ninety mark is because after that, our anchor pathways begin to degrade. I'm having to do constant repairs and it's sucking me dry."

"But if Ager decreases their zone of influence, people die," Canto finished.

"So Ager is here as a living example of the stupidity of our forefathers?" Arms folded, feet apart, Arran was a storm barely contained.

Ager's bones creaked as they angled their head toward Arran. "No, wolf child, I'm here because I was born at the start of the stupidity and have more knowledge in my old skull than your young brain can imagine."

Suriana found her voice, her Australian twang impossible to miss despite the quietness of her voice. "Ager? Were we always forgotten?"

"Yes." Ager coughed again and there was a painful rattle to it. "But the old As back when I first took over my zone, they told me they liked it. The politicians left them alone to get on with their job, and no one ever questioned how anchors managed the flows of the PsyNet—it was just accepted that they did. It meant our kind didn't have to play politics or show our faces to the media."

Payal spoke for the first time, her voice pushing against the bruise she'd put on Canto with her request that he sever the emotional ties between them, stop caring for her. "I'd agree with their stance were the situation the same—with all of us in a stable network."

Suriana nodded, while Bjorn appeared thoughtful. "Do you know if the Council consulted Designation A when they first came up with the idea for Silence?"

Ager gestured to a bottle of nutrients. It was lifted, uncapped, and in the elder's hands before Canto could see which Tk had done it. The look Arran shot Payal gave him the answer: she was faster and had more fine control than Arran, her ability cool and focused where Arran's was hot and more erratic.

After taking their time to have a sip, Ager said, "As far as I know, As were never consulted. I don't know if it would've made much difference if they had been."

"Seriously?" Arran was pacing again. "Our forebears couldn't figure out the mess Silence would make of the Net?"

"According to the old ones, the Substrate was in chaos prior to Silence. Massive turbulence, 'emotional fires' that burned out minds in their path, sudden and unpredictable flash floods of data that literally crushed biofeedback links and led to deaths termed 'unexplained' by the medics."

"Why isn't this in the records?" Bjorn asked with the intellectual skepticism of a man who worked in academia.

"Because no one talks to anchors," Payal said, crisp and to the point.

"Exactly so." Ager's hand shook as they placed the bottle on the table. "The Psy Council of the time was made aware of the incidents, but they were absorbed by the problem of how to fix the insanity and violence affecting our race. I suppose the information just became lost in the chaos."

Ager rasped in a breath. "My mentors, the old anchors, they preferred Silence. They said they'd felt peace for the first time in the years after it was implemented—the waves calmed at last, the flash fires and floods coming to a halt."

"Does that mean there's no hope for the PsyNet?" Suriana whispered, her hand rising to her mouth; on the back of it was what appeared to be a burn scar. "We bring it back to equilibrium, and it just fails again in a different way? An endless loop? Is that how it's always been?"

"Not according to all the history I know," Ager responded before wetting their throat with the nutrient liquid once more. "We've always been the most unstable of the three races, but prior to the first crash, we were never on the edge of chaos. Something went critically wrong at least a generation before Silence came into effect—a wound of which we have no comprehension."

This was why Canto had asked Ager to join them, despite the other anchor's precarious health. So much information had been lost because anchors lived isolated lives, knowing only their sub-anchors and perhaps the anchors in the next zone over. No longer were they close enough to mentor each other, the zones too stretched out. Their "pack" had been decimated.

Canto was determined to change that, pull them back together.

"This, what we're going to attempt, it's critical for the future of our race," he said. "You're either in or out. Make the choice. If you're in, loyalty is a prerequisite. Both to the As in this group and As as a whole—Payal is to be our face, but we stand as equals within."

"I agree to the terms," Payal said. "Unless the anchor is psychopathic and has turned to murder. Then I'll take them down."

Arran stared at Payal. "I like you. You say things without bullshit." A glance at Canto. "What she said."

"Yes." Suriana's whisper.

"I'm also in agreement," Bjorn said, "though I do think you're being naive to take our words for it, child. You should have us sign legal documentation."

"Would you betray us, Professor?" Ager asked after signaling their acquiescence with the terms.

"No, but we're all different individuals."

"We're anchors," Canto said, a sense of stretching deep inside him. "No one but another A will ever understand who we are and what we do. No one else even considers the board on which the game is played. We must be our champions."

Payal would be their champion. Intelligent, calculating, ruthless— and capable of a far fiercer allegiance than she would ever acknowledge— the woman the world knew as the hard-nosed Rao CEO was going to stand for Designation A.

Chapter 17

If you control the anchors, you control the Net.

—Bjorn Thorsen (2081)

PAYAL FOUGHT HER need to look at Canto; the gravitational pull of him acted as a tide on her senses. To feel such a visceral compulsion toward anyone, it was a new thing, a craving unknown. She never took her attention off Lalit or her father, but that wasn't the same. She didn't want to look at them. She had to look at them. With Canto Mercant, want was very much a component of her response.

Want. Desire. Hunger.

All words for a single potent emotion. For Payal, such violence of need equaled a chaos of the mind that could leave her vulnerable to her father's or brother's machinations. Even knowing this, every part of her wanted to reach out to Canto, a painful ache deep within her that only he could assuage.

Her eyes wanted to go to the gift he'd given her.

Food.

Again.

Not just food, a thing she'd asked for as a child.

He hadn't forgotten.

All these years and he hadn't forgotten.

That awareness had threatened to break all the restraints on that screaming, obsessive girl in her mind. Panic had set in. It still fluttered in the back of her throat, a small trapped creature that wanted to show itself in fluctuations in her breath, splotches of blood on her face.

Payal kept it in check with teeth-gritted will—and by refusing to make eye contact with Canto. Those galaxies made her want too much, made her dream. She wasn't in a position to dream, would never be in a position to dream even if her father and Lalit were both gone.

Because the meds only stabilized the imbalance in her brain—and what was wrong with her wasn't only organic. She was quite certain a strong component of it came from the PsyNet.

And the neosentience of the Net was now quite fragmented and mad.

"Tell us about the Ruling Coalition plan you mentioned." Ager's voice broke the silence, shattering the ice that crawled over her inner landscape as she tried to reinitialize the defenses that kept her robotic and uninvolved with the world.

"It's called Project Sentinel." The black strands of Canto's hair glinted in the sun now just angling into the shelter, catching her eye despite her every attempt to maintain visual detachment. "The Ruling Coalition wants to break off a test section of the PsyNet. It's an experiment to see if the smaller section will be more stable and less prone to fractures."

Payal thought of another deal she'd just made. "Did they get the idea from the Forgotten?" When Arran and Suriana looked blank, she said, "Not all our ancestors agreed with Silence. The ones that didn't left the PsyNet, and as their descendants are still alive, they must have their own network." Psy brains needed the biofeedback generated by a psychic network. Cut that off and those brains died—an established biological fact.

"I've never heard of them," Suriana said softly.

Ager coughed. "The Council liked to pretend they didn't exist. But back when I was a young'un, a few of the old-timers used to keep in sporadic contact with Forgotten relatives. Wasn't allowed, but people are people."

Canto's constellation eyes met hers, and those dreams, they threatened to awaken all over again. "How do you know about them?"

"I've done a number of deals with Devraj Santos." The leader of the Forgotten and a man whose gold- and bronze-flecked brown eyes appeared to be undergoing a transformation that made her wonder if enough Psy genes had coalesced in him to create a cardinal. "Rao also keeps excellent histories."

It had turned out that she and Santos were—*very*—distant cousins, linking up at an ancestor who'd left the PsyNet with the defectors. "The Forgotten also don't hide their heritage as they once did," she added. "I've heard that the Council used to hunt them." Likely because anyone with psychic power outside the Net was a threat.

"Now the Council's defunct and we have bigger problems." Canto leaned forward, his forearms braced on his thighs and his gaze direct. "I think you're right that the Ruling Coalition looked to the Forgotten, but it won't have been the only factor."

He paused to take a drink before continuing. "Per Sentinel, Kaleb Krychek would shift his mind into the initial experimental section and go with the broken piece—the island, so to speak. We all know he's powerful enough to hold the piece together if it's about to go into cataclysmic failure—but he's not an anchor. He can only hold back a collapse, not create a foundation."

"They taking an anchor with the island?" Arms folded, Arran leaned against one side of the open end of the shelter.

"That's the plan, but there's a problem that seems to have escaped everyone's notice, probably because anchors just keep on with the job."

He showed the others the graphic representation of Designation A in the Substrate that he'd already shown Payal—the lack of overlaps between anchor zones, the sheer thinness of the coverage. As Suriana, Arran, Ager, and Bjorn asked their questions, Payal sat back and distracted herself from obsessing over Canto by processing what she thought of the others.

Each had an element to them that could be dangerous if used against the group, but it was inescapable that the most dangerous person in the group was Canto, who held all their attention even now. He had that unknown quality that turned people into followers. It was a rare thing, but she'd seen it in both Devraj Santos and Ivy Jane Zen, the high-Gradient empath who was the president of the Empathic Collective.

She'd also seen it in a local human guru who used his charisma to leech money from his followers.

The difference between a user and a leader was what they did with the adulation.

Mercants had never had a reputation for selflessness.

Yes, Silver Mercant was head of EmNet, the largest humanitarian network in the world, but Silver Mercant was also mated to a changeling bear. She couldn't be taken as an exemplar of the proto-Mercant.

He'd given her food. He'd remembered her.

Her fingers curled into her palms, her nails digging into her flesh.

"That isolated hub will crash and burn in weeks if not days." Hands shoved into his pockets, Arran glared at no one and everyone. "How can they *not know* that we zone shift? It's been getting harder and harder, but we can still do it."

Payal had realized the latter, too. While the zones no longer overlapped in the vast majority of the world, one A could extend while another shrank back for a few days, and vice versa. Taking the pressure off in turns, to give all of them a chance to rest and recharge.

Canto's scowl was dark enough that Arran focused all his attention on him, belatedly realizing what Payal already had: that Canto Mercant was the apex predator in this space. "They don't know because there's no A on the Ruling Coalition—and nobody on the Coalition is old enough to remember how As worked before Silence."

"Probably didn't even know back then," Ager croaked out, waving a hand. "I don't know if any political leadership has ever understood the mechanics of the A network, probably because our predecessors were less than generous with the information. A bit of mystery intended to protect us—no one can chain us if they don't know how we work."

"I can see the sense in that," Bjorn muttered. "We all saw what Pure Psy did with the limited knowledge that is available."

"Be that as it may," Payal said, conscious her voice sounded flat and hard, "staying enigmatic is no longer viable or wise. Canto is correct: we need a voice on the Ruling Coalition."

"What makes you the best choice?" Arran's "smile" was nothing like Lalit's, but neither was it anything akin to warmth. No, it was a thing of razors.

"You can volunteer, but your anger issues would cause you to strike out at the first meeting. As Kaleb Krychek is stronger and deadlier than you, you'd then be dead and we'd have one less anchor."

Suriana sucked in a breath, Bjorn winced, Ager cackled.

Arran stared at her before inclining his head. "Point."

"Canto is the only other viable candidate," she added. "It's not only about brute power, but associated power." Because no matter if Psy thought themselves more advanced than changelings, they weren't; power mattered, the sense of authority mattered. "I have the Rao group; he has his family."

Canto's eyes seemed to burn when he looked at her. "I'm not much better than Arran when it comes to patience," he said, and she knew he was repeating the point for the benefit of the others. "I'll be far better as your backup."

"As long as you remember you're backup," she said, driven by her weakness where he was concerned. "Don't attempt to manipulate me."

Everyone else went quiet, while darkness eclipsed the stars in his eyes. She knew he understood what she was saying, understood what she was asking of him. Their past could not color this interaction, not if they were going to do this right.

"IF I'd wanted a doll to manipulate," Canto all but growled, furious with her for taking one step into trust, then two steps back, "I'd have picked anyone but you. I picked a gladiator for a reason. Anchors need a leader who'll stand and fight against the biggest predators in the Net." The Ruling Coalition might not think of themselves that way, but they were all—each and every one—huge powers.

Kaleb was a rumored dual cardinal with fingers in every pie in the Net. Payal and Canto might hold two cardinal designations, but they weren't dual cardinals. The term was one of art and did not include anchors—because a cardinal A could only access and use their anchor powers within the Substrate.

Outside that, they were reliant on their secondary abilities. The same applied in reverse—their secondary powers were effectively useless to them when they acted as anchors. The two different abilities simply did not interact. There was also the fact that many, *many* As were so mentally wiped by their anchor duties that they barely utilized their secondary abilities.

During his research into the designation, Canto had run across a very old—and cruel—joke made at the expense of Designation A: *What do you call a group of anchors? A waste of cardinals.* If he had to guess, he'd say it was an A behind the joke, a person who understood the price they paid to stand as the iron foundation of the Net.

Kaleb, however, if the rumors were true, had no restrictions on his abilities. He could access both cardinal-level telekinetic and telepathic powers *at the same time—and at any point he wanted.* The man could level cities and erase minds with the ease of a wave crashing to shore and wiping the sand clean.

Aden Kai was a huge psychic power in his own right, but he also had the might of the entire Arrow Squad behind him. The specialist black-ops squad was composed of soldiers deadly and relentless.

Ivy Jane Zen was the softest of the group, but she brought with her the Empathic Collective—who were backed by the Arrow Squad.

Nikita Duncan was a former Councilor with knowledge of more secrets than almost anyone else in the Net; she was also a massive financial powerhouse.

Anthony Kyriakus hadn't been a Councilor for long prior to the Council's collapse, but his power came from another source altogether— he headed the strongest clan of foreseers in the world. PsyClan Night-Star knew more about the future than was wise or sane.

Canto's anchors needed a person of equal weight and steel to stand against that wall of power. To be a fighter who would not flinch, would not back away, would not stop until they listened to her.

Payal gave him a measuring glance that betrayed nothing of what they were to each other before she looked around at the group. "You all feel emotion."

"So do you," Suriana whispered back, this anchor who'd been terrified of Canto's approach yet had stepped up. "You're an anchor. You can't be immune to everything that's happened, all the emotions the Es are pumping into the Net. It was powerful even when they were in a forced sleep. Now that they're awake, there's no way to avoid their colors in the river that is the Net."

Suriana had spoken in a rapid burst, as if she'd had to psych herself up to get out the words. She collapsed in the aftermath, her shoulders hunching inward.

Someone hurt her. Cold, crisp Payal in his mind.

His parched cells drank in the psychic touch. *Yes. I haven't figured out who yet, but I will.*

Payal gave him the slightest nod. Because she'd committed, and when Payal committed, she gave it her all. Suriana was one of hers now.

"I always felt something." Ager's voice was a bit croaky but not tired—as if this gathering had given them a new lease on life. "I don't know if it was because I was raised around people who were alive prior to Silence, but I've felt tendrils of emotion in the PsyNet all my life."

"I'm the same," Bjorn admitted. "It wasn't difficult to throw off the shackles of Silence. They never fit well, though I'm of the generation that had the dissonance embedded in our minds—for you young ones, dissonance is a pain loop designed to punish Psy for feeling emotion."

He winced, as if being hit by that programming for daring to speak of it. "But it's been fading in strength for a long time under the weight of what I do as an anchor. I don't think the Councils bothered to program dissonance into As after us. Our shields are impregnable— even were we to cry and laugh, nothing would leak into the Net."

Arran had gone motionless as Bjorn spoke, a whiteness to his jawline. Canto was certain Arran had been so programmed. He hadn't been pulled out of martial training until he was eleven and someone finally realized he was an A.

For an initialized anchor to be punished for emotion when droplets of emotion had leaked into and run through the pathways of the Net even during Silence? They were fucking lucky Arran and Bjorn were sane.

He made it a priority to find out how to disable that programming. Because these people were his now, too. Payal and he, they had this in common: they were possessive about those they claimed.

He wanted to throw back his head and yell his fury up at the sky. Because the first person he'd ever claimed was her. And she was the one person he could never have. Not if he was to keep his promise. Not if he was to be the knight on whom she could depend to defend her against all threats—including the one in her mind.

Chapter 18

Cor meum familia est.
My heart is family.

—Motto of the Mercant family

THOUGH PAYAL HADN'T looked at Canto, didn't need his answer when it came to emotion, he knew the others did. "I didn't see the point in pretending to be Silent when I so obviously wasn't."

Ager gave him a curious look. "No one has ever questioned Ena Mercant's Silence."

Canto could've blocked the reference to his family, but if he wanted commitment, he had to commit in turn.

"You can't expect to receive if you don't give," Arwen had said once. "No one likes feeling exposed."

Coming from an E who wore his heart on his sleeve where family was concerned, it had made an impact.

"My grandmother is many things." Canto's respect for Ena was one of the foundations of his life. "First and foremost, she is a warrior for our family. No Mercant will ever be betrayed to outsiders—not even the ones who don't fit the mold of so-called perfection."

He made eye contact with everyone but Payal—because shit, he needed time to handle that. "That's who I am and where I come from and what I want for us as a group."

"Big goals," Arran muttered.

Suriana stirred. "It would be nice, to have a group I could trust without question."

"After so long, I am content alone," Bjorn said, exchanging a quiet nod with Ager, "but a union of minds in sync . . . Yes, I see how it could make things better for the future of all As."

"You gonna pretend you're Silent?" Arran challenged Payal.

"I understand and feel emotion." Cool as ice. "But I've trained myself to keep it at a distance. I function far better that way."

Canto wanted to argue with her about her stance, wanted to ask if she'd ever considered anything other than a total shutdown of her emotions, not out of arrogance or his own need, but because his childhood had shown him that the environment in which a person grew could alter everything about how they thought, what they believed.

He would not be *this* Canto had he come to adulthood in the household of his father.

That Payal's mental wiring was distinctive, he didn't doubt. But she'd also had to learn to wall off her emotions in order to survive her childhood. There were suggestions—hidden, underground—that Pranath Rao had either killed or arranged for the death of his firstborn. Add in her psychopathic surviving brother, and that wasn't a home in which a small, sensitive little girl could endure without hardening herself.

"Fascinating." Ager flexed then closed their hand back around the head of their cane. "You realize you are what the architects of Silence actually envisioned? A being born with emotion who can nonetheless keep that emotion from overwhelming her."

"No," Payal said with her customary directness. "If you go back and read up on the original aims of Silence, it best matches a psycho-pathic personality profile."

A bark of laughter from Arran that made Suriana jump and Bjorn jerk upright. But the other anchor wasn't looking at either of them. He was grinning at Payal. "I definitely want her representing us," he said to Canto, his body more relaxed than Canto had ever seen it. "Can you imagine her using that take-no-shit voice against Krychek?"

"It's not about 'against,'" Payal said before Canto could reply. "The members of the Ruling Coalition aren't our enemies. They are allies."

"Agreed," Canto said. "Their only mistake was in not bringing anchors to the table—but that was a decision put into play generations ago, well before any of us were born—and Designation A played a major role in our invisibility." Canto wasn't about to allow his designation to skate on past mistakes.

"So," he said, "do we have a consensus? That we're now a team that represents anchors, with Payal as our public voice?" Their general forged in a burn of ice and survival.

A round of nods—and a small salute from Arran.

Payal, meanwhile, showed no outward reaction to the outcome. She simply uncrossed her legs and said, "Then it's time to make our first move."

SOPHIA Russo's official title was special advisor to Ruling Coalition member Nikita Duncan. Her duties and responsibilities, however, had grown significantly since she took on the position. She'd told Nikita that she'd never lie to her—and that she wasn't afraid of her, either.

Both facts were true.

Not much scared a former Justice-Psy who'd walked in the minds of serial killers.

Sophia had openly opposed her boss's stance on a number of matters; that she was still here spoke to the strength of their relationship. Sophia didn't think she'd ever like Nikita, not when she knew so much of what the other woman had done, but she respected her.

Nikita had blood on her hands—but she also had a cardinal empath daughter she'd raised to adulthood. The same cardinal daughter who'd created the first major chink in Silence when she defected from the PsyNet. Also, unlike a number of notable others, Nikita had felt the winds of change and was moving with them rather than attempting to keep the Psy locked in a cold and Silent past.

So when the other woman asked her to look over Project Sentinel and give feedback, Sophia took care with the task. A headache pulsed at the back of her head by the time she was done, but that was nothing new. She'd been getting small headaches for weeks now, and she knew it had to do with the problems in the PsyNet.

Most Psy were anchored into the PsyNet by a single biofeedback link. Sophia, however, was interwoven so deeply into its fabric that she could never extricate herself. She felt no such desire—not when she knew how important her mind was to the Net. It was a tiny weight in the grand scheme of things, a tiny anchor at best, but it *was* an anchor. It also didn't matter that she hadn't been born an anchor, her attachment to the Net a result of childhood trauma; that her anchor point existed was now fact.

"That's the problem with this plan," she said to Nikita as the two of them walked down a long bridge that connected two parts of Duncan HQ in San Francisco. Clear water flowed under the bridge from the large water feature to the right—a flat wall of veined granite that had water running down it. The minerals in the rock sparkled in the morning sunlight in this part of the world.

"Explain," Nikita said.

Sophia halted in the center of the bridge. "It has to do with the anchor who'll be attached to the island."

"The individual hasn't yet been chosen." The wedge of Nikita's black hair was newly cut, the edges blunt and perfect. Her skirt-suit was a dark gray, the shirt she wore underneath a pristine white.

Sophia had gone for a dark green pantsuit today, paired with a white top that featured a ribbon woven through the high neckline. It wasn't crisply Psy, but it was very Sophia—as she'd come to realize in the time since her emancipation from Silence.

"But," Nikita continued, "it will be a strong and stable cardinal."

Frowning, Sophia shook her head. "You need the input of a hub-A before things get to that point." As a strange minor A, Sophia couldn't quite see the shape of the problem, though it hovered on the edge of her consciousness. "I have a strong feeling a single anchor won't be able to hold the island."

Nikita glanced at her timepiece. "I have to go in for the buyout meeting. We'll discuss this later—but I can tell you from my time on the Council that anchors are generally unstable. It may prove difficult to find one rational enough to participate in such talks."

Sophia refrained from rolling her eyes; she'd picked up the action from one of the DarkRiver leopard teens, and a more apt one she couldn't at this moment imagine. "Think about what you just said, Nikita." She held the brown of her boss's gaze. "Santano Enrique was a Councilor."

Nikita paused in the act of turning away, was still, then gave a crisp nod. "I'll add this to the Ruling Coalition's agenda—but if you're correct, any number of As should have contacted us by now to warn against the current shape of Sentinel."

"That assumes they're in the information loop." Nikita tended to forget that not everyone had such access—she had been in power for decades, was unused to being in the dark on any important matter.

The two of them began to walk together again.

Nikita's hair was black glass under the sun as she said, "The fact is, we're in a time crunch." In front of them, the doors to the building slid open. "There's no sign of a slowdown in the Scarab issue—the damage being done is long-term and destructive."

Sophia didn't follow Nikita inside. Frowning in thought, she made her way slowly back across the bridge. She knew a lot of people—but as a former J-Psy, her major network was in Justice. She had no contacts in Designation A. Even if she did, what would she ask them? Her feeling of unease was exactly that, a *feeling*.

No facts, no rationale behind it.

Stopping near the center of the bridge once more, she stared down at the running water as her headache pulsed, slow and steady. When she looked on the PsyNet, at the small section she anchored, she saw that it remained calm, stable, and yet the knots in her stomach wound themselves into painful rocks.

The NetMind and DarkMind had once been whole when they wove through her section of the Net—she'd become an uncategorizable focus, one that helped the twin neosentiences find cohesion. Perhaps because she, too, had once been fragmented. Into so many pieces that her personality and mind were a scarred mélange.

"Beautiful signs of your will to survive, Sophie darling." Max's dimpled smile as he ran a finger over her chin, after she'd spoken aloud about her piecemeal self. "You kicked the scrawny ass of anyone stupid enough to write you off, and I'm a smug shit about it."

Today, hoping her mind could help the twin neosentiences of the Net hold on to coherence, she "listened" for their presence and heard only the wind. As if they'd gone beyond madness and into a final death. But no . . . *There*. A brush against her mind, another.

Inhaling on a sob, she clenched one hand on the bridge railing. She couldn't speak to the NetMind or the DarkMind, but she'd never needed to; theirs was a bond of emotion. Now she staggered under a melancholy wave of sadness and heartbreak.

Their sadness. Their heartbreak.

The PsyNet was dying. And they were dying with it.

Chapter 19

The volcanic eruption came without warning, and it led to the death of an entire city. Included in that number were twenty members of Designation A. It is said that the loss changed the face of the designation forever.

—From *Disasters of the Ancient World* by Antonio Flavia (1957)

EIGHT HOURS AFTER the meeting, Payal lay awake in bed, staring up at the ceiling. In her fist was a small white stone she'd stolen from the oasis when Canto wasn't looking. A stone he'd touched, held. Her larceny had been an impulsive emotional act that had nothing of reason in it, another sign of the deleterious effects of her response to him.

She squeezed the stone hard . . . and teleported herself back to the desert, barefoot, and wearing only a sleep tee and pajama pants. Moonlight kissed the oasis, so she was in the same hemisphere—and from the position of the moon, not so very far from Delhi. Padding down the path, the sand gritty under her soles, she checked the areas she'd altered while he'd watched with interest. None of them had been changed back.

Sitting down on a fractionally misaligned paving so she wouldn't have to look at it, Payal soaked in the peace and quiet. No wind stirred the trees or made the sands whisper closer. No other voices split the air. If she'd tripped a silent alarm, no one came to kick her out.

In front of her lay a small area she'd fixed so it was harmonious to her mind.

"It's compulsive, your need for mathematical perfection." Her father's voice when he'd discovered her arranging her childhood belongings exactly so on her shelves. "Coloring between the lines will never get you anywhere. Our race likes rules, but the people who gain power are the ones who understand that the rules need to be bent and broken."

Pranath Rao had never seemed to understand that though his daughter far preferred to color inside the lines, she saw *all* the options, the decision-making system in her mind a multilayered and multidimensional matrix. Her preference for order over chaos wasn't heavily weighted in that matrix.

Rising, she went to the next little garden area. It had been planted with care but remained out of alignment. She knew Canto wouldn't mind the small alterations she wanted to make to bring it back to harmony. This place was his, but . . . it felt a little bit hers, too. It was a terrible thing, this emotional response, another strike at the walls that protected her sanity, but she couldn't make herself teleport home.

She began to work.

Sitting back with a satisfied sigh some time afterward, she looked at her sand- and dirt-covered hands, then up at the night sky. The galaxies of Canto Mercant's eyes dazzled her inner vision. The part of her that had learned to survive in Vara hissed at her to remember that he was a Mercant.

Don't trust him, it whispered.

It was silenced by the furious echo of the wild-eyed girl she'd once been. *He'd bleed for you!* she yelled over the warning whisper. The intensity of Canto's loyalty was a kind of subvocal hum that disturbed the tiny hairs on her arms and caused her ears to attune themselves to the deep timbre of his voice.

"You're imagining it," she told herself. "You've never been great at reading emotional cues."

The girl inside her remained stubborn, mutinous. That girl had no doubts.

Canto Mercant would not betray Payal Rao.

The knowledge kept on causing breaks in the wall of her mind, kept on making her want to retreat from her own request to him. She'd made that request in a blind panic, stunned by how fast her walls were crumbling. Now, as she sat in the cold night air, hugging her knees to her chest, she was afraid, so afraid that she'd given up the only thing in her life that had ever made her feel . . . good. Just good.

The insane girl inside her smashed her fisted hands against the iron bars of the cage Payal had built to keep her contained, wanting out, wanting freedom. Wanting Canto. Bending her head toward her knees, her eyes hot and her throat thick, Payal rocked back and forth.

A telepathic knock had her jolting. She recognized the mental signature as that of Arran Gabriel. Prior to ending their first meeting, the six of them—in what they'd decided to name the Anchor Representative Association or ARA for short—had exchanged telepathic conversation in order to make such contact more seamless.

Arran, she said, guard raised. *How may I assist you?*

I've been thinking, he said in a mental voice far colder than the angry heat of his physical presence, *and I still can't work out if Canto is for real. So I reckoned I'd ask the most rational person in the room. You figure this for a con?*

Payal wondered if she should disclose her conflict of interest. No, the past was between her and Canto, a private thing. She could answer Arran's question using pure robotic reason, her own terrifying sense of trust no part of the equation.

Mercants always plan multiple moves ahead in multiple dimensions, she said, *but right now, Canto is planning for Designation A. The foundation of the PsyNet is in trouble. There's no faking that. Anchors must be part of the solution—Canto and the Mercants gain nothing from this gambit that we all also do not gain.*

Huh, Arran said. *Guess so.*

He ended the communication as abruptly as he'd begun it.

But the interaction had been enough to break her out of her cycling thoughts. After taking one last look around the oasis, she returned home to sleep and prepare for what was to come, the small white stone clutched safely in her hand.

She slept with the heaviness of exhaustion and woke to the feel of a massive pressure wave at the back of her brain. The gravity of it was familiar, the conclusion inexorable: the PsyNet in her region was buckling under bombardment from multiple sources.

Leaving Krychek and other powerful minds to deal with the assault on the main level of the PsyNet, she dived into the Substrate. The grid with which she made sense of this space wasn't broken. It was warped.

Severely.

Net failure imminent.

She shifted into anchor mode, her entire attention zeroing in on that warped section that was no longer a healthy glowing blue, but a dull and muddy green.

As if the warping had cut off the blood flow to critical arteries.

Weaving through it all were the strange and thick fibers of dull brown that had begun to grow a couple of decades earlier. As far as Payal knew, none of the As had ever been able to get rid of the fibers, and the stuff was clogging up the flow of the Substrate.

But that was a problem for another day.

The rest of her zone would be fine with nothing but a ghost anchor for a short period. But no matter how much energy she fed into the matrix, she couldn't correct the warp. It hadn't, she belatedly realized, been caused only by the newest attack—this was a mutation in the Substrate, part of the rot in the Net.

When she rose up out of the Substrate, it was to see a huge mind working on the breach—a mind that wasn't Kaleb's obsidian, but darker, more cloaked in shadow. *Aden Kai*, leader of the Arrow Squad. Only recognizable because he wasn't in stealth mode.

She could see what he was trying to do, knew it wouldn't work, not given the extent of the damage in the Substrate.

Payal didn't like touching unknown minds, but this was an extenuating circumstance; she made the effort to send a message to the man working with such merciless concentration in front of her: *You need Krychek, too. The Substrate is badly damaged, and I require a bigger window of time to fix it.*

In truth, she wasn't certain she had the raw psychic energy to do such a massive repair on her own—but she couldn't pull in her subanchors. With her focused on the repair, her subs were bearing the bulk of the zone's load.

The mental voice that replied to hers was black ice. *Who are you, and how did you telepath me through blackout shields?*

I'm the hub-anchor for this region, and I sent the message through your biofeedback link. It was a clunky way to talk even for anchors, so this second message she sent through the telepathic pathway he'd opened. *I have to fix the Substrate or your repair will collapse. Get Krychek.*

She returned to the foundations of the Net without waiting for an answer. As she did so, she thought of Canto . . . and was reaching for him before she'd processed the need that was a bruise inside her. Once again, he was too far away for her to touch. But she did hit another familiar mind.

She could've stopped then, returned to rationality, but she spoke to that familiar mind: *Suriana, can you bounce a message to Canto?*

Suriana's telepathic voice was sweet and clear. *I just tried, but I'm too far. I can message him on the number he gave us.*

Do it. Tell Canto I need him.

A crystalline mind brushed against Payal's mere seconds later. *I'm here.* Absolute attention. *Is this about the attack on the Net in your area? I can see the turbulence in the Substrate.*

Aware that he was listening for her now, his telepathic "ear" far stronger than her voice, she said, *I can't do it alone. Not enough energy.* It was a mathematical truth, yet she kept on working. Anchors did not give up. Anchors went down with the Net if necessary, but until then, they fought.

I can give you ten minutes, he said. *My anchor point will hold for that duration even without me.*

Never did she ask for help for anything, but this was Canto. Her 7J. *Come.*

ADEN was an Arrow, privy to secrets dark and dangerous, but he had no experience with a communication such as the one that had just taken place. The initial contact hadn't been telepathic, had come from inside him. Ostensibly through his biofeedback link. Which was an impossibility, unless he was losing his mind. As he knew he was sane, he decided to do as the eerie and clipped voice had commanded, and contacted Kaleb.

The dual cardinal arrived within a short period, and they began to work with a rhythm they'd long since perfected. It felt akin to gluing the holes in a leaking bucket that was so eggshell-thin and brittle it kept cracking and breaking.

I was contacted by the hub-anchor for this region through my biofeedback link.

Anchors don't talk to anyone. Not directly.

This one ordered me to get you because what she termed the Substrate is damaged, and I wouldn't be able to do the repair on my own. She also stated that the repair would fail unless she fixed the Substrate.

She?

Yes. Her telepathic voice had fallen into a register rarely found in males. *Who's the hub for this region?*

I don't have the information at hand. But whoever she is, she was right. Krychek indicated a patch that was already unraveling even with both of them using every ounce of their abilities to keep it in place. As if the Net was crumbing so fast that their stitches couldn't hold. *Let's hope she can fix this mysterious Substrate.*

The Architect

While most patients with Scarab Syndrome show signs of confusion and memory loss, a small segment remain fully cognizant—and deeply damaged as a result. They are aware of their decline and unable to stop it.

The most dangerous group, however, are those with delusions of omnipotence—this pool is limited, but the delusion, when it takes hold, is all-consuming. Such patients want no assistance, refuse to believe that their brain is degrading, and consider health professionals enemies envious of their power.

—Report to the Psy Ruling Coalition from Dr. Maia Ndiaye, PsyMed SF Echo

THE ARCHITECT "WOKE" to the realization that her memory was an ominous blank.

Unalarmed, she accessed her telepathic recorder and played back the time.

Nothing of note. It appeared she'd simply been sitting at her desk, staring into nothingness. A dangerous sign, but not one that she couldn't find a way to mitigate. Her deeper concern was what her children had done during her time of "sleep."

She glanced at the chains that bound her children to her.

Three had snapped their leashes and gone rogue, and from the waves rolling through the PsyNet, they'd done what might be irreparable damage. Her children might be the next evolution of Psy, brilliant and too big for the current world, but nonetheless, she couldn't permit such rebellion.

It would only foment more at a time when that could collapse all her plans for the future. Regrettable as it was, she had to do what she so rarely did and end their existence. The three believed they'd attained freedom by snapping the leash, but the Architect had been a power for many years. She understood never to rely only on a single factor.

Which was why she'd put ticking time bombs in their minds.

It took a single telepathic command to detonate those bombs: *Sleep, my child. Your work is done.*

Three huge minds fell under the weight of devastating aneurysms.

The Architect sighed and ran her hands down the front of her pristine black dress. An undesirable choice, but a necessary one. She'd made it clear to her children that they were to do no more damage to the PsyNet. Not until things had stabilized to the point that the threat of further damage could be used as a bargaining chip.

The Psy would give her anything once they understood she held the foundation of their lives in her hand. She intended to get to the point where her children could collapse specific parts of the Net, executing hundreds or thousands at a whim and as a reminder of her power.

Once she had the Psy, she would take the humans, and last, the changelings. They were the most dangerous, but they would not be able to stand against the combined power she intended to wield.

The world would belong to her, with her children her successors.

Chapter 20

The stars are moving. Leaving . . . migrating.

—Faith NightStar, Cardinal Foreseer,
PsyClan NightStar/DarkRiver leopard pack

PAYAL WRESTLED WITH the warping, trying to pull the lines of the grid back into shape.

The system did not move back into alignment.

Then a pair of arms formed of starlight joined hers, the hands closing over her fists. Warm, masculine, a hint of roughness. Canto. He made no attempt to take the lead, just fed his energy into her actions. It was the most intimate she'd ever been with any being, yet she felt no shock, nothing but a sense of rightness so pure it hurt.

Together, they wrenched the first line into alignment.

Muddy green morphed into glowing blue along that line.

How bad is it? His voice was music in her mind.

Catastrophic. Payal could sense all the lives being impacted by the carnage, each and every one a flickering pinpoint of light in her awareness. *We're going to have casualties.* The people at the very center of the wound in the Net would've died before Payal could respond, their minds crushed by a roaring wave of data as pieces of the Net impacted one on top of the other.

But we can save those who remain if we fix this. A repair below impacted the space above and vice versa. That was why anchors had quietly mirrored every upper-level repair.

Just part of their job. Nothing to mention or make a fuss over.

Arran will replace me when I have to return, Canto told her. *Then Suriana, followed by Bjorn. Ager last, because they are the oldest with the least energy to spare. I'll work on increasing the network for future incidents.*

Payal fought the visceral urge to reject such potent psychic contact with anyone but him. She needed every bit of help she could get. Held in Canto's starlight arms, she worked with a focus that burned blue fire.

She knew the instant he fell away, the vastness of his power sucked back to his anchor point. Arran arrived on his heels, his power angry in a way that made it turbulent. But he didn't try to take over and that was all that mattered. There was also no sense of an embrace with him; he simply stood with her and fed power where she needed it.

Relieved at the lack of intimacy, she worked on. Canto had helped her with the most difficult part, the twisted center. Arran assisted her to smooth out the surrounding section. Then he was gone, Suriana slipping into the void left behind.

Her energy was as gentle and as soft as her voice.

Weaving her power with Payal's, she helped until the matrix was back in place. Battered and heavily patched, with the odd remaining kink, but good enough to keep people alive. *Tell Bjorn and Ager to stand down.* She threw the thought out to Canto, certain he was still listening for her.

Canto would always now listen for her. It was an illogical but confident belief.

Done, he responded at once. *We'll talk after you've recovered.*

After managing to thank Suriana for her assistance, Payal dropped out of the Substrate and straight into her physical body. It ached, as if all her muscles had cramped. Stabs of pain shot down her jaw at her first breath, her tendons pulled taut for far too long as she unknowingly gritted her teeth.

The last thought she had was that she was glad she turned her room into a walled castle every night before she went to bed. No one would violate her sanctuary while she was unconscious.

Because her mind was fried, her power close to flatlining.

Her anchor point would hold, but barely.

The veil fell.

CANTO had gotten to work as soon as his anchor point hauled him back to his zone. If he couldn't help Payal one way, he'd find another. His first act had been to touch base with ten other anchors who had the mental strength and capability to assist should it be required—Bjorn had agreed to watch the situation and send in those anchors as needed.

That set up, Canto hacked into Vara.

His family didn't advertise his ability to hack into various databases and locations, preferring to keep that particular trick up their sleeves for exigent circumstances. The Mercant information network was fed by living informants—data hacking had too many pitfalls to be useful as part of normal operations.

Driven by his obsession to confirm beyond any doubt that Payal wasn't 3K, Canto had tried to get into Vara many times over the years. He'd failed. Over and over again. Now that he'd witnessed how Payal's mind worked, it was clear that the beautiful layers of code that protected Vara were her work.

Had her code been left alone, he'd have been out in the cold. But Lalit Rao had, seven days earlier, used his administrator access to create a back door into the system—likely so he could slip in and out were he ever shut out of legal access to Vara.

Unfortunately, he wasn't as good as Payal, and Canto had found that door. He'd never used it, had instead intended to tell Payal of the weakness at their first meeting so she could fix it—a calculated offer of trust.

Then she'd said "7J" and it had all flown out of his mind.

Fate must've been looking out for them both, because his forgetfulness meant he could slip into Vara and watch over Payal at a time when she wasn't able to protect herself.

There.

He was inside.

Throwing up the security visuals on his screens, he zeroed in on the section he knew held her apartment. The information had come in via an informant long before they'd reconnected, when he'd simply been doing his due diligence on an influential PsyNet family. That informant—a relatively new hire—had since lost his position inside Vara due to his slapdash work. Canto's current informant was violently loyal to Payal—a loyalty Canto had seen reflected over and over again in members of staff both junior and senior.

Payal had no idea how much her people loved her for her fairness and kindness.

Compliance out of fear and compliance out of devotion were two very different things.

Today, Canto spoke telepathically to his contact inside Vara. *Sunita. I need you to keep an eye on Payal's quarters. Tell me if anyone tries to enter.* An older member of staff, Sunita had sung like a gleeful canary when it came to Lalit and Pranath Rao, but her lips had always been tightly zipped on the subject of Payal. *This is for her safety.*

He needed a pair of eyes on the ground in case the system sensed his intrusion and rejected him.

Yes, I will do that, Sunita replied with her usual formal way of speaking. *There is disruption in Vara. Miss Payal missed two big meetings. Is she in trouble?*

She's fine, but she needs to rest. His pulse rapid and his gut tight, he'd looked in the Substrate three times in the past five minutes, confirmed each time that her anchor zone was holding steady. 3K had to be okay for that to be the case. *We just have to give her the time she needs to recover.*

I will watch, Sunita promised.

A ping on Canto's system alerted him to another hack in progress. Frowning, he glanced at the data and realized Lalit Rao was attempting to get into Payal's private files while she was incommunicado. The man wouldn't succeed—he didn't have a brain half as dazzling as his sister's.

Canto would stand guard regardless. Lalit *would not* hurt Payal while she was down. Only another anchor might ever understand what she'd done, the death she'd courted by standing so close to the vortex, but that took nothing away from her courage and her ferocity.

Sending a targeted worm through the system, he set it to corrupting the other man's files. The security subsystems would soon hit Lalit with an emergency alert that should distract him for hours.

Canto could've asked Genara to teleport him into Vara since he now had the necessary visuals, but right now he was more useful to Payal as a dangerous ally hidden in the shadows.

He was also fully capable of killing Lalit Rao from a distance.

It was amazing how much current could be fed through a single point if you shut off the safety features. All Canto would need was for Lalit to make contact with a computronic point—such as Payal's secure doorknob. It wouldn't be pretty, but it would get the job done.

Never again would anyone hurt or hunt Canto's 3K.

Chapter 21

Without you, I would be a monster.

—Kaleb Krychek to Sahara Kyriakus

KALEB ASSISTED ADEN to finish the repair. The two of them then checked it sector by sector. "It'll hold, but it's like the other recent ones." A repair they'd have to strengthen again and again in the coming months to maintain its integrity.

"Are you tired?"

"Yes." Psychic tiredness was a rare thing for Kaleb—as a dual cardinal, he could access more energy than most Psy could even imagine. "Nowhere close to flameout, but this was a difficult repair. The worst we've had to date."

"I agree. Maybe that was why the anchor spoke to me."

"Possible. But we've had critical incidents in the past without any anchor contact." Yet PsyNet logistics dictated that the As had to have been working alongside them the entire time.

Aden put his thoughts into words. "The anchors must have been adapting to the changes in the PsyNet for the PsyNet to retain any kind of stability. It was a mistake to think of them as a passive presence."

"We have a dangerous blind spot." Not words Kaleb had ever expected to say when he'd spent his entire adult life gathering information—because in that lay power. Yet he'd permitted Designation A to slip under his radar.

"I'll find out the name of the anchor in this region." He'd also touch base with Ena regarding the Mercant anchor who'd asked for data on Sentinel. Clearly, that A was taking a serious and active interest in current matters.

"Intake nutrients first," Aden said.

Unspoken was the fact that even with a corps of other strong Psy now trained to counter breaches, Aden and Kaleb remained the strongest and most skilled at the task. They had to be ready to respond at a moment's notice. "I'll give you the same advice." He and Aden weren't friends, but they'd become brothers-in-arms after so long fighting together.

The two of them parted without further words.

When Kaleb opened his eyes to the cold dark of very early morning in Moscow, it was to see Sahara standing in the doorway that led into their house, a glass of nutrient liquid in her hand. She wore one of his shirts with the sleeves folded back, the color an ice white, paired with dark gray leggings that were stretchy and soft.

Padding out onto the deck on socked feet, she handed over the drink. "I felt you go."

Both he and Sahara had been meant to have early meetings with other time zones today, and he'd been outside exercising to shake off the night when Aden sent him the emergency alert. His naked upper body was now covered in sweat, and the thin black fabric of his pants stuck to his skin.

The cool bite of the morning air was welcome against his overheated flesh.

Accepting the drink, he swallowed it down to the last drop. Sahara had made sure it wasn't one of the flavored varieties she preferred. She might be the reason Kaleb wasn't a ravening monster, every cell of his body hers to command—but he drew the line at peach- and cherry-flavored nutrients.

She smiled after he teleported the glass back to the kitchen. "How about banana?"

"It should remain a fruit."

Her laughter was soft and husky, sparks of delight in the midnight blue of her eyes. But it faded too fast. Placing a hand on his back, touching him as she so often did—just because she wanted to be close—she said, "That was a hard one, wasn't it?"

"Major cascading breach." As she listened, he told her about the anchor who'd spoken to Aden.

Wide eyes. "Anchors don't talk to anyone, I mean, I'm sure they do—but they never talk about anchor business. They just . . . do it."

"Unless the situation is now so critical that they have no choice." Grabbing the towel he'd left on an outdoor chair, he began to rub his face and hair dry. "I need a shower."

"Go, have a long one." She pressed her fingers to his lips when he would've spoken. "Finding out about the anchor can wait a few more minutes. Look after yourself first."

She kept on doing that. Looking after him. *Protecting* him. Him, a man who could topple cities with the power of his mind alone. Seeing the fine lines flaring out from the corners of her eyes, sensing her concern in the way she ran her hand over him, he did as she'd ordered and got himself to a bathroom lush with plants his lover babied every morning.

When a naked Sahara stepped into the large space minutes later, he welcomed her with open arms and a hungry mouth. He hadn't understood pleasure before her, hadn't understood that touch could be wanted and not simply borne. All slippery limbs and possessive lips, she kissed and bit and claimed him all over again as he found home inside her. Always, he'd find home with Sahara.

Afterward, he pulled on a pair of sweatpants while she threw on a loose sweater-dress that came to halfway down her thighs. Hit by a wave of raw possessiveness, he gripped her by the waist, held her. If he ever lost her . . .

Her fingers on his jaw, her charm bracelet sliding over her wrist, she rose on tiptoe to brush her mouth over his. "Don't go there. Into the dark." An order. "Stay in the now. In the here. With me."

Pressing his forehead to hers, he exhaled before nodding. Sometimes the demons tried to claw him back into the relentless fury in which he'd lived after she'd been taken from him, but that past held nothing but pain. This, where they were now—despite all the problems in the PsyNet—it held only beauty of a kind he hadn't known could exist.

Hands linked, they walked to the kitchen, where she made him a second drink.

Lips curving, she said, "Kiwi?"

"Is a bird."

Laughter in the air again as she pushed across the drink. Her bracelet tinkled gently, and he caught sight of the most recent charm he'd given her: a flower in full bloom, its petals pink sapphires and its heart a yellow diamond.

For his birthday, she'd talked his admin into ensuring that his schedule was free of all meetings—and then she'd "kidnapped" him for a visit to a theme park where, disguised to avoid recognition, they'd ridden all the rides and eaten the bad food, and he'd won her a stuffed creature of indeterminate origin that she kept in her home office.

Giving him, giving *them*, the kind of innocent joy they'd never had as children.

Seated at the counter, he waited for her to join him before he said,

"I need to track down that A, find out what she means when she talks about the Substrate."

"You're *extremely* annoyed you don't know this already." She rubbed the back of his neck. "It's okay, I won't tell anyone."

He scowled at her, the gentle teasing something else to which he'd become accustomed. She kept on doing things to pull him into the light, keep him from giving in to his tendencies toward cold-eyed power. "I was a Councilor and yet this subject never came up."

"We both know our race has managed frankly remarkable feats of memory loss—we even forgot an entire designation. In comparison to that, this is a minor oversight."

The most dangerous thing was that she was right. It made Kaleb wonder what other critical data lay mothballed in the past, gathering dust while the PsyNet floundered. Today, however, his priority was the Delhi hub-A.

"The entire anchor database now has dual protections—I have to get Ivy Jane's authorization as well as my own." Everyone knew Kaleb could breach almost any wall put in place to keep him out, but he had no reason to breach this one. He had no ill intent.

Sahara picked up the phone she'd left on the breakfast counter. "She was online just before—it's early evening for her." Her fingers flew over the screen. "If you're right about the A working as hard as you and Aden, you'll have to wait to talk to her. You're tired, so she has to be close to flameout."

A reply popped onto Sahara's phone screen at the same instant: *Tell Kaleb I'll meet him at the vault that holds the data.*

That vault was on the PsyNet. But, courtesy of the Pure Psy attacks in 2081, it didn't hold information on every A in the world. The information had been split into myriad pieces, much of it held safe by trusted parties, and the rest scattered across seven PsyNet vaults. It was a safeguard so a breach wouldn't expose all the anchors in the network.

Each member of the Ruling Coalition knew which data guardian or vault held which segment of information, the reason why Ivy Jane hadn't had to specify it for him. The president of the Empathic Collective also had to be the second person to authorize any request for access. Of them all, she was the one most likely to hold on to her ethical center.

On the PsyNet, Ivy Jane's presence held an echo of empath-gold. "Who are you looking for?" she asked once they were inside the vault.

"The main anchor for the region that fractured today. Around Delhi." It was at times hard to tell which physical location correlated to the psychic, but not with such a major city—and not when fatalities had reached over two hundred and fifty. People had collapsed where they stood, their minds crushed in the initial assault.

"Here." Ivy pointed out the segment of data that related to northern India.

It only took him half a minute to find the name: *Payal Rao.*

Chapter 22

We are not meant to be alone.

As a species, we're designed to be social. Yet we've told ourselves for over a hundred years that Psy are different from humans and changelings, that we can function at full capacity within the cold loneliness of Silence—denying ourselves all bonds, including those formed in spaces such as the PsyNet and the Internet.

Each of us must accept that that was a mistake. To move forward, we must embrace the truth: that Psy need connections as much as changelings and humans—and that such need isn't a flaw or a weakness.

—*PsyNet Beacon* social interaction column by Jaya Laila Storm

PAYAL.

Mmm.

Wake up, baby. Or I could send an electrical shock through the door and fry your brother's brains. Sounds like a better idea to me.

Payal's eyes snapped open. *Canto?*

Even as she reached for him with her mind, she winced at the high-pitched sounds emanating from her organizer—the emergency alarm from her security system. Coming immediately out of her groggy state, she turned off the alarm, then got out of bed and scanned outward with her telepathic senses.

Multiple minds beyond the door.

They can't get in. Canto's voice, as clear as an ice-cold lake. *But I'm picking up chatter that they're considering a battering ram. Want me to melt Lalit's brain?*

He sounded serious.

No, that'll just cause questions.

She should've been grilling him about his security access, but ignoring that, she pulled up the external visual feed on her organizer. A maintenance team stood outside, with her brother giving them orders. "Lalit," she said through the intercom, "what are you doing?"

He stilled, then looked up at the door camera. "You've been incommunicado for hours, dearest *bahena.*" He made the word for "sister" sound slimy. "Father asked me to check on you."

"My apartment is fitted with sensors that would've sent out a medical alert had I been incapacitated." Her father was the one who'd suggested it—though Payal had sourced her own tech so he couldn't sneak in subtle surveillance. The fact was, her tumors could grow in the time between scans, leading to a sudden collapse; a medical alarm was a sensible precaution. "Leave now."

Muting Lalit's response, she contacted her father through the comm, audio only. "Father, did you receive a medical alert?"

"No, but you weren't responding to any attempt to contact you. I assumed you'd had a psychic breakdown."

Breakdown.

The word choice was intentional, a reminder that she was "unstable." Having been born with the intelligence to see through his manipulation was one of the strongest weapons in her arsenal. She'd been more vulnerable as a child, but she hadn't been a child for a long time. "I had to deal with the possible collapse of the PsyNet over Delhi. I'm sure you heard of it." No one in this area of the PsyNet could've missed the massive fissure.

Pranath's pause went on a beat too long. "You were involved in that?"

"I'm an anchor, Father. The Delhi hub. What do you think I do? Now I need to be left alone to finish my work. Or would you rather the Net collapse and take us all with it?"

No response, but the maintenance crew outside her door began to disperse. Lalit shot a malicious smile toward the camera, and she knew this was just another imagined slight her brother was adding to his list of grievances. She'd never understood if his brain was miswired, or if it was simply his personality, but he hoarded grievances the same way he hoarded money and power.

The first thing she did was check the number of fatalities: two hundred and sixty-three. Three hundred and seven more noted as injured, half of them badly.

Her stomach lurched.

Forcing herself to breathe through the punch of it, she read through the rest of the bulletin sent out by Anthony Kyriakus on behalf of the Ruling Coalition. The city's medical system had switched into disaster mode, had hauled in all standby medics, and was coping with the influx with the assistance of EmNet—which had organized the teleportation of more medics and supplies from outside the affected zone.

No one was missing out on medical care.

So much death and pain, but she had to remember it could've been far worse, or the thought would paralyze her. *Canto?*

I'm here.

Why were you watching when Lalit came?

I knew he'd try some bullshit, and you needed your rest. He sounded like he was growling, a ferocious dragon who'd hunched his lethal mind over her vulnerable form, his claws extended and teeth bared. *Your data security kept him out of your files, but then the manipulative shit went running to your father. Few hours earlier and I'd have run that current through him without hesitation.*

Payal had no idea which element of that to address first, so she did what she always did when she got overwhelmed. She broke his reply down into its component parts. And went straight to the point that shook her the most. *Thank you for protecting me.*

You never have to thank me for looking out for you. Pure voice, rough words.

She swallowed hard. *I'll be perfectly capable when I contact the Ruling Coalition.*

I don't care about that. I was worried about you, 3K.

What had once been a moniker that indicated pain and horror had become a thing far more tender. As if Canto had claimed it, put his stamp on it.

Payal stood motionless at her kitchenette counter, her eyes hot and her walls tumbling down all over again. She always ate in her apartment and ordered her own food via private delivery because she didn't trust anyone in the house, not even those who'd professed their loyalty.

She'd been fine alone for years. She'd been functional.

And sad, whispered the lost, broken part of her. Sad and so alone. She didn't want to be that way today, didn't want to live in an isolated bubble where she could never let down her guard.

Canto was so dangerous to her—and her craving for him was a storm.

She looked down at her pajamas. A pair of thin cotton pants of blue with fine yellow stripes, paired with a white T-shirt in a silky fabric that felt good against her skin. *My mind has regrouped*, she telepathed to him, her heart a drumbeat. *I might teleport to the oasis after I have my nutrients.*

If he didn't want to acknowledge her implied invitation, he could just tell her she was welcome to go there.

Nothing in her words made her need obvious.

Nothing laid her soft inner core bare to him.

No, Canto said. *Come here.*

The image that entered her mind was of a room with comfortable sofas of chocolate brown and warm wooden flooring striped by what looked to be midmorning sunshine.

Okay. Her fingers trembled.

Breathing slow and deep, slow and deep until her mind no longer skittered, she drank the first glass of nutrients with focused concentration. She couldn't so quickly intake the second, decided to leave it for later.

Hurry, hurry, whispered the madness in her. *Go to him. To 7J.*

She thought about brushing her hair into its usual tail, thought about putting on the cosmetics she'd learned to use because they created a shield against the world. Then she thought about the image Canto had sent her. Her heartbeat jerked. She was near certain what he'd done, but it made no rational sense to her. Yet she teleported into that space—into danger—while barefoot and in her pajamas.

The ghost of the little girl she'd once been, wanting to see the friend in him.

Her mind responded with red warning sirens an instant afterward, but it was too late to take back her action. She'd arrived.

CANTO couldn't believe she was here. All sleep-tumbled hair, a line yet marking her cheek from when she'd curled onto her side, her body clad in soft fabrics that made him want to touch, and her feet bare.

Her toenails were neatly buffed and polished with a clear coat, her toes small, as befitted her overall size. He'd never before noticed anyone's toes. It was probably strange and creepy to find himself fascinated by them, but he couldn't stop noticing things about her—couldn't stop being fascinated by her.

His heart was thunder.

"Don't get mad, but I got you food." He scowled, aggravated by the shadows under her eyes. "Actual solid food." Payal needed fuel, especially since he'd made her teleport here; he'd thrown the items together in the short minutes since she'd said she'd go to the desert . . . and he'd hoped she'd come to him.

"I can't *not* help you. Don't ask that of me." He picked up a fortified roll and thrust it at her, even knowing she'd probably be furious with him for doing it. He couldn't help it, not with her shoeless and sleep-mussed and looking at him with those big cardinal eyes, her face devoid of makeup.

But what she said had nothing to do with the food. "This is your home." She sounded . . . appalled.

Appalled.

His chest expanded, fire in his blood. She hadn't stepped back, hadn't told him to stop taking care of her. No, she was glaring at him as if he'd lost his goddamn mind. Canto wanted to fucking dance. "Yes."

Everyone in his family would lose their shit when they discovered what he'd done. But if Canto knew one thing, it was that he had to be the naked and defenseless one in this first step into pure trust. Payal didn't have that capacity and he couldn't ask it of her. While Canto might've had a cold bastard for a father, he'd then been embraced by a pack of Mercants who'd gut anyone who dared lay a finger on him.

Payal had never had anyone.

Well, fuck that. She had him now, and he'd show her until she accepted that indelible truth.

"You just gave a *teleporter* access to your *home*." Appalled was morphing into furious. Grabbing the bread roll, she shook it at him. "Do you know what I could do with that information?"

Canto shrugged, fighting a grin. "Teleport in and murder me." Unless he did major renovations—including blocking out the view beyond the automatic balcony sliders—she could now enter his home as she wished.

"Why?" She spread her arms on either side of her body, and the sun speared through the white of her tee to reveal the protrusion of her rib cage.

"*Eat.*" It came out a growl and he didn't fucking care; he couldn't concentrate when he knew she was hurting herself. "You've lost weight."

Glaring, she took a deliberate bite of the roll, chewed.

Mollified, he huffed out a breath. "You planning to use this information to cause harm to me or mine?"

"No," she snapped, nothing muted or distant about her. "But you couldn't have known that. You shouldn't just *trust* people, Canto." Her emotions were brilliant and dazzling, a crackle of energy in the air.

This was the wild heart she kept caged. It was a shine in her eyes, a rapid jerkiness in her movements, a hyper energy that had her pacing.

He was as compelled by this side of her as he was the other. "I know an empath—he says my instincts are generally good."

"Empaths have a tendency to get in trouble because they trust the wrong people." Payal took another feral bite of the roll, chewed, and swallowed, before adding, "The last time we hired a commercial empath, I had to run interference the entire time because they kept going into rooms with unauthorized people who are controlled by Lalit."

She waved the roll in the air. "At least they had the sense not to want to be alone with *him*."

"Too late now." He fought the urge to thrust a chocolate drink at her. "I've given you the key to my home. I've burdened you with my trust."

A hard look from glittering eyes. "I won't reciprocate." She still held half the roll.

"I know." This wasn't about quid pro quo. "Have something to drink." *Great.* That restraint had lasted exactly ten seconds. He truly was channeling a bear now. The last time he'd visited Denhome, they'd plied him with so much food he'd asked Silver if her packmates thought Psy had prodigious appetites.

His cousin had given him an amused look. "No. They just like you."

Now Payal gave him the same look he'd probably given those bears. But she did deign to curl up on the sofa. It happened to be his favorite seat, and seeing her there . . . Good. It was good. After moving his chair to the other side of the low coffee table, he nudged across a sealed bottle of chocolate-flavored nutrients.

She took it, before freezing and staring at the partially eaten roll in her hand. "I ate this."

He didn't get it for a second. Then he did—it had been unsealed, could've held poison.

Payal lived in a world where food was a weapon.

Canto gritted his teeth. Anger was a familiar friend from his childhood, a hot flame that scalded from the inside out, but that wouldn't be helpful here. "Throw it to me."

When she did nothing, he held out his hands. She finally chucked it over. Holding her gaze, he finished it in two bites. "If I wanted to kill you," he muttered, "I'd just shoot you. I wouldn't waste handmade fucking rolls."

A sudden intense burst of laughter from her that turned him to stone, it was so bright and sharp and beautiful.

Chapter 23

Yesterday, someone I was assisting yelled at me to stop being so damn
naive, to stop expecting the best of people! I had to inform them it was
congenital—and that it wasn't a bug but a feature. Never, my fellow Es,
let anyone tell you otherwise. One by one, we're going to change hearts
and minds . . . and the world.

—Ivy Jane Zen, President, Empathic Collective,
in a letter to the Collective membership

SNAPPING HER MOUTH shut, Payal swallowed and blinked hard.
"Do you see?" It came out a rasp. "I'm manic. My shields are down and
I'm like a bullet that keeps ricocheting."

Canto made himself breathe past the shock of hearing her laughter
for that one dazzling moment, made himself *listen*. He needed to talk
to Arwen, find out more about how a mind like Payal's worked—
without ever mentioning Payal. But for now, he just wanted her in
any way she wanted to be with him.

Payal drank from the chocolate drink, gave it a long look afterward. "Too rich. I like the fruit ones better." Putting the drink aside
with a rapid movement, she teleported a fruit drink from the table to
hover in front of her.

Tilting her head to the side, she made the bottle tumble end over end while they both watched. Grabbing it without warning, she twisted off the lid and took two gulps before meeting Canto's gaze again. "Do you see? I'm unstable." It was a challenge. "No one normal acts this way."

"What I see is a telekinetic with fine control over her ability," he pointed out. "You're also having a fully rational conversation with me." He had his suspicions about why she had such a negative view of her natural emotional inclinations, but he didn't have enough information to know if he was right.

Payal "threw" the bottle almost to the ceiling, held it there, then allowed it to drop into her hands. "My mind zigs and zags," she muttered. "I can't hold on to a single thought for long." She jumped up, went to the balcony doors. "Why is it so green outside?" Her hand hovered over the touch-activated door control, but she looked back at him rather than making contact.

"Yes," he said, fascinated by the primal complexity of her.

Opening the doors on a shush of sound, she ran out onto the deck that overlooked lush green foliage and, beyond it, a road bordered by more foliage. Farther back rose huge forest goliaths—as they did behind his property.

Having reached the railing, Payal craned her neck left, then right. "There are no other houses. Only trees."

Canto didn't tell her they were on the edge of StoneWater bear territory, even though this part of their land was technically accessible to the public. While he could put himself in Payal's hands without a qualm, he couldn't do that with the bears.

He'd have to talk to Valentin, ask permission to give a teleporter this information.

"It's so quiet here." Payal stepped back from the edge, then went to it again. This time, she leaned over the railing until her feet were off the deck boards. "You planted flowers!"

"They were a gift. I couldn't let them die." It would've broken Arwen's heart, and that Canto would never do.

Running to the other edge of the balcony, Payal looked over there, too, then came back and said, "I'm hungry. I have a migraine. It hurts."

Canto scowled. "Do you need—"

"Food," she interrupted, dropping her fingers from her temple. "Food will make me feel better."

The two of them went inside, and she curled up on his sofa again, tangled hair, wild eyes, and a frenetic energy tightly contained as she wrapped her arms around her knees and began to rock. "See, Canto? See? I'm quite mad outside the cage."

"I see bright, wild energy. A little jagged at the edges, sure. But I don't see any sign of dangerous mental instability." With no other data at hand, he had to go on his gut instinct and on his knowledge of Payal on the mental plane.

That she was disturbed by herself, he accepted. But he also knew that she'd never received positive feedback from those around her.

"Kindness matters, Canto," Arwen had said to him once, his empath's heart pinned to his sleeve and his eyes shining. "Tell a child enough times that he's brave and smart and good, and it becomes a self-fulfilling prophecy."

Not ever would Canto gainsay Payal in any decision she made about her mind—but he damn well was going to be that positive voice, the one that shone light on the other side of the coin and made her realize that all her feedback to date had been skewed heavily to the negative.

When she continued to rock silently, he picked up a piece of toast, spread it with butter, then took a bite. The salt hit hard and strong. "I'm a fan of butter and baked goods." He held out the half-eaten toast to her. "Bite?"

A halt to the rocking.

She stared suspiciously at the bread, then snatched it and took an experimental bite. "Maybe," she said, but she didn't give it back.

He made another piece for himself, began to eat.

As she nibbled on the piece she'd claimed, Payal watched him with an intensity that should've been unnerving. It wasn't. Payal wasn't looking at him with murder in mind—but as if he were some unknown animal. "My father told me I was a feral and insane beast. That's why he put me in that place."

"My father told me I was a blot on their genetic history, too broken to be worth saving even for my cardinal status."

Half the furniture in the room rose up off its legs before slamming back down. Hard. "I'll kill him," Payal said firmly, then frowned. "No, he's already dead."

"And long forgotten." Since she'd finished her toast, Canto threw her a piece of Chaos's homemade muesli slice. "Want me to kill your father for you?"

A pause as she chewed on a bite of the slice. Two deep vertical lines furrowed her brow. "No," she said after swallowing. "He's a monster, but it'd cause too much chaos if he died without warning—thousands of people rely on the Rao empire to feed their families."

Leaning forward in his chair, Canto raised an eyebrow. "Baby, you sound lucid to me."

She ate two bites in quick succession, her breathing short and jagged. "The jittering in my head. It's not . . . good, Canto."

He heard the incipient panic, frowned. "Can you shield partway? So you're not shutting away all of you?" He was compelled by her in all her guises, but he wouldn't have her hurting. Payal deserved a life of joy, not pain. "Or is it all or nothing?"

She parted her lips to reply, but shut her mouth before saying a word. For a while she just focused on the muesli slice, interspersed with drinks of the fruit-flavored nutrients she'd chosen. When she'd finished the slice, she looked at what else he had on offer, and chose a piece of mild cheese. "I don't know," she said after she'd finished that. "As a child, it was all or nothing."

"You're not a child anymore," he said softly, holding her gaze as his heart squeezed. "You were also doing it alone. If you want, I can get you access to an empath who'll never ever betray anything you tell him. He might be able to assist."

Payal ate another piece of cheese before throwing her arms open without warning. "What are we doing? *This.*" Moving her arm around to indicate the two of them in his living room.

"Being us." It was a risk, to remind her that they were just Canto and Payal. 3K and 7J, with a bond fierce and unbreakable.

Payal hugged her knees to her chest again. "I have to go," she blurted out. "I'll send you the details of my contact with the Ruling Coalition."

She was gone before he could respond.

His heart kicked and he hoped like hell he hadn't made a mistake, hadn't terrified her away.

A flicker of movement to his left had him jerking his attention that way. The last thing he expected to see was a small bear with dark brown fur climbing up the balcony strut to reach the beam at the top. Seeing him, the little bear made excited sounds and jumped onto the balcony before running over to him.

The doors were still open, so the cub ran right in.

Heart thundering—this level of his home was high above the ground—Canto leaned down and scooped up the small, furry weight. "What are you doing here?" He nipped the cub's ear as he'd seen Valentin do; he needed the outlet for his fear, but he made sure not to do it too hard.

The cub made more sounds and snuggled into him.

Holding the cub's warmth against his chest, Canto forced himself to breathe. What if Payal had been here when this happened? She'd have realized they were in bear country. He knew she wouldn't have used the information in any ugly way, but he still needed to let Valentin know.

The only reason he'd invited her here was that Denhome was some distance away. Just because he'd decided to move closer to his cousin didn't mean he actually wanted to live with bears who didn't know the meaning of personal space.

He'd once put out a sign saying: *I don't want visitors.*

It had been replaced by a sign that read: *We're not visitors. We're bears.*

Hilarious.

But baby bears were not allowed out alone in this public-accessible area.

He stroked his hand over the small bear in his arms. A bear who'd begun to tremble. "I have you," he said roughly, patting its back—he was no expert in affection, but he had eyes; he'd seen how Chaos handled Dima, how Valentin interacted with all the cubs.

"I'll get you home." He opened the buttons of his shirt so the cub could lie against his skin—such contact was important to changelings, especially such a small and scared one. "You know you're safe." He couldn't yet recognize most bears in their bear form, but he knew the child must've met him when he'd visited Denhome.

Even a lost, scared changeling child wouldn't have run so joyfully toward a stranger. Kid must've caught his scent by the house, come toward it out of panic.

"Come on, let's go call your pack." It came out rougher than he'd intended, but the cub didn't flinch. Used to grumbling bear voices, it snuggled closer to the vibration of his chest and dug small claws into his chest to hold on—but the child was careful not to pierce his skin. This was someone's baby; they'd been taught their manners.

Spotting the food at that instant, the cub made hungry sounds but didn't pounce.

He put the cub on the sofa. "Sit here. I'm getting something." He was aware of the cub getting to its feet and watching him over the top of the sofa as he went into the kitchen. All the counters in the space were hydraulic, so they could be raised or lowered at will. Mostly, they stayed set to the levels he preferred, but the system gave him the flexibility to accommodate Arwen—his cousin loved to cook. Not that a lack of customization had ever stopped Arwen; for Canto's last place, he'd just gone ahead and bought himself a riser that he'd placed on any surface where he wanted to work standing up.

Stubborn empath.

Now Canto grabbed the jar of hazelnut-chocolate spread that same stubborn empath had bought him. He'd tried it once and nearly died from the sugar overdose.

But the cub jumped happily when he held it up.

Satisfied he was handling this in a way that wouldn't traumatize the kid, he went back around and shifted himself from his chair to the sofa. The cub immediately snuggled itself to his side, where the child waited patiently while Canto put the spread on a piece of toast.

The cub ate neatly after Canto offered it to him.

He was about to dig out his phone when a much larger figure jumped onto his deck.

Chapter 24

Dear Canto,

Attached is a drawing Dima made for you. He tells me it's of you if you were a bear. He thinks you would make a good bear. He wanted me to make sure you noticed the stars in the bear's eyes, because it's a cardinal bear.

He's frowning because he didn't get your bear-sized wheelchair exactly as he wanted, but he is very proud of the rocket he put on the back—so you can "go zoom faster." He is on tenterhooks awaiting your response.

Love, Nova

—Note from Dima's mother, Nova, on his behalf

CANTO WAS READY to strike out with his mind, the protective urge pure instinct born of a time when he'd protected another child, but one glance and he stood down. He didn't much know what to do with small bears, but the man who entered the living area the next second was an expert.

The cub beside Canto abandoned its half-eaten toast on the table and jumped toward Valentin. The bear alpha caught the desperate cub close to his bare chest, his body devoid of clothing. He must've been in bear form before shifting to climb up to the deck—Valentin was huge as a bear, and Canto was fairly sure he couldn't climb in that form.

The alpha bear was currently growling out a stream of Russian. Canto had a good command of the language, enough to know the words were a mix of reassurance and rebuke. The cub clung to Valentin.

Canto, meanwhile, got back in his chair and went to find something Valentin could put around himself. Changelings were confident naked, since they came out of the shift in that state, but Canto hadn't yet been around them enough to be nonchalant about it. He settled on a large bath towel.

"*Spasibo*," Valentin said when Canto emerged with the towel. Leaving the cub to cling to him—the child had half climbed onto his shoulder by this point—Valentin grabbed the towel out of the air when Canto threw it, and wrapped it around his waist.

After which, he kissed the cub on its furry face, then pulled it around to sit on his lap as he took a seat on the sofa. "Eat," he said, picking up and passing over the half-eaten toast.

Only after the cub was eating with careful paws did Valentin say, "This troublemaker's family went for a morning walk together, but he decided to wander off while his parents were distracted pulling his twin from a mudhole she'd somehow managed to discover. All my life I've lived here and I've never found a mudhole that big." Valentin shook his head. "The cubs have radar."

When Canto tapped the side of his nose, not sure if he should ask the question aloud, Valentin said, "He's too young—and he decided to cross a few streams after getting disoriented."

So his parents couldn't track him, and the cub's own sense of smell wasn't well developed enough to lead him home. Yet Valentin had found him. Because whatever it was that created a pack alpha, it included a wild kind of psychic bond. "His parents must be frantic."

"Can I borrow your phone? I need to call them. They're search-ing, too."

Canto passed over the device and Valentin made the call. The cub's ears pricked up at whatever he heard from the device, because Valen-tin pressed the phone to one furry ear afterward.

The sounds the cub made were—okay, fine, they were cute. Though Canto would go to his grave never saying that word aloud.

Valentin ended the call by assuring the boy's parents he'd bring their boy to them.

The cub went through two pieces of toast loaded with the spread before curling up against Valentin's chest and falling fast asleep.

Small snores erupted from his furry body.

The bear alpha shook his head, his eyes still the amber of his bear. "Canto, never ever have cubs. They will drive you insane, I promise you this. I am swearing off them." The words were a verifiable lie, because the alpha then pressed his lips to the top of the sleeping boy's head.

"Will he be all right?" Canto hated seeing children afraid.

"A little scare won't keep this future tiny gangster down for long." A petting stroke of the boy's back. "But he is going to be grounded for a while to teach him that cubs have to follow rules set for their own good. He's barely beyond a baby, far too young to go roaming on his own."

Bear eyes held Canto's, the power in them a primal thing that made his skin prickle. "It's good you're here. To have a friend on our public border, it's something we appreciate."

"Like you said, we're family." Canto's grandmother had famously said that trust to a Mercant was a "complicated thing" that required "years of acquaintance, several background checks, and a probationary period." The bears had flown way over that barrier—and not simply because Silver was mated to Valentin, and Arwen was tangled up with Pavel.

"It's because of their innate goodness," his grandmother had said to Canto after she first visited Denhome. "I know they're big and tough and that Valentin could bloody us both in battle—and yes, there might be some with evil in their hearts, but that isn't their natural inclination.

"Now that Silver is part of their pack, they'll defend her with their own lives without hesitation—and they will love her with every cell of those big hearts. We must honor that—for one of us to betray one of StoneWater would be a grave insult against the integrity and loyalty that is at the core of our family."

Canto hadn't understood then. Then he'd met the bears, seen the openness with which they embraced the world, and wanted to put up a fence around their entire territory so no one could ever hurt their huge hearts.

Valentin's was the biggest of them all.

Mercants, in comparison, were cynical and skeptical when it came to dealing with anyone outside their family unit. Now Canto and the others had taken on the task of being cynical on the bears' behalf, too. He felt the same protective urge toward Payal, but it was deeper, stronger, more primal.

"I better go," Valentin said, but it was only once they were downstairs and by the front door that he added, "Canto, I scented a stranger in your living space. Is all well?"

"A friend. A teleport-capable Tk." It was too simple a word for what was going on with Payal, but it'd do as a placeholder. "I didn't think you'd consider it a security risk on this part of the border, but after this . . ." He nodded at the cub.

"This doesn't alter the security situation," Valentin said. "To have a cub stumble so far out without being spotted by a sentry is so unusual that this is the first time it's happened in my memory. You can feel free to invite your friends." He raised an eyebrow, a faint smile edging his lips. "A woman, yes?"

Canto scowled. "I hate changeling noses."

Valentin's laughter was a boom that made the cub in his arms startle awake and try to join in, its voice far higher-pitched. And goddamn it, adorable. Chuckling, Valentin kissed the cub's head before handing him over to Canto and dropping the towel aside. He shifted in a shower of light.

When Canto next looked, a huge Kamchatka bear stood where the man had been. It shook its body as if settling its fur into place. Waiting until the bear glanced at him, Canto placed the cub on his back, where the boy took a solid grip. Valentin left with a nod, a predator who could move with lethal speed despite his size.

Canto watched after him, still with that inexplicable sense of protectiveness in his gut. Sometimes danger didn't come from the biggest and most obvious predators. Sometimes it came from the quieter, deadlier ones.

He knew Payal was one of those quieter, deadlier threats.

He also knew that she'd fight with vicious fury to protect the innocent. It was part of her core, unalterable and forever. His 3K was still alive beyond the carapace Payal had created to protect her bruised and abused heart.

His wrist unit vibrated discreetly. A surveillance alert. Lalit Rao had just made an interesting financial maneuver. Canto's eyes narrowed. He knew what the other man was doing—attempting to box Payal out. He wouldn't succeed, but he might make things difficult for her if he got enough others on his side.

He tapped out a message to Payal with the info.

PAYAL didn't teleport to her apartment after leaving Canto's house. She went to the desert oasis. Her brain was a place of jittery chaos; she needed to find her cool, calm center again. Locating an area in the garden she hadn't already mathematically balanced, she began to move things around.

As she restructured and reconfigured under the brilliant desert sun that almost hurt the eye, she didn't try to think, just let herself be.

Until at last she could breathe, her heartbeat no longer irregular and her skin temperature even.

You're not a child anymore.

Canto's words reverberated in her soul. She'd never considered that there might be another way, that controlling her aberrant tendencies didn't have to be a brutal crushing hammer, that a more subtle approach might work as well.

Nothing but a false hope, whispered another part of her. *It's a thing of madness you carry inside you. That's why your father put you in that place.*

"No." Payal would not permit that old voice to rear its ugly head. Yes, she'd been unstable, but she'd also had a brother who'd tortured her, until the only way she could fight was to lose herself and turn into a berserker.

This was a far different situation.

She *wasn't* a child—and the empaths were brilliant lights in the world. They hadn't been permitted to exist openly during her childhood, and even if they had been, her father would've never taken her to see one. Too high a risk of exposure, he'd have said, too high a chance she'd become known as defective.

Yet in the time since the Empathic Collective came into being, Payal had heard of no leaks of personal psychological information. *None.* The empaths of the Collective took their vow of privacy dead seriously.

Canto had also offered to introduce her to an empath who would hold all her secrets, but if Payal did this, she'd choose her own E. Not because she believed Canto would point her toward anyone less than

stellar, but because this had to be on her. She had to make the choice—
as she'd made the choice as a child, to cage the screaming girl.

Canto had *trusted* her.

A sudden, panicked reminder of the act that had shattered her
psychic distance, turned her manic.

No one ever just trusted anyone.

That wasn't how the world worked.

People maneuvered and negotiated and formed alliances for spec-
ified endeavors. As she, Canto, Arran, Suriana, Ager, and Bjorn had
done on the anchor issue. As 3K and 7J had done in that long-ago
past. It had been about survival; they'd clung to each other because
they'd had no one else.

But this, what had just happened . . .

Was it possible that despite everything, he was setting up a cunning double cross? Had he researched her brain, figured out that this
tactic would confuse and put her off-balance? The Mercants were
known for their ability to get their hands on information, and Canto
was a key player in that network.

There was logic to her train of thought for a woman who'd grown
up in a family where trust was considered a fatal weakness. It was easy
to believe that Canto Mercant was playing a dangerous and finely
balanced game.

Eat.

His care was a rough echo in her head. No one but Kari cared
about Payal. Yet Canto had watched over her while she'd been at her
most vulnerable; he'd taken no advantage. Not once.

She'd shown him her madness, and he hadn't been disgusted as her
father had been disgusted with her as a child. He hadn't gotten an
avaricious gleam in his eye as Lalit had done when he realized he
could push and manipulate his younger sister by activating particular
emotional triggers.

Canto had looked at her as he always did, with an amalgam of what she wanted to see as fascination and tenderness—mixed with a little aggravated frustration. The latter element made her memories seem more real, more quintessentially him. She could almost hear the gruff rumble of his voice.

He'd also asked her to look within, see if she needed to stay inside the prison she'd built for herself. He hadn't told her she was wrong, that her brain wasn't strong enough to make such decisions. He'd just asked her to look again at a problem she'd solved in childhood, to check if she could structure a more elegant solution.

Her head hurt, nothing fitting quite right.

After one last look at this tranquil paradise, she teleported to her apartment . . . and to chaos. A scream echoed through the telepathic channel she used with the other As she'd met, and it was an agonized plea for help.

Ager.

Chapter 25

Grandmother, I found her.
Her? Oh. I see. Is she doing well?
She's Payal Rao.
Well, Canto. You do like to keep my life interesting.

—Conversation between Canto Mercant and Ena Mercant

PAYAL RESPONDED INSTINCTIVELY, her body collapsing like a doll's onto her bed as she threw her full energy into the Substrate. The oldest A of them all was being battered by massive waves of glowing blue cracked with fissures of bleeding black—as if the fabric of the PsyNet was tearing itself apart.

Look for the answer, Payal! Canto's piercingly clear voice. *Suriana and I will help Ager!*

Payal didn't take offense at the order. She saw it as a logical division of labor, given her detail-oriented mind and ability to see the grid in the Substrate. She found the part of the grid that correlated to Ager's zone.

It was contorted into a stomach-churning "ball" in one section—but there were no smooth edges. Only hard, jagged "bones" that split the fabric of the Substrate and sheared off sections that bled viscous black. When she looked at the mirror section on the PsyNet, she saw an assemblage of minds that blazed so hot they were burning out one by one. Bright fires extinguished after a short flash.

Scarabs who'd gathered in one location?

Another mind appeared in the distance. Martial, with strange—almost invisible—shimmers of black fluctuating through it. Empath? If so, a very unique one. More likely, it was an Arrow with unusual shields.

Then a mind of obsidian darkness: Kaleb Krychek.

But they were too late. The dazzling minds burned out of existence one by one, all within a matter of split seconds. Seeing that Krychek and the unfamiliar mind were already working on the resulting hole in the fabric of the Net, she dived back down and told Canto what she'd discovered as she began to straighten the grid.

The shards cut her psychic hands, but that couldn't be helped. She worked on.

Canto vanished from her vicinity halfway through. *Ager?*

I'm well, young Rao. But Canto gave me too much of himself. He may have flamed out. He kicked Suriana out of the merge when she was teetering on the edge, but stayed too long himself.

Panic fluttered in Payal's throat, but she made herself finish the grid repair—she would not let Canto down. That done, she checked that Ager was well enough to hold their zone before touching base with Arran and Bjorn.

The two had been dealing with a smaller riptide, had come through unscathed.

Opening her eyes on the physical plane, she scrabbled for her phone and found the direct line for Silver Mercant. She had that number because EmNet had needed her cooperation to spread out in this region.

The phone was answered by a mellifluous male voice. "Director Mercant's office."

"This is Payal Rao. I need to talk to the director at once. It's an emergency."

The assistant was well trained, because he made no attempt to divert Payal or block her access to Silver. "She is currently in a meeting, but I'll break in. Please hold."

Silver came on the line five seconds later. "Payal," she said in her crisp, clear tone. "What's the problem and what resources—"

"You need to check on Canto," Payal interrupted. "He may have flamed out after an anchor emergency." And Payal couldn't teleport to him after her own energy output. She'd flatline halfway through, end up in a random location for which her brain had an image.

It might be a safe place—or it might be the middle of a freeway.

Silver hung up without a response. Payal was fine with that. She'd rather the other woman move with rapid speed than be polite. But her stomach ached as she worried and wondered. Would Silver think to call her back? She had no reason to do so. Payal was nothing to the Mercant family.

Silver's name flashed on her phone screen.

Payal couldn't answer fast enough. "Is Canto all right?"

"Groggy but conscious. He did flame out, so he'll be crashing soon."

Relief smashed into Payal, obliterating what control she'd achieved. "You're an A?"

When Payal confirmed that, Silver said, "He won't be able to assist with the A network for twenty-four hours at least—it could be up to forty-eight. I've never known Canto to flame out—do we have to prepare for a collapse?"

"His anchor point will hold." Payal pushed her hair behind her ears. "Being an A is who we are, flameout or not. I'll handle any more active issues while he recovers." As he'd watched over her, she'd now watch over the interwoven system he was working so hard to create.

Payal would make sure the As didn't fall while Canto was down.

. . .

AFTER hanging up with Payal Rao, Silver sat in her office and thought about the past few minutes. It was pure luck that she'd known Pavel was heading out to visit Canto, even better that he'd had his phone—he tended that way now that he'd talked Arwen into playing with his thoroughly disreputable bear self.

As it was, Pavel had almost reached Canto's place when she got in touch, and he'd been able to confirm that Canto was okay but "wiped." Not a surprise given what she was hearing about the most recent assault against the Net. No official reports yet, but the *Beacon* livestream had eyewitness statements that seemed to point to a group of Scarabs doing something so dangerous they'd basically exploded their brains.

She'd ask Canto for the details of his involvement when he woke. She'd grown up with him in her life, but their relationship wasn't of siblings. Older by nine years and scarred by life as a child, he tended to ask more after her and Arwen than speak on himself. Only today did she realize how little she knew about the technical aspects of his base designation.

Then there was Payal Rao. Ruthless operator, cardinal Tk who'd never been in the Council's control, and major CEO. Also an anchor. One friendly enough with Canto to get him emergency assistance. *Mercants*. Always had to keep a few secrets. Valentin was right. Sneaky was in her family's DNA.

Lips curving at the thought of her bear mate—who'd nuzzled a kiss into her neck this morning before he'd let her leave for work—she picked up the phone and called Pavel. "Did you talk him into bed?"

"Am I a bear?" was the insulted response. "Of course I talked him into bed. Even if he is the grumpiest Mercant alive." A rustling. "I'm sneaking into his room. Yep, he's down for the count. Let me throw a blanket over him."

After stepping back out, he said, "I'll hang here until he comes out of it. Yasha's happy to cover my security shift. Is there anything special I should do?"

"Have a nutrient drink prepped for him for when he wakes, but that won't be for hours yet." She bit back the next question she wanted to ask, well aware it'd be a serious invasion of Canto's privacy.

Ethically, it was the right choice, but her protective instincts were a far more primal element of her psyche, and they struggled with it. Canto had protected her for years, even more so after she became the head of EmNet—Grandmother thought Silver didn't know that her oft-scowling cousin with reclusive tendencies was the computronic genius who'd hacked his way through half the world to keep her safe.

It was time for Silver to balance the scales, have his back. Because Payal Rao was a shark with great big teeth. A woman cold-eyed, merciless, and with zero loyalty to kin.

Then Pavel said, "Hey, looks like you don't have to worry about Canto so much. He's had company." The way the bear drew out the last word made it clear the company had been female.

"Family?"

"No. I know the Mercant scent—you all share a thread. This is new." A deep breath. "Different. Layers to it. None of them are Mercant layers."

Which meant whatever the relationship, it wasn't one that involved physical intimacy. "Tell me if he wakes," she said before hanging up.

Silver would talk to Canto directly about this, warn him about the predator with whom he was tangling.

But when she mentioned her decision to Arwen later in the day, after he dropped by Denhome, her brother threw back his head and laughed so hard that he fell back on her and Valentin's bed. He'd followed her into the bedroom when she went inside to take off her jewelry.

"What is so amusing?" she asked in her iciest tone.

It had zero effect on her empath brother—he knew she loved him down to the bone. "You. Mated. A. *Bear.*"

"You're currently playing with one," she pointed out.

"*I'm* not the one thinking of poking my nose into Canto's business." Sitting up on the bed, his fashionably cut black hair tousled but the pale blue of his shirt still crisp against the dove gray of his suit jacket, Arwen raised an eyebrow. His eyes were the same silver as hers, but uptilted sharply at the corners, his bones striking. "Do you really think Canto can't handle himself against Payal Rao if something is going on?"

"He has no experience dealing with people like her. Not when it comes to a personal relationship."

"Bear." Arwen pointed. "*Alpha* bear."

Silver gave him a quelling look, but she got the point. She'd keep from interfering. But she'd also do some research on Payal Rao that wasn't about the business or the work, but about who she was as a person. Because while Canto might be grumpy and nonsociable, he was family. He was also one of the rocks on which she stood—one of the quiet foundations of Mercant power.

Silver would cut Payal Rao to pieces before she allowed her to harm Canto.

"What if she's Canto's person?"

Silver stared at her brother. "Payal Rao?"

"Bear."

"Be quiet. I'm your elder."

"By ten minutes." Laughing, he came over to hug her from the back, her brother with his snobby taste in clothes and a heart huge enough to contain the world. "But what if, Silver?"

Putting aside her need to protect, Silver made herself consider the question. "I want Canto to have what I have," she said at last. "He has such aloneness inside him. If Payal can reach him in a way I don't think even Grandmother has . . . then I'll back her all the way."

"And they call me the empath." Arwen squeezed her tight. "I want that for him, too. He's one of the best people I know—his heart, Silver, it's a thing of courage and loyalty and stubborn will."

"Payal Rao took over five corporations last week in a bloodless coup."

"Alpha bear who can break you in half with his hands."

Silver took off her bracelet. "I'm still going to spy on her." Just in case.

"It's the Mercant way."

Chapter 26

A well-read bear is a dangerous creature.

—Unknown bear philosopher

PAYAL WAS GOOD at putting things in boxes, at shutting off parts of herself so the others could function. But though she crashed that night, a single need pulsed continuously at the back of her mind when she woke the next day. She kept on wanting to reach out to Canto even knowing he wouldn't hear her.

She was all too aware it was dangerous to be so distracted, especially when she was summoned to a meeting with her father. Lalit was already in the room, as smooth and polished as ever. Neither one of them spoke as they waited for Pranath's attention.

"Payal," Lalit said when their father continued to ignore them, "you're hiding out a lot in your room lately. Being overwhelmed, are you?"

Before Payal could point out that they were here to discuss a major deal she'd negotiated, Pranath lifted his head from the organizer on which he was working. "This is work, Lalit. If you wish to play games, do so on your own time."

Lalit took a step forward, his hands in his suit pockets. A shove of telekinetic power pushed him back past Payal. That was . . . unexpected. Their father was a Tk, but not at the level evidenced by the strength of that shove. Which meant he had guards who were watching the goings-on in this room.

Watching, not listening.

Pranath Rao would never permit strangers to listen in on private family business. But those mirrors behind his bed? Yes, they could be one-way. Good to know.

Lalit stopped before slamming into the far wall. "That was unnecessary, Father." He hitched his jacket back into place.

"Just a reminder that while I may be in this bed, I am the Rao king." He made eye contact with them both. "You are only pawns on the chessboard."

"You seem to forget that I bring in billions every year," Payal said with cool pragmatism. "Shall I add up the value of my most recent deals?" She didn't care about credit—it was about being seen as powerful rather than weak.

"You bring in those deals because I allow it." Pranath's voice was poisonous silk. "How long would you survive should I withdraw my protection?" A subtle reminder of the life-giving medicine that allowed him to act the puppet master.

"As for you." He swung the pale sharpness of his gaze toward Lalit. "You have no self-control. That makes you a waste of time except for the fact that you're my secondary heir."

Was it any wonder, Payal thought, that Lalit regularly tried to find ways to assassinate her? Their father would like nothing more than for his two oldest living children to be vicious pit bulls straining at the leash to attack each other. Unfortunately, the psychological manipulation had taken with Lalit.

"Did you bring us here for anything useful?" Payal took no pleasure in any of this; her brother was a psychopath and had probably been born so, but the way they'd been raised hadn't helped when it came to his pathology. Perhaps if he'd been given therapy in child-hood, he'd have become a garden-variety psychopath instead of a serial killer in training.

Pranath tapped his organizer. "I've been approached by the Jannik-Kao Family Group with a possible opportunity. Lalit, I want you to run the financials. Payal, I want you to look at the overall possibilities. Sending information to you now."

Then he dismissed them.

As they exited the rooms, Lalit murmured, "He created us both, you know that, don't you?"

"Undeniable," she said, keeping it to the facts because she'd long ago realized there could be no common ground with Lalit. If he ever reached out, it was to dig up her weaknesses.

Only once had she fallen for it: she'd been five at the time.

She'd ended up with burns all up one leg as a result. They hadn't been of the worst degree and had mostly faded after all this time, but her skin was just a little tight there. Just enough to remind her to never trust any olive branch he might hold out. That branch would always be coated with poison—or broken shards of glass.

"Don't you want to murder him sometimes?"

Did he really think she was foolish enough to answer that? "I have work to do, and so do you." Turning right, she left him at the cross-roads of the hallway, and she knew he was staring. Thinking again if he could take her.

She halted, looked over her shoulder, made sure he met her eyes.

His mouth tightened at the silent reminder that she was a cardinal, but he shifted on his heel and went the other way. That didn't mean she was safe. It just meant he'd be cunning when he came after her. But then, she'd known that nearly all her life.

Canto.

His name was a beat inside her, but she could do nothing about it. What she'd done yesterday had drained her. If she teleported now,

she'd make it to him—but only just. She'd have to stay with him until
she recovered.

Her step hitched, her craving a current dragging her out into
deeper and deeper water. But she couldn't give in. She needed to stand
sentinel, watch over the newly healed damage until he woke.

Things calmed further and further as the hours passed.

Until it got to the point that there were no more ripples and night
had fallen over Delhi. Alone in her apartment, the Substrate stable,
she couldn't fight the urge any longer. She teleported to Canto . . . and
came face-to-face with an unknown male with skin of mid-brown
who had to have moved with predator speed to get to her in the heartbeat since she'd teleported in.

She teleported to another area before the man could slam into her,
only to realize he was frantically pulling back his punch and wobbling
on his feet as he attempted to shift his center of gravity.

"Izvinite!" he yelled, his head swiveling to where she'd gone, before
switching to English accented in the way of someone who normally
spoke a Slavic tongue. According to her quick Net search, *izvinite* was
"sorry" in Russian. "Didn't know it was you."

Payal had no major business interests in Russian-speaking locations and had never met this man with a compactly muscular build,
his eyes a stunning aqua green behind wire-rimmed spectacles. Yet he
knew her. She'd have asked him how except that her body swayed.

She'd miscalculated what the anchor work yesterday had taken out
of her. This was what came of being irrational, of going with emotion.

Yet still, she said, "Canto?"

"Fine. He's in the bedroom." Shoving the mahogany-colored
strands of his choppily cut hair back from his face, the stranger walked
closer on cautious feet. "Put your arm around my shoulders."

Because he'd asked instead of taken advantage of her obvious
weakness, she did as he'd suggested, and he helped her walk to Canto's
bedroom doorway and look in.

Long lashes shaded Canto's cheeks as his chest rose and fell in an easy rhythm.

"You want the other side of the bed?"

Startled, she looked at the stranger . . . and saw eyes that were glowing just a little behind the clear lenses of his spectacles. A ring of amber encircled the aqua green, shooting light through his irises. Wild. Changeling. *Sense of smell. Knowledge of Payal in Canto's space.* It added up to a conclusion of intimacy for him. "No," she said. "The sofa."

He frowned but didn't argue. He just helped her to that sofa and, after she lay down, found a blanket and opened it over her with gentle hands. Panic was metal on her tongue. "Who . . ."

"Pavel. Friends call me Pasha." He crouched down to meet her eyes. "Bear. Madly in love with a Mercant who's leading me on a dance."

Madly in love with a Mercant.

He wouldn't hurt Canto.

By extension, he wouldn't hurt Payal—because he thought she belonged to Canto. And still the panic threatened to strangle her. He was an unknown, a threat. Heat built under her skin, her breathing turning jagged.

She *had* to stay awake.

A brush across her mind, a sense of Canto wrapping her up in his arms. *Sleep*, she heard on a level beyond telepathy. *I'll keep you safe.*

I'm going mad, but it's a beautiful madness was her last conscious thought before she slipped into sleep.

PAVEL got a call from Silver not long after Payal's arrival. "Stay home," he told his alpha's mate. "You just pulled a big day with that EmNet meeting and I'm set here." Silver had already dropped by that morning to check on her cousin—and bring Pavel a change of clothing.

Food wasn't an issue; Canto had an open-cupboard policy for hungry bears.

"Pasha," she said very precisely, "there's an unfamiliar cardinal telekinetic in Canto's house."

"She's asleep. Super scary." He grinned at the sound that came down the line. "Seriously, Siva," he said, using the name Dima and the other cubs called her, "she was more worried about Canto than anything. You rest. I'll keep you updated."

Silver argued for two more minutes before she interrupted herself with a huge yawn and finally admitted to her exhaustion. Not that it would stop her. Soon as she woke, she'd be driving over.

Still, it was better than nothing.

That sorted, he grabbed a spare unsecured organizer of Canto's that he knew the other man was okay with him borrowing, and went out on the deck to finish a book he'd started earlier. He wasn't a total barbarian. And Arwen had a thing for men who read.

Tucking one arm behind his head, he dived in.

It was an hour later that he tiptoed in from the deck. He'd heard the cardinal's breathing drop into an intensely slow and deep rhythm, wanted to check she wasn't in trouble. The last thing he needed was for Canto to tear him a new one because he hadn't looked out for Canto's woman.

The damn Psy was as prickly as a grizzly right out of hibernation.

What did it say about Pavel that he liked him not in spite of it, but because of it? Contrary bear, that was what he was.

The cardinal was fast asleep.

No signs of distress. Not like the dangerous tension he'd sensed in her before she surrendered to sleep. Dangerous, that was, to him. A cardinal telekinetic could do a lot of damage to a bear. That was why there was only one rule when fighting Tks: hit first and hit hard. Any delay and you might as well plan your funeral.

But Canto's Tk hadn't tried to hurt him even when startled.

Now she lay motionless, unguarded.

Maybe it had taken her this long to actually relax. Couldn't blame her, not when he'd almost tackled her to the floor when she first arrived. In his defense, she'd been nothing but a flicker at the corner of his eye, a threat that had appeared out of nowhere.

Bozhe moi! Imagine if he'd concussed Canto's lover!

Dead meat, he'd have been bear-flavored dead meat.

Chapter 27

To say Mercants are a tight-knit unit is a *slight* understatement. More correct would be to say that if they consider you a threat to one of their own, they will cut out your liver, fry it in front of you, then offer it to you with a side dish of your poison of choice.

—Quote by an anonymous source for the *PsyNet Beacon* (2082)

DESPITE HIS TWIN Yakov calling him as subtle as an elephant, Pavel could be pretty light of foot for a bear, so he padded over to tuck the blanket more firmly around Canto's cardinal, frowning at the dark shadows under her eyes. He'd seen Arwen get that way—it happened when Psy burned too hot and used up all their psychic energy.

Canto had looked the same when Pavel arrived.

Grumbling under his breath about "Psy who don't take care of themselves," he turned off the one light he'd left on while Payal was falling asleep. She might as well sleep in nice cozy darkness. But he didn't lower the blinds over the sliding doors—the moonlight would allow her to orient herself if she woke.

The next thing he did was check on Canto. Also in a deep natural sleep. Pavel had never seen anyone sleep that way—almost as if the body were in hibernation—but Silver had told him it was normal after a psychic burn so severe it flatlined the user's powers.

A scent caught his nose just as he exited the bedroom, and suddenly, he felt like a high school bear with his first crush. He wanted to bounce on his toes. Would it always be like this? Probably. Was he fine with that?

Hell yeah.

He grabbed Arwen in his arms the instant the more slender man hit the top stair. He was as impeccably dressed as always, today in a suit of black paired with a dark gray shirt and perfectly knotted black tie. His hair was combed to within an inch of its life, his black leather shoes shined to a polish.

He looked as if he'd walked off the page of a high-end menswear catalog.

Pavel, meanwhile, wore old blue jeans, a once-green tee that had seen better days, and beat-up sneakers. Yet Arwen's delight wrapped around him like a hug even as he looked snootily down his perfect aristocratic nose and said, "You're creasing my jacket."

Laughing, Pavel kissed him on that gorgeous mouth. The thing with empaths was that they could be as snooty as they liked—if they loved you, it showed. Hell, it surrounded you until it was in every cell of your being. Pavel had told Yakov that it was like being enfolded in Arwen-scented sunshine.

The kiss was a wild, familiar thing until Arwen pushed at his shoulders.

Pavel let go at once. Arwen wasn't a dominant, not the way changelings saw things. He wasn't a submissive, either. He was closer to a healer than anything else. And healers were to be protected. Though Pavel wasn't stupid enough to say that out loud; Arwen would cut him to shreds with his tone alone.

He'd taken lessons at Ena Mercant's knee, after all.

But the crux of it all was that Pavel was far, far physically stronger. The only way this could work—whatever it was they were doing—was for him to listen to and follow Arwen's physical cues. "Silver sent you, didn't she?"

"Of course she did—not just because of Canto, either. She's worried about you hanging around an unknown Tk." Arwen looked him up and down. "You seem whole." Cool words, but the happy sunshine wove through his hair, sank into his skin, was a near-taste on his tongue.

Arwen fixed his jacket back into place, then leaned over and nudged Pavel's glasses up his nose. "Cute."

Pavel grinned, even though he'd pound anyone else who dared call him cute. "Your cousin's asleep. Looks normal to me, but you want to check?" He nudged his head toward the sofa. "She's out like a light, too. Not a stir despite our noise." He'd kept a bearish ear out for any sign of disturbance.

After a curious glance at the cardinal—whose face was obscured by the way the blanket had bunched there—Arwen walked into the bedroom, his stride as fluid as Silver's. That they weren't changeling was clear, but Mercants had a deadly grace about them.

When Arwen exited, he went to stare down at the cardinal. "Shit, it really is Payal Rao," he said, his breath hitching in his throat and his voice an octave higher than normal. "She's in Canto's house, *asleep*."

Blinking rapidly, he reached down to undo his suit jacket, then put his hands on his hips, pushing the jacket back as he did so—to reveal a black leather belt initialed with a discreet designer logo. "Canto and Payal Rao." He sounded as agog as many people did when they said *Valentin Nikolaev and Silver Mercant*.

A shake of his head. "I told Silver to leave it be, but it was all theoretical then."

"Come here before you hyperventilate." Pavel dragged him out onto the deck.

Arwen came but he was still muttering. "Grandmother must know. Canto wouldn't go behind her back."

"Your grandmother knows everything." Swinging his arm around the other man's shoulders, Pavel drew him out to the railing. "And Canto will kick your ass if you interfere."

Arwen looked mutinous for a second before wincing. "You're right."

"So, you consider my invite?" Because their relationship? It wasn't settled like Silver and Valentin's or Chaos and Nova's. The two of them had been playing this game of back and forth for months.

"Aren't you frustrated?" Yakov had asked him the other day.

Pavel's answer had been easy. "No. He's an E who's been in hiding all his life. Not from his family, but from the rest of the world. This is the first time he's been free to be himself. He needs to do that first before he can come to me."

"If he decides he doesn't want that? To come to you?"

"Why are you so mean? What did I ever do to you?"

"Kick me in the womb."

"*Mudak*," Pavel had muttered, but hadn't pounced on his twin for a fight that let their bears out. "If he doesn't want me after, I have to let him go. That's who we are. StoneWater bears court our lovers. We might occasionally try to kidnap them, but we don't force."

Long, elegant fingers with nails buffed and squared stroked his jaw. "What's the matter, Pasha bear?" Arwen murmured, looking at him with those empathic eyes that saw too much.

Pasha bear.

If Yakov ever heard that, he'd die laughing, then come back from the grave to laugh some more. But Pavel melted. "Big bear thoughts," he said with a grin, because he wouldn't put that pressure on Arwen.

His E had to come to him on his own terms.

"Tell me about this Payal Rao," he said. "She sounds like your sister."

An immediate scowl, the gentle touch gone. "Silver is not like

Payal." Arwen folded his arms. "From what I know, she's ruthless and calculated and doesn't care about anything but power."

Pavel's lips twitched. "*Moy luchik*, do you think Silver is a fluffy kitten?"

Growling low in his throat—and yes, Pavel was proud of having taught him that—Arwen turned and leaned on the balcony railing. "Silver is loyal to family. She'd die to protect us. Payal, as far as I know, has no deep family connections."

"Her fault?"

Arwen took a moment before shrugging. "I don't know. It's not my job in the family to keep track of stuff like that." He sighed. "I have to apologize to Silver for being so smug—I can't stop worrying, either, now that it's real. She's so dangerous, Pasha."

Shifting to lean on the railing beside him, but facing the house, Pavel said, "Canto can take care of himself, you know. Man's a cardinal and as tough as any bear." He watched the wind riffle its fingers through Arwen's hair, and his fingers itched to do the same.

Later, he promised himself.

"You don't understand." Arwen's fingers tightened on the railing. "Canto's about to hit thirty-nine, and the only people he's ever trusted are family—and family adjacent, like you." Shoulders tense, he stood to his full height. "I just . . . I don't know if he understands the power of emotion. I don't know if he understands that it can be used to manipulate."

"I gotta disagree, Arwen. Canto's about as un-Psy a Psy I've ever met." Grumpy, open, generous. "I say you should worry about Payal. Is she good at emotions?"

Arwen hesitated, then reached over to pull Pavel's phone out of his back jeans pocket and did a search. They both watched the video that came up—an interview with Payal in relation to a recent merger.

Afterward, Pavel raised an eyebrow. "Payal Rao has no fucking idea how to deal with a sneaky Mercant."

"Canto isn't sneaky," Arwen muttered. "He's a straight arrow."

Chuckling, Pavel slid his hand around the back of Arwen's neck. "Sneaky is in your blood," he said against his lover's lips. "You can't help it." Then, as his bear stirred against the inside of his skin, its fur rich and luxuriant, he kissed the man who held his wild changeling heart.

And he wished Payal Rao luck.

She'd need it with her Mercant.

Chapter 28

Trust is a fragile glass bird. Drop it once, and it will shatter into shards innumerable.

—Inshara Rao, essayist (1892)

CANTO WOKE TO the awareness that he wasn't alone. His telepathic senses had scanned out automatically on waking, a security measure he'd built into his brain in childhood. It had been a way to control what was happening to him.

He hit a changeling mind he couldn't read, then a Psy one that was open enough to Canto to tell him it was Arwen. Which, given the current proximity of the two minds, meant the other one had to be Pavel.

The final proximate mind was Psy and locked against intrusion in a way that sang "anchor" to him.

Payal.

No response to his attempt at telepathic contact, though when he checked in the Substrate, he found her zone calm and controlled. So was the rest of the Net. The situation had been contained.

Not bothering to throw water on his face or pull a pair of sweatpants over his boxer briefs, he got in his chair and made his way to her.

He couldn't see Pavel and Arwen, which meant they were probably downstairs. Pavel's keen hearing would've caught his movements—if the two younger men were smart, they'd fade discreetly away.

He found Payal asleep on his couch. Her breathing was even and she seemed to be in a genuine resting state. His fingers flexed, wanting to touch, but he wouldn't steal touch. Not from Payal, this woman who was so careful about intimacy of any kind.

Heading to the elevator, he made it downstairs just in time to catch sight of a laughing Pavel tugging Arwen into the trees in the distance. Canto's cousin wasn't exactly fighting, and the fact he was wearing a suit in the early-morning fog told Canto he must've kept Pavel company overnight.

Tell your bear thanks, Canto telepathed.

He's not my bear, Arwen replied utterly unconvincingly. *But he says you're welcome. Does Grandmother know about Payal?*

Canto didn't answer to anyone but Ena, but he couldn't ignore the open concern in Arwen's tone. Empath. Always caring so much, always trying to make sure the family was happy. *Yes. So you can stop worrying, little old man.* A childhood nickname given in affection.

Payal . . . you'll be careful? She's ruthless.

So is Grandmother.

That made Arwen go quiet for several long seconds. When he did reply, he sounded peeved. *I made the mistake of telling Pasha what you said, and he's rolling around on the forest floor laughing so hard he can't talk.*

Canto understood the bear's amusement. *The men in our family don't go for weak, Arwen. Have you not figured that out?* Especially since he was tangled up with a bear lieutenant.

But she's like a razor-sharp knife at the throat. A bit extreme.

Go ask Valentin about Silver Fucking Mercant. Those were the exact words the bear alpha had been known to yell in pride about his mate.

You're grumpy when you wake up, Arwen muttered. *I'm going to go find some cold water to throw on Pasha.*

Meanwhile, Canto sat there and realized he'd just talked about Mercant men and the lovers they fell for; yeah, he'd gone well past friendship based on his and Payal's shared past. But as with Arwen and his laughing bear, this would not be a fast courtship.

Courtship.

More bear influence.

Psy didn't court each other.

But Valentin had courted Silver and won her. Pavel was courting Arwen with what appeared to be slow but joyous success. Psy *could* be courted. The question was, Did Canto know how to do it?

"I'm very good at research," he muttered to himself, and went back upstairs to get cleaned up.

After drying off following his shower, he put on a pair of gray sweatpants and a faded olive green tee that hugged his biceps—he'd seen Payal's eyes go to his arms more than once, and the first rule of Mercant life was to use every advantage. His jaw was stubbled, but Payal didn't seem to mind that, so he left it, and his hair was short enough to require nothing but a quick comb with his fingers.

He didn't bother with socks or shoes.

Ready, he hit the kitchen and made himself a sandwich. He was just finishing it off when he heard stirring in the lounge. "Payal," he said out loud as he wheeled himself to her.

She was sitting with her hair tumbled around her face, her black pants and silky green top mussed. Her eyes were hazy, her lips plump and relaxed. "Canto?"

"Hello, sleepy." He fought the urge to go over, cuddle her warm, sleep-dazed body against his.

A flare of her eyes, her body leaning toward his . . . then she took a deep breath and squeezed her eyes shut. Her muscles lost their softness, her features no longer open.

Canto shoved aside his frustration, killed his anger dead. No fucking way would he ever lash out at Payal for doing what she needed to do to survive. "Hungry?"

"Starving," she admitted, one hand on her stomach. "And I need to fix my hair."

"Guest bathroom's that way. There's stuff in there you can use. Brushes and things."

PAYAL was still a little drugged from her deep sleep, so it took her a few minutes to notice that all of the makeup in the basket of "stuff" for guests was designed for her skin tone. Not her preferred brands, as there was no way Canto could've known those—but he'd done the research to find the things she needed to feel whole.

Feel as if her armor weren't cracked.

She opened a new brush and used it to comb out her hair, then pulled it back into a tight ponytail. Next, she fixed her face and re-arranged her clothing so it didn't look so much like she'd slept in it.

When she glanced in the mirror again, she looked like the Payal Rao people saw in the media. Except for one thing. She hadn't been wearing shoes when she teleported in, and now her feet felt naked.

Canto was just coming in from the deck. "I put the food out on the deck table."

His feet were bare, too, his toenails squared and his skin tanned enough to tell her he sat in the sun without shoes. "Thank you," she said, her voice husky.

"Hey, you'll get frozen feet. Let me grab you a pair of socks."

Her chest felt as if it were compressing on itself. "What about you?" she managed to say as he disappeared into the bedroom.

"I'm used to the colder temps here—and, after all these years, I've got a good handle on how to regulate my lower body temperature. You're at hothouse heat in Delhi right now." He emerged with a pair of black socks.

They were too big for her feet and warm, and she was going to steal them so she'd have a piece of Canto with her in Vara. Her stomach clenched. She should go there now, away from this man who made the mad girl inside her agitate to be free. But she took her socked feet out into the pale gray of early morning and onto the wooden boards of the deck.

Then she sat with Canto and, as the sun rose in a glory of washed gold, ate with no concern of poison.

It scared her, just how safe she felt with him, causing tremors that cracked her shields and threatened to set her madness free. Her fingers ached to make contact with his skin, her eyes going over and over to the musculature of his arms, the strong tendons of his neck, the damp strands of his hair . . . the mobile firmness of his mouth.

Pain stabbed behind her left eye even as she struggled with her need. She was an expert at hiding such attacks, but Canto's eyes narrowed. "What's the matter?" He reached out a hand.

Despite the terrible danger of it, she leaned into the touch. The rough pads of his fingertips brushed her cheek. "Migraine."

"That's the second one in the past few days." Scowl dark, Canto brushed the pad of his thumb over her cheekbone.

Payal jerked away. Not because it felt bad. But because it didn't. She wanted to crawl into his lap, take off his tee, bare her own body, and rub skin against skin.

It was a red warning sign.

And still, she stayed.

Canto continued to scowl. "Have you had scans to make sure it's not due to a recurrence of your childhood tumor?"

All at once, she'd had enough of secrets with her 7J. If she couldn't trust Canto, then she was so badly broken that she could have no hope of a life beyond mere robotic existence.

It would mean her father and brother had succeeded in breaking her.

No.

"I have small tumors the surgeons were never able to remove—they're in a location that can't be excised without the risk of significant and irreparable damage to my mental capacity and possible physical function."

A muscle ticked in Canto's jaw. "Are they growing?"

"No. A type of chemotherapy keeps it in check." Her pulse beat in her mouth, her skin too hot, then too cold. "Unfortunately, the 'recipe' was created by a chemist hired by my father. That chemist then conveniently died. I've attempted to have other chemists reverse engineer it without success."

"He's using it as a leash, isn't he?" Canto's voice was an unsheathed blade. "That's why we sense Pranath Rao's stamp on many of your family's actions, though you're the CEO."

"Don't use this knowledge against me, Canto." It was the first time she could remember asking someone not to hurt her.

Canto moved quickly, shifting his chair so that he was right next to her. Reaching out, he cupped the back of her neck when she didn't make any move to stop him. "Understand this, Payal. I will protect you always. *Never* will I hurt you."

No one had ever before cared if she was hurt or used. It was too much . . . almost. "I have to go," she whispered, but didn't wrench away. "It's time for a dose."

Eyes full of constellations shifted to pure darkness. "How long between doses?"

"It should last seven days, but things can be accelerated by power usage—and we've had to deal with two major incidents." She'd used too much psychic energy in too close a time frame.

"Can you get me a sample?"

"I've hired the best of the best in the world."

"You haven't hired everyone." His fingers tightened on her nape, the heat of his skin a rough warmth. "Give me the chance to try to set you free."

The offer froze her blood, then shattered it, tiny shards ricocheting around her bloodstream and smashing into her already fragmented shields. Making a sharp, pained sound, she gave in to clawing need and pressed her lips to his, her hands on the wall of his chest.

She didn't know how to kiss, but the contact, the way his hands came immediately to cup her face, it was everything. So many years of loneliness inside her, so much *need. I'll overwhelm you*, she warned. *I'll take and take and take.*

Take as much as you want. His hand wrapping itself in her ponytail, the taste of him turning her hunger into an addiction. *I'll always have more for you.*

Madness sparking like electricity in her veins, she broke the contact as fast as she'd made it. "Please don't forget me, Canto." Words torn out of her. To ask someone to care for her enough to remember her, it was the hardest thing she'd ever asked of anyone. If Canto forgot her . . . she'd break.

She teleported out before he could answer.

The Architect

I am God. Death is meaningless.

—Suicide note left by participant in Operation Scarab (circa 2003)

THE ARCHITECT STARED at the back of her hand, at the fine blue veins that made her heart pump, her brain work. How was it possible that someone like her, someone of the ascendent race, was still bound by flesh?

Picking up a letter opener with a razor-sharp edge, she cut a line on her skin. Blood blossomed wet and a bright, bright red. She tilted her head, watched the line of it form, bubble, then slowly drip down the side of her hand when she angled that mortal thing of bone and skin and distasteful organics.

She was beyond this, her body nothing but a weight holding her down.

There had to be a better way to exist, to grow, to become all that she was meant to be.

Chapter 29

To the end.

—Motto of the Anchor Society (1701)

IT TOOK A full hour for Payal to rebuild her carapace enough to face the world without feeling like a turtle without its shell. Armored in a fitted gray dress and heels of dark scarlet that matched her lipstick, she teleported straight from her bedroom to her office just before nine thirty.

Her brother was seated in her visitor chair, his legs stretched out in front of him and his hands clasped over the white shirt he'd paired with a navy suit. She felt no surprise; Ruhi had messaged her a half hour prior, when Lalit first turned up.

He'd once sat in her chair. She'd teleported him to the visitor one.

He'd never forgiven her for the "humiliation"—but that was par for the course with Lalit. "How can I help you?" she asked after taking her seat.

"Wanted to see how you were doing with my own eyes," he said with that chilling smile. "You know Father is worried, don't you?

When you took on this position, we all assumed you could keep the anchor business from interfering."

He'd always been better at words than her, better at doing verbal damage. But this time around, his words were so foolish that she reconsidered his intelligence. "I'll be sure to allow the PsyNet to collapse next time."

His smile didn't fade. "All at once you're so important that the PsyNet will collapse without you." Rising to his feet, he buttoned his jacket. "I think you need another psych consult, little sister. Looks like your delusions are taking over." Then he reached out and, holding eye contact, deliberately nudged her pens out of alignment. "Oops."

Payal didn't fix the small incursion of chaos. Her need for balance wasn't a compulsion. It could've been, but that would've given Lalit a weakness to exploit—and that was the one thing Payal would not do. "Did you finish the financial report?" She picked up an organizer. "Father wants it on his desk today."

"Of course. I know how to do my job." He teleported out instead of using the door.

Picking up one of the pens he'd misaligned, she looked at it, then put it back without fixing the error. A test to make sure she *wasn't* becoming tied to compulsion.

Rising, she walked to stand by the glass doors that looked out over Delhi. The city was wide awake, the markets in the distance going full bore, and the chai-wallah at the far corner already pouring steaming hot cups of tea for commuters.

Once centered by the beat of her city, she returned to her desk and asked Ruhi to contact Kaleb Krychek's office to set up a meeting.

Her intercom buzzed a bare minute later. "Ms. Rao." Ruhi's voice was pitched high. "Mr. Krychek is in the outer office."

Payal had heard that the cardinal could lock onto faces as well as places. Polite of him to lock onto Ruhi's face rather than Payal's; in-

teresting, however, that he'd had Ruhi's on file. "Send him in." To rise
or to sit, it was normally a calculated choice, but since he'd been polite,
she did the same and met him halfway across her office. "Thank you
for the quick response."

He was a handsome man. In a league far beyond Lalit's surface
flash. Black hair, cardinal eyes—and a sense of confidence so deep
that he had no need to posture and play games. Power pulsed off him.

Payal felt neither attraction nor fear. No, what she felt was a cautious sense of hope that he'd be sensible, listen to what she had to say.

Leading him to the small meeting table to one side of her office,
she took one seat while waving him into the opposing one. Cardinal
eyes met her own, impenetrable and unreadable. Kaleb Krychek had
that down to an art. He was also unquestionably one of the most
powerful people in the PsyNet. Yet he had a bond with another Psy:
Sahara Kyriakus. That meant he had an emotional link. A weakness.

But no one would dare call Kaleb Krychek weak. Even outwardly
relaxed, the force of his psychic strength was a weight in the air; Payal
had no illusions about who would win a battle between the two of
them. She was a cardinal. He was obsidian death. But that wouldn't
stop her from going toe-to-toe with him when it came to Designation A.

Kaleb was dangerous but he was no psychopath.

"This is important," he said, and raised an eyebrow. "We're not
used to anchors speaking up."

"A choice made in the past that is no longer relevant." She threw
her telepathic voice toward Canto, her need for him a raw bruise.

It was as if he'd been listening for her all this time, because he
responded at once: *Payal.*

I'm with Krychek. Stand by for questions. It was hard, so hard to find
a way to tell him what he was to her, but she could do this, could be
practical and logical and hold on to him using their shared need to
protect the Net.

"True," Krychek said. "Tell me about the Substrate you mentioned to Aden."

"The Substrate is where anchors exist. In simple terms, it's the foundation of the PsyNet."

"The fractures we see, have they been on an upper level?"

"No, the breaches go all the way through. Anchors have assisted you with every breach in one form or another." She continued on when he didn't ask further questions. "Designation A wants a seat at the table. You can't discuss the future of the PsyNet without an anchor presence."

His expression cooled, black ice to him. "I thought you'd decided to stay out of politics."

Realizing her misstep, she contacted Canto. *He thinks I'm trying to get into power.*

Tell him to contact me if he wants verification of your status as the A rep.

Payal relied on no one. But she had no difficulty relying on Canto, her 7J who'd never forgotten her. "You can contact Canto Mercant for confirmation that I've been chosen to represent Designation A."

No visible signs of surprise, but she hadn't expected any from a man as pitiless and experienced in politics as Kaleb Krychek. He just said, "I didn't realize anchors talked to one another."

"You aren't all-knowing and all-seeing," she said, because Krychek understood power, understood standing your ground.

"What do the anchors want?"

"A seat at the table," she repeated. "We aren't political, not in the way you believe. Santano Enrique was a true outlier. I never aimed myself at the Psy Council—that was more my father's ambition."

"If this isn't about politics, then why a seat at the table?"

"Because none of you, not even the empaths, understand the Substrate. You can't even see it. There are also major issues with Sentinel."

"You're well informed. Or should I say, Canto is."

"I'm the voice of the As." She didn't break the eye contact. "Don't try doing an end run around me—you won't succeed. As for the politics—once we have this situation under control, I would become a silent member of the Ruling Coalition except when it comes to anchor business. Our priority is the health of the PsyNet."

Kaleb got to his feet. "I'll organize a meeting of the Coalition to discuss your request."

Having risen with him, Payal went to answer when a massive shake tore through her body. It felt like a physical quake, but she knew it wasn't. The PsyNet was fracturing again, and somewhere close.

It was dangerous to leave her body unguarded around Krychek while she jumped into the psychic plane, but she was an A. There was no choice.

She jumped.

The Substrate twisted around her, but her area held strong. Following the chaos east to Uttar Pradesh and the beginning of Chandika Das's zone, she felt her blood run cold. *Canto, Chandika—the anchor on the eastern edge of my zone—is dead.*

KALEB reacted out of instinct when Payal's body went liquid. Catching her using his Tk, he placed her back in the chair. The only reason he wasn't in the PsyNet was that it was Aden's turn to take the breach—it went against his natural instincts to hold back, but it would do more harm than good if they were both wiped out.

Then he took a look in the PsyNet.

Unadulterated chaos, an entire section of the Net spiraling inward. *Aden, do you need assistance?*

Yes. It was short, clipped.

Kaleb took a moment to lock Payal's office from the inside before he shot his mind into the psychic space. He could've teleported to the security of his home, but Payal was clearly more vulnerable than he was right now; even while on the PsyNet, he had a level of awareness of the outside world and could react to danger.

Kaleb.

He didn't recognize the painful clarity of the voice that hit his mind as he entered the PsyNet, but it had to be a cardinal if he could make himself heard though he was a stranger. Kaleb's mind was well-shielded against unwanted contact.

It's Canto. Sending confirmation of my identity to your phone.

The other man's telepathic voice had a rare quality that was hard to put into words, but it reached places in Kaleb that weren't exactly comfortable. *Do you know why Payal's unconscious?*

It's what happens to anchors when we do a major Substrate repair. We can't exist on both planes. We have to choose one.

That was another thing Kaleb hadn't known about anchors. Perhaps the very reason they'd begun to prefer to live lives of isolation, where no one could harm them while they were vulnerable. So many things concealed, kept secret—or just forgotten.

How is she? Canto made no attempt to hide his taut concern—because to the Mercants, Kaleb was now family. And no Mercant ever betrayed another. *She's barely recovered from the previous incident.*

Seemed physically fine when I checked.

Good. Don't leave her alone.

I won't, he promised, because it was rare for a Mercant to ask a favor of him—and Canto in particular had never before done so, while feeding Kaleb interesting tidbits of information through Ena. Ena always gave credit where it was due, so Kaleb had known of Canto long before he found out the other man was a hub.

The reason for the psychic quake is the death of a neighboring anchor, Canto told him.

Their fail-safes should've kicked in. Kaleb frowned. *Why aren't they holding the Net steady until an anchor like Payal can step in?*

Canto's answer was a thing of death and devastation. *There aren't enough anchors anymore. Chandika Das was old—as a result, her anchor point was already on our critical short list.*

We just didn't expect to lose her so soon. Crisp, clear, with a rough edge of sorrow. *Her sub-anchors were already taking incredible pressure as a result of her age and health—they're too worn out to hold on now that she's gone. The entire zone is unraveling from the center.*

On the PsyNet, Kaleb saw a voracious spiral, with Aden fighting to keep it from pulling more minds into its murderous fury. *Is there anything we can do to make things easier for the As attempting a fix?*

Do what you've always done. The more you do on the Net level, the less strain on the Substrate.

Kaleb was already working with Aden. He didn't mention the loss of an anchor to the leader of the Arrow Squad—Aden's brain was already at full capacity. This information could wait. But the knowledge pulsed at the back of his head. He'd known they had an issue with anchors, but not that it was at a deadly juncture.

Because anchors were always there.

The foundation of the entire Psy way of life.

A knock on the door to Payal's office. He ignored it, while using a minute percentage of his telekinetic power to press against the door so no one could get inside.

A bead of sweat dripped down Payal's temple.

Kaleb closed his eyes to better focus on the repair.

Each mind that blinked out as it disappeared into the spiraling void was a person who had ceased to exist, their biofeedback link disconnected without warning.

Kaleb kept his mind calm, black ice on which nothing could stick. It was the only way to work in this type of a situation. He couldn't think of all the people lost; he had to think of those who still had a chance of survival.

Because Sahara had asked him to save the Psy instead of condemning them to the darkness—and Kaleb kept his promises.

Chapter 30

Payal Rao: Anchor—Delhi. Actual zone is the largest in India, stretching as far as Budaun in Uttar Pradesh on her eastern border. I'm still working on figuring out her reach in the other directions, but it's apt to be of similar significance. If she falls, it will cause a chain reaction across Asia.

—Inventory of anchors created by Canto Mercant (2082)

AS AN EMERGENCY measure, Payal took Chandika's place, becoming the sun with her stars around her. The hub and the subs. She could only maintain the position for a short burst of time before her own region began to collapse, but this area was in a dire situation.

Chandika's death must've been sudden, else she'd have contacted her neighboring hubs to set up a succession plan—though what they might have been able to do, Payal couldn't imagine, not when their zones were already edge to edge.

She wasn't the only neighboring hub who'd responded. Prabhyx, Shanta, and Virat—all of whom Payal knew because she made it her business to know her region—had also just appeared inside Chandika's zone. This close, they could talk to each other as most Psy did on the PsyNet. "We need to cover this zone," she said. "There is no replacement."

Prabhyx had always been high-strung. Now his mind flared with panic. "That's impossible! We're all stretched to the max."

Virat was more pragmatic. "We can do ten-minute sessions," he said, "but it'll be a twenty-four-hour rotation and it'll wear us out, even if we pull in anchors from farther out."

Shanta, older and more experienced, said, "Let me check the zones. There may be room for expansion from each of us. Stressful, yes, but not as bad as a rotation."

Payal held Chandika's zone while they waited. She'd sensed the horror of minds blinking out at a sickening rate when she first arrived, but the losses had stopped the instant she wrenched the Substrate back into shape. However, with many of Chandika's sub-anchors having collapsed under the initial surge after her death, the strain on Payal's mind was enormous.

Shanta returned. "Prabhyx, you have capacity in your southern quadrant. Can you see if you can reshape your zone to take a segment of the weight?"

High-strung or not, Prabhyx was an anchor and he reacted to try to save lives, save the Net. Payal felt a small amount of pressure exit her mind. "That's good," she said. "Shanta, who else has capacity?"

"Nobody" was the quiet answer. "You were already taking on a big chunk of Chandika's zone and so was I. Virat's got extra weight with Pallavi's zone—she's aging, too."

All of them must've stretched out automatically, their brains reacting as designed. *Canto, there is no cover.*

Check the grid. See if there are any answers there. I'm searching to see if we can get cover from an A based in a more stable zone.

The grid was faded and crumbling. As with plants deprived of water, every part of the Net suffered when deprived of anchor energy.

Water. Energy. ENERGY.

A puzzle piece slotted into place in her mind, then another and another.

"I'll build conduits," she said to the others, as well as telepathically to Canto. "It'll feed our energy into this zone."

"That won't last." She could hear tears in Prabhyx's voice. "It needs to be one of *us*."

"I know." She tempered her tone—there was no point in yelling at someone who simply couldn't help the way they were; Prabhyx was a good anchor. That was all he had to be. She'd take care of the rest. "But it'll give us time to try to find a solution. Canto's currently searching for an area of the world with an extra anchor." It'd be a hardship for that A to relocate, but such sacrifices were part of being an A.

When the Net bled, so did anchors.

Santano Enrique had once covered three zones for a heroic five minutes when twin anchors passed away within seconds of each other. He'd been a psychopath, but he'd also been an A.

"Okay, yes. Yes, that makes sense." Prabhyx repeated that multiple times as he helped her build the conduits. One from each neighboring anchor, so that their combined energies fed the grid and made it stronger.

"It's like a spiderweb," Shanta said afterward, as the conduit network glowed blue and began to pump anchor energy into the region; the only things that didn't alter in color were the intrusive brown fibers. "A web fed with our psychic blood."

"It's going to drain all of us." Payal was far more concerned with the practical than the metaphysical. "Eat and drink double your usual amount. I think we can maintain this for up to a month at the absolute maximum—but only if you fuel yourselves."

All three communicated their acceptance of the plan.

Virat said, "Thank you, Payal. When Canto reached out about this anchor union, I didn't appreciate why he'd chosen you to represent us, but now I see. You can think even when the Net is falling around us."

"Yes," Shanta murmured. "But we know you can't do magic. We'll help you in any and every way we can. It hurts to watch the Net die."

They separated on that simple, profound truth.

Already able to feel the energy drain, she opened her eyes on the physical plane to find herself still sitting across from Kaleb Krychek. His eyes were closed, and the dark gray of his shirt stuck to his body. He'd discarded his jacket at some point and loosened his tie.

"Kaleb?"

"Five more minutes."

Her legs shaky, she was glad to have the opportunity to just sit there. She hadn't flamed out, so she was able to teleport in two nutrient drinks. As she knew exactly where they were in her apartment, the small "fetch" was easy to pull off.

Payal, how are you? I can see the change in the Substrate.

That beautiful voice. Of a man who remembered her, who saw her. *I'm fine. Kaleb's still here.*

Kaleb came back fully into his body at that moment. The transformation was subtle and intense at the same time. His muscles held a touch more tension, his obsidian gaze acute, the sheer power of him focused on her.

Many people were afraid of Kaleb Krychek. A logical response. Payal, though, felt no fear—she was an A. He would never touch her. But more than that, she saw something in Kaleb that felt familiar.

Spotting the drink, he picked it up and unscrewed the tamper-proof seal. "The repair is fragile at best," he said afterward. "We have an Arrow babysitting it, but it's not going to hold."

"That's because there's no anchor there." Rising, she grabbed a jotter pad off her desk and sketched out the system she and the others had put in place. "Best-case scenario is that it'll hold for a month, but we can't guarantee anything beyond two weeks. Especially should another linked anchor fall."

Krychek looked at her with eyes still devoid of stars. "What's this conduit mean for you and the other hubs?"

"Exhaustion." Payal wasn't here to pull punches. She was here to be a battle tank. "A short stint won't do permanent injury, but much longer and you'll lose five anchors instead of one."

Kaleb's face stayed expressionless. She could see why he'd not only made the Psy Council at such a young age but survived it. Either he had a stone-cold heart or he'd learned to school his emotions in the same kind of deadly crucible in which she'd come of age.

Yet Kaleb had what changelings would call a mate. "May I ask a personal question?"

He looked directly at her face, as if trying to see through to her brain. "I can't promise to answer it."

Payal didn't retreat. This was too important. "How do you do it?" She returned that direct stare. "Feel enough emotion to be bonded to another while remaining ice-cold in your daily interactions."

A single blink was the only giveaway that she'd surprised him. For a long second, she thought he wouldn't answer, but then he said, "It's Canto, isn't it?" He crossed one ankle over the knee of his other leg, his hand lying loosely on the crossed leg. "I knew as soon as he asked me to protect you while you were out."

Things shifted and twisted inside her, the screaming girl fierce with joy, a bright and defiant flame.

Even though she didn't confirm his supposition, Kaleb continued. "I had a childhood where—let's just say trust would've been a weakness that saw me destroyed. So I learned to build impenetrable shields."

Startled that he'd shared such a personal thing, Payal leaned forward. "Why did you tell me that?"

Another intent look. "The same reason you asked the question of a man most people never dare to approach on personal topics."

A sense of familiarity, of like knowing like.

"The shields aren't the problem," she admitted. "I can hold those forever if I truly wish to."

"It's a cold place to live, isn't it? That cage of walls?"

"But it's safe."

"Do you want to die feeling safe?" His words were soft. "Or do you want to die feeling free?"

It was as if the two of them were in a bubble, cold and dark. "What if freedom equals destruction?"

"Might depend on the reason you asked your initial question." Rising, he grabbed his jacket. "According to Ena Mercant, Canto is one of the rocks of the family. He could be your safe place to stand, as Sahara is mine."

The idea of it was so breathtakingly seductive that it stole her breath. "Thank you," she managed to get out. "You didn't have to answer me, but you did." It meant something.

"Sahara's obviously a bad influence." No change in his tone or expression, Krychek glanced at his timepiece. "We need a Coalition meeting," he said. "Can you do it after this?"

"Give me a half hour." Not only did she need to refuel, she had to deal with a couple of business issues to keep her father and brother at bay.

"I'll send you the comm codes." He nodded toward the door. "By the way, someone's been shoving telekinetically at your door for the past ten minutes."

She glanced toward the door, only then realizing he had to be holding it shut against any attempt to enter. "I appreciate the notice. I have it."

Krychek left it to her, but before he teleported out, he looked her in the eye and said, "Some choices define us, Payal."

She inclined her head, her heart in a fist, and when she looked up, he was gone.

"Payal!" Lalit's voice yelling her name. "Stop playing games and open this damn door."

She rubbed her forehead. She was tired and needed time to rest and refuel, not deal with her psychopathic brother. She also needed the tumor-control medication, but the pain wasn't yet to the point where things were critical. What was Lalit even doing here?

A single glance at her organizer told her the answer: their father had been attempting to contact her. Too bad.

She teleported out, leaving Lalit to fall into an empty office.

Chapter 31

"I think I might actually have been kind. It's disturbing."
"And people say you have no sense of humor. Come here so I can
kiss you."

—Sahara Kyriakus to Kaleb Krychek

CANTO NEARLY RAN into Payal when she appeared in front of the
glass doors that opened out onto his deck.

She swayed.

"Hey, hey." Heart thundering, he gripped her hips.

She swayed again.

Shifting his hold, he eased her down into a seated position on the
only possible seat: his lap. Warm and soft, she was a jolt to his system.

"Sorry." Her voice was slurred as her head slumped against his shoulder. "Thought I was stable, but conduit drain kicked in midteleport."

"It's all right, baby. I have you." He made sure she was settled in a
comfortable position, then took them straight to the kitchen using
hover mode—he couldn't push the chair with one arm holding her
tight against him. He could've shifted her to the sofa on his way past,
but his muscles were rigid, his chest a drum. Feeling the warm puffs
of her breath on his skin—he needed that.

Needed to have her alive and breathing, his 3K who'd always been a fighter.

Grabbing a bottle of nutrients, he twisted it open, then poured the thick liquid into a glass, all the while aware of her living warmth. Payal was considerably lighter than him, but she also had a lot more softness to her—a cushion of curves that might've distracted had he not been so worried about the sluggish nature of her pulse.

Cupping the back of her head, he put the edge of the glass to her lips. "Payal, you need this." He made his voice a harsh order. "Can you drink?"

She lifted her hands, but they were weak and barely touched the glass before sliding off. But she was swallowing, so sip by sip, he got the whole glass into her. When she laid her head back down against his shoulder afterward, he didn't try to repeat his success. The first glass should be enough to give her a boost.

Moving them out of the kitchen, he dragged a small knitted blanket off his sofa. Magdalene had made it for him after taking up the craft as a calming exercise in the years after he returned to her life—his ostensibly Silent mother had carried a lot of guilt for what Binh had done to Canto.

"I ran full background checks," she'd told him when he was older. "Our family never agrees to such contracts with the cruel or evil. We never send our blood into harm. But I did. I failed you."

Their relationship would've withered if he'd held on to anger and she on to guilt. As it was, she was now one of the stable foundations of his life, and he was glad of the warmth of her blanket around Payal's body as he moved back outside. He wanted Payal in the fresh air and sunlight. Anchors were too often in darkened rooms, their minds overwhelming all other senses.

Once he'd parked the chair, he moved his free hand to cup her nape, then went into the Substrate, to the location of the construct meant to cover Chandika Das's zone. He saw the problem at once. The construct had cracked at a critical point, which meant the entire thing was feeding off only Payal.

Canto got to work.

Payal stirred in his arms the instant he completed the final repair. Dropping from the Substrate, he stroked a hand down her back over the top of the knitted blanket.

She snuggled into him, her nose cold when it touched his neck.

Canto cuddled her closer. It came naturally—because it was her. 3K. The girl who'd held his hand with fierce loyalty when he was at his most broken.

There were no walls inside him when it came to her.

She came out of it with a yawn, then froze before her muscles went lax again. "I'm sitting on your lap," she said, snuggling into him with no sign of discomfort.

"It was the closest chair."

"I like how you smell." Eyes heavy-lidded, she slid her arms around him.

He knew something then: she could get whatever she wanted, win every argument, if she spoke to him with that particular affectionate tone in her voice. "How are you feeling?"

"Better, but my legs are still regaining sensation." Fewer vestiges of drowsiness in her voice—but she didn't break contact. "Does it hurt you to have me on your lap?"

"No," he said roughly. Now that he knew she was fine, he was viscerally aware of the softness and warmth of her curves, and of how pretty *she* smelled. Gritting his teeth against the urge to sniff at her— he was definitely spending too much time around bears—he told her what had happened.

She sat up, cardinal eyes on his. "Thank you." A solemn statement.

"Don't thank me. Not for looking after you. You're mine to care for, mine to hold." The possessive words just came out, and he wasn't fucking sorry. "You know it and I know it. It might've begun in child-hood, but it's a bigger, stronger, far more powerful thing now."

Looking away, she moved her fingers over the stitches of the knit-ted blanket. "This is fine work."

"Stop trying to change the subject."

Sparks literally snapped off her. "You're being needlessly aggravat-ing." She got up off him—while bracing one hand against the balcony railing.

Canto shifted forward, ready to catch her.

But she soon let go of the railing and stood balanced on heels thin and sharp. As he watched, she bent and picked up the blanket. His gaze went straight to the curvy roundness of her backside.

His hand itched to shape over it.

Skin hot, he tugged his shirt collar away from his neck. He knew what this was, had seen it between Silver and Valentin, Arwen and Pavel. Physical attraction. Strong physical attraction.

And because he was clearly off his head today, he almost gave in and stroked the tempting curve.

Skin privileges, yelled a more rational part of him, *are to be given, not taken!*

He fisted his hand and, when she rose to her feet, said, "Come here."

A suspicious frown. "Why?"

"I want to touch you." Might as well be blunt since he wasn't ex-actly sophisticated in this arena. "I want the softness of you on me, and I want your skin under my palms." Tugging off his gloves, he threw them aside.

HEAT flushed Payal's face, her own fingers itching to trace the bristled angle of his jawline, the curves of that gruff, growly mouth. Her defenses had already been shaky at best—after waking to find him holding her with such care, they were all but decimated.

It was madness, a sure mistake, but Payal did it anyway. She returned to his lap, his thighs hard under her and his body all angles.

Shuddering, he cupped the side of her neck, squeezed. "Have you decided then, 3K?"

She felt claimed, owned. It should've been disturbing—except that she felt the same possessive drive toward him. "It can never work." But she pressed her hand flat to the heat of his chest, the fine cotton of his shirt doing little to block that raw masculine heat.

His muscled arm around her back, his eyes locked with hers, Canto said, "Never say that to a Mercant. We're masters at finding the loopholes." A rough murmur, his breath brushing against her lips, the two of them were so close.

Her body felt oddly full, as if her skin were too small to contain her; the touch of his lips on her own was even more startling and shocking than the first time.

She jolted back, her lips burning.

His own chest heaved, streaks of color on his cheekbones.

Fascinated, she brushed her fingers over that color. He closed his eyes, and she found herself fascinated again because his eyelashes were long and lush. When she brushed her fingertips lightly over the edges of those lashes, he shuddered, his fingers sinking into her hips.

"Is this new for you, too?" she asked, then felt foolish. He was far further into a post-Silent life . . . and she'd rather not know if he'd been on this journey with another woman.

Irrational, illogical, jealous.

But it was too late; she couldn't call back the question.

Opening those eyes full of galaxies, he said, "Yeah," in a rough voice.

"Oh."

When he used his renewed hold on the side of her neck to haul her closer, she didn't resist. Their lips touched once more. Though braced for the impact, she shivered. So close to Canto, his body a wall of muscled heat, she felt a rapacious greed awaken inside her.

She wanted more. She wanted everything.

When he moved his hand to the back of her head, the survivor in her told her to teleport away, that he now had access to an incredibly vulnerable part of her nape. But the echo of 3K said the opposite.

She didn't pull away.

Canto's hand was big and warm as he cradled her head, his other hand still gripping her hip. She'd never been so possessed by someone else before, never wanted to be. But this felt good. As if she was being cherished.

Their noses bumped.

They broke off, stared at one another. Then Canto grinned—and things inside her broke.

"Guess we should practice more," he rumbled, and, reinitiating the kiss, opened his mouth over hers.

The depth of intimacy made her moan, as together they figured out the sensual mechanics of kissing. For the first time in her adult life, she was being terrible at a skill and she didn't care.

Then, just because she wanted to, she flicked out her tongue to brush his.

A deep groan emanating from his chest, Canto pressed his hand against the back of her head even as he leaned harder into her. Payal didn't feel the slightest urge to resist. He wasn't hurting her.

He'd never hurt her.

She could trust Canto. Her 7J.

CANTO was drowning in the decadent influx of sensation, and he didn't care for rescue. He'd fuck up anyone who dared interrupt them.

Payal shifted on his lap just then; he sucked in a breath.

"Am I hurting you?" A murmur against his lips.

"I'm aroused." Not as if he could hide it. "I've never been so hard in my life." Even Psy couldn't control autonomic reflexes, so he'd woken with an erection at times in his life, but it had never been like this.

So rigid it was painful.

When Payal looked down at his lap, her eyes wide and lips parted, he suddenly realized something. "I'm sexually able," he ground out, his muscles locking. "The surgeons who worked on me weren't thinking about sexual contact, just giving me back as much function as possible, but yeah, I'm able.

"Though that might one day change." A bitter pill to swallow, to reveal. "Like I said before, there are no guarantees."

Payal looked up, tiny frown lines between her eyebrows. "That makes you sad." She stroked her fingers through his hair. "But it wouldn't affect this, you know."

He scowled. "Payal, of course it would." It was one thing to be supportive, another to ignore harsh reality.

A wave of sensation licking down his body, right to his rigid penis . . . and beyond, to thighs he hadn't felt in decades. He sucked in a breath. "What did you just do?" It came out a gritty rasp.

"I don't know." A shrug. "I touched you through your mind. Like this."

"Fucking hell!" It felt as if she had her fingers around his rigid penis, was squeezing.

Telepathic contact didn't allow this kind of mental stimulation. It was as if she was directly accessing sensory controls in his mind, then bypassing the damaged section of his spinal cord with some kind of a neural connector. A connector formed by her own mind? For that to happen, they'd need to have—"A bond," he rasped. "There's a bond between us."

"I can't see it," Payal murmured, leaning in to take a kiss as if she couldn't get enough of him. "But I feel you."

He tried to feed sensation to her . . . and there she was: an icy flame he could sense with every psychic muscle. He sent his own erotic need through to her. She moaned and gripped at the short strands of his hair.

They came together in a tangled, wet kiss, the taste of her a kick to his senses and the feel of her inside him a thing the possessive heart of him hoarded close. When they broke apart this time, she touched her fingers to his lips. He kissed those fingers.

She shivered, went to lean inward. Her timepiece sounded a cool bell.

Inhaling shakily, she glanced down at it. "Ruling Coalition is ready to meet."

He wanted her with a feral desperation. But they were anchors. The Net came first. Lifting her hand, he pressed his lips to the softness of her inner wrist. "To be continued."

Her eyes flared. "I can take the call here, since it'll be on the comm." Sliding off him and to her feet, she smoothed her hands down her dress. "Unless you have an issue with me using your devices?"

"Baby, you can use anything of mine you want." He held her gaze. "I'm assuming you want my input. Do you?" A question that sounded so simple but was a thing of trust, of bonds, of loyalty.

She didn't look away, didn't put distance between them. "Yes."

"Come on." He led her to the elevator. "Comm room's downstairs."

Payal halted, her voice hard when she said, "No."

Chapter 32

We have lost too many of our brightest. We are broken.

—Fragment of text in the *Journal of Shora Nek* (no other identifiers found), held in the archives of the British Museum

CANTO GLANCED BACK at Payal, a frown carving his forehead. "You don't like enclosed spaces?" Gentle words in a gruff tone. "You take the stairs, I'll do the elevator. Meet downstairs."

His tenderness threatened to break her. "This has nothing to do with that. Give me a lower-floor view and there is no way you can ever keep me out of this location." At present, all her visuals were from this upper floor—and telekinetics needed precise visual coordinates.

Which meant, if need be, Canto could raze his house to the ground and rebuild in a way that altered the viewpoints from here. He couldn't do that if she'd been at ground level—she could then teleport in outside his home even if he rebuilt. "Protect yourself, Canto."

"No." A flat refusal. "You aren't going to hurt me or mine."

Payal wanted to rage at him, her walls in tatters at her feet. "Don't trust me! What if my mind goes? What if it leaves me open to manipulation by my brother or father?" It was her greatest fear, that they'd use her to hurt him.

Canto grabbed her hand, tugging her down toward him. "I'll be the first to know." One hand squeezing the back of her neck. "Whatever this bond is that exists between us, I'll be the first to see your flame flicker."

Payal hesitated, looked within, and there he was: a solid column of light that blazed bright and clear. "I'll know, too." It came out a shaken whisper. "If anything happens to you."

His dark expression didn't soften. "I didn't force this bond. I don't know what it is."

"I know." Whatever it was, it was too raw and violent. "I can't see it in the PsyNet."

Canto shrugged. "We're anchors. Who knows how that affects things." A hard kiss. "You gonna come with me now?"

Payal stood to her full height, nodded. "You have a bad temper," she pointed out, though his "bad" temper was nothing frightening or dangerous. Even at his most growly, Canto was . . . warm. His eyes never went hard like Lalit's or cold like her father's.

"Is that a problem?" he muttered, after summoning the elevator. "Because if it is, too bad. I'm keeping you."

Payal blinked and stepped into the elevator with him. "You can't just keep a person."

"Yeah?" He glanced up. "Watch me."

Payal frowned, then said, "Then I'll keep you, too." It only seemed fair, and made absolute sense to the screaming girl trapped inside her mind.

They reached the bottom floor.

And Canto tugged at her hand.

The action already part of their personal lexicon, she bent toward him. One big hand sliding around to her nape, warm and rough, he kissed her. "Done deal," he said. "No take-backs."

It felt as if his scent were caught in the threads of her clothing, embedded in her skin. Payal hugged it close, a dragon with its gold. She'd forever associate Canto's scent with being held with care, with being claimed by a man who saw no flaws in her.

They said nothing further until they were inside his tech center, a room without windows that had been set up with multiple comm screens and other computronic equipment. "I need to make the call within the next three minutes." She bent to check her hair and makeup in a comm screen clear enough to function as a mirror.

The next two minutes were taken up with the technical. Canto's tech room was set up to his specifications, but together, he and Payal were able to jerry-rig a comm screen to accommodate her preference for taking comm meetings standing up. "The posture helps me contain my natural tendency to fidget," she admitted.

Tenderness bloomed inside him. He wondered when she'd realize she'd long conquered any such inclination, but today wasn't the day to bring it up; if the stance was what it took for her to feel comfortable in this situation, so be it.

Switching to hover mode once the comm screen was ready, he dragged across a chair that he kept in the room for when Arwen dropped by. "Just in case the conduit drain goes haywire again."

"Yes, good idea."

That sorted, he shifted out of view and watched Payal—*his* Payal—go to work.

The faces of the Ruling Coalition appeared on the screen one by one. Kaleb Krychek, Aden Kai, Ivy Jane Zen, Nikita Duncan, and Anthony Kyriakus. Each chosen for their personal power or for who and what they represented—power of another kind. Because with Psy, power mattered. Their race could never have democracy as espoused by humans—what was the point of being an elected head if a man like Krychek could do as he pleased, with no one able to stop him?

Psy were more akin to changelings in that sense.

He listened as Payal laid out the problem with Sentinel, her words succinct and her tone cool. No longer was she the soft, curvy woman who'd sat in his lap. This was the CEO, the anchor, the general.

"I didn't realize the situation with Designation A was so dire." Nikita Duncan's face was a seamless canvas that gave away nothing. "Santano was the one in charge of that portfolio, and after his death, we all but forgot about it." Not an excuse, just a statement of fact.

"The problem didn't begin with your generation," Payal said. "It began much earlier, but regardless, we're stuck with the consequences."

"Is it still happening?" Ivy Jane's unusual eyes—clear copper ringed by gold, her pupils jet black—were stark against the cream hue of her skin. "Young anchors not making it to adulthood because they're considered flawed?"

"Unknown. We don't have the data and no one is collecting it. That's something that needs to be put in place, but right this instant, our first problem is the issue in my region."

"The repair is fluctuating." Aden Kai, all square angles, olive skin, and short black hair, was as expressionless as Ivy Jane was distressed. "Payal's right to assume it won't last much beyond two weeks. A month might be possible, but it'd probably burn out all the anchors involved."

"Confirmed," Payal said when Aden shot her a questioning look.

Kaleb spoke for the first time, a living green wall at his back that offered no clues as to his physical location. "Suggestions?"

The result of the discussion was confirmation that there weren't *any* free anchors who could take over the area. Canto had already come to the same conclusion, but it was important for the Coalition to reach that conclusion on their own, be confronted by the brutal reality of the problem.

"We may have another option," Anthony Kyriakus said, his dark hair silvered at the temples and his body clad in a tailored black jacket with a rounded collar that was buttoned up on both sides of his chest with polished black buttons. The head of PsyClan NightStar was a man of dignified appearance and bearing.

At this moment, he had everyone's attention. "One of my foreseers has twice this week reported visions of what she termed 'a great migration of stars.' She could make no sense of it at the time, but if we look at it in the context of shifting minds out of a dangerous PsyNet zone, it fits."

NightStar foreseers were the best in the world. And if Anthony was mentioning it, the vision had to have been seen by one of their senior F-Psy, possibly even Faith NightStar, the jewel in the NightStar crown.

"Is a move viable from an anchor perspective?" Nikita, pragmatic and ruthless. "The same number of As handling a significantly larger number of minds?"

"Yes." Payal held her own with one of the deadliest women in the Net. "Our zones are limited by geography, not by the number of minds."

Because anchors, Canto thought, worked for the PsyNet. That was the critical difference between them and empaths. The Honeycomb helped protect the PsyNet, but the basis of the empaths' work was to protect and provide succor to the people within it.

An anchor's first priority, by contrast, was to the Net.

That was why the loss of the NetMind and DarkMind had hurt Designation A so much. Every anchor in the world had been connected to the twin neosentiences in some way, even psychopathic Santano Enrique. The twins had sickened as *they* sickened. Or perhaps it was the other way around.

That As and the Net were entwined was beyond question.

"We still have the problem of logistics," Nikita pointed out. "Such a large psychic migration has never before been attempted. Most Psy won't even know how to sever their PsyNet link, then reconnect."

Canto acknowledged the point. The biofeedback link was necessary for life. Unless the Psy in question had another psychic network in which to link, to cut it was to die, so what was the point of learning?

Still, there was something . . .

"Panic will kill the majority." Ivy Jane rubbed her face, the purplish shadows under her eyes a silent statement of the strain on Designation E.

Canto's brain worked, his mind finally unearthing the piece of random information he'd stored away at some point in his teens. *It's been done before*, he telepathed Payal. *Hundreds of years ago. No detailed information available in any of my databases, but it was precipitated by an accident that took out twenty anchors at once.*

Payal kept her eyes on the screen as she replied. *Why were the twenty anchors together? Anchors are never physically together in such a big number.*

From what I was able to dig up at the time, they were having a regional meeting. Perhaps that was where he'd gotten the kernel of his idea of an association to represent anchors, and it had grown to fullness in the back of his mind. *A violent and unforeseen volcanic eruption destroyed the city in which they were staying, burying them before anyone could get help. No teleporters in the group.*

Payal's response was thoughtful. *That could explain the strong prohibition against anchors gathering in one place. Because too many of us died once. A prohibition passed on through time with the explanation lost.*

Sounds right. Canto's head spun with the implications—past and present—but for now, he dug through his files for further information. *The Catari Incident. That's how the migration was listed in the records I found, but it says in my notes that those records were in human-authored history books. I couldn't find any Psy corroboration.*

I am shocked. Our race, after all, does not have a tendency to hide things. Payal followed up her acerbic telepathic statement by interrupting the discussion onscreen. "The Catari Incident. What do you know of it?"

Blank faces.

She shared the few facts they had, then said, "If it happened, the records must exist in some dusty archive—I see no reason why any Psy Council would've prioritized destroying it. The problem will be in finding that information with the NetMind no longer capable of offering assistance."

"Did the NetMind talk to anchors?" Krychek asked, and as always, Canto was struck by how the man had managed to fly under the radar for years when power fairly pulsed off him. Kaleb Krychek's will had to be a thing of vicious strength.

"We had a connection that meant such communication was unnecessary," Payal explained, though no one but an anchor could understand the depth of that link. "The NetMind existed as part of the PsyNet, as do we. We knew and understood one another." She glanced at her timepiece. "The clock is counting down. What are our chances of tracking down the relevant information?"

"There's an old historical archive that we always ignored while I was on the Council." Nikita Duncan's eyes were acute with intelligence, and it was only when those eyes went to the left for a split second—and Anthony Kyriakus's went right at the same instant—that Canto zeroed in on their physical backgrounds.

Nikita was at her desk, a night-cloaked San Francisco glittering with lights beyond the large plate glass window to her back. Anthony, meanwhile, had nothing but a blank wall behind him. But Canto was nearly one hundred percent sure they were in the same room. He couldn't figure out what that might mean—could be nothing, the two might have been in a meeting before this one—or it could be confirmation of a rumor he'd picked up.

That Nikita and Anthony had a relationship beyond the political.

His hand tightened on the arm of his chair. He wanted that rumor to be true. Not so he could use it in some way, but because it would mean he and Payal had a chance. Neither former Councilor, after all, had ever betrayed emotion . . . except in how they'd protected their children.

As Payal protected Karishma.

Nikita's next statement snapped him back to the moment. "The archive was full of ancient data that we believed had no relevance to today. But it was also too large to erase without indexing it to check that it didn't hold anything important—the task kept getting put on the back burner. If the information is anywhere, it's there."

"I'll help you search," Payal said, and when Nikita raised an eyebrow, added, "I am now a part of the Ruling Coalition. Accept it and cooperate, or die, because without us, the PsyNet will collapse."

"An arrogant stance."

"No, only the truth."

"Payal is right." Anthony Kyriakus's voice. "Whatever the reason anchors were omitted from our leadership structure, that reason can no longer stand. Not now, in the face of total PsyNet failure."

"Welcome to the Ruling Coalition." Ivy Jane's smile was genuine. "Let's go hunt in this archive."

"Not yet." Krychek's shoulders moved slightly, as if he'd slid his hands into his pockets. "Not if it's the database I'm thinking of— Sigma18, Nikita?"

"Yes, that's the one."

"It's been shuttered," Kaleb told them. "Automatic security precaution during mothballing. It'll take time to track down the codes and open it up in line with a step-by-step reactivation protocol. Otherwise, with a database this old—and given the archaic process most likely used to shutter it—there's a distinct risk of fading."

Shit, he's right, Canto telepathed to Payal. *Old PsyNet databases that aren't regularly maintained can lose coherence.*

"Will you undertake the task of reopening the database?" Payal asked Krychek. "It's critical."

"I'll make it my priority. How long it takes will depend on if we have any Net failures or Scarab incursions in the interim."

"It makes more sense for me to take on the task," Nikita inserted. "It doesn't require major power, just subtlety. I have that."

Since Nikita Duncan was said to possess the power to infect minds with mental viruses, Canto had no doubt of her ability to do delicate psychic work. She wasn't a woman he'd ever trust, but she also had a lot to lose should the PsyNet collapse—her empire had diversified of late, but it was still heavily Psy-based.

"As long as it's done." Payal's words came out cool, almost autocratic.

"You'd do well to remember that we don't work for you," Nikita said, icicles dripping off each syllable.

"Right this moment, you do." Payal's tone was blunt. "After it's done, I'll work for you—as all anchors do on a daily basis. I reiterate again that we have no wish to be involved in politics for politics' sake. Our only priority is the PsyNet and how to save it."

To Canto's surprise, Nikita reacted well to the plain speaking. "A fair exchange," she said, then went silent while everyone talked over the plan. But once they'd begun to sign off, Nikita lingered until she was the only one onscreen.

"A problem?" Payal asked.

"No. I have a J-Psy in my organization. Sophia Russo."

She's an anchor, Canto told Payal. *A very interesting one. We need to talk to her.* Making contact with Sophia had been on his to-do list, but then had come the Delhi fracture and he'd had to shove it aside.

"We know of her," Payal said with smooth fluidity. "In point of fact, we wish to make contact."

"I thought as much. I'll give Sophia your contact information and tell her to touch base."

"Thank you." Payal held Nikita's eyes. "Why did you not eliminate your child when you became aware she was a cardinal empath?"

Canto didn't know which one of them was more surprised at the question—him or Nikita.

Chapter 33

I would do it all again. To save my child, I would bathe in blood a
thousand times over. I have no morality where her life is concerned.

—Nikita Duncan to Anthony Kyriakus

"THAT IS NONE of your concern." The ice was back, frigid enough to
burn.

"It is," Payal insisted. "Anchor infants are dying before they initialize. We need to know how to stop it, how to make their parents bond
to them enough to keep them alive—because there is no way to identify child As before initialization."

Nikita shifted in her chair, the sleek strands of her hair falling back
in perfect alignment after the movement. "I can't help you," she said,
but it didn't sound like a rejection.

That, Canto thought, was about all the answer they'd get from
Nikita.

Again, she surprised him.

"But," the former Councilor added, "our race has been about power
for a long time—long before Silence. You need to leverage your power
as Designation A. Telekinetics are currently considered one of the

most useful designations in the Net and are of considerable value and offer prestige to the families who produce them. But Tks are worthless should the Net collapse."

Nikita's image blinked out.

Payal glanced at Canto. "Did I misunderstand, or did Nikita just tell us that our problem is public relations?"

"You didn't misunderstand." Canto rubbed his jaw, his stubble rasping under his fingertips. "It's brilliant, you know. The reason no one watches for anchor children is because we're just there, doing our work in the background. I think it's time we step out of the shadows."

"I just met with the Ruling Coalition."

"But who knows about that?" He tapped the arm of his chair. "Are you up for an interview with the *PsyNet Beacon?*"

"Me? The robot?" Payal folded her arms and spread her legs apart. "You do it."

He adored her. And he was not a man to use that kind of word. But he did. Adore her. "You're our gladiator, my beautiful, intelligent, fascinating Payal. Also, wouldn't you like to rub Gia Khan's face in your rise to power?"

Her eyes narrowed. "I don't feel such petty emotions . . . but set up the interview."

Canto crossed the floor to grip her hips. "You dazzle me."

A sudden hesitancy to her. "What if it doesn't work?" Soft words. "What if the only way I can stay functional is to keep up the iron walls?" Her fingers lingering delicately against his jaw, as if he'd break if she pushed too hard. "I let them fall today with you, and I feel stable enough, but what if it's a false hope?"

"It doesn't matter. We've had this conversation—no matter what, no matter how, we *stick.*"

"7J and 3K?" she whispered.

"Always. *Always.*" Sometimes it wasn't a childhood thing; sometimes you found your person early. She was his person and always would be.

"I don't want to go back to Vara." It came out naked, her face devoid of protective shields. "The repair is holding for now. It might be the only window of stability we have for some time."

"Can you stay?" She was the CEO of a major family. More, she was being watched by unfriendly eyes. "The medication?" he asked, biting back his rage at the ugly drug leash her father had put on her.

"I need a dose of the meds—that's the biggest hurdle." Payal chewed her lower lip. "I can do a lot of work remotely." A small nod. "I'll tell Lalit and Father that I've been inducted into the Ruling Coalition and asked to remain close to Krychek so I can shadow him and learn my new duties."

"Payal, you don't have to hide me from them." It came out hard, a near-snarl.

"Yes, I do." A solemn statement that cut him to the bone. "Because you're my person. The only one I have. I need to protect you."

Canto chafed against restrictions, protections, but when she put it that way . . . when she looked at him with such raw vulnerability . . . Fucked. He was fucked. He'd give her anything she wanted. He couldn't, however, stop himself from muttering, "I'd prefer to just shoot your father and brother, but yeah, that should work. Chances they have a spy in Krychek's base?"

"Nil. His HQ is airtight—Kaleb is a man who inspires loyalty."

"I'll ask him to cover for you."

He squeezed her hips when she parted her lips to reply. "It won't be an official request like you'd make, it'll be one among friends." Krychek and Mercant were now entwined. "It's the less complicated way."

Payal frowned. "No, let me ask. In an unofficial way."

The way she said it had Canto holding his words. He watched as her gaze went distant, as if she was telepathing. She was back within seconds. "He's agreed," she murmured. "He also said he'd answer any other questions I want to ask him."

A stab of quite ridiculous jealousy had Canto scowling. "Why are you asking him questions?"

"Because he's like me." A whisper as her body jerked a little toward Canto. "And he has the life I want."

Love smashed through every bone in his body, a love so pure and so visceral that it devastated pride and jealousy and anything but the desire to give her what she needed. "Come here, baby."

She all but melted into him, curling into his lap with her head against his shoulder and one hand on his chest. He wrapped her up, holding her close, this woman who was powerful and complicated and had been deprived of tenderness all her life.

Canto knew zilch about tenderness, but he was a quick study. He'd watched how the bears treated their mates, seen how Arwen was with his bear. And the thing was, it came naturally with Payal. He wanted to hold her, wanted to kiss her stupid, wanted to keep her warm and safe in his arms.

PAYAL could still feel Canto wrapped around her as she stood in front of the comm screen later that afternoon, ready to make the call to her father. Canto himself was upstairs, but she knew he'd be with her in a heartbeat should she need him, their minds entwined.

The broken girl inside her had learned that it wasn't only okay to lean on him, such things were unremarkable between the two of them. The watchful, robotic part of her had come to the same conclusion: there was no ledger between 3K and 7J. Canto Mercant would give Payal Rao whatever she needed and vice versa.

Because they were each other's person.

"Payal," her father said coldly when his aristocratic face appeared onscreen. "What's the meaning of this disappearing act?"

Her head was heavy, the pain a constant now, but she allowed none of that to show on her face. "I have been inducted into the Ruling Coalition. I wasn't permitted to speak about the possibility until it was final."

Pranath Rao was a man who'd long perfected an expressionless— if cold—countenance, but even he blinked in surprise, his posture suddenly straighter. "I've heard nothing of this."

"The official press release will be going out within the next hour." Ivy Jane had sent her a message alerting her to that fact. "I was permitted that time to advise my family unit."

"I must admit you've caught me unprepared," Pranath confessed. "Why did they approach you? Gia Khan has always been the front-runner in our region when it comes to politics."

"I'm a hub-anchor, Father. A powerful one who is currently holding Delhi together." This wasn't the time to be modest about her abilities; her father reacted to power and she'd use that weakness against him. "The Coalition wants an anchor presence, and they need an A who is both stable and able to understand business. As for the approach, I made it on behalf of Designation A."

Before Pranath could interrupt, she continued, "Given my sudden elevation to Coalition-member status, I've been asked to stay in Moscow and liaise with Kaleb Krychek for approximately two weeks, to ensure that I know my duties and can access all necessary databases." It was the longest she could be physically away from her anchor zone.

Avarice fairly pulsed off her father. "Payal, I could've never predicted this, and I'm certain I won't believe it until I see the release, but well done, daughter."

She inclined her head. "I can deal with family business matters remotely, but I don't also need to be dealing with Lalit. At present, he's attempting to break into my personal quarters." An angry Canto had just passed her that information.

Her father nodded. "I'll pull him into line—and I'll put aside two vials of your medication for you to pick up."

"I'd appreciate it if you could courier it to my secure Coalition box in Moscow." A service that had been put automatically in place once she was accepted into the group and had stated her aim of staying in Moscow for the time being. "I need to maintain my energy levels to deal with Krychek."

"Agreed."

"Father, courtesy of the recent fractures in the Net in our area, I'll need a dose within the next two hours. Can you have a teleport courier make the delivery by then?"

"I'll organize it now." A ten-second pause in his feed. When he reappeared, he said, "It'll be there within the next five minutes." His eyes bore into her. "Remember your family, Payal. You wouldn't have been chosen for this position if you weren't the Rao CEO. *I* put you there."

No, Payal had put herself there, after outperforming Lalit in every way. "Of course, Father. I won't be able to report in regularly, due to my heavy schedule, but I'll give you a full debrief when I can return home."

"Understood." Pranath Rao was nothing if not practical when it came to matters of power. "Do you need us to teleport across your clothing and personal items?"

"There's no need." And no reason for Pranath's people to enter her apartment. "I'll make local purchases. A small way to get my face and name out among Psy businesses once the news hits the public channels."

"You've always been a clever child." Pranath smiled that cold, false smile. "Do the family proud, Payal."

After signing off, Payal glanced at her timepiece. *Hmm . . .*

Exiting the tech room, she went to head upstairs but heard a sound to the left and went that way instead. She found Canto stripped to the waist, his lower body clad only in black exercise shorts. His upper body gleamed with sweat, but he was currently exercising his legs using robotic braces that had him gritting his teeth as he lifted his legs up and down.

The brace was a webwork carapace of gleaming black that went over his legs, up his arms, and partially along his spine. Payal knew the devices were designed to function even on a fully passive patient, but it appeared Canto had set it so he had to use his ab and arm muscles to power the device.

That took brutal strength—his legs would've become dead weights multiplied by the weight force he'd programmed on the device the instant he turned off the robotic lift assist. From the lights along one side of his thigh, she could see that he'd left on the muscle-stimulation function that kept his muscles from atrophying.

But it was the teeth-gritted grimace on his face that held her attention. "This is not comfortable for you."

He grunted, clearly unsurprised by her presence. "Fucking thing feels like biting ants across my spine." He lifted up again, his shoulder muscles defined as he curled up his arms to lift his legs as the brace pulsed his leg muscles to keep them strong and active. "But it's the best way to keep my legs from turning into twigs."

Perspiration gleamed on his skin. His hair was damp at the temples, the scent of him a mix of fresh sweat and Canto. The primal nature of the scene spoke to the wild part of her she'd so long locked away.

Walking closer, she waited until he'd lowered his legs.

Then she leaned down and pressed a kiss to an exposed section of his shoulder. He groaned as the taste of salt and him entered her mouth. "That is doing nothing for my concentration, 3K."

3K.

What had once been a dehumanizing label now felt like a kiss. "You look like you've worked hard enough."

A glance up. "I need to do ten more minutes. Stay?"

Payal ran her hand through his hair, feeling a sense of ownership that was as primal as how he looked right now. Then she moved to take a seat on an exercise machine across from the one he was using. It had weights; Canto probably used it for his upper body. Which she admired openly while he finished up his routine.

"Baby," he said five minutes later, "you can't keep looking at me like that." A harsh order, but there was nothing angry about it. "My damn erection is like a steel pole right now."

Baby.

A term of affection when used as he used it with her. For Payal Rao, the robot. "Can I touch it after you're done?"

He dropped his legs so fast the machine screamed an alarm. He slammed it off with his palm. "Yeah," he rasped. "You can touch anything on me you want. Full, no-holds-barred skin privileges."

She'd heard that term from one of the Delhi tigers at some point during negotiations, when they'd spoken about handshakes. This, however, was nothing so mundane. "You had five minutes to go." Her skin was hot, her pulse a rocket. "I didn't mean to interrupt."

His eyes glittered. "I'll do another session later. Come 'ere."

CANTO'S mind blanked as Payal walked to him. As he watched, she kicked off her heels, her feet soundless on the special matting of the gym.

He went to tell her to wait while he removed the robotic brace, so she could sit on his lap, but she hitched up her fitted dress to straddle one side of the bench seat on which he sat. "Hell." Those legs, the creamy brown of her upper thighs . . .

He wanted to goddamn bite into her.

But Payal had other priorities, her eyes on the jut of his erection. His chest heaved.

And she wrapped her fingers around his rigid length, over the top of the thin fabric of his shorts. He bit back a shout, the tendons on his neck feeling like they'd burst out of his skin.

"It's so hot and hard."

Canto's brain blazed a dangerous red. Shifting his hand to her wrist, he squeezed. "I think we should stop."

She released him at once but didn't tug her wrist free. "You didn't like it?"

"Hell yes, I liked it." So much that it hurt. "But I don't want to lose control."

Terrible darkness eclipsed the stars in her eyes.

Chapter 34

The child displays significant ongoing trauma.

—Therapeutic notes on Canto Mercant (age 14)

REALIZING WHAT HE'D said, Canto let go of Payal's hand before he squeezed it too hard. "Shit. *Shit.*" Leaning forward with his elbows on his thighs, he shoved his hands through his hair. "I'm sorry. I'm screwing this up."

He'd spent all this time trying to teach her that she could trust him with everything, and here he was, stumbling at the first step. "It's not about trust, Payal. I—"

A gentle hand on his shoulder, stroking slowly down his back. "I understand." Soft words that held no anger or confusion. "It's why I have such rigid shields. Control." Leaning in, she pressed a kiss to the side of his neck. "We had it stolen from us, and now we can't let go."

Had anyone else said they understood, he would've ignored them. But this was Payal. His 3K. Dropping his hands to his thighs, he looked at her . . . and spoke about a part of his life that he spoke of to no one else. "I was all but immobile in a hospital bed for months."

He released a shuddering exhale. "My grandmother did every-thing in her power to give me freedom—she took me on long flights through the PsyNet, had a family teleporter move my hospital bed to different locations to give me variety. Once, my uncle teleported me out to this lonely stretch of beach and it was incredible."

"But it wasn't the same as controlling your own body," Payal said, sliding her hand down to tangle it with his.

"Yeah." He coughed, swallowed. "Grandmother made me attend a ton of psych sessions to help me make sense of the world—and to prepare me for a possible future where I might *always* be only my mind—but the experience left a scar." His jaw worked. "I keep telling myself I'm so fucking lucky. Not many children have someone like Ena come for them, rescue them, but—" He shook his head. "I can't forget all that went before."

Payal touched her hand to part of his robotic brace. "Let's look at this logically."

It was a response he hadn't expected—and it was so very Payal. "Yeah?" He wove his fingers through hers, squeezed.

"You're no longer a child without agency. Neither are you injured as you were when your grandmother first found you. You could walk using a brace if you wished. It would be irritating, but you certainly wouldn't be confined to bed." Another kiss, this one to his jaw. "You also have me. I would take you anywhere you wanted to go."

Canto didn't rely on anyone, had spent nearly thirty years making sure of that. But this was 3K, who curled into his lap because she needed the contact, and who reached for their strange bond every few minutes. He didn't know if she was aware of doing it, but he was; he felt every light brush.

As if she was checking it was still there and taking strength from it.

Lifting their clasped hands, he pressed a kiss to her knuckles in a silent acceptance of her offer. "If the worst ever happens, I'm one hun-dred percent still going to be an ass about it at times."

Payal imitated his shrug. "I'm still going to be a total robot some-times, when I get scared and retreat behind my walls."

"Guess we're both screwed up." He shifted so he could cup the side of her face with his free hand. Part of the brace spiderwebbed the back and a fine mesh overlay his palm, but she turned into the touch.

"Perfection is overrated." Inside him, it was as if she'd wrapped him in her cold flame, a possessive embrace that would shield him from the world. "I heard Sascha Duncan say that in an interview once. She also said that flaws are what make us unique. That perfect people would just be simulacrums of each other."

Payal hadn't believed the cardinal empath at the time—all her life, she'd been told she was a mistake, an error. But with Canto, she understood at last. Neither one of them would be who they were if they'd been born "perfect" by the standards of a Silent society. Their scars had shaped them.

And Canto, brash and stubborn, had far deeper scars than she'd realized.

He was so tough and emotionally stable that she hadn't understood the extent to which his childhood haunted him. Today, she saw the ghosts in his eyes, saw the echoes of the boy who'd lost the use of his legs and almost lost control over his whole body, the boy who'd been unable to defend himself—*or her*—against a monster.

The latter would matter to a man like Canto. He was a protector. Yet he'd failed her. That was how he'd see it, her Mercant knight.

Payal understood something about herself at that moment: she'd built her life on control, but for Canto, she could be "weaker," more exposed. Between the two of them, he needed that rock of control more than she did . . . because her rock was Canto. Kaleb had been right. That bond she could sense but couldn't see? It had given her a safe harbor to cling to when the screams got too bad.

"Would you like to touch me as I touched you?" she asked. She'd lay herself bare to him without hesitation if that was what he needed.

Canto's hand tightened on hers. "Hell yeah, but I think we might be going too fast." A narrow-eyed look. "Have you talked to an empath? We don't know how us getting physical will affect you."

Payal tried to wrench back her hand, but he held on.

"Hey," he whispered roughly. "I want you with every fiber of my being, but I will *never* hurt you." A fierce vow. "This could hurt you if we don't do it right."

Payal wanted to argue with him, wanted to ignore the panicky feeling that lived in the back of her head and that she could only assuage by touching their bond. "Kaleb said you could be my safe place to stand."

"Always. Fucking *always*," Canto answered. "But Kaleb isn't you. He and his mate aren't us. We're anchors, baby, and that changes everything."

She knew he was right, but she couldn't deal with it yet, couldn't face it. Because facing it meant facing the broken, devastated, screaming girl inside her. "I need clothes and personal items. I've said I'll visit the shops."

Canto looked at her for a long moment before nodding. "I'll drive you. If I stay in the vehicle, no one will pay attention to your driver."

Confused and unsettled, she pulled at her hand again. "Don't you want to be seen with me?" she demanded utterly irrationally.

"3K, I want to tattoo your name on my damn forehead so everyone will know I'm yours and you're mine"—a hard kiss, his hand cradling her nape with roughly tender possessiveness—"but this is your time to shine."

FOR IMMEDIATE RELEASE
NEW MEMBER OF RULING COALITION: PAYAL RAO, SPEAKER FOR THE ANCHOR
REPRESENTATIVE ASSOCIATION (ARA)

The members of the Ruling Coalition are pleased to welcome Payal Rao, Cardinal A-Tk and CEO of the Rao Conglomerate, to their ranks. Payal is the chosen Speaker of the Anchor Representative Association and has full power to deal on their behalf.

Having a member of the critical A designation on the Ruling Coalition is an important step as we face the turbulence in the PsyNet. We will need to rely on anchors more than ever—it's vital that their voices be heard. They must be represented at all levels of the decision-making process, including at the very highest.

Interview requests with Payal Rao can be sent through the Ruling Coalition's media liaison, Jin Verkamp-Jeong.

END OF RELEASE

Chapter 35

Canto, you and Payal are invited to after-dinner tea. I shall see you at seven this evening.

—Message from Ena Mercant to Canto Mercant

CANTO SAT IN the sleek car the color of darkest smoke that had been designed according to his preferences, complete with hand and voice controls, doors that went straight up in a smooth glide, and a driver's-seat area with an automatic ramp and a convertible seat that meant he didn't have to store his chair while driving unless he felt like it.

Payal had just stepped out of the passenger door, beautiful and contained, and already, he could see passersby taking surreptitious photographs that they'd no doubt feed out into the PsyNet—and into the human/changeling media. The makeup of the Ruling Coalition was of interest to a lot of people, and Payal's ascension especially so; to the vast majority of the world, she'd come out of nowhere.

As he'd predicted, no one paid any attention to her driver—not that they could see him. He'd opaqued all the glass after he parked. He could see out, but they couldn't see in.

As he sat there, he thought about contacting Arwen, then immediately vetoed the idea. Payal needed to decide to see an empath on her own, without pressure. It was obvious she wasn't yet ready, but she was tough, his 3K. She'd get there.

Then, as if he'd imagined his cousin up out of thin air, he saw Arwen on the sidewalk, accompanied by his bear. Arwen was in a pristine gray-on-gray suit he'd paired with a charcoal tie, his shoes polished and every strand of hair in place. His lover, in contrast, had tumbled hair of dark brown and was wearing a rough navy shirt with the tails hanging out and torn jeans.

Pavel's sneakers had seen better days.

But the way he looked at Arwen out of those bright green-blue eyes behind clear spectacles . . . Yes, the bears knew how to treat their people.

Arwen had never appeared so happy, so at peace.

Canto liked Pavel for how he treated Arwen.

Ena loved him for it.

Silver had been known to kiss him.

Now Arwen's eyes swiveled toward Canto without warning. Even though his cousin had been out of Canto's shields for a long time, they still had a strong connection. Of all the people toward whom Canto felt protective, Payal and Arwen were at the top of the list.

His cousin smiled and made an immediate beeline toward him.

Lowering his window, Canto scowled. "I'm trying to be incognito. Go away."

Instead, Arwen laughed and went around to get in the passenger seat, closing the door behind him, then lowering his own window. Pavel put his head in that window and said, "This car smells like a woman." He sniffed ostentatiously. "*Definitely* a woman. A certain specific cardinal-eyed woman."

Arwen's eyes widened at the same instant. "*Canto*, you're linked to her." He pretended to punch Canto. "You couldn't have told me?" The light comment nonetheless held a smidgen of hurt.

And because this was his baby brother for all intents and purposes, Canto said, "It's new. No one else knows. Not even Grandmother." Though Ena's all-seeing antenna was working just fine, if the invite that had appeared on his phone an hour earlier was any indication.

Arwen's gaze softened at once. "It's different, too." He frowned, gaze turning inward. "I can't see a bond like I could with Silver and Valentin when they mated."

We're anchors. That changes everything.

His own words reverberated inside his head. "It might be in the Substrate," he murmured, because he hadn't looked there—and it made sense that for two anchors, the bond would show on their home ground.

"So?" Pavel waggled his eyebrows. "Where is she?"

Arwen kissed Pavel on the cheek. "What he said."

"In the boutique." Canto nodded toward the store.

Arwen grinned. "I'm going to go spy on her fashion choices." He got out of the car on that cheerful declaration.

Pavel and Canto both watched Arwen walk into the boutique, a sharply dressed and handsome man who drew eyes from all kinds of people. Canto felt no need to warn Payal. Arwen was a kitten in comparison to her shark.

"How is he?" he said quietly, because he and Pavel had an unspoken understanding about Arwen—the bear knew that Canto had watched over Arwen for a long time, couldn't just stop.

"Good. Better than good." His smile was delighted as he slipped into Arwen's abandoned seat. "He's still tight with his empath buds Jaya and Ruslan—I've met them, like how they are with him. I also nudged him to go on playdates with some local empaths who have no idea he's a Mercant. He clicked with a few—his circle's growing."

"Good. We worry about him becoming isolated." Arwen had been so fiercely protected by the Mercant family that even Ena had begun to wonder if they'd clipped his wings.

"No, Arwen just likes to take his time with people." Pavel lifted his shirt away from his body, as if he were fixing the lapels of a suit. "Because he picks the best people."

Arwen exited the boutique soon afterward, to come over and get into the back seat.

"I want to meet her," he said, open protectiveness in his voice. "Just to be sure she's not taking advantage of you."

Pavel doubled over laughing. When Arwen poked him in the side, the bear said, "It's like a butterfly trying to protect a Rottweiler. Adorable."

That got him another poke.

Grabbing Arwen's hand, Pavel threatened to bite it.

Canto groaned as Arwen went all blushing and happy. "*Out,*" he muttered.

Of course they didn't listen to him. Instead, Pavel clambered into the back with Arwen. Sighing, Canto reached out to Payal with his mind. *My cousin Arwen and his disreputable bear beloved—who you've already met—are in the car, waiting to see you. I'll get rid of them if you want.*

The response came after a few seconds. *I would be happy to talk to them. I'll be there in about ten more minutes.*

Arwen told Canto about his new friends as the three of them waited, while Pavel checked his phone for work purposes. He was StoneWater's tech specialist, and he and Canto had taught each other a few things.

Then there she was, walking out of the shop with a bag in hand, sunglasses covering her eyes. The cameras clicked again as she walked to get into the car. He pulled away as soon as she was safely inside, making the introductions as they drove.

PAYAL had barely recovered from the shock of Ena Mercant's invitation. Now this.

She hadn't expected to speak to any of Canto's family anytime soon, but she wasn't going to run from such contacts. These people were important to him—so even if they didn't like her, even if Ena's invitation turned out to be a slap of rejection, she would persevere. She'd spent a lifetime surviving people who didn't like or respect her. But now she had Canto. For him, she'd bear anything.

Angling her head to look at the man in the back seat who had a very different build from Canto—and silver eyes watchful and quiet—she said, "I'm glad to meet you, Arwen."

She used the mirror to meet the gaze of the bear who sat directly behind her. "It's nice to see you again, Pavel."

The bear smiled at her, but Arwen had an assessing look on his face when she glanced at him once more. He only said a few words as Canto drove them out of the city. She'd already stopped at three boutiques and had everything she needed—especially for her tea with Ena in a few short hours.

Once they were at the house and had carried her purchases inside, Canto left to deal with a minor work matter, while Pavel excused himself to return a call.

It left Payal and Arwen alone on the deck.

They stood side by side in awkward silence until Arwen blurted out, "Sorry."

Payal looked at him to see a blush painting the razor-sharp lines of his cheekbones. "For what?"

"For acting like a jealous kid." His hands tightened on the deck railing. "Canto was mine for a long time. He protected me inside his shields when I was born—I don't know how it happened, but we were in the hospital at the same time, and it just did."

This was the empath Canto had mentioned, Payal realized. Not just a trusted empath. *A beloved Mercant.* "I don't intend to take him from you." Canto's family was part of his foundations, part of his heartbeat.

"I know. I was being stupid." He gave her a hesitant smile that was so open it sliced right through her shields. "Can we start again?" He held out a hand. "I'm Arwen, and I adore Canto. He's the best big brother I could've ever had."

Physical contact wasn't an easy thing for her, but this was important enough that she slipped her hand into Arwen's. "Payal. Canto is . . . extraordinary." She didn't know why, but she added a private truth. "We met as children before you were born."

Arwen's eyes flared. "You're *her*. The girl he's been searching for all this time."

A tight hotness inside her chest. "I thought he'd forget me, but he never did."

"Canto never forgets the people he loves."

That last word made her entire soul quake. She clung to the railing to keep her stability. "Arwen, if I talk to you as an empath, will you keep my confidence?" Now that she'd met him, now that they'd come to terms, she felt his gentleness, his kindness.

"Yes," Arwen said. "But I have a conflict of interest because of my relationship with Canto. Can I recommend a friend?" When Payal nodded, he said, "Her name is Jaya and she's a senior empath. She usually works with patients in comas or who are otherwise trapped in their bodies and minds, but she's also just . . . wise. As if she was born that way. I talk to her, too, about everything."

Payal had just taken Jaya's details when Canto returned, and the heart of her, it arrowed in toward him. As if he were her star, and she the circling planet. She wanted to pull back, step away, protect herself, but it was too late. Her walls were cracked and damaged so badly that there was no hope.

Chapter 36

You are one of mine. I will allow nothing and no one to cause
you harm. Ever.

—Ena Mercant to Canto Mercant (September 2053)

ENA HAD SPENT a lifetime watching out for her family. She'd been
taught to do it by her grandmother, who'd been taught by her mother.
Theirs was a matriarchal line—though when there were boys who
showed leadership qualities, they were never pushed aside. Ena's
great-grandmother had been taught her duties by her father.

Canto could've been the next male to lead the clan; for a long time,
Ena had believed he would be her successor. The angry boy she'd first
met had grown into a strong, stable youth who made her proud. He
was also intensely protective of the younger children in the clan—he'd
held Arwen inside his shields, and even now, he watched over Silver.

When it became clear that Silver was more suited to succeed her,
she'd wondered if Canto would resent her choice—they'd both understood that the boy had never been Silent, that his emotions could burn
flashfire hot. But Canto had supported her.

"I was hoping you'd see that," he'd said to her in his direct way.

"I'm not suited to stand where you stand, Grandmother. Silver has the patience and diplomacy to take the family into the future."

When that future came, when Silver stood in Ena's place, she knew Canto would be staunch in his support. Magdalene's boy knew how to back his people. Once given, his loyalty was a hard thing to break. Which was why Ena wanted to put her eyes on Payal Rao.

From her research on the woman—research Ena and Magdalene had done together, without involving anyone else in the clan—there was little to commend Payal as Canto's partner in life. Ena's grandson might have his rough edges, but the boy overflowed with emotion. He loved Ena even though Ena had been raised in Silence, had come to adulthood in Silence, and could never openly show him what he was to her.

Payal Rao was like Ena. Hard. Distant. Calculating.

Canto deserved so much more.

Not that Ena would get in his way—she'd known from their first meeting that this boy had inherited the Mercant will. He would not be manipulated, would not be molded. He would be who he chose to be. So she'd leave him be, but she would make sure Payal Rao understood that she wasn't a Mercant and never would be—and if that was her reason for playing off Canto's memories and worming her way into his life, she could just worm her way back out.

Ena would wait to pay her back for hurting Canto. She could be as patient as a spider waiting for prey—and she had no mercy in her for those who hurt the children of her family.

Today, she stared out at the manicured grounds of the small residence she kept in Moscow now that three of her grandchildren were based here. The evening sun gilded everything in sight. A lovely place, but she didn't truly need it; Valentin had assigned her a residence within the bear den, and all the small bears there toddled after her and called her "Babushka Ena."

She spent far more time in that residence than she'd believed she would; after a lifetime in Silence, she'd expected to be overwhelmed. She could never live in the den as Silver did, but she could tolerate it for days at a time. So if she had to sacrifice this residence once Payal Rao knew of it, so be it.

This was just a place to rest her head now and then. It wasn't her home. Only family and a rare few others were ever granted the privilege of visiting her clifftop residence. Payal Rao was unlikely to ever be one of those people.

Canto's vehicle turned in to her short drive.

As he knew all her entry codes, Ena took a seat in an elegant chair of gray velvet with curved legs on one side of a round table set with a tea service. An identical chair faced her, while she'd left ample space in between for Canto's chair.

"Grandmother." His voice preceded him into the room, his presence as big and stubbornly *him* as always.

"Canto." Ena didn't smile; she had been too long in this world in Silence. But her heart warmed at seeing him, this grandson of hers who argued with her the most of all.

He took the hand of the woman who stood at his side. "Payal, meet my grandmother. Grandmother, this is Payal."

Ena took in the other woman at a glance: a simple but well-tailored dress in burgundy, black heels, her hair in a neat ponytail, and her makeup subtle. The perfect Psy CEO. Not at all the kind of woman who was suited to Canto's wild heart.

"A pleasure," Ena said, because she hadn't been raised by feral wolves. "Please take a seat."

"Thank you for the invitation," Payal said as she sat. "I'm honored to meet the elder of Canto's family."

Pretty words, Ena thought, but what else would one expect from the daughter of Pranath Rao? The man was as slick as a snake, a cobra hiding in plain sight. "Of course," she said, and picked up the teapot. "I would be remiss not to greet the chosen partner of my grandchild."

"I can pour," Payal offered.

Ena allowed it, better to watch her as she did so. Canto, meanwhile, glanced at Ena, then Payal. Ena waited for a telepathic defense of Payal, but surprisingly, her grandson said nothing. Confident Payal didn't need it? Poor child. He was clearly blinded by the past in which a child Payal had saved his life.

But that had been a long time ago.

They spoke of polite things, of the Anchor Representative Association, and of Payal's rise to the Ruling Coalition. Canto also told her he'd seen Arwen and Pavel, and Ena updated him on another family member.

It was all terribly pleasant, the daggers hidden away.

Then Canto's body went rigid, his jaw working. Payal's attention whiplashed to him.

"Back spasm," he bit out, taking a short, sharp breath. "Side effect of surgery." His chest rose and fell, his skin stretched tight.

Ena wanted to wrap him up in cotton wool, protect him from the world, but she'd learned that for an impossibility long ago. Canto had demanded to be left alone to fight such battles.

In front of her, Payal moved her hand to place it over Canto's fisted one. He flipped his fist, wove his fingers through hers. Their hands locked. Then Payal turned back to Ena, and her expression, it was as closed as it had been when they began . . . but the pulse in her neck, it jumped.

Ena frowned inwardly.

"Payal, stop it." A harsh order from Canto.

Jaw set, Payal shook her head. "No." Clipped, hard, unmoving.

Ena had no idea what was going on, but Canto was glaring at Payal—who was now holding his gaze without flinching.

Ena felt a stirring of approval. She'd always known that Canto had a strong personality. The boy did like to get his own way—and he often succeeded, even with Ena. But it appeared Payal Rao was strong enough to stand against him—*and* not inclined to pander to him in an effort to get in his good graces. Hmm . . .

A bead of sweat formed on Payal's temple, and her pulse, it was even more jagged now.

"I swear—" Canto began, his words a growl.

That was when Payal's mask slipped . . . but not in the way Ena had expected. Eyes going inky black, she glared at Canto. "Would you stand by if I was in pain?" she demanded, her cheeks flushed. "Especially when you could do something about it?" She wrenched at her hand.

Canto refused to let go. "This is different."

Payal leaned toward him. "Why?"

"Because," Canto all but growled.

Payal took a deep breath and shifted the conversation to the telepathic plane. Ena could sense it in the energy that arced between them, in the emotions that pulsed off Canto . . . and were tightly, *tightly* contained in Payal.

She saw also that Canto wasn't in as much pain as he should be— she'd witnessed a spasm a couple of years ago, had seen how it made his tendons arch white against his skin, sweat pop out on his brow, while his eyes went blank as he turned all his energy into riding the agony.

Ena took another look at Payal.

She was sweating, her pulse still erratic, and her skin bloodless. *Well then.*

Ena was not a woman without prejudice, but she was also not a woman who held on to those prejudices when faced with uncomfortable truths. That Payal was assisting Canto in some way was clear, and for that alone, Ena would've been in charity with her. But what sealed the deal was when a fuming Payal reached over and brushed a strand of hair off Canto's forehead.

The two had forgotten Ena was in the room.

Payal Rao, cutthroat CEO, was so focused on Canto that she'd forgotten about the other predator in the room. Not only was she focused on Canto, she couldn't help caring for him even when so angry that steam was coming out of her ears.

Canto was furious, too—and he could be intimidating when angry. Which was why he made it a point to hold back most of the time. He wasn't holding back today, and Payal wasn't shrinking away in the least.

Making a rumbling sound in his throat, he lifted their clasped hands and kissed her knuckles. Only then did Payal startle and turn to Ena. Color a sudden hot flush on her face, she said, "My apologies. That was incredibly rude."

"No, it was rather interesting." Ena took a sip of her tea. "Feeling better, Canto dear?"

Her grandson gave her a narrow-eyed look, pain no longer a shadow on his beautiful features. He'd never worked that out, had Canto, just how beautiful he was as a man. Despite his paternity, he reminded Ena very strongly of her own father. He'd been a beautiful man, too. And a kind one.

Canto had inherited that core of kindness, too, albeit with a rougher edge.

"Spasm is over," he muttered, and grabbed a teacup, then made a face and put it back. "I'm going to make coffee." Then her bad-tempered grandson turned his chair around and headed out to her kitchen area.

Ena didn't cook, but the residence had come fully stocked.

"Tell me," Ena said to Payal. "Is he truly not in pain any longer?"

"Yes." Payal turned from where she'd been looking at the doorway through which Canto had left. "It's gone. He told me it happens very rarely. This is the first one in two years."

Ena nodded. "Yes. It has to do with the wiring in his spine—it builds up some type of tension. There's no safe way to release it."

"He says a minute or two of pain every two years is worth it," Payal said, not sounding like she agreed.

Of course she wouldn't. Because coldhearted Payal Rao cared for gruff, softhearted Canto Mercant. How did Ena's grandchildren keep doing this to her? Silver with an alpha bear. Arwen with another bear. Now this. "You saved his life as a child. For this, I thank you."

Payal met her eyes the same way she'd met Canto's—without flinching. "The teacher was hurting Canto. I stopped him. As you stopped Binh Fernandez."

Canto wheeled his chair back into the room right then, no coffee in hand. "It's percolating," he muttered, then raised an eyebrow at Ena. "You've never told me—why did Binh have to go when you already had a contractual way to take over guardianship?"

Ena considered her words, decided it was time. "My dear Canto, it wasn't me."

He frowned, parted his lips, closed his mouth. "An actual accident?"

"No," Payal murmured, her eyes on Ena, "it was your mother."

Ena inclined her head, as Canto sucked in a breath. "Magdalene?" Shaking his head, he said, "My mother is the least aggressive person in the family."

"She's also Ena Mercant's daughter," Payal said. "And Ena Mercant protects her own."

The child understood this family, Ena thought. Not only that, she thought like them. And she protected like them. Ena knew all about Karishma Rao, buried in a lovely boarding school that had strict laws of confidentiality. Enough to protect a girl who wouldn't rise to Pranath Rao's standards of perfection.

All of it paid for through one of Payal Rao's private accounts.

"Mother, huh." Canto rubbed his smooth-shaven jawline. "She never said."

"She didn't do it to buy a way out of your anger," Ena said. "She did it because Binh Fernandez hurt her child after promising to care for him. Magdalene does not forgive such slights."

What Ena didn't say was that giving up Canto had fractured something in Magdalene. That was why she'd never had another child, though she could've made another fertilization agreement after she and Binh dissolved the agreement that had produced Canto.

To then learn that Binh had abused the child she'd wanted to keep with every ounce of her being? No, Magdalene would never forgive. As Ena wouldn't forgive herself for not foreseeing Magdalene's reaction to giving birth.

Given their possessive natures, Mercants rarely, *rarely* entered into agreements where their children would be raised fully by others, but it was Magdalene herself who'd brought forward the proposal when Fernandez approached her. She'd been very interested in the genetic match and confirmed that she had no problem with a dual agreement as requested by the Fernandez family.

Ena had thought her Silent, had believed in her pragmatic take on the situation.

They'd both been wrong.

"The final decision was mine, Mother," Magdalene had said to her some years ago, after Ena apologized for her mistake. "You told me to think long and hard on it, advised me to do my research. I thought I could handle it." A hand pressed to her belly. "But then I carried him for nine months, and I felt his mind awaken . . ."

The only good thing in it all was that they'd been able to save Canto.

Such an angry boy he'd been, but even then, he'd been fiercely loyal. To 3K, the little girl who'd murdered for him.

Watching the two of them together now, Ena was quite convinced the adult Payal Rao would murder for him, too. So. "We'll have tea at the Sea House next time," she said as the two were about to leave.

Canto was still scowling, but his lips tugged up into a slight smile, and the voice that touched her mind was smug in a way he rarely was: *I knew you'd like her.*

One does not gloat, Canto.

He laughed out loud as he exited, causing Payal to look at him with soft eyes . . . and Ena's long-frozen heart to threaten to thaw. "It appears," she said to the slinky black cat that had prowled into the room, "the family is to expand again."

CLINICAL NOTES ON PAYAL RAO

JAYA STORM, E.

Patient is very self-aware and conscious of the damage inflicted by her childhood, and is searching for a way to balance her powerful emotional response to the man she loves* against her need to maintain psychic and mental stability.

Her childhood protections did the job required, but they were a blunt tool. I have advised her that we can use more subtle methods to allow her to find the control she needs without losing herself. I have also received permission to speak about her case on an anonymous basis with other Es who have more specialized knowledge in certain areas.

Most specifically, I intend to speak to Sascha Duncan regarding custom shields, and to Dr. Farukh Duvall about the issue of childhood trauma and how it interacts with brain chemistry. I also need to find—or become—an expert in how childhood trauma may affect the development of psychic pathways in all children, and anchors in particular.

There do not appear to be any anchors who are also empaths, which is a critical piece of information in itself, but I intend to further my knowledge of anchors to the highest degree to better serve my patient— and any future patients from Designation A.

While this is not my area of specialization, my skills appear to transfer over very well to this particular anchor. When I work with patients in a coma, it is to coax them back to consciousness. With Payal, I feel as if I'm teaching her how to walk out of a different kind of darkness.

She is an incredibly intelligent woman and—given her past—could easily have gone off the rails, yet she has risen to her current high-level position through sheer grit and the help of a limited slate of medications, none of which are calibrated correctly for her current psychic and mental state. I will be consulting with a prescribing physician to get those levels corrected—with Payal having a final say on who that physician will be, though I will offer my recommendations.

For now, I've given her mental exercises that should begin to bring peace to her mind without the bluntness of her previous shields.

This is my view. The patient has not yet put a label on what she feels for him.

Chapter 37

I'd like to book it out for the entire day. I'll make the payment
immediately on receipt of your invoice.

—E-mail sent by Canto Mercant

JUST OVER A week after surviving Ena, and seven days after her first
meeting with Jaya, Payal was happier than she'd been in her entire
life. She'd had nine whole days with Canto, nine days with a man she
trusted with all of herself, nine days where she could just be Payal
without the masks she wore in the world.

It had been aggravating at times, frustrating often, and wonderful
always.

Now she looked at the image Canto had given her and tried to
work out where it was that he was asking her to teleport them. But the
image, while distinctive enough for a teleport lock, was of a stone wall
marred by multiple small pieces of carved-in graffiti. All seemed to be
entwined initials.

"Ready?" he asked.

Payal nodded and put her hand on his shoulder. Other than clasped
hands, they hadn't had any intimate contact since the day she'd

touched him in the gym, and to feel his muscle and warmth now made her breath catch.

The distance was her fault.

Her reactions were too strong, too manic when it came to him—and it had only gotten worse after that incident in the gym. After a lifetime deprived of pleasure, she wanted to be a glutton, just gorge on Canto. She'd withdrawn because she needed to find a middle path between unrestrained and frenzied sensual gluttony and cold control.

But she thought she might've made a mistake in taking that backward step—Canto had been increasingly gruff with her. "Are you angry?" She had to ask, had to know; he was the most important person in her life. She couldn't bear it if he was angry with her.

He scowled up at her, the galaxies missing. "Only that I can't help you with whatever's happening. I want to fight all your battles, take all the battle damage."

She scowled back at him. "Yet I'm not allowed to help take your pain?" It had been a beautiful surprise to find out that their bond permitted her to share the load.

He growled at her, *growled*. "Are you ever going to let that go?"

"No." Because that was her line in the sand; there were a lot of ways in which she would bend for Canto, but not when it led to pain and hurt for him.

A glare was her reward . . . but he also reached up to take her hand and press a kiss to the back. Things melted inside her. This was something else she'd learned—fighting with Canto didn't have to mean rejection or hurt. He'd always be there, no matter how much they disagreed. Never had she had that kind of certainty, that kind of a stable place on which to stand.

Bending, she kissed him on one bristled cheek. "I think you're wonderful, Canto." It came out solemn, not playful like she'd seen in the human/changeling shows she'd started to watch on the comm screen.

His smile was slow, a brush of dark red on his cheekbones. "Well, okay." It came out gruff, but then he "kissed" her using their bond, the psychic touch tender.

Her toes curled inside her shoes. Those shoes were soft sneakers and went well with the dark blue jeans and simple white vee-necked knitted top that she'd bought purposefully loose. "Shall we go?"

Canto nodded, his chest clenched and hot with the impact of the words Payal had spoken. So serious and intense. So Payal. He wanted to wrap her up in his arms and cuddle her close, but today he had another priority. He'd spent hours searching for a suitable place that was close enough not to tire her, but also remote enough that they were unlikely to see anyone else.

He didn't give a flying fuck about being exposed to her family, but it'd distract her from the healing she'd begun to do since she'd had the freedom to stop watching constantly for a knife in the back.

It'd be a long journey, but she'd begun.

The world blinked out, then blinked back into place a heartbeat later.

In front of them was the old stone wall he'd used as a marker. Scratched within it were love hearts with initials, other messages old and new. But that wasn't what he'd brought her here to see. "Turn around."

He did it with her, saw the moment she realized.

Her breath caught, her body going motionless. Then she stepped forward, her eyes lifted to the spray of soft blooms even now dropping petals on her in a delicate pink rain. This greenhouse was one of the largest in Russia, and it was planted not with fruits or vegetables, but with flowers.

Including an avenue of cherry blossom trees currently in riotous bloom.

The greenhouse was the brainchild of a human gardener who'd put all his money into it—but was now reaping the rewards, as people came from far and wide to walk in beauty. It sold out every winter, as residents sought out a glimpse of the colors of spring and summer, but—thanks to its range of exotic flora—wasn't exactly quiet in the warmer months.

Arwen had come here with Pavel; he was the one who'd given Canto the photo of the wall, to add to their files as a teleport reference.

Today, Canto and Payal had it to themselves. He'd arranged it in advance, paid the hefty fee without hesitation. He'd have paid double if asked. Because the wonder on Payal's face as she walked under the blooms . . .

"It's even more lovely than I imagined." Her voice was a breath, her hands held out to catch the falling petals.

Canto stayed with her as she walked on. She stopped every few steps to pick up a petal or touch a leaf or just stand under a falling shower of pink.

Entranced by her, Canto didn't bother to pick off the petals that clung to his hair and clothing.

But when she looked at him after tipping back her head to bathe in the blossoms, he saw a single tear rolling down her cheek. "Hey." He immediately curled his arm around her hips. "Baby, what's wrong?"

Moving into him, she curled herself into his lap, allowed him to put his arms around her. "We can go home," he said, devastated at the idea of having hurt her.

"No." An immediate negative, a kiss pressed to his jaw. "I'm just . . . overwhelmed. You *remembered*."

Nuzzling the top of her head with his chin, he said, "Don't you know by now? I remember everything you've ever said to me." He wanted to give her the world, give her his heart, give her whatever she wanted.

The only thing that stopped him was the need to give her freedom.

He wouldn't hold Payal to him by force or with emotional demands. Her wings were opening wider with each day that passed. She had to choose whether to stay with him or fly.

Soft kisses on his jaw that led to his lips. Shuddering, he held her tight as she explored his lips, tasted him. His heart punched against his rib cage, his breathing going erratic. "Payal," he rasped.

Sliding her hand over his cheek, she broke the kiss to say, "I don't want to slow down."

He saw the glitter in her eyes, knew her shields were fracturing. "What about—"

"I am this broken, fragmented patchwork person," Payal said, sitting up and facing the beautiful man who'd once held her bloody hand. "I'll always be some version of this." Nothing would ever "fix" her, and she didn't want to be *fixed*.

She just wanted to be Payal without the screams and the chaos, wanted to be a woman in control of her mind. "Today, here, in this dream from the past"—she held out her hand to catch the falling petals—"I remembered how fast life can change, how quickly blood can flow."

Canto's face twisted, shadows in his eyes. "Baby, I never intended—"

Payal pressed her fingers to his lips, the petals she held falling onto the faded blue of his chambray shirt. "No, it's not a bad thing. I got scared, Canto. Not today, before." A whisper. "Terrified by the power of what I feel for you." It was in every cell of her body, until it had become a defining feature of the person who was Payal Rao—there would never be any going back from this.

"I thought I was doing a good thing in stepping back, assessing, but that's how I control the world. A good skill . . . but there is no controlling this, controlling us." She pressed her forehead to his. "No matter how much I assess, how much I regulate, I will always be a little crazy when it comes to you."

Canto, this man who was always on her side, gripped her jaw. "It's fine to be afraid. This is one hell of a change."

Her eyes burned. "I know. But I don't want to stop living while I figure out the best way to be me." She traced the edges of his eyelashes with a careful fingertip; it was a strange thing, but he allowed it because Canto allowed her everything. "The Substrate is in trouble like we've never before known—what if it falls? What if? I don't want to fall with it knowing I was too scared to grab onto joy, grab onto you."

CANTO ran his hand to her nape, squeezed. "It'd destroy me to hurt you." His voice fractured with the force of his emotions.

Huge, starless eyes looking into his. "Don't you understand, Canto?" Fingers brushing his lips. "That's why I can risk this. Because it's you."

She broke him. Into a million pieces.

Surrendering to the need that had built and built inside him, he pressed a hungry kiss to her lips. When she responded as passionately, her hands fisting in his hair and her mouth opening over his, he knew he couldn't allow his protectiveness to ruin this. He had to honor her choice. *What about the greenhouse?*

Pulling back from the kiss, her breath ragged and a feverish glitter in her eyes, Payal glanced around. "Can we come back later today?"

"Yes." He'd paid for the whole day, and it wasn't so far that the teleports would wipe her out.

"Then let's go home." The world blinked out.

She'd brought them back into the living area of his home, but—not wanting to jostle Payal with the motion of the wheels—he quickly used hover mode to move them both into the bedroom and shut the door. Just in case a bear decided to pay a visit. They'd get the hint.

Shifting back a little, Payal reached for the bottom of her top and stripped it off. All she wore underneath was a white bra with lace edging. It glowed against the honey brown hue of her skin.

His mouth dried up. Gloved hands clasping the dip of her waist, he bent to kiss the tops of her breasts, the curves plump and very, very bad for his concentration. Shivering, she held his head to her, her body warm and silky and oh so soft. He licked and tasted and stroked even as his erection swelled with dark heat.

"I should've done research on this," she muttered before kissing him again.

It's all right, he told her telepathically since their mouths were busy. *A friend decided I needed an education and gave me a few tips.*

The bears found it fascinating that many Psy had never indulged in sexual skin privileges. After the first time Canto visited Denhome—and found himself the target of flirtation from bear women who'd decided he was a "snack," as described by Pavel's twin Yakov—Valentin had taken him aside and given him the "talk."

Not the biology of it. Of course Canto knew that. Valentin had told him things far beyond the biological act.

"Most important," the bear alpha had boomed, slapping Canto on the shoulder, "listen to your woman. Shy or loud, she'll find a way to tell you what she needs."

Back then, Canto had muttered that he'd never need the information, he was quite content being alone. He'd never been so happy to be wrong. "We're going to mess this up the first time around," he told Payal as he pulled off his gloves, loath to have any barrier between them. "Apparently, 'fumbling' is a given the first time around, so the recommendation was to practice. A lot."

"We won't mess up." Payal's voice was firm. "I'm a Tk. I know how to move."

He fucking loved her blunt confidence.

When she began to unbutton his shirt, he pulled it off over the top of his head instead and threw it aside. She ran her hands over his shoulders with a little moan, as if she found him as beautiful as he found her. Her touch was electric fire in his veins, the sounds she made as he pulled down the cup of her bra to expose her nipple a kiss to the most sensitive, most vulnerable part of him.

He sucked on the rich brown of her nipple.

Payal's body jerked and then she was holding him to her, telling him without words that she liked it, that he could continue.

Molding and squeezing her other breast with his hand because he wanted to touch her everywhere all at once, he suddenly froze. "Shit, I forgot about my calluses." Gloves or not, his palms were never going to be anything but hardened—and Payal's skin was like velvet.

"What?" An uncomprehending look.

He held up a hand. "My skin is rough."

"Oh, I like the texture of your hands and your warmth and how you touch me." She caressed her fingers over his palm. "It all feels really, *really* good."

Simple. Direct. Payal.

Thanking his lucky stars, he got back to his delicious adoration of her breasts. Cupping one, he rolled her nipple with his tongue. When she whimpered as if it was too much, he kissed the tip, then switched breasts.

"Canto." A breathy sigh.

He tugged at the clasp of her bra. "How the hell does this thing come off?"

The bra was suddenly gone, her gorgeous breasts bare for his delectation.

"Did you just teleport it off?" Groaning, he closed his hands over both mounds.

Lips plump and kiss-wet, she cupped his face in her hands and devoured him. Senses on fire, he kissed her back with little finesse and no damn control while her breasts were crushed against his chest. She was so soft and so curvy and so damn lush that he wanted to eat her up.

Even the small voice of panic that yelled he was losing control, losing himself, couldn't stop him.

Accessing the hover controls with one hand, his mouth locked with hers, he moved them closer to the bed. When they broke apart to gasp in air, he lifted her up and dropped her lightly on the mattress, his upper body plenty strong enough to handle her small frame that way. She watched him with hungry eyes as he lifted himself up onto the mattress.

It wasn't until he was pressed lengthwise along her that he realized she could've teleported him. She hadn't. Because this was his 3K. She understood what he could and couldn't bear, understood his scars as he understood hers.

A shudder rocked through him as he buried his face against her neck.

"Canto, my Canto." She kissed his neck, his shoulder, stroked her hands down his back, melting him from the inside out.

Lifting his head as the thread of panic retreated under the tenderness of her loving, he took her lips again. She rocked her lower body up against him.

Pressing up on his hands, he looked down at her. Her hair was all tumbled, her face flushed, and her nipples wet from his caresses. Small red marks lingered from where his stubble had brushed against her, but she didn't seem to mind the roughness. He pressed down, moved to kiss the softness of her stomach.

She arched up . . . and the bed lifted off the floor.

Chapter 38

Strong telekinetics may cause physical destruction during emotional and sexual intimacy, especially in the first instances. Control is possible, but the nature of it depends on the individual. Listed below are strategies used by other Tks who have contributed to this document.

—The Manual (private document)

CANTO LOOKED UP to see that Payal's eyes were closed, her breathing erratic. He grinned. If he was going to get naked with a telekinetic, he had to be ready for a few interesting side effects.

Ignoring the fact that their bed was levitating, he used his arms to move down the bed, then braced himself on one hand and used his other to undo the top of her pants. And . . . they were gone. Teleported away.

Laughing at her impatience, he kissed the top of her navel.

He also noticed that she hadn't done the same to his jeans. His 3K. Remembering what he needed even when desire was screwing with her control.

Because it's you.

Her words came back to him, and he found himself saying, "Teleport off my jeans, baby." He could accept that small loss of control when it came to this intimate act.

Because it was her.

She met his eyes, her own hazy . . . and then she moved her hands to the top button of his jeans. Groaning, he let her take the manual route, let her unbutton and unzip him. He wasn't wearing underwear, and the little gasp-moan she made when she set sight on him almost made him break then and there.

The only thing that helped him maintain control was the knowledge that pleasure was a foreign concept to Payal.

Canto wasn't going to be another taker in her life.

When she finally teleported away his jeans to leave him naked, he watched her breath catch, her skin flush as she ran her hands over him from shoulder to the part of his thighs she could reach.

He couldn't feel that section of his thighs, but it didn't matter—the visual impact was visceral. Pressing down on both arms, he kissed her lips, then made his way to her throat. She arched up against him, her nails digging into his shoulders.

Canto made a note in his Manual of Loving Payal: *Throat extremely sensitive.*

Her breasts were even more so and he couldn't resist adoring them, his own body held in a fierce kind of check that might've been impossible had he not spent so many years learning to contain his anger and frustration and pain as he lay at the mercy of physicians.

He put that willpower to use today to pleasure his 3K. The musk of her was thick in the air by the time he reached the dip of her waist and pressed a kiss there.

She pulled at his shoulders. *"Canto."* It was a plea.

His back perspiration-damp, Canto made his way up her body. Bracing himself with one arm beside her head, he ran his free hand down to the juncture between her thighs. No cotton hindered his touch. Payal had teleported off her panties.

"*Payal.*" He held on to his fractured willpower with gritted teeth.

A single touch and she jerked so hard she almost bucked him off. Their bed banged onto the floor with enough force to jar his teeth, then rose up again while other loose items in the room began flying around them in a silent tornado.

Her surrender made his brain haze so badly he thought he felt the earth shake.

He stroked deeper, found her silken and wet and tight.

Sweat beaded on his temples. His hand trembled.

And Payal spread her thighs before gripping his erection to pull him to her. He saw stars. Flipping off her, he brought himself to a seated position against the solid support of the headboard. Payal moved with him, straddled him, her expression dazed.

"This way," he said, his voice harsh with need. "So I can see your face."

She touched her fingers to his lips, then looked down between them and positioned herself just right. The first touch of her scalding heat on his cock snapped his spine rigid and made his hands clench on her. He fought to loosen his hold, but Payal murmured that it was okay.

Then his telekinetic lover, movement her gift, undulated her hips as she sank onto him. Canto felt *her* pleasure in his mind, felt her break even as he broke. They rocked together hard and fast and probably without rhythm.

But it didn't matter.

What mattered was her desperate kiss. What mattered were his arms wrapped around her. What mattered was the pleasure he felt shake her body before the same wild pleasure erupted in him, shattering him to pieces.

PAYAL lay cradled in Canto's arms, her inner shields in shards at her feet, and the screaming madness in her oddly quiescent. As if it, too, had been drugged by the pleasure that had turned her body boneless.

She thought about moving, did nothing about it. She just kept her head against Canto's shoulder, one hand on his chest, the scent of salt and sweat and Canto in her every breath, and wallowed in this moment.

Stirring, he brushed a kiss over her shoulder.

Payal snuggled into him even more. The way he'd touched her . . . the way he held her . . . She'd never be the same. If he ever decided against her, it would break a fundamental part of her.

Unable to stop, she reached out to touch their bond.

It was still there, deep in the Substrate, a gossamer thread as strong as steel. It made her happy to touch it, to know that she wasn't alone as she'd been for so long. It felt even better with Canto wrapped around her.

He nuzzled at her hair, strands of it catching on his stubble. "That's nice," he murmured, his voice a lazy lion's. "Like you're stroking me."

Shy, startled, she pulled back her psychic hand . . . but then because he'd sounded like it was a good thing, she touched the bond again. He made a rumbling sound of contentment in his chest before saying, "I'm sweaty as hell."

Payal could feel the stickiness between them, the stickiness between her thighs, but she didn't care. "I don't want to move." It'd probably get uncomfortable in a while, but not yet. She wanted to wrap this moment around herself until nothing could take it away, wanted to hoard it deep inside her mind, a secret treasure.

"Me, either." He yawned. "God, I feel like I could sleep and sleep. As if you've wrung a lifetime of tension out of me."

Her own eyes were heavy. "Hmm."

She didn't know which one of them fell asleep first, but when she woke, Canto was flat on his back and she was on top of him. He stirred with her, and when his lashes lifted, she saw galaxies. "I love your eyes," she whispered. "You carry the universe in them."

"They're weird eyes," he said with a laugh that made lines fan out from the corners of his eyes, then kissed her with an ease and an affection that made her want more and more. "But they meant you knew me when we met again, so they're my lucky charm." Another kiss.

Smiling wasn't an act Payal had ever tried, but she didn't fight it when the warmth within her wanted to reach her face. "Do you have a bath? I've never had a bath." Showers were far more efficient.

"No," Canto said. "But let me send you an image."

A clear pond surrounded by lush green forest shimmered into her mind. "It looks cold." She shivered.

"Dare you."

She teleported them both into the water. A shriek was torn out of her at the cold, while Canto said, "Fuck!" Then he dived underneath. When he came back up, he was a sleek seal of a man. Even though he could only use his upper body for floating, he had no trouble, having clearly spent a lot of time in water.

"How often do you come here?" she asked.

"Few times a week. It's not far from the house." Then he splashed her.

Crying out at the cold, Payal manipulated the water using her Tk so that it fell on him in gentle waves. He grinned and began to "chase" her around the pond. It was silly and fun and it was a wonderful coda to the most pleasurable experience of her life . . . even though her mind was already going sideways, her thoughts skittering out of her control.

She barely got them home, her ability to maintain a teleport lock erratic as her concentration fractured. "I can't think." Wrapped in a large towel, she walked jaggedly back and forth across the bedroom floor. "Broken things inside my head." She held the sides of that head. "The screaming part is awake." A whimper escaped her control. "Mad. Mad. Mad."

Canto was already in his chair, having pulled on a pair of sweat-pants in the interim. Intercepting her, he gripped her hips and said, "Focus on the calming exercise the empath taught you."

"I can't remember!" It came out a scream, panic jabbering inside her. "I'm mad! I'm mad! I'm mad!" A singsong litany. "Insane murderous Payal who stabs people and isn't sorry. Mad. Mad. Mad."

Hauling her down into his lap, he crushed her in his arms. "Shh. You're safe. And you're not mad. You just have to learn to deal with a kind of mental paralysis, as I had to do with my legs."

Payal clung to that imagery with feral claws. "You've adapted."

"Using tools. Remember?" He continued to squeeze her close, as if aware that being contained this way by him, warm and safe, helped her find coherence. "You need the help of the framework your E has started to teach you. Reach for it."

Wet heat in her eyes. "I can't. It's lost in the chaos." Pieces of a thousand memories and thoughts floated in her mind.

"Hold on to our bond." He pressed his lips to her temple. "Use it, *use me*, as you made me use you to handle my pain."

Payal clung and clung and he didn't shove her away, didn't tell her it was uncomfortable or unwanted. Not even when her jittering self pulled at the bond in jagged bursts, desperation making her rough. He just held her to his heartbeat until her breathing evened and she found her footing.

No longer too confused to think, she did what she should've done from the start and began to build the framework Jaya had begun to teach her. It was less solid than her shields, and it allowed her to be herself while corralling the part of her mind that was damaged and broken.

"You're not broken," the E had said in her gentle voice. "You have trauma that's calcified and exacerbated a chemical imbalance in your brain. We work with one element at a time, step-by-step, to bring you to a place where *you* feel good. No one else gets to make that call. Just you."

Shaky in the aftermath of the build, she whispered, "I lost control." Shame was a wildfire in her veins.

"Baby, I threw full-on tantrums when I was initially in the hospital." He kissed her hair in that way that had already become so familiar, so affectionate that it made her feel precious. "Cut yourself some slack—you've held it together for three decades on your own. It's okay if you lose it now and then. Jaya didn't promise overnight success, remember? You have to build those muscles as I build my leg muscles."

Again, the analogy worked for the way she thought, giving her a physical analogue that offered her something to grip. She'd been falling back on thinking of the new framework as ropes around her mind, handcuffs to keep the madness at bay. She had to consider it a tool, as Canto considered his robotic exercise machinery.

"I'm not broken." It was the first time in her life she'd ever verbalized such a thing. "I just function differently than other people."

"Got it in one." Another one of those nuzzles that made her feel so warm and . . . There was another word she couldn't say, couldn't think, because it was too big, too huge a promise.

So she just lay against him and used the tools she'd been given.

MESSAGE STREAM BETWEEN YAKOV AND PAVEL STEPYREV

Pasha, the weirdest thing just happened.

What? A woman looked at your ugly face and didn't turn to stone in fright?

I'm going to tell on you to Mama.

Tattletale. Also, if you tell, I'll tell her who stole that entire chocolate cake when we were thirteen. What happened anyway?

I'm just walking through the forest, minding my own business, when this big old tree starts creaking and groaning . . .

???? I'm growing old here.

It fell over. Right in front of me!

You okay?

Yeah, yeah, it was making so much noise before it fell that no one could've missed it. And even when it began to fall, it was in slow motion. The thing came down with a boom that I swear caused a quake.

A tree falls in the forest. And thanks to the great explorer Yasha, we know it made a noise.

You suck. But it fell down for no reason! Like it was pushed over by a giant hand. But that's not the weirdest part.

You have my interest, young man. Proceed.

It AVOIDED all the other trees in its path, and managed to lie down right in this fine gap. Like the giant finger couldn't stop from pushing it over, but they controlled it.

Huh.

Yeah.

Log it.

You think?

Yeah, just in case. I mean, I don't think rogue telekinetics are out there pushing over our trees, but you never know.

PSYNET BEACON: INTERVIEW WITH PAYAL RAO

COCO RAMIREZ

No one expected Payal Rao.

That statement is no hyperbole. We're all used to hearing of Ms. Rao's business dealings, but even those mentions are never anything but restrained references in financial newspapers. She has a reputation for keeping her head down and getting on with the work of running a major family empire.

Certainly, none of the political pundits predicted this move, and yet to have a hub-anchor as part of the Ruling Coalition makes sense in every possible way, especially given the PsyNet's current instability.

Today, I sit down with Payal Rao and attempt to uncover the anchor behind the enigma.

Beacon: Were you surprised when the Ruling Coalition approached you?

Rao: They didn't. I approached them as the chosen representative of Designation A. There is every reason to have an anchor at the highest level of power, and no reason to keep us out.

Beacon: Do I have this right? You demanded a seat at the table?

Rao: Yes.

Beacon: Not many would dare such against the most powerful people in the PsyNet.

Rao: Do you know what happens to the PsyNet if the anchors go on strike? The PsyNet disappears and we all die. The end.

Beacon: Are you saying Designation A is the most important designation of them all?

Rao: Anchors would be drowning in a sea of insanity without the empaths, would've fallen to Pure Psy and others with warlike ambitions without the strength of the telekinetics and telepaths and more who protected

us. Foreseers have saved us from countless disasters, while psycho-
metrics and Justice-Psy and many others solve problem after problem.
We are the foundation. The foundation holds, but it can't actively do
battle.

To state the skillset of one designation does not negate those of every
other—the hierarchy is a continuous flux based on need, and right now,
A is the critical designation.

Beacon: You don't pull your punches.

Rao: I know my own value—and I know the value of the designation I represent. We were once content to be the silent party to the health of
the PsyNet. But since the powers that be made such a mess of that
over the past century, a passive presence is no longer a viable option.

Beacon: Do you blame the current Ruling Coalition, too?

Rao: Your comprehension skills need work. I made it clear that my problem
is with past leaders. That includes past anchors. Our ancestors in the
designation are not blameless.

Beacon: What will your new responsibilities mean for your duties as the
Rao CEO?

Rao: Why don't you ask Kaleb Krychek what his responsibilities mean for
his status as the head of Krychek Industries?

Beacon: A good point, but the question had to be asked.

Rao: No, it didn't—it was nonsensical and I have little time to waste.

Beacon: Then let us ask a very important question—as an A, what do you
see in our future? Can the PsyNet be saved? Or are we fighting a losing
battle, death a whisper on the horizon?

Rao: I'm no foreseer. All I can tell you is that I have the cooperation of
every single A in the world, and we intend to work with the empaths
and with every other power in the Net to repair the psychic fabric on
which we all depend for life. If we fail, you'll die. If we succeed, you'll
forget about anchors all over again—except this time, forgetting us will
no longer be an option.

Chapter 39

We are Designation J.
Justice.
But where is our justice?
Where is our peace?
I'm so tired of the horror that lives inside me now.

—Note left by Arnaud Smith, J-Psy (missing, presumed dead)

CANTO BURST OUT laughing as he read the *Beacon* interview. "God, you're magnificent." He kissed the woman who was sitting on the sofa next to him, her back leaning up against his side.

She had an organizer on her lap and was doing complex financial transactions as part of her job as the Rao CEO.

"That comeback about asking Krychek was perfection."

"Interviewer was an idiot. Does she ask Nikita the same question? Does she ask Aden Kai if he can still run the Arrows?" She continued on with her transactions. "Entire thing was a waste of time."

"No." Shifting his arm around so he could put his organizer in front of her face, he showed her the trending subjects in the PsyNet—once collated by the NetMind and available to any Psy who wanted to look, they were now collected by psychic bots seeded by the media.

Those bots had nowhere near the NetMind's scope, but it was better than nothing.

"I'm at the top of the list." She did not sound impressed. "At least Designation A is number two."

"Visibility helps us." Canto pulled back his organizer when he saw an incoming message. "Sophia Russo is happy to meet with us." It had taken this long to organize a meeting because Sophia had been involved in an emergency situation to do with a former Justice colleague.

"I know what you're asking is important," she'd said, "but the PsyNet won't fall in two days. My colleague may." The rich blue-violet of her eyes had been potent with emotion, the thin tracery of scars on her face—whitish against skin of a cream hue—speaking to a violent past that had come up in none of the research Canto had done about her.

He hadn't known too much about J-Psy at that point, but he'd dug deep in the time since. Both he and Payal had been stunned by the level of attrition in the designation. So many dead and damaged, so much pain. There had to be a better way.

SOPHIA didn't know what she was expecting from the mysterious Canto Mercant and Payal Rao. After reading the *Beacon* interview with Payal, she'd braced herself for an abrasive personality who took no bullshit, but that wasn't quite what she got when they teleported into a small outdoor garden at Duncan HQ.

Payal was wearing flowing pants in dark gray, matched with a pale green top with sleeves cuffed at the wrist. Her hair was up in a ponytail, but that ponytail was loose, not tight. There was nothing sleek about her. She was . . . softer than she'd come across in that interview, at least on the outside.

As for Canto Mercant, she was surprised by the chair, but only because she knew her race's desire for perfection had meant terrible, criminal acts in the past. It was rare to see a Psy adult who used assistive devices; those who'd survived childhood but ended up injured later tended to either disappear or be hidden away.

Yet so-called perfect Psy were often the worst monsters of them all—she carried the marks of that cold truth on her face, and in her memories of three innocent children who'd never gotten the chance to live. Sophia would never forget them—and she'd made sure the world wouldn't forget them, either.

Carrie O'Brien.

Lin Wong.

Bilar Baramichai.

All three names were now listed as "lost on duty" in the official J-rolls. A small thing, but it mattered. Their names mattered. Their lives had mattered.

As did the lives of Designation A.

Canto Mercant's hair was silky black like her husband Max's, and he had eyes with just a hint of an upward tilt. Those eyes were the most unusual cardinal eyes she'd ever seen. Her overall impression was of a handsome man, but one with a dangerous edge to him.

"Hello." Meeting them halfway, she kept her hands loosely linked in front of her. "We can sit over there." She nodded to an outdoor seating arrangement put in place when Nikita began to make deals with non-Psy.

She saw both Payal and Canto glance at the fine black leather of her gloves. When neither asked a question about them, she figured they'd dug around and knew she was a Sensitive after her years of work as a J. Skin-to-skin contact led to a telepathic connection she couldn't control and didn't want.

To be buried in another person's thoughts and memories, fears and horrors, it was akin to being buried alive, having the life suffocated out of her. In the worst-case scenario, the overload could crush the brain, collapse the psychic pathways, and kill.

Her friend and fellow J, Cèlian, had turned Sensitive six months earlier. Touch could kill him—yet he was starved of it, too. The divergent needs had been tearing him apart, pushing him closer and closer to choosing self-termination. Sophia had lost too many friends to that terrible final choice, and she refused, *refused* to let anyone else fall. She'd managed to haul Cèlian back thanks to Max and his huge heart: her husband had natural shields that nothing could crack.

For a Sensitive, he was an oasis of peace, of silence.

After Sophia convinced Cèlian to let Max touch him—and though Sophia's husband wasn't a big cuddler of strangers—Max had hugged the other J. Not once. As many times as Cèlian needed in the days since. Cèlian had sobbed the first time and clung to Max's muscled frame. Her ex-cop husband had stroked the other man's back and held him without a single sign of impatience.

Later, he'd told her they needed to talk to Bowen Knight at the Human Alliance to build a list of naturally shielded humans who wouldn't mind interacting with hurt Js. "Back when I was in Enforcement," he'd said, "I knew some pros on the street who had clients who came to them just for friendly touch, not sexual stuff."

He'd frowned. "It's not only Js who ache for touch. I think touch therapy might actually already be a thing, but we need to set up a subgroup of therapists who have airtight shields. And it's not like Js have never helped humans—the Council only interfered in major cases. Rest of the time, Js did as much good for humans as they did for Psy, so I don't think it'll be a hard sell to get help for your friends. Let me talk to Bo."

Just another reason Sophia would love Max to the end of time.

"Thank you for meeting with us." Payal took a seat at the edge of the seating area, so Canto could park his chair next to her.

Sophia chose a seat opposite the other woman, putting the three of them in a rough semicircle. "Of course." Sophia rubbed her forehead, the dull pain behind her eyelids a constant. "The NetMind is so scared and lost and I can't help it. I need—" She looked up and halted. The two As were staring at her. "What?"

"The NetMind is alive?" Canto Mercant's voice was harsh—with a piercing note of hope. "All we sense in the Net are fragments."

"It exists," Sophia confirmed. "Not as the huge presence it once was, but the core remains. My anchor point—I'm sorry, that's what I've always called it, though I know it's not correct."

"It *is* an anchor point." Payal Rao's tone brooked no argument. "We can see you in the Substrate. While you can't communicate in that sphere with the rest of us, your anchor lines are rooted deep."

Sophia didn't understand all of what Payal had just said, but she didn't need to, not for this. "The NetMind seems to have hidden a piece of itself in my anchor point—*in me.*" In the very pathways of her brain.

Canto frowned. "May we see?"

When she inclined her head, they joined her on the PsyNet. At one point, they both disappeared after telling her they were examining her anchor point in the Substrate.

Later, when all three of them opened their eyes in the garden again, she saw Canto glance at Payal. Payal, in turn, looked first to Canto. Unspoken things passed between them.

"Is the DarkMind there, too?" Payal asked afterward.

"Yes. They're not two separate presences anymore but one complete one." A single point of hope that made her want to believe they could stop the spiral of loss. "When I say NetMind, I mean both."

Canto said something to Payal about the "weeds" in the Substrate; Payal responded with technical jargon. Allowing their discussion to flow past her, she considered the two of them, and who they were together.

Inside her mind, the NetMind threw a bouquet of flowers into the air.

Sophia sucked in a silent breath. *Is this what you need? Anchors who've begun to bloom into their full selves?*

A sense of terrible sadness, then the image of wilting flowers. No, not wilting. Flowers that had begun to curl up and die because of a lack of sunlight, a lack of care.

As it fragmented in the rest of the PsyNet, the NetMind had grown stronger in her mind. It also brought with it images and thoughts and hopes. Today, it showed her sunlight on the drooping blooms.

Those blooms opened again.

I understand. She tried to encompass the neosentience in love, as protective toward it as she was toward the nascent life cradled in her womb. It was the tiniest collection of cells at this moment in time, so very small that no one outside could sense it. Only she and Max knew. They'd tell River after the first-trimester mark; Max's brother would be an astonishing uncle, devoted and gentle.

The neosentience of the Net "leaned" into her. It was difficult to describe the sensation fully, but it was as if it was asking for comfort. She embraced it with her mind, held it close. *I'll tell them*, she promised, and it calmed.

"I have to pass on a message," she said, interrupting Canto and Payal's technical discussion.

They turned as one to her, both so startlingly beautiful that it was a shock each time she looked at them. She had the idea that neither one of them was aware of their physical beauty. Payal struck Sophia as atypical in her thinking and reactions. Not flawed. *Never* would Sophia call anyone flawed. It was simply a difference.

The same way Sophia's touch sensitivity was a difference.

As for Canto, given the lack of information on him on the PsyNet, he probably kept a low profile. Those within his trusted circle would be used to his looks. Canto Mercant also struck her as a man who didn't much care for the opinions of many; the reactions of others would only matter to him in how they affected his goals.

Sophia liked them both.

"The NetMind," she said, "wants the anchors to emerge into the light, to live full lives. I think that's just the tip of the iceberg—it wants *all* Psy to live full lives, but anchors are the foundation." She often understood such subtleties instinctively, as if the NetMind was so deep a part of her mind that it didn't need to speak to her to communicate. "If you fade away into the darkness, so does it."

Canto frowned, but it was Payal—her expression modulated to give nothing away—who spoke. "Does it know if anchors have always been this way? Withdrawn from the world? Or was there a trigger that set this chain of events in motion?"

An excellent question. "I'll ask, but—for me at least—speaking to the NetMind isn't like a conversation between me and you. It thinks and responds in a unique way." She did her best to put Payal's question to the NetMind.

Its response was slow in coming, and it was a grouping of images.

Blooms, wild and colorful in a field.

A black cloud.

The blooms curling inward until they were shriveled and small.

Sophia blew out a breath. "There was an inciting incident. Time is a fluid concept to the NetMind—I can't tell you when the incident took place. But it had a catastrophic effect and led to the seclusion of Designation A."

"The volcanic eruption?" Payal mused. "But that was so long ago—it doesn't explain the psychic fires and flash floods that Ager mentioned."

"So many secrets," Canto bit out. "Our ancestors kicked us all in the guts by hiding anything deemed dark or bad."

As a J who'd walked in the minds of serial killers the Council refused to acknowledge, Sophia well knew his anger. "I can help you with the research on the inciting incident—but we have to accept that it might've been too long ago for there to be any records."

"You're one of us, Sophia." Canto leaned forward, forearms on his thighs. "Unless you don't want to be?"

"I'm not a normal A. I can't see your Substrate."

"You do as much as a minor hub in holding this area stable. You're an A."

Sophia was part of a tight fraternity of current and former Js, but this, too, was an element of her identity. To be welcomed in . . . It meant more than she'd realized. "Thank you."

"Do you want to take the lead on the research?" Canto's haunting eyes held her own. "I'll put you in touch with Ager, who is one of our oldest members, and I'll forward you what we know about the volcanic eruption that killed twenty anchors, but the historical can't be our priority."

"I agree." The Net was falling apart too quickly. "You have to focus on the now. I'll take care of the historical hunt."

"We also need to start working on a plan to reintegrate Designation A into society," Payal said. "It's going to be a difficult task—many of us are near agoraphobic after a lifetime of being told we needed to be sheltered."

"Ask the Es for an assist?" Sophia suggested.

"A good idea, but their workload is already significant." Payal looked off into the distance, and Sophia could almost see her mind working. "If it's to last, it has to come from us," she said finally. "From within."

"What do you think the reaction will be? How many As will make the attempt?"

To her surprise, Payal said, "All of them."

Canto's face was grim. "An anchor's job is to protect the Net. If that means leaving the walls of safety, so be it." He glanced at Payal.

Who picked up the thread at once . . . because these two were bonded. It was a hum in the air between them, a quiet knowledge the NetMind whispered into Sophia's ear.

"The correct question," Payal said, "is how many will succeed and how many will fail." No expression on her face, but Sophia knew her well enough by now to know that meant little. "Some of us have no knowledge of how to be free—those As are akin to caged animals, knowing only their enclosures."

Sophia flexed her hand, staring down at the black of her glove. She'd never been isolated like an anchor, but she'd been in a cage nonetheless. "If there's hope," she said, raising her head to meet Payal's eyes, "they'll try and try again. As long as there is light in the darkness, a reason to keep fighting."

For her, that hope had come in the form of Max. Her lover. Her husband. Her mate.

But love wasn't a jealous thing, and from its roots had grown so many other tendrils of affection and love and joy. Sophia wanted that for Canto and Payal and every other anchor in the world. "Give them that hope. Let your bond blaze like a candle in the dark."

Chapter 40

To forget our history is to forget ourselves.

—From *The Dying Light* by Harissa Mercant (1947)

CANTO AND PAYAL took Sophia's advice to heart, pushing away the weeds around their bond so it burned a glowing azure that was a beacon. There was an infinite amount of work to do, so many bricks to lay to build a strong new foundation for Designation A, but every spare moment they had, they spent together. Neither one of them said it aloud, but the ticking clock in Payal's brain accompanied them every second of every day.

Not many more days and she'd have to return home to ensure that her anchor point stayed stable—and to get a shot of the medication that was a leash on her life. The thirteenth day after she'd arrived in Moscow, and she'd used up the second dose Pranath Rao had couriered over.

One—maybe two—more days till she went critical.

Canto had used her access passwords to break into the Rao systems, had even managed to work his way into her father's private files, but Pranath Rao was a smart man. There was nothing useful in the available files.

"He'll have it in his head," Payal murmured, pressing a kiss to Canto's shoulder as they lay face-to-face in bed, both of them bare to the skin.

Intimate skin privileges were extraordinary, but this kind of affectionate contact, it was better even than that. Especially now that Payal sometimes just went to him and said, "I need you."

He'd open his arms, and she'd curl into his lap, and he'd hold her until she could breathe past the panic building in her brain. Because that panic hadn't magically disappeared after her continuing work with Jaya. It had too long been a part of her to be so easily vanquished.

She still had agitated episodes at times, but increasingly, she could now calm herself down rather than going into a chaotic spiral. Jaya had taught—was still teaching—her tools to help herself. It was the best thing the empath could've done; Payal understood and valued such strategic mental work. Her recalibrated medications were also helping her to maintain a more even keel in day-to-day life.

The hardest thing she'd had to learn was that it was all right to be a little different.

"Quirky isn't a bad thing, Payal," Jaya had said as the two of them walked through a wooded area cool and green. "Some of the most admired people in human and changeling societies are the ones who walk to the beat of their own drummer."

Then there was Canto. He kept telling her he adored her exactly as she was—reminding her that she'd been his favorite even when she'd been totally feral. The latter held weight because it was true. She could still remember the pieces of dried apple thrust into her hand, the way he'd found methods to give her hints to questions asked by the teacher, how he'd held her hand that final day.

How he'd *remembered* her.

Payal didn't know when she'd be willing to allow her true self out in public, but she let Canto see her more and more. So when she felt the urge to lean over and kiss his nose, then nuzzle at his throat, she did it. He chuckled and cuddled her tight and almost suffocatingly close, exactly as she liked. "Are you sure you're not a small changeling bear? A sun bear, maybe?"

She pretended to claw him, the game one she would've *never* played with anyone else, lest they see it as a sign of mental instability. But with Canto, she was free. She didn't have to pretend.

Growling in his throat, he made as if to bite at her. The two of them were rolling around the bed, skin sliding on skin and breaths mingling, when Nikita Duncan's cool voice entered her mind.

I have unlocked and reinitialized the archive.

PAYAL and Canto had together decided it'd be best for her to be in the tech room when she went into the archive, in case she needed to meet with the others on visual comms.

Having changed into a work-suitable outfit in preparation for that eventuality, Payal took a seat before stepping into the PsyNet. Unlike when she did anchor work, she was present in the physical space to a degree, while also in the psychic space. But it wasn't until she was deep in the old vault that she realized she hadn't given even a single thought to the fact Canto was present in the same space.

He could knife her and she'd never see it coming, but she knew he wouldn't. She trusted him. No walls. No shields. Pure trust.

Because Canto would always choose to use his power to protect her, not hurt.

She entered the vault together with the rest of the Ruling Coalition. Of them all, Aden proved the most efficient searcher. Possibly because Arrows were hunters and not just for people, but for data. He got them to the right time period in the vault, then they spread out.

Payal considered her search strategy, thought of what an efficient A would've done, and dropped into the Substrate.

A small beacon pulsed below the fabric of the PsyNet.

Having fixed the location of the beacon in her mind, she returned to the PsyNet, overlaid the Substrate grid on it, and made her way to the correct point. It took her only four minutes and twenty-seven seconds to locate the file. "I have it."

Her words reverberated around the massive vault.

"Fast," commented the vast obsidian mind that was Krychek.

"An anchor stored this here—and they left a marker."

Not waiting for further questions, she opened up the file. The information rose to float on the black walls of the PsyNet. She reached out to Canto at the same time: *Shadow my mind. We have the data.*

The two of them looked at the data. It was a pale and silvery ghost against the black of the Net, data so old that it was in danger of fading away. Someone, however, was reinforcing it as it emerged—a person clever enough to make the fix without altering the data or otherwise causing damage.

Her first thought was that it had to be Aden. Arrows were skilled at subtle maneuvers. Then, all at once, she understood that she was behind the correction. *I don't have this skill.* She was a cardinal telekinetic with low-level Tp; such delicate power dynamics required a level of telepathic subtlety she simply didn't possess.

I can do it. Canto had a frown in his voice. *I'm not feeding you anything but you* are *in my anchor zone. So is this vault. It could be I'm fixing it instinctively.*

It's okay, Canto. Even if you are feeding me the information, I don't mind. Because it was him. Her 7J. *Isn't it strange, though, that the vault exists in the same psychic space as you?*

Coincidence.

Or the NetMind playing a very long game.

His response was a gruff sound that made her blood warm. Smile.

"Excellent work," Nikita murmured. "It took me many years to be so proficient in such delicate repairs."

Payal didn't respond, choosing instead to focus on the data in an effort to capture the secret of how the other As had pulled off . . . "An occlusion," she said. "That's what they called it. Look."

Her brain began to pull pieces of the puzzle together without her conscious command, each piece flaring with light in a coordinated cascade so she couldn't miss it.

It's been coded for anchor brains. Canto's crystalline voice, sharp with an excitement that echoed her own. *The others have no idea.*

"How did you see it?" Ivy Jane said at the same time. "I only saw chaos until you pointed out that one area."

"Because only anchors are meant to know this," Payal said shortly, not because she was annoyed—the question was relevant and she liked Ivy Jane—but because she was processing too much data at once and needed to understand it.

She blanked everyone but Canto. Working together, they unraveled the information left behind for them by anchors long turned to dust. But their legacy might yet save hundreds of thousands of lives. Because there, in the encoded data, was a plan that meant they didn't have to move people one by one.

Fucking beautiful, Canto declared. *I can see how they did it, how they encoded it so only an anchor would understand the message.*

Because it's dangerous. Anyone else who tried this would collapse the Net. She double-checked their final conclusion. *We'll need twenty hub-anchors to pull it off. Five more for backup in case anyone overloads.*

I can make it happen. They'll follow your lead.

She knew at once that was wrong. *No, Canto. I might be the battle tank, but you're the navigational star. They'll follow you.* Payal could talk people into doing as she wanted by showing them that it was the logical course of action because of her skills or contacts—but Canto could make people follow him simply by being who he was.

Charisma?

No. Something more.

Perhaps his tendency to just aggressively *trust* people. A man like that . . . Well, it was hard not to trust him in return. Especially once you figured out that he had no hidden agenda. He was fighting for Designation A exactly as he'd said.

"I have it," she said into the vault, not sure how long she'd blanked the rest of the Ruling Coalition. "It can be done by a syndicate of anchors acting in concert."

The other minds around her sparked with questions, but it was Anthony who asked the most important one. "Can you explain the process?"

"No. Your brains aren't designed to comprehend the Substrate."

Ouch. Canto sounded like he was laughing, the rough warmth of it firelight in her blood. *I bet you no one has ever told Anthony Kyriakus his brain isn't good enough.*

It isn't. Not for this.

"You're asking us to take you on faith," Nikita said. "You're asking countless people to take you on faith."

"You do that every day." Payal wasn't here to play word games. "When was the last time you thought about the anchor in your region or wondered at their political leanings?"

"Touché," Kaleb murmured softly. "Do you? Have political affiliations?"

"As Payal Rao, CEO? Yes. As Payal Rao, anchor? No." It was that simple, her world split in two. Both were her. "Would you like to waste time on further discussion, or shall I get this started?"

"What can we do to assist?" said a dark voice that hadn't spoken until now—Aden Kai. "Will there be confusion or other disruption on the physical plane or on the psychic?"

Payal had to take a moment to think about that, consult with Canto, then check the vital information left by past anchors. "It's possible," she said at last. "All most people should feel is a headache that should pass within the hour, but a few may panic."

We'll need Krychek's voice.

Payal agreed. "Kaleb, you have the loudest psychic voice in the room. We'll need you to blast a message across that area of the PsyNet, warning people of what is to come—we don't need cooperation, but it might stave off the panic."

"Give me the text of the warning, and I'll adapt it to what'll make the populace behave as needed."

That was why Kaleb had become a Councilor while Payal hadn't; he understood how to manipulate people in ways she never had. Lalit had the same skill. So did the empaths—though they didn't think of it as manipulation. Es had a tendency to gently nudge people toward certain behaviors with the full cooperation of the patient.

Jaya, for example, was teaching Payal how to modify her own behavior.

But even empaths must have their bad seeds, so the same skills could conceivably be used for evil.

"I have to leave to work on the occlusion," she said. "Our aim is to do this within the next twenty-four hours, though that will depend on technical considerations. We have some room to maneuver, but the longer we wait, the harder it'll be on the anchors in Delhi."

Payal had managed to maintain to date, but it was getting more difficult with each day that passed, psychic exhaustion a constant threat on the horizon. Prabhyx and Virat were the same, while Shanta—the oldest of them—was starting to sleep fourteen hours a day as her mind and body began to overload. Payal would've urged Nikita to hurry if she hadn't been aware of the intricate series of actions required to open the archive without damaging the data; Nikita had sent a copy of the process to her, so she could follow along as it progressed.

Now Payal opened her eyes on the physical plane and looked at the man who would take the next step. "Do you have it?"

He nodded. "They were brilliant, our psychic forefathers. Why did we forget?"

"Because our people like to forget things. Apparently, we believe ignoring and forgetting is as good as actually fixing problems."

"Wish I could argue with you on that." Scowling, he turned to the door. "I'll contact the others. Arran and Suriana will assist, I know. We'll leave Ager and Bjorn out of it unless we're desperate."

"Yes, they've earned their rest." She glanced at her organizer. "Ruhi has been trying to get in touch with me. I'll need to make a few calls to keep certain balls in the air."

"You can do that while I gather our team."

Payal held his eyes when he glanced back at her. "I'll have to go back to Delhi for the occlusion." She'd have had to return soon regardless, but she'd been hoping that her brain—calm and rested—would allow her to push things a little, give her an extra day or two before her need for the tumor medication went critical.

Yet there was no other viable choice.

They were anchors.

The first and last guard of a failing system.

This was their duty.

Canto turned right back around and moved until his chair was beside where she sat, the two of them facing in opposite directions. Reaching out to cup the back of her neck, he tugged her close for a kiss long and deep. "I'll always be there." Hot breath against her lips, his forehead pressed to hers. "A single thought and I'll find a way to be by your side."

Payal fisted her hand in his shirt. "Maintain the surveillance inside Vara." Some might consider that a strange choice, but for Payal, it meant that in a place filled with enemies, she'd have one person on her side.

Her Mercant knight.

"A single thought, Payal." Canto squeezed her neck. "And if I see a threat to you, I'll take care of it."

Payal felt no need to argue with him—she'd destroy anyone who hurt him, too. That was what it meant to be someone's person.

Her temple pulsed softly, a whisper from the tumors growing deep in her brain.

Chapter 41

AFTER CANTO PUT together the anchors who'd assist with the occlusion, they practiced the maneuver in the Substrate. "It's so simple," Canto said, his mind already working on multiple other possibilities using this technique. "Hard on my energy levels, but the merging with other anchor minds? It's not difficult. Actually feels like I'm stretching out kinked muscles."

Payal gave him a penetrating look. "For you," she said precisely. "I've shadowed you on every merge, and I think you were born with the ability to be the nucleus for such large-scale actions."

The nucleus.

That was exactly what it felt like, as if the other anchors were becoming part of him, part of a living cell. "What if I couldn't do it?" he asked, his jaw clenching. "We'd have had the plan, but no one capable of putting it into play."

Payal turned the full force of those beautiful, intelligent eyes on him, unblinking in her focus. "Canto, do you really believe it's a coincidence that the anchor who reached out to bring us all together is also the same anchor with the ability to be the nucleus of a large-scale action?"

"I hear sarcasm, 3K."

"You're imagining it." Straight face, but he felt her amusement in the bond between them. "I'm just asking a fact-based question." She held up a hand when he would've argued—regal as a queen—and said, "What set you on the course of connecting us all? Do you remember?"

"Seeing the empaths rise and gather." A once-stifled designation that was now a powerhouse.

"Was that the trigger, or did it just help you form your thoughts?"

Canto frowned, considered it. "I had a dream," he said softly. "I'd almost forgotten that. It was this crazy, disjointed dream that showed anchors linked together in a constellation rather than as separate stars."

Again, the image flared vividly against the screen of his mind. Of that constellation linked by lines of energy, so vivid and strong. Far stronger than the lonely stars alone in the Substrate. "It was so broken, that dream. But that image, it stuck with me."

"Broken like the NetMind is broken?"

He sucked in a breath, stared at her. "Fuck, it was a message." Now that she'd dragged him to the damn water, he couldn't help but drink. "It's still trying to help us, even though it's dying." Anger knotted his spine. The NetMind was as much a part of the Net as any one of them. It was a child and it was dying of a cancer they couldn't fix.

Payal's hand closed over his fisted one. Opening out his fingers, he turned his hand and wove his fingers through hers. It felt natural, as if they'd always been meant to be entwined.

"How do we achieve occlusion?" she said. "Work it through with me one more time."

His "robotic" Payal had felt his rage and was trying to help him fight it. Fuck, he was gone for her. Lifting their linked hands, he kissed the back of hers. Then he began to go step-by-step through the plan his mind had fathomed from his first glimpse of it.

It involved shrinking the PsyNet rather than cutting off a piece. In simple terms, Canto and the twenty merged hubs would become a superanchor for the duration of the occlusion, and that superanchor would haul the Substrate toward itself, bringing with it all the minds in the vicinity.

The PsyNet could exist with sparse psychic energy, the reason why it existed in the most remote regions in the world, but it could not exist with *zero* psychic energy. As a result, the empty sections would "collapse" inward, leaving the Net permanently smaller. "Simple."

Payal gave him a *look*.

Grumbling at her, he hauled her in for a kiss. Somehow they both ended up naked on the sofa, the forest a darkness pressing against the glass of the balcony doors. Canto set his mind to do an automatic scan—no way in hell did he want to share the sight of his lover with anyone who might decide to drop by for a visit.

She sat on his lap, soft and welcoming and curious. "I did a bit of research." Her hands doing that thing on his shoulders, that soft petting that made him turn to mush.

A slow smile spread across his face. "So did I."

Big eyes.

A luscious kiss—then he set her beside him. She watched with a confused expression as he got into his chair, which he'd parked right next to the sofa. "The bedroom?" she asked.

"Nope." Shifting so he faced the sofa, he engaged the brakes, then crooked a finger.

She came, retook her position on his lap. It felt so good to have her soft weight on him, to see her eyes as they touched, as they learned one another. She shivered when he nipped at her breasts. He shuddered when she scraped her nails gently down his chest. Her wet heat rubbed against his hard cock with every movement.

He ran his hands down her back, squeezed her lower cheeks. "Soft," he murmured appreciatively, loving that softness as he loved the gentle curve of her stomach and the roundness of her thighs.

"Hard," she whispered in return, shaping his biceps.

Payal had a thing for his arms. Canto wasn't complaining.

Sucking at her neck, he gripped her hips to still her when she began to move faster on his cock. "Remember that research?"

Her hand in his hair, she held him to her throat. "What?"

Nipping lightly at her, he pulled back. "On the sofa."

"*Canto*," she complained.

He bit down gently on her plump lower lip. "Promise it'll be worth it."

Face flushed and nipples hard and inviting, she teleported herself to the sofa even though it was only a few inches. He laughed at her small display of temper and released the brakes to edge a bit closer, then engaged them again. "Impatient cat." Putting his hands on her thighs, he tugged her forward. "Hmm, not quite right."

He reached to her left, grabbed a couple of cushions. "Sit on these?"

A scowl. "You want me higher? I'm a Tk." Then she levitated . . . at the perfect level to his face. "See? Now can we get back to intimate skin privileges?"

His brain short-circuited. Grabbing her under the thighs, he hauled her toward him. And put his research to good use between her thighs. Her scream was short, sharp before her body crashed to the sofa—or would have, if he hadn't used his upper-body strength to ease her down.

Shoving the pillows under her hips to raise her to the perfect height, he went back to his pleasurable task. His research had taken him to a clinical sex manual, but there was nothing clinical about the taste of Payal on his tongue, nothing clinical about how her short, breathy screams made his cock pulse, nothing clinical at all in what it did to him to have to hold her hips tight because she was thrashing too hard in pleasure.

He knew it was pleasure because she was wide-open to him on the mental level. And right now, her brain was hazed by wave upon wave of orgasm. Turned out positive feedback worked on Canto—and made him want to wring even more pleasure out of her. He licked, he sucked, he learned the folds and softness of her body.

He even slipped his tongue into her.

"Canto!" It was a scream as her thighs clamped around his head.

Things crashed and broke. He thought it might have been the other sofa. He didn't give a shit. Because Payal was orgasming so hard that the feedback through their link was threatening to make him come.

Lifting his head before it was too late, he hauled her back into his lap . . . and thrust into her while her body yet rippled from the final echoes of her pleasure. Wrapping her arms around his head, she pressed her face to the side of his and let him move her lax, lazy body as he wished.

To have her so limp and sated, it was all the validation he needed that he'd gotten it right. If there was a touch of desperation in the way he thrust into her, the kisses he demanded, the way his fingers dug into her curves, it had nothing to do with their upcoming separation. Because no matter what, Canto wasn't about to let her go.

The Architect

Once the delusion takes hold, it's proven impossible to treat, though we continue to make the attempt.

—Report to the Psy Ruling Coalition from Dr. Maia Ndiaye,
PsyMed SF Echo

SOMETHING WAS HAPPENING in the Net, but the Architect's contacts had let her down this time. The Ruling Coalition was being very closemouthed about what was to take place, so she had to wait, see.

The Architect did not like being outside the loop of knowledge.

It simmered in her, the awareness that she was the rightful queen of them all. The queen of a newer, better race of people. And a queen waited for no one, least of all these pitiful things called Psy.

"No matter," she said aloud. "I can be patient." None of her children had acted out since seeing that one rebellious group annihilate itself in an attempt to take power from her. They'd thought they could join forces. All they'd done was burn up in their combined fire.

Only the Architect was immune from those flames.

She could snuff them out at any time.

Let the so-called Ruling Coalition play their little games. She would watch, she would learn, and she would strike at the moment when they were the most vulnerable. Soon, she would be the one who reigned, the one who made the decisions, the one who determined who lived and who died.

Chapter 42

Two hours to occlusion.

—Substrate timer set by Canto Mercant

CANTO STROLLED WITH Payal through the fog-bound trees in the pale light of dawn. He'd switched to the outdoor chair he preferred for uneven terrain, and she'd put on sneakers. Soon she'd leave him, get ready to do her part from Delhi.

"Look, Canto." Voice full of wonder, she pointed to the dark form of a bear passing in the distance, the fog blurring its outline into a mirage.

He scowled and yelled, "Stop being so goddamn nosy, you furry asshole!"

Payal stared at him—while the bear turned around and bared its teeth in what he knew full well was a bearish grin, before the big creature lumbered off into the trees. Another bear padded along in the other one's wake—but first he rose up onto his hindquarters and waved.

"Changelings, I presume?" Payal murmured.

"Ignore them." He glared in the general direction of where the bears had disappeared. "They know you're with me and they can't help but poke their noses in—damn bears want to know all my business."

Payal held out a hand, and when he took it, she said, "Are they your friends?"

"Worse. Family."

"It's true, then? I heard rumors the bears had claimed the entire Mercant clan as family after your cousin's mating with their alpha."

"The bears like to hold on to their people."

A bright, stunning burst of laughter from her that owned him. Just *owned* him.

"What?"

"Just like Mercants."

He made a face at her. "Don't be rude."

Solemn lines carving away the laughter. "To have such a family: it's a gift."

He squeezed her hand. "They're yours now, too. I was going to tell you post-occlusion, but Grandmother and Mother have *both* requested your presence at dinner next week—to be held at Grandmother's private residence, the Sea House."

The minutest flaring at the corners of Payal's eyes. "I can handle meeting your mother," she said, her voice firm. "I can. I survived Ena, didn't I?"

"Yes, you can. She'll love you." Magdalene would see what Ena already had—that Payal's hard outer shell protected a heart capable of fierce loyalty and raw devotion.

A bear lumbered out of the misty woods, its eyes bright with interest. Canto's glare had no effect.

Of course it didn't. This was Pavel's twin, Yakov.

It had taken Canto a while to learn bear markings, but he could now identify the bears with whom he interacted most. "I thought I told you to get lost."

The bear walked right up to a fascinated Payal and bent to butt her hand with its head. Sucking in a breath, she lifted that hand and petted the top of the bear's head. Said bear gave Canto a smug look.

"I'll shoot you in your big furry butt if you don't stop smirking," Canto threatened.

Payal gave him a dark look. "Be polite to your friends."

Yakov gave her big brown eyes, with no hint of the glow that turned them yellowish-amber at night. If you didn't know he was one of Valentin's most dangerous people, you'd fall for the teddy bear act. Payal certainly did, petting him with gentle hands.

When Yakov ambled away at last, her face fell. A little jealous, Canto muttered, "You could just stroke me, you know."

She gave him a long look. "Yes," she said in that way she had, as when she'd worked through a mathematical problem. "I will." A sudden smile and she was in his lap, kissing him stupid.

His heart was thunder by the time she was done.

"You're my favorite," she whispered. "No matter how many bears I pet."

He squeezed her hips. "You're not funny." But she was—wickedly funny when she allowed her shields to drop. Only the thing was . . . he loved her in all her moods and facets. Whether it was the cool-eyed CEO, contained Payal Rao, or his wild 3K.

The light faded from her eyes moment by moment. "I have to go."

"You take care of yourself, 3K. Or you'll answer to me."

A solemn look, a delicate touch . . . and he was holding on to nothing but air.

Time to occlusion: zero minutes.

In the Substrate, Canto relocated himself to the Delhi region.

Payal was the first to link herself to him, a burst of icy light in his veins.

Then Arran and Suriana. The other As saw what they'd done, copied their linking technique. The final link. The superanchor formed. And suddenly, Canto was heavier than he'd ever before been in his life. As if every cell of his body held a massive weight.

Pulling, pulling, *pulling.*

He was the core of the superanchor, wrenching minds toward him with inexorable force. They came, hundreds at once, sliding across the Net toward him without ever breaking their biofeedback link.

Hundreds turned into thousands.

Thousands turned into tens of thousands.

More. And more. And more. Minds upon minds held within his grasp so huge and powerful . . . but he could feel all the separate strands of the anchors who made him this nucleus.

The strongest thread of all was her.

His Payal.

Occlusion complete.

Now!

The other As disconnected from him at the same time.

Several of those minds were far too close to where Canto's superanchor had been. If he hadn't broken it off when he had, they'd have slammed into him. He didn't think it would've impacted him—not with how huge he'd become—but it would've probably killed them.

Now he allowed his mind to return to his body, to his zone, while Payal and the other Delhi anchors absorbed all those new minds into their zones. There had to come a point where anchor zones would overload and break, but it wasn't now.

Payal spoke across the vast distance between them, his mind automatically catching her voice because he listened for her always.

The minds are already attempting to stretch. That's how the PsyNet grows—a natural progression that keeps anchor points from strain and collapse. The effect is magnified by the fact that these people are no longer in a region of the PsyNet that correlates exactly to their usual physical residence.

How long?

I don't know, but this fix buys us time to dig deeper, find more answers. We can do the same for other fractured areas, gain a few more months. Until then, we stand guard. We watch. We protect.

Because they were anchors, and this was what they'd been born to do. *Have you had a fatality report?*

No, I—wait. It's coming in.

Canto braced himself.

Zero. Joy seared their bond. *A number of people had panic attacks, but there were no deaths and no major injuries.*

Exhaling hard, Canto shoved both hands through his hair. But his worry lingered. *How are you feeling?*

Tired, but not exhausted. I expected to be, but the merge seemed to magnify our power in some way.

I noticed that, too. Can you rest?

No. My father is impatient. Better I take the lead, see him now.

Canto's jaw worked, his abdomen a steel board. *I'll be there, watching over you.*

I know.

3K?

Yes?

Be careful, darling.

The Architect

What we witnessed today was the most breathtaking act of psychic management that has ever occurred in any of our lifetimes. Bravo, Designation A. We salute you.

—Editorial, *PsyNet Beacon*

THE ARCHITECT STOOD cloaked in the section of the Net where minds had been repositioned in an awesome display of power, and knew she needed to control the mind behind the maneuver. Whoever had done this must be one of hers—no one but a Scarab, one of the new people, had that much power. She just had to find that Scarab and pull them to her, collect them in her web.

In the meantime, she had to keep making room for her children in this Net. There were too many Psy, that was the problem. Why couldn't everyone see it? That was why the Net was collapsing. Their race had never been meant to be millions. Bring it down to a small number and it would be far more pure, far more powerful.

Taking a deep breath on the physical plane, she reached out to one group of her children. *It's time. Wash the Net clean of the disease.* Remove all the weak old players from the network. Create space for the new-born Scarabs to thrive.

Her children stirred and began to act. They trusted her in every way.

Yes, Mother.

Chapter 43

We aim not to conceal the break, but to give respect to it—for it is an integral aspect of the item's character, to be cherished for the story it tells.

—Tomoko Aoki, *kintsugi* master (1998)

BE CAREFUL, DARLING.

Unable to deal with the emotion she could hear in Canto's telepathic tone when she was about to face her father, Payal cut the contact. She knew he'd understand. He was 7J. He got 3K and her oddities and flaws and . . . uniqueness.

He'd know that she couldn't be anything but a robot when she met with Pranath or Lalit. Robots had metallic armor, couldn't be easily wounded or taken advantage of; most of all, robots were logical—and that was the biggest advantage she'd ever had when it came to her family.

On the flip side, she could now also access a level of emotional intelligence that she'd locked away when she'd segregated the part of herself she'd always seen as the screaming girl.

She wasn't. She was simply a less restrained aspect of Payal's nature.

The Payal Rao who walked out of her apartment was a woman in charge of her life, and a worthy adversary. She'd decided not to teleport, because she needed to keep energy in reserve. Being vulnerable in this house was a recipe for fatal disaster—

The psychic shock wave hit without warning.

She slammed one hand against the nearest wall to keep her footing.

Her phone buzzed at the same time. "Suriana," she said, after seeing the ID. "What's the problem?"

"I'm stretched." Short, sharp breaths. "Major cascading fracture."

Payal. Canto's crystalline voice entered her mind as Suriana hung up abruptly. *Massive Scarab assault. I'm heading to assist Arran.*

I'm with Suriana. Do you need help assigning tasks?

No, I've pulled in Sophia.

Returning to her room, she locked the door, ran to lie down in her bed to lessen the risk of injury from a collapse, then entered the Substrate.

The shock wave in the PsyNet had to be huge, but Designation A couldn't worry about that. Their job was to hold the Substrate together.

Her head rang, her blood pounding in her mouth, but she and other As assisted Suriana in putting the seal in place before their minds whiplashed back to their home zones.

The scent of wet iron filled the air.

Looking down at her bedspread, she saw the small spread of red: she was bleeding from the nose. Only the fact she'd lain down on her side had stopped the blood from staining her clothing.

She dug out a tissue from her pocket and used that to try to stop the blood. It was a sign that she'd pushed too hard. But as her brain was still functional and she still had all her physical abilities, it was nothing beyond a minor overload.

Canto.

She'd never before needed anyone, and when he didn't respond, it was a stark reminder that such need was a weakness. She felt adrift without him. If this was what it was like to be someone's person, and to have them be yours, she wasn't sure she liked it.

But the idea of letting go? No, she would *never*. He was hers now.

And he needed her to function both as an anchor and as Payal. So she mopped up the blood, then took stock of the situation. The massive—and *immediate*—coordinated response by anchors had squelched the shock wave at its mouth. That in turn had helped powerful Psy in the Net fix the damage and find the perpetrators.

A telepathic message slipped into her mind via the channel she'd set up for the Ruling Coalition. *Alert to Ruling Coalition from Aden Kai: Attacking Scarabs captured in seventy-five percent of cases. One large eruption of the virus. An E is taking care of that. Situation contained.*

So quickly, Payal thought, but when she glanced at the time on her phone, it was to see that two hours had passed. Yet neither Lalit nor her father had tried to contact her. It appeared they were finally beginning to understand what she did. While she could understand her father considering that a plus now that she was on the Ruling Coalition, it could augur nothing good when it came to her brother.

Lalit would see her newfound power as an insult to him.

Rising, she ate a nutrient bar, then stripped the bloody sheet off her bed and put it in the laundry basket she'd teleport to the cleaning team later. That done, she made sure her makeup was undisturbed. Given all that had occurred, she needed an injection of the meds as soon as possible, so this meeting wasn't negotiable.

Already, her head throbbed.

For once, her father didn't make a production of giving her the medication. He was too busy on an audio-only call, and though she saw his need to interrogate her, he allowed her to come and go in a matter of three minutes. She had no trouble swapping out the vial for another one.

Her pain was brutal by the time she got into her apartment and injected herself, but she was able to save ten percent of the vial to give to Canto. Such a small amount wouldn't make much of a difference to her, and she could blame continuing anchor duties—and duties to the Ruling Coalition—on any necessary increase in her dosage.

She teleported the vial and its precious cargo onto Canto's desk. Not all teleport-capable telekinetics could do this kind of a fetch or send, but Payal had understood the psychic mechanics of it from childhood. And given the small mass of the vial, it took little of her depleted energy resources.

I have it, baby. The pure clarity of Canto's voice in her mind, the bond between them awash in primal protectiveness.

Payal hugged that sensation around herself; she could protect herself, had done so all her life, but to know that he thought she was worth protecting? It meant everything. The sensation triggered another thought, and as she returned to her work, she found herself gnawing on a question that had first emerged in her mind during their meeting with Sophia Russo.

The NetMind had done so much to protect the Es. Why hadn't it protected the anchors? They were as critical to the survival of the Net. Just as without Es there would eventually be no sane Psy, without As there was no PsyNet. The psychic fabric would ripple and fold and collapse.

Which left only one answer: the NetMind *had* done something.

From all she'd learned since her induction into the Ruling Coalition—thanks to her newfound access to a number of top secret databases—the neosentience had made too many long-game moves to have dropped this one ball so badly. But whatever it had done, they couldn't see it. So Payal would look and keep looking until she found the answer.

The first thing she did was log into Canto's private database on Designation A and start reading. He'd collated a lot of information. It scrolled in her mind, piece after piece after piece. Until by the time she lay down to sleep, her brain was on autopilot, moving the pieces from one place to the other, checking details, finding connections.

Connections.

It was the first word she thought of when she woke. "But there are no overlap zones," she muttered as she readied herself for the day.

The problem occupied her mind as she chose a skirt in black that hugged her hips and came to the knee, and paired it with a sleeveless silk shell with a high neck, in vivid red. Black heels and a wide black belt finished off the outfit.

She kept her makeup nude today, but for the pop of red on her lips. Her hair, she pulled back into a neat bun. *Canto? Are you awake?*

Yes. I've been trying to figure out a solution to the connective tissue problem.

Connective tissue.

Payal halted in the act of doing her makeup, the answer almost within reach, but it slipped away before she could capture it. Frustrated, she nonetheless let it go for the time being. *Nikita's sent out a notice about another Coalition meeting. I'd better log in. Come with me.*

KALEB knew the meeting was necessary, given the devastation throughout the Net. There was just too much damage, too many broken pieces, too many tears. He'd still rather be out there trying to fix the damage than in this comm meeting.

"We stand on a cracked eggshell," Payal said in her blunt and precise way.

"No," he responded. "There is no way to repair a cracked egg. We *will* repair this." Because Sahara had asked him to save the world, and he'd made her a promise. It was a promise the twisted darkness inside him would go to the ends of the earth to keep—the only thing he wouldn't sacrifice was Sahara.

That was why he'd finally made the call that the Net had to be cut into pieces. There'd been no other way to maintain its damaged psychic fabric. That the plan had proved flawed wasn't a failure—but that they had no backup *was*; the occlusion had bought them time, nothing more.

Payal gave him a long glance, then inclined her head a little. "Perhaps I should call us a cracked vessel. In Japan, there is an art called *kintsugi*—the masters of the art use gold and other fine metals to mend such cracks, so that the resulting artefact is more beautiful because of its scars, not regardless of them." Starless eyes held his. "We just need to find our gold."

But there were no answers that day, and Kaleb logged off as frustrated as when he'd logged on.

PAYAL glanced at her organizer after leaving the meeting. A single priority message sat at the top of the queue: *Your father requires your presence.*

A hot ball of fire in her stomach, dark and dangerous.

Canto's voice hit her mind the next instant. *I got your sample to Ashaya and Amara Aleine.*

She knew those names. Everybody with *any* interest in science knew those names. The twin scientists were said to be geniuses alone—and beyond that when together. *How?* Payal had a lot of contacts, but she'd never managed to get close to the Aleines.

Silver to Valentin; Valentin to Lucas Hunter, alpha of DarkRiver; Lucas to Ashaya, as she's a member of his pack now. A touch along their bond. *Mercants are all about connections.*

Again that word: *connections.*

Her brain scrabbled for what it was that she couldn't see, fell short.

She forced her mind back to the point at hand. *But why would they take it on?* Payal was nobody to them.

Scientific interest—and because I passed on the information that this was for an anchor. The Aleines were high up enough in the Council super-structure that they're aware of the dearth of anchors. Amara, from all I know of her, likely wasn't swayed by that, since the twins are no longer in the PsyNet, but Ashaya has a child and must've thought of the lives in the Net.

Payal didn't know much about the Aleines in terms of their personalities, but she'd once heard her father say that Lalit was the Rao family's Amara Aleine. It had been a while ago, and she hadn't really understood what he was talking about—only that he'd been displeased with Lalit at the time.

Did they say anything yet?

No. But if anyone can find the solution, they will.

The two of them ended the conversation there, without good-byes. They weren't necessary, because even separated by thousands of miles, Payal and Canto were never apart, the bond between them a living thing luminous with emotion.

He lived inside her, as she lived inside him.

The Payal before, the one who hadn't yet met Canto again, she would've believed such a thing must be intrusive—but it wasn't. They didn't surveil one another. No, it was more akin to knowing that if she held out a hand, he'd be there to grab onto it. Always, he'd be there.

A word hovered on the tip of her tongue, such a huge word, such a massive emotion.

Breath shuddering, she pushed it away. Not yet. She wasn't ready to face that . . . to hope for that. It felt like asking for too much.

After doing breathing exercises to compose herself, she took one last look in the mirror before she headed to her father. Sunita, her long gray hair neatly braided and her black staff uniform pressed to within an inch of its life, was hovering outside her room when she exited. "Miss Payal," she whispered, fear a tremor in her voice.

Payal immediately stepped close to the taller but far thinner woman. "What's the matter?"

Chapter 44

Murder most foul, as in the best it is. But this most foul, strange and unnatural.

—From *Hamlet* by the human playwright William Shakespeare (17th century)

"YOUR BROTHER," SUNITA said, darting looks up the hallway. "He destroyed his suite last night." She twisted her hands. "He hasn't lost control like that since the day you saved Visha."

Payal's mind flashed to an image of Visha's wounds, the slick of red on the brown of her skin. "Thank you. Now, I want you to disappear for a few days—log health leave into the system. I'll authorize it." If her brother was in a rage, then the older woman wasn't safe. Lalit might ignore the servants, but she couldn't take the risk that he hadn't worked out that Sunita was Payal's.

The older woman—who put on a good Silent front most of the time, but who'd clearly thrown off the shackles of the protocol with far more success than most Psy her age—looked at her with distressed eyes. "You'll be all alone."

Payal had always thought theirs a strictly mercenary relationship, but there was fear and worry in the other woman's eyes. She could see it clear as day now that she was no longer blocking her emotional center. It shook her to know she'd blinded herself in such a destructive way.

"I'm a cardinal Tk," she said gently. "He's never going to be as strong as I am."

Sunita resisted. "He won't fight in the open. He'll be like a snake, sliding in under the door while you sleep—it's how he was as a boy, so cunning that he hurt you while your father wasn't looking. I tried to watch, to find ways to distract him, but I was only a maid."

No doubt in Payal's mind of the depth of Sunita's concern. "I'll make sure I never drop my guard." She put a gentle hand on Sunita's shoulder, felt the jut of bone there; she'd looked into Sunita's nutrition in the past, learned that the other woman ate a normal diet—the thin stature was a family trait and not a cause for medical concern. "But I need you out of the way so I don't have to worry about anyone else."

Sunita hesitated again before nodding at last. "I should leave now?"

"Yes. Go." A storm had been gathering on the horizon for a long time—her ascension to the Ruling Coalition would've only fueled Lalit's fury.

After Sunita hurried away, Payal deliberately called her brother on the phone to keep him distracted. "Has Father summoned you to his apartment, too?" she asked. "I need to discuss something with both of you."

"No," Lalit purred, and it held venom. "I'm not part of the Ruling Coalition, after all."

Yes, the storm would break soon. "Meet me there. Bring an updated version of the Tirawa file." She made it an order because she had to act as she'd always done with him—anything else, and he'd suspect she'd been warned of his tantrum. "Ten minutes." It'd take him most of that time to put together the old file, and Sunita would be long out of the house by then.

"Yes, boss."

She stopped herself from glancing up at one of the security cameras as she spoke to Canto. *Can you see me now?*

Yes. Not being creepy—I just need to watch over you in that place.

I don't mind. She wasn't "normal" and neither was he. This was their normal. *I'm going to see my father.*

I have no feed in your father's apartment. Grim words. *You'll have to alert me if there's a problem.*

Shouldn't be. He likely wants to talk politics and how I can use my position to advantage the family.

I'll keep you in sight as long as possible.

Payal walked on feeling as if he were right there beside her.

Arriving at the door to her father's apartment not long afterward, she put all extraneous thoughts aside. Pranath Rao's assistant showed her into her father's room, where Pranath sat in bed, showered and dressed in a crisp white shirt with a raised collar. A blanket of fine black wool covered his lower half.

His bed desk was busy with documents and organizers.

"A moment, Payal."

She used that time to make a subtle scan of the room. The mirrors at the back were still in place, but she felt no minds in that area. That might be true—or it might be a complex shield. It could be done, though it was hard work. As far as she knew, the only people who regularly maintained such shields were those like the Arrows.

Her father wouldn't have hired just anyone for his guards; his people would be highly trained. Not Arrows, since Arrows couldn't be bought. Mercenaries, then. Possibly leftovers from the Council superstructure, people who'd managed to get away because they'd kept their heads down.

"Father." Lalit walked into the room.

Pranath looked up. "I was informed you were here." A reminder that he knew everything that happened in Vara. "But this is a private meeting, Lalit."

"To which Payal invited me," Lalit said with apparent equanimity.

"We need to discuss the Tirawa offer that just came in." Payal held her father's gaze. "I want Lalit to run that negotiation."

Lalit's head swiveled toward her, but he said nothing. Pranath, in contrast, put aside the organizer on which he'd been focused, and said, "Is there a reason you don't want to personally handle such a major deal?"

"I'm part of the Ruling Coalition," she pointed out. "There are certain duties I must perform that will take me away at times. Lalit's more than capable of closing this."

"Are you?" Pranath demanded of her brother. "You've been slipping of late. Did you really think I wouldn't hear of you demolishing your suite? That kind of a lack of control is of a child."

She didn't expect it. Not then.

Lalit had used his telekinesis to pick up Pranath and break his neck before their father was even aware of what was happening. "Goodbye, Father dearest."

No guards responded.

Pranath hadn't had anyone on standby. He'd been expecting only Payal. Whom he had on a leash.

She shoved Lalit telekinetically to the other end of the room as he began to turn toward her. He smashed into the wall, cracks going out in every direction . . . then smiled and said, "You and me, little sister. Oh wait, we have another sibling, don't we?" Then he vanished.

Canto, Lalit just killed our father! I think he's going for Karishma! She teleported the split second afterward, right into Karishma's living space at the school . . . just in time to see Lalit blink out of there. It happened so fast that she couldn't tell if he'd had anyone with him. "Kari!"

She's not at the school, remember? Canto's calm, clear voice. *You told me she and Visha Ramachandran went on a small vacation to a rural property that you own.*

Payal's panic flatlined. *Yes, and Lalit has no knowledge of that property.*

I just used your passwords to access the security system of the vacation property, Canto added. *I can see them—they're fine, doing a puzzle in the living area. If Lalit could get there, he'd be there already.*

Thank you. Her mind snapping back into focus, she returned to her father's suite.

The doors flung open at the same instant, Pranath Rao's guards arriving too late.

She slammed them back with her Tk before they could raise their weapons. "My brother is now a murderer." One who was on tape, because she had zero doubts her father had a security system that recorded everything. Including Lalit's vicious and mocking good-bye, and the way he'd just slightly raised his right hand at the exact moment Pranath was killed. A small tell, but one Lalit had developed young; it wouldn't be hard to prove that, of the two of them, he was the one who'd committed the murder.

"Call Enforcement and send out an alert that he is dangerous and wanted for the murder of his father." Lalit's plan must be to take her out, too, then seize control of the entire Rao empire. But the instant she made his crime public, she would throw a massive spanner in the works—and might just flush him out.

Her father's secretary coughed. "Are you sure, ma'am? This is family business."

"I'm sure," she said, her voice arctic. "This is *my* family now. If I *ever* need to repeat an order again, you won't like it."

No flinch, no reaction, but the middle-aged man began to make the call.

His cooperation wouldn't equal a position at Payal's side, or even in the sprawl of Rao businesses. The secretary had seen far too much and allowed far too much. Payal would never trust him.

Releasing the guards, she said, "Get out." Safe in the knowledge that Canto was watching over her sister, she'd stand guard over her father's corpse until the arrival of the investigators. She didn't trust the secretary and others not to decide Lalit was the better option and attempt to help him by removing Pranath's body.

What she didn't do was search her father. He would've kept nothing on him that would give her an answer when it came to the drug. No, he'd taken that secret to the grave with him. "Bravo, Father. You won this round." But the game wasn't yet over.

Six more days before her tumor would begin to go active.

CANTO made sure he had Karishma and Visha on his center screen.

Around them were the feeds from the cameras in Vara. He'd also reached out to all his moles in Lalit's camp. No one had spotted him, and the security cameras couldn't see him, either.

Then there he was, literally smashing his way into Payal's suite.

Payal, he's broken through a wall into your apartment. I'm going to handle this. He'd fucking had enough. The man was a psychopath and a murderer, and Canto wasn't about to allow him to skulk away and start hunting Payal from the shadows. *Don't stop me.*

Do it, she said. *I don't want Kari looking over her shoulder all her life. That's why he's in my apartment—trying to find some way to get to her.*

There was his 3K. Thinking about someone else rather than herself. But all that mattered was that she wouldn't stand in his way. *I need to get into your private organizer.* She'd messaged him from it last night, but she hadn't had it with her when she exited the apartment, which meant there was a high chance it was in her bedroom.

Payal telepathed him the necessary information.

"Thank you, baby," he muttered, his fingers flying over the keyboard. "It's time to take out the garbage." He pinged her organizer;

he'd already turned off the screen control remotely and upped the volume.

As if Payal had made a mistake and left it unlocked.

His message was simple: *Hi, Didi.* Payal had shared what Karishma called her, told him the import of Karishma's chosen form of address.

Lalit spoke the same language, would recognize it.

If Payal's brother had already teleported out, it wouldn't work, but Canto didn't think that was a possibility. Lalit wanted to destroy Payal—and he'd somehow worked out that Karishma mattered to her. He was in that apartment, searching.

A reply pinged on Canto's screen: *Hello, Karishma. What are you doing?*

Adrenaline pumping, Canto messaged back: *Waiting for you to visit. You said you'd come today.*

I keep my promises. Just send me a photograph of where you are—I've been distracted, seem to have misfiled the image.

Canto's lips curved. While waiting for Lalit's reply, he'd pulled up a number of suitable images and edited out the people in them. Leaving only the location. Then he sent the message: *Oh, okay! Here's a picture. Can't wait to see you!*

A second later, he heard a step upstairs. Right where he'd wanted Lalit to 'port in.

The man had raised a telepathic shield and was moving with care.

Switching on his recording equipment, Canto turned his chair to face the door into his comm room, his mind calm and the weapon he slid into his hand as cool as glass.

"Kari, oh sweet Kari." Lalit's voice was singsong as he came down the stairs. "What are you doing in this place with so many trees? I've come to take you home, little sister." A small laugh. "I'm going to send you to see Father."

Canto didn't take his attention off the door.

Lalit's surprise at coming face-to-face not with his youngest sibling but with an armed Canto was almost comical. His eyes flared.

That single moment of indecision was all Canto needed.

Single shot. Center of the forehead.

There was no other way to win against a powerful telekinetic.

Lalit crashed to the floor, dead before he hit it, but Canto went across and checked to make sure he really was gone. "Grandmother," he murmured, "you'd be proud of my accuracy."

Ena had made him practice as a teen until he could shoot a fly off an apple. Today, that training had ended one nightmare for Payal. Now they had to figure out the answer to the second one—because even the Aleines weren't magic. They couldn't come up with answers in a matter of days.

He and Payal had to locate Pranath's stash of the medication, buy her time.

Canto, Lalit's mind just disappeared from the PsyNet.

Sliding away his weapon, Canto said, *He came here. I took care of him. Where do you want his body?* Lalit couldn't vanish; people had to know he was dead.

Sounds from upstairs, feet flying down the stairs. The woman who appeared in the doorway was his 3K, fury in her face and determination in her body. "You're okay." Ignoring her dead sibling, she crossed over to brace her hands on his shoulders, her chest heaving. "Canto, you're okay. He came here to kill you."

"No. He wanted to kill your sister." Canto felt no guilt whatsoever.

Gripping her nape with one hand, he kissed her hard. "I think you need to reappear with him so no one doubts your power. Tell them the truth—that he invaded the home of a Mercant and was shot as a result." No one was going to come after Canto for eliminating a man who'd already committed one murder this day. "Because the two of us? We're in the open now."

Payal frowned. "You don't like being in public."

"I like being by your side." Then he scowled. "Baby, you're exhausted. Your fucking cheekbones are like glass. Let me get you some food, then you can teleport home."

Payal just looked at him for a long time, before giving the smallest smile. "Okay, 7J."

Chapter 45

The NetMind feels like a kitten in my head today, Max. Excited and jumpy and so very young. As if it can sense something on the horizon that makes it happy.

—Sophia Russo to Max Shannon

THE FALLOUT FROM her father's murder and Lalit's death took Payal less time to handle than she might've predicted. It turned out Lalit had very few loyalists, and those she fired off the bat. As for her father's people, that was more complicated—many were highly skilled and necessary to the business.

In the end, she kept most of them. Not the ones like the secretary, but there were very few in that innermost circle. As for the others . . . while they weren't people she would ever trust as she'd trust those who'd been loyal to her when she had little power, they *were* now hers. They knew she hadn't murdered the man to whom they'd been faithful, and thus they'd transferred their loyalty from father to child.

She was also planning for a certain level of attrition. The Rao family was never again going to function as it'd done under Pranath. For one, her sister was coming home—*after* Payal cleared Vara of anyone who might make Kari feel flawed or like a mistake or in any way less.

As for Lalit, Enforcement had interviewed Canto, decided he was telling the truth after viewing the surveillance footage from the stand-off, and that was the end of it. She'd had the feeling the entire thing had been nothing but theater, the decision already made behind the scenes.

"So much power, Canto," Payal said to him in the aftermath, as she stood beside him on the highest external vantage point in Vara, Delhi cloaked in the first flush of night around them. "Aren't you afraid it'll corrupt you?" Mercants had tentacles everywhere, could conceivably pervert any system.

"Arwen lived inside me for ten years of his life. I couldn't be evil if I tried my hardest." He placed one hand on her lower back, the contact as familiar as the touch of their bond.

"But even without that," he added, "you've met my grandmother. She is the fountainhead from which all of us flow, as she flowed from the fountainhead of her grandmother, all the way back to the Mercant who was knight to a king. We've never forgotten who we are." He nudged her toward him.

Curling into his lap was second nature to her now, and she did so with ease, laying her head against his shoulder as he wrapped his arms around her. "I want to build that same kind of honor into the Rao line," she confessed. "I want those who come after me to be good people."

"Then it'll happen," Canto said. "Nothing stands in the way of Payal Rao when she's decided on something."

A point of pain in Payal's temple, a reminder that she faced one obstacle that she couldn't strategize away and that even the Mercant network couldn't fix. Canto had gone so far as to locate a Tk who worked on the micro-med level—such a *rare, rare* ability—and they'd discussed 'porting the tumors out of her brain.

But the thing was, the disease that created the tumors came from her connection to the Substrate. They would grow again and again, and the position of the tumors meant even the gentlest telekinetic surgical removal could cause permanent damage.

"You're hurting." Canto hated that he couldn't fix this for Payal, *hated* it. He'd used every possible connection, as had every member of his family, and still nothing.

Sitting up, Payal locked eyes with him. "They put us in that place to die, Canto. Yet here we are, alive and thriving, and they're both dead." A feral smile from the wildness in her. "We're going to win this, too."

"Yes, we fucking are." No way was he ever letting her go. He wanted to fill her life with joy to the brim, then more. Wanted to love her until she expected it, until she took it for granted.

Their kiss was a wild tangle interrupted by tremors at the edge of their minds.

Separating, they looked inward, saw the ripples in the Net. Another fracture. Not in their zones and not large enough that they had to respond to assist. But it was enough to break the moment in two, because they were anchors, and it was their duty to hold the Net in place.

A keen filled Canto's mind, the whispered tears of other anchors carried by the Substrate. He hadn't been able to hear them before he began to set up the anchor network, but it was as if with contact had come a connection. "All our anchors are on the verge of a total breakdown."

"It's crushing to not be able to do the one thing you were born to do." Payal's eyes held no stars, the night air blowing her unbound hair back from her face.

"How could the NetMind have allowed it to get this bad?" Canto wasn't blaming the neosentience—never would he do that. He just didn't understand why it had made this choice. "It protected the Es. Why not do the same for the designation without which the PsyNet can't exist? Do you think it was devolving long before we realized?" It had been so vibrant, so young during his childhood, a vast and grow-ing neosentience.

A sudden burst of starlight in the obsidian of Payal's gaze. "I want to check something."

SHE dived into the Substrate without waiting for an answer because she knew Canto would follow her here to this place that was their psychic home. The weeds tangled her up, thicker than ever.

Then there he was: *her* Canto. Whose language of love was food and physical contact, and who understood that hers was a feral pos-sessiveness that meant she touched their bond constantly.

"I can't believe how fast these things have taken over the Sub-strate," he said, pushing away one of the thorn-heavy weeds. "How long's it been? Twenty, twenty-five years since it first began?"

Sparks of light in Payal's brain, coalescing into a stunning whole. "How old are the variant Es? The ones who clean the PsyNet?" She'd been told of them as part of her Ruling Coalition briefing, and Canto knew because Mercants liked to know things.

"I can find out," Canto said. "Why?"

"Because the NetMind would never abandon us."

"You think these aren't weeds?" Canto's mind danced in and out of the rough brown strands. "I don't know, baby. The things do nothing but take up space in the Substrate."

"Are we sure? Have we ever truly looked at them?" She ran her hand along one of the weeds. It sparked with light as the weeds always did when an anchor brushed them. "Remember how Arran mentioned he got stuck in a cluster and had to fight his way out?"

"It's dangerously aggressive."

"What if it wasn't trying to hurt him?"

"Payal, wait!"

But her mind saw the possibilities, and she knew Canto would rescue her if she needed rescue. Because she was his person. She dived straight into the midst of a heavy thicket of weeds, not fighting when they wrapped around her psychic presence. It felt like being wrapped up in ropes, but only at first.

Payal! I can't see you anymore!

I'm fine. I think I know what to do. Because the ropes were now part of her psychic presence, part of her *anchor.*

Opening herself out with those ropes attached to her, she spread and spread. All the little thorny hooks gripped the Substrate to give her more stability as she sent her anchor energy out along each of the interlocking ropes in a way that turned her into the center of a huge psychic organism.

She touched Shanta's zone, overlapped it to the very center. She touched Prabhyx's zone, overlapped that, too. Then the As on her remaining sides. She was now the biggest anchor in the entire Substrate.

CANTO'S breath caught.

She was glorious. The fibrous "weeds" had softened and taken on the blue glow of an anchor mind in the Substrate, Payal the nucleus of a huge living cell that had veins and arteries that flowed with energy. The NetMind had given them one final gift before the Psy race burned it out with their terrible choices and their inability to embrace their natures. "You're magnificent."

"I feel bigger. Stronger." Energy pulsed along the veins and arteries, a stunning light show that cleared out all the smog that had erased the clarity of the Substrate.

He forced himself to pay attention to the practicalities. "The thorns, they only attach to the Substrate if an anchor is feeding them energy."

"Yes. But they're not feeding off me. More . . . amplifying."

A sudden cold fear in his gut. "Can you disengage?"

"There's no need," she said. "These weeds—we need another

word—are now a part of my anchor point. They allow us to spread ourselves far thinner, because the anchor point will hold as a result of all the tiny anchor points created by the thorns along the way."

Canto's mind was pulling him back to his anchor point—because even while he existed in the same physical space as Payal, his anchor remained locked in place. "We need to talk more about this."

"I'll follow you to your zone."

Canto allowed himself to whiplash back to his zone, only relaxed when her mind appeared after his, as normal. Her anchor point might have bloomed into an unearthly entity, but it hadn't tangled her up in ropes she couldn't escape.

As she stood watch, he moved into a thicket of weeds.

They closed around him, the tendrils becoming a part of his mind, until he saw why Payal wasn't worried. *He* now controlled these tendrils, and as they unfurled, his anchor point grew and grew.

And grew.

"You're a constellation, Canto," Payal whispered before whiplashing back to her zone.

The next time they spoke, it was telepathically, both of them in their bodies on the physical plane in Vara, their minds entwined in a dance of glowing blue.

Did you see the small white sparks on the weeds?

Children. Joy seared him. *Baby anchors. We can pinpoint them, protect them.*

Is this the answer? Can we save the Net this way?

No. It was a terrible thing to say but it was the truth. *The Substrate is only one part of the Net. And the rot continues above. Anchors continue to die. But this gives us time to find another solution. Not months. I think two or three years.*

We should test it. See if it works for all of us.

They asked Suriana and Arran. Suriana took a deep breath and agreed, while Arran was leery but game. Both soon exclaimed at the acute clarity of their minds, the sudden abundance of life in the Substrate, no sluggishness to it.

Bjorn went next . . . and he cried. They heard the tears in his voice. "The wonder . . . My heart aches for the NetMind, this child we broke too young. And still, it watches over us."

Canto's own anguish was intermingled with a brittle anger—and sharp shards of hope. He needed to talk to Sophia, see if she was okay with sharing her knowledge of the NetMind's survival with the rest of Designation A.

Ager they'd left for last, as they were the oldest and most apt to suffer from shock if it went wrong—but they would not be deterred. And the effect on them was the most astonishing of all. "I can breathe," they said on the comm the day after the experiment, their face fuller and less lined, their eyes bright sparks. "I feel twenty years younger!"

They began the next level of experiments the following day.

Each of the merged As brought in a neighboring A and had them merge, too. All succeeded.

But the real surprise came when Canto said, "Let's see if we can attach tendrils to each other, so that if one day we do have no choice but to cut the Net into pieces, we can keep the Substrate together so no one anchor starves."

It turned out Canto couldn't attach to anyone. But he could be *attached to*.

"You're built to be the nucleus of any such strategy," Payal said. "It makes logical sense. For this to work, we need someone really heavy at the center, to make sure it holds. You don't move. Everyone else moves around you."

Canto wasn't sure he liked being stuck in place—it reminded him too much of his childhood. But then Payal's telepathic voice entered his mind: *You're the protector. The one who'll hold us all stable. Without you, we fail. And we fall.*

Her words took away his breath.

Payal Rao, I love you.

Heart exploding with a joy so big she couldn't bear it, she kissed him as they sat once more under the Delhi sky, sunset a dark orange fire around them. When they parted, she touched her fingers to his jaw. "There's only one of you, Canto. A single superanchor can't save the entire Net."

Canto leaned into her touch. "No, if that option ever needs to be used, the rest of the Net will have failed. Millions will be dead."

"So we have to make sure we never have to use it," Payal said. "The weeds are our circulatory system. The NetMind has given us a chance."

"We have to do as it's asked—we have to become more than isolated stars in the darkness."

Payal held his gaze. "Single steps out of the void. With each step we take, we bring the NetMind into the light."

"Single steps," he agreed. "I'm going to make that my priority, while you deal with the Coalition."

"Agreed."

Then Canto wrapped his arms around her as she did him. Holding on against the cells dividing and growing inside her head, killing her with every moment that passed.

Chapter 46

Dear Dima, I'm very happy you like the rocket-powered wheelchair design
I sent you. At the moment, I'm in Delhi, but we can discuss it more after
I'm back home. Also, I'm trying to think bear thoughts, but I need more
time to get it right. Being a bear isn't as easy as it looks.

—Message from Canto to Dima

KALEB LISTENED AS Payal laid out what the anchors had discovered
to the Ruling Coalition.

"This is no magic bullet that will erase our problems," she said on
the comm, "but it will buy us a little more time. If the clock was hovering a few minutes to midnight, it's now been turned back by fifteen
minutes."

Ivy Jane Zen, her face thinner than it had been only months ago,
her exhaustion imprinted on her skin, said, "It's enough. For all of us
to catch a breath."

Nikita parted her lips as if to argue, then shut them. No one else
refuted Payal's statement, either. Because Ivy Jane was right. Yes,
they'd all wanted a solution, but that solution had to hold. Or it would
all fall apart again—perhaps at a time when the PsyNet didn't have so
many powerful Psy willing to work together for their survival.

Had this happened in the time of the Council, half the population would already be dead, sacrificed because they weren't powerful or connected enough.

"In that fifteen minutes, Designation A has a demand."

Nikita raised an eyebrow at the wording of the statement but, oddly for Nikita, kept her silence once again. Something was going on there. Perhaps Anthony's influence? No, the head of PsyClan Night-Star knew nothing of anchors. Had to be another person closer to Nikita who held sway with her.

Possibly her daughter.

"We can now ID young As before they initialize." Payal's words were massive boulders crashing into the earth. "What we want is the Coalition's backing to formally tag those children as newborn As and maintain a health watch on them as they grow."

She wasn't asking their permission, Kaleb thought. The As *would* do this. They just wanted to know if they'd have the support of the Coalition.

"Accepted," Aden said, speaking for the first time. "If you need Arrow escorts during the checkups, I'll make them available."

"And if you need Es to scope out the emotional situation," Ivy Jane added, "you can have us on call."

Arrow-Empath-Anchor.

Looked like a new kind of network was being born right in front of him.

"I see no issue with this," Nikita said, and Anthony concurred.

"Children should never be hurt or tortured or killed." Kaleb held Payal's eyes, knowing her secrets without knowing them. "The simple fact that a child is an A should protect them as a result of A now being a hotly coveted designation." Payal's ascension to the Council, her repeated interviews, as well as the interviews given by a number of other As, had helped achieve that outcome.

The Psy now understood that it was on the shoulders of anchors that they all stood. That many As required high-level care from those around them didn't alter the fact that they were critical to the PsyNet's survival.

"I'm glad we are all in accord on this point." Payal's voice was as crisp and detached as always—yet Ena had mentioned that Payal had bonded with Canto. A little piece of family information dropped into the conversation, a quiet statement that Payal was now part of the wider Mercant family.

Just like Kaleb.

Do you think anyone realizes the Mercants are slowly growing into the most powerful family in the Net? asked the woman who'd been with him throughout this meeting. *Silver runs EmNet. They call you family and have claimed the bears as kin. Now they have within their ranks the leadership of the anchors.*

I don't think it's a pursuit of power, Kaleb said. *I think it's the other way around. I pursued them because of who they are.* Loyal. Intelligent. Relentless. *If they become an even bigger power than they are now, the Net has nothing to fear.*

Warmth along his bond with Sahara. *Admit it, you have a crush on Ena.*

The twisted darkness in him laughed, delighted with her. *I will take that secret to the grave.*

Her laughter filled him to the brim, even as the Coalition meeting broke up. As Payal's face blinked out, he was certain he saw her wince. Likely another Net rupture, but nothing echoed to him along the pathways of the Net, so it couldn't have been a significant one.

He teleported home to Sahara.

PAYAL'S nose was bleeding, and a pulse pounded at the back of her skull. She cleaned up the blood with quick efficiency. This had happened a few times before, when she'd waited too long before taking her dose.

She had about two more days before things went critical.

Canto entered her office, the two of them having come up with a residence schedule that worked for their anchor points.

Two weeks in one zone, two weeks in the other. Both anchor points would remain stable, and they could live together. They could do that for a lifetime. Karishma had asked to stay at her school for the time being, since it was familiar and comfortable, but when she came to Vara for the holidays—which she was excited to do—Payal would stay in Delhi for the duration.

All these plans they had.

Because she was going to survive. Payal was a survivor. So was Canto. "Any word from the Aleines?" she asked, making no attempt to hide her pain.

He knew. He always knew.

White lines around his mouth, he said, "Ashaya says it's an incredibly complex piece of work. They will break it down and be able to engineer it backward, but it's a question of how long it'll take." He came around her desk. She swiveled her chair so she faced him. "The Aleines are working all possible hours. They know we're fighting a ticking clock."

"Two women who I've never met are fighting for me. I would've never imagined such a thing possible before you." She touched her hand to the bristles of his jaw, the wildness in her angry at the shadows under his eyes, the tension across his shoulders.

Put there by a man so in love with control that he'd rather his heir die than live without him. "I've sent word to every branch of the Rao empire alerting them to the transfer in power—and the circumstances of my father's death. It's possible his scientists might reach out to me."

Payal hadn't expected such family-defeating arrogance of her father—he'd always been about building an empire, an unbroken line.

But he'd also thought he'd hold on to power forever, so dying with the secret of the drug might not have been a purposeful decision.

Payal might die because her father had believed himself immortal.

FORTY-EIGHT hours later, with pain a constant throb in the back of her skull, Payal continued on with putting a line of succession in place. Too many lives and livelihoods depended on the Rao empire for her to leave it to flounder. She hadn't yet notified any of the parties, but she *had* taken up Canto's offer to have Arwen in the room when she had meetings with various people.

She let it get around that she was interviewing him for a possible secondary assistant position, and he played the part, taking notes and fetching documents as needed. Ruhi, sure of her position since Payal had made it a point to tell her that she was to remain the most senior member of the office staff, had taken him under her wing.

One thing was non-negotiable: the succession could not be put on Karishma's shoulders. Payal's sister was an artist, a gifted one. She no more understood business than Payal understood how to put paint together in such a way that it came alive on the canvas. But ownership of all Rao enterprises would remain hers, to be passed on to her children if she so wished.

Payal intended to leave the oversight of her plan in Canto's hands.

He refused to discuss it with her, gritting his jaw and changing the subject anytime she tried to bring it up. But she knew that should the worst happen, he'd take care of it, take care of Kari. Because he was in her corner. Always.

"Payal?" Arwen hesitated in the act of rising from the chair across from her own.

The two of them had finished their final meeting of the day, and he was now free to do as he wished. He'd mentioned going to see the art that lined the walls of the lower floor of Vara.

Her headache dull rather than sharp thanks to medication, she looked up. "Yes?" Protectiveness was a pulse in her veins. There was a gentleness to Arwen that made her want to wrap him up in cotton wool.

Eyes of clear silver searched her face. "You're not mad with Canto for how he's acting, are you?" He swallowed. "He loves *so* hard—and the idea that he might lose you, it's making him act angry and grumpy. He feels helpless and he hates that beyond anything."

"I know." She still touched their bond compulsively, felt it grow stronger with every hour that passed. "I don't know how to shield him from this, Arwen." It devastated the feral girl in her that Canto would hurt after she was gone.

Because it turned out even a survivor couldn't outrace this clock.

Eyes shining with wetness, Arwen shook his head. "You can't shield from life—that's what got our race into trouble in the first place."

She was still thinking of his words when Canto rolled his chair into her office. Darkness was falling outside, the lights of Delhi beginning to flicker to life. Stopping her work the instant he appeared, she rose to go over to him.

He glowered at her but wove his fingers through hers. "You look exhausted. Have you eaten?"

"I love you." No more hiding from that huge emotion, no more cowardice. "Do you know?"

"Yeah." It came out as rough as his bristled cheek. "But it's nice to hear it."

"Shall we go for a walk in the streets of Delhi?" She wanted to show him her city, the vibrancy and the chaos and the stark contrast of new and old.

Canto's eyes held no galaxies, his jaw a brutal line, but he nodded.

He was a tense, alert presence at her side as they exited through the main gates of Vara.

Which was why it didn't surprise her in the least when he said, "Stop," in a cold tone to a short and skinny man who'd darted toward her—from behind a tree outside the gates. He wore a satchel crosswise across his body.

The man skidded to a halt, his dark eyes shifting to Payal. "Miss Payal, I have information for you," he said in the local dialect.

Canto had subtly angled his chair so he—and his hidden weapon— were in front of her.

Wait, Canto. Payal put a hand on his shoulder. *I think I recognize him.* The memory was a few years old, and she couldn't quite place the man, but he wasn't a stranger. "Why are you lurking outside? You could have contacted me in other ways." As the Rao CEO, she wasn't easily accessible, but neither was she insulated from the outside world.

He looked around, as if searching for watchers. "I wasn't sure who to trust."

Canto, able to understand the dialect because she was permitting him to link to her in a way that was beyond telepathic, said, *He's Psy. Good shields, but nothing martial or extraordinary. No weapons that I can spot, though the satchel is suspect, and his body language isn't threatening. More scared.*

Payal processed that, said, "All right. Let's speak." And because she saw his jittery gaze and constant swallowing, she invited him through the gates of Vara. Once safe from outside eyes, she led him into the garden and said, "You can speak freely. My home has been cleared of those not loyal to me."

Payal didn't seek devotion from those who worked for her, but she did want to know that she could walk the halls of her home without worrying about a knife in the back. To Sunita, the member of staff who had been so very loyal to her, she'd offered a generous pension should the woman wish to retire, but Sunita was basking in her promotion to head of domestic staff and had no intention of retiring.

It was a promotion long overdue; skilled and hardworking Sunita had been overlooked too many times in favor of Pranath's favorites.

"What is your name?" she asked the man who'd stopped her, the garden lights a soft glow against the falling night, and the leaves of the guava tree rustling in the gentle breeze.

"Nikhil Varma." Perspiration dotted his dark skin, though it wasn't a hot night by Delhi standards. "I'm a cleaner. Chemical and medical waste."

Payal inclined her head. "A job with a degree of risk." It was significantly higher paid than general cleaning, but it meant bulky protective gear and a chance of exposure if something went wrong.

"I work at a Rao subsidiary," he said, and used the back of his hand to wipe off his brow.

"Is there a problem with the cleanup standards?" All of Rao was meant to be following the long-agreed-upon international environmental standards that protected the earth. Psy, changeling, or human, breaches of those laws were punished harshly and could tarnish the Rao name. Even Psy didn't enjoy living in polluted surroundings.

"What?" His eyes widened. "No, no. I do my work. I do it well."

"I didn't mean to imply otherwise. Which subsidiary do you work at?"

"Raja MedChem."

"That isn't one of my companies." Payal had the name of every major and minor company listed in an internal mental database.

"That's just it." Nikhil darted a look toward Canto before shifting his attention back to Payal. "We heard in the lab that you'd sent out a change-of-ownership notice to the entire business, but nothing came to Raja MedChem. We waited and waited, but still nothing."

He wiped his forehead again. "I've been the cleaner there for years. No one considers me a threat. They talk around me . . . and I heard them talking about just quietly taking over the lab. Changing the documents to make it look like they were always independent."

I have to admire their ability to seize the day. Canto's telepathic voice held a growl.

"I appreciate this information," Payal said, a hot, urgent thought blooming in the back of her mind. *Canto. A secret lab.*

Fierce exultation in the bond that connected them.

Chapter 47

Our capacity for love may yet save us.

—From *The Dying Light* by Harissa Mercant (1947)

"I JUST . . . YOU helped her." Nikhil's face softened. "Visha."

"Visha Ramachandran?"

A jerky nod. "I knew I wasn't supposed to feel anything—we were meant to be Silent then, but it made me feel good to be around her. I used to work in the small Vara lab then. I heard what he did to her, what *you* did." Quick blinking. "I heard that you looked after her."

"She's doing well," Payal told him. "If you wish, I can pass on your details to her, for when she next visits Delhi."

If hope could be said to have a face, it was this man's. "Oh, yes, please." He fumbled with the catch of his satchel. "I have more information."

Payal.

I'm ready.

Nikhil didn't notice their alertness, he was so involved with opening his satchel. "I knew we had to be doing something important—your father was our only point of contact in Rao. That meant high-level."

He pushed his hand in, returned with a sheaf of papers. "I stole this," he admitted. "Specs of the compounds we make at Raja. The top one is the priority." Another dive into his bag, as Payal accepted the papers.

"Here, I stole two vials of the newly made batch. I hope you won't fire me, but I couldn't work out how else to show you what we did. I thought you'd know." He held out his palm . . . on which lay vials that glowed a piercing green.

Payal's entire world went silent. *It has to be tested*, she said to Canto with an almost preternatural calm. *To make sure it's what we're looking for.*

Yes. A single gritty word.

"Did . . . did I do the wrong thing?" Nikhil's shaky question had her snapping out of her frozen state.

Passing the papers to Canto, she took the vials and slipped them into her pockets. "No, you did exactly the right thing. Now, I need you to tell me everything about Raja MedChem."

THE small specialized lab was back under Rao control in a matter of hours. The scientists who'd considered rebellion quickly changed their minds once they realized they were known to the Rao successor after all.

Theirs had been a rebellion of opportunity, not passion.

Canto had, by then, wiped all security footage of Nikhil's actions, so that the man could slip back into his position like nothing had happened. It'd be a temporary one, as once they'd checked they had every detail about the manufacture of the drug, Payal intended to disband the lab and have her medication produced by a small, trusted unit. For now, the Aleines had done an emergency test on the vials Nikhil had appropriated, and confirmed it was her medication, so she'd been able to take a dose.

As for Nikhil, he'd be receiving a serious promotion very soon.

"Reward people who do the right thing," Ena Mercant said to her when she visited Delhi the day following. "Make it clear by your actions that good work and ethics will get a person further along in your organization than corruption. Blind loyalty can't be the first yardstick."

"Blind loyalty?"

"Loyalty is a good thing," Ena confirmed, "but you want people in your organization who aren't afraid to challenge you or bring you ideas that break the rules. Your father rewarded *only* the loyal, and so was surrounded by toadies.

"You want the kind of loyalty you have with Canto—where you know the person will back you, but they remain their own person, willing to stand against you if required. Nurture the strong who are faithful. That is true leadership."

"I understand," Payal said, adding that piece of data to the decision matrix in her mind.

"Most of all, keep on being who you are, Payal." Ena's eyes held approval when she turned them on Payal . . . and the older woman's approbation mattered. A great deal. "You stand here today because you acted on your conscience and saved the life of a young woman— and in so doing, you set in motion a chain of events that led to the answer to your problems coming to your door. He came not because you are powerful, but because he trusts you."

Payal intended to follow Ena's advice. "In the meantime," she told Canto as the two of them lay in a hanging bed on a sprawling verandah in the back of Vara, "I passed on Nikhil's regards to Visha." The bed—which Payal had found in deep storage—swung gently in the evening light.

"You romantic."

Payal laughed, wild and unfettered. It came easier now, finding a balance between sanity and total erasure of self. "She blushed because she remembered him, too. She was also proud, I think, when I told her that Nikhil had risked himself to warn me of insurrection. Her shoulders grew straighter, and her eyes shone."

"The man is a hero to her now." His arm her pillow, Canto now curved his hand around to rub his knuckles over her cheek. "You'd better get ready for a wedding invitation soon."

Payal moved to lean over him—a maneuver it should've been impossible to make easily in this bed designed to swing, but there were advantages to being a telekinetic. Including the fact she could freeze the bed in place when Canto wanted to shift in or out of his chair.

His beloved face was relaxed as he looked up at her, galaxies in his eyes and his hair damp from the swim they'd just taken in the secluded lake to which she'd teleported them. Soon Vara would have a pool. Being in the water was important to Canto, and so it was important to Payal.

"Should we?" she asked him.

"Should we?" He raised an eyebrow.

"Get married." It wasn't a Psy thing, but weddings in Delhi were always loud, colorful events, and Payal felt like making a loud, colorful start to her new life.

Canto's lips curved in a slow smile. "Are you asking me to marry you?"

She grinned, kicking up her legs. "Yes."

"Okay, but you have to get me a ring. And I'm not budging on a small, pretty cake for our private—and naked—post-wedding celebrations."

Laughing, she climbed on top of him, her 7J who had never forgotten a single one of her dreams. "Agreed. Done deal."

This man, he was hers. For always.

Divergence

Coherence, connection, bonds, that has always been the answer. We must fight to hold on to that which makes us a sentient society capable of empathy and hope and joy.

—From *The Dying Light* by Harissa Mercant (1947)

If enough believe, does delusion become reality? What is reality but the will of the masses?

—Discussion question: Philosophy 101

IN THE HEART of the Substrate, an unbreakable tendril that connected two anchors sparked with blue fire that began other small fires. As they burned, the waters of the Substrate grew clearer, until parts were translucent limned with blue. Even Ager was astonished, such purity of Substrate flow unseen in their long lifetime.

Deep in the PsyNet, in the mind of an anchor unlike any other, a neosentience in danger of losing itself forever took its first clear "breath" in hundreds of years. It wasn't Psy, changeling, or human, its thought patterns unknowable, but it watched the bond deep beneath the starlit sky of the PsyNet as a mother watches her children.

With hope. With fear. With wonder.

It sent the mind in which it hid images of a drop of water falling onto a dry seabed, a single blade of grass coming to life in a desert, a tiny iridescent butterfly in a huge rocky gorge.

Even as that mind woke and asked, "Is it enough?" another, far more twisted mind came to wakefulness.

The Queen of the Scarabs, she called herself now, though others still said the Architect. The name didn't matter, only what she was, what she'd become. A spider with endless tentacles, endless disciples.

The Psy, those inferior minds, had stopped the first wave, but unbeknownst to all but the queen, that had been a test strike to evaluate the enemy. She'd held back many of her children, sacrificed others.

No more.

It was time to unleash their full might while the Net was in good enough shape to handle the deluge—but not so strong that it could repel so many of her children acting in concert. Because she knew what to do now. To be a true queen, she had to first rule her own kingdom.

The easiest way to do that was to take the action the Ruling Coalition had been too cowardly to complete—tear off a piece of the PsyNet, isolate it so it was an island on which the Scarabs ruled. Where *she* ruled.

She had everything she needed, *everyone* she needed. Because amongst her children were three of the bright minds needed to anchor a broken piece. So mad they were, quite out of control had she not squeezed walls around their minds that made them appear sane to their brethren, but they could do their task.

They would sit below her island and hold it up.

Are you ready, my children?

Yes, Mother.

It is time. Cut the threads, make the excision. Let the Net bleed.

ACKNOWLEDGMENTS

A very special thank-you to Hasna Saadani for reading a draft of this book and taking the time to provide honest and in-depth feedback. You are incredibly kind and generous, and *Last Guard* is a better book because of you.

My thanks also to Karen Lamming and Vladimir Samozvanov, for coming to my rescue once again on a Russian question.

Any errors are mine.